Back in the USSA

Back in the USSA

A Novel

Eugene Byrne & Kim Newman

MARK V. ZIESING BOOKS
SHINGLETOWN, CA · 1997

Back In The USSA
Copyright © 1997 by Eugene Byrne and Kim Newman

A Mark V. Ziesing Book
PO Box 76
Shingletown, CA 96088
ziesing@bigchair.com
http://www.bigchair.com/ziesing
By arrangement with the Author. All rights reserved.

Artwork and Interior design by Arnie Fenner
Composition by John Snowden

FIRST EDITION
ISBN   0-929480-84-8

ACKNOWLEDGMENTS

For support, advice, inspiration, etc.

Tom Tunney for lots of technical help on planes and Newcastle; David Pringle for publishing the stories in *Interzone* and on one occasion giving us half the magazine; to Brian Smedley for letting us pick his brain on all sorts of collapse-of-communism issues, and for taking us on a dream holiday to the Czech Republic; Alex Dunn for being there a lot of the time when we were talking about these stories; Meg Davis for moral support; Monique Brocklesby for cooking and hoovering (but not ironing); Martina Drnkova for demonstrating that absinthe and cricket are not mutually exclusive; Paul J. McAuley for snickering; Harlan Ellison for letting himself appear; Sergei Paradjanov for heroism and style; Maura McHugh for being there; Cindy Moul for make-up; Pat Cadigan, for leaving Kansas; Mark V. Ziesing for not caring how many Americans have heard of *The Likely Lads*. We also owe a small debt to Vaclav Havel, whom history will judge one of the greatest figures of the 20th century, for giving us the idea in the first place.

For characters we've sampled and re-mixed

Eddie Albert, Robert Aldrich, Robert Altman, Raymond Allen, Sir Kingsley Amis, Gerry Anderson, Sylvia Anderson, Edwin Apps, Dan Aykroyd, Peter Barnes, James Warner Bellah, John Belushi, Robert Bloch, Humphrey Bogart, John Boulting, Malcolm Bradbury, David Bradley, Bernard Bresslaw, Norman Brooks, Anthony Buckeridge, James Cagney, Michael Caine, Ian Carmichael, John Carradine, Sir Charles Chaplin, Ronald Chesney, Julie Christie, Brian Clemens, Dick Clement, James Coburn, Francis Ford Coppola, John Russell Coryell, Nicholas Courtney, Tom Courtenay, Michael Crawford, David Croft, Richmal Crompton, Windsor Davies, R.F. Delderfield, Pauline Devaney, E.L. Doctorow, Michael Dobbs, Sergio Donati, Michael Douglas, Harry Driver, Paul Eddington, Lee Ermey, W.C. Fields, Albert Finney, F. Scott Fitzgerald, Ian Fleming, Henry Fonda, Peter Fonda, John Ford, Bill Fraser, Willis Goldbeck, Julie Goodyear, Maxim Gorki, Andy Griffith, Walon Green, Davis Grubb, Alan Hackney, Mervyn Haisman, Willis Hall, Earl Hamner Jr, Thomas Harris, Gustav Hasford, Joseph Heller, Marc Hellinger, Michael Herr, Patricia Highsmith, Nat Hiken, Barry Hines, Mike Hodges, Anthony Hope, Dennis Hopper, Norman Hudis, John Huston, David Jacobs, Anthony Jay, Joseph Kesselring, Stephen King, Walter Koenig, Dorothy M. Johnson, Ian La Frenais, John Landis, Charles Laughton, Henry Lincoln, Sergio Leone, Ira Levin, Sinclair Lewis, Ted Lewis, Ken Loach, Jonathan Lynn, David McCallum, Patrick MacNee, Herman Mankiewicz, Derek Marlowe, W. Somerset Maugham, John Milius, Robert Mitchum, David Morrell, Jack Palance, Boris Pasternak, Sam Peckinpah, Jimmy Perry, James Poe, Roman Polanski, Melville Davisson Post, Vince Powell, Frederic Raphael, Ian Richardson, Diana Rigg, Tim Robbins, Gene Roddenberry, Peter Rogers, Sam Rolfe, John Schlesinger, Charles G. Schultz, Ronald Searle, Antony Sher, Alan Sillitoe, Phil Silvers, Jack Smethurst, Ormond G. Smith, Terry Southern, John Steinbeck, James Stewart, Oliver Stone, Booth Tarkington, Gerald Thomas, Richard Thomas, Jim Thompson, David Thomson, Leo Tolstoi, Robert Towne, B. Traven, S.S. Van Dyne, Luciano Vincenzoini, Rudolph Walker, Raoul Walsh, Tony Warren, Keith Waterhouse, Colin Welland, Orson Welles, William Wharton, Geoffrey Williams, Ronald Wolfe.

To Monique — EB

To Maura — KN

"What a country! Afraid of Debs and proud of Dempsey! It's too silly."

George Bernard Shaw

IN THE AIR

1989

The PPC had offered to send an official car to the hotel, but he decided he'd rather walk. He would learn more from a stroll among the bustle of ordinary America than a cruise in a Detroit Streetmaster with a Party Suit.

Getting It Together might be in progress, but there were still long, impatient queues outside the grocery stores. Straight Talking might be the buzzword, but there were still only Party papers—*Newsweek*, *Workboy*, *MAD*—on the newsstands. It was chilly, and everyone was hurrying, thin overcoat collars turned up against the windblast. This was a busy city, with no time to lose. Very different from the London Lowe had left two days ago. There, it had been Autumn; here, Fall had fallen, and it was Winter. He was breathing dirty ice-chips. He had been coughing off and on since the plane touched down at Hillquit Field. In the industrial USSA, you could always taste the air. There was already a light dandruff of snow, soon the glaciation level would sweep across Lake Michigan and the city would be like Reykjavik or Petrograd, carpeted with filthy slush. All Americans were equal, but those here with bearskin hats and gloves had a bitterly resented edge.

He came off Michigan Avenue, into Alphonse Capone Plaza. Soon, unless he misjudged First Secretary Vonnegut, to be renamed Something Else Plaza. He looked up at the triumphal statue, and wondered how long it would last. Apart from anything else, it was monumentally ugly. No larger than the *Hindenburg* Zeppelin, the bronze depicted a slimmer-than-the-newsreels Al on a rearing steed, riding down Robber Barons like Buffalo Bill pursuing Apaches. The bloated, top-hatted figures

1

crawling away from the horse's hooves were grotesque caricature Vanderbilts, Rockefellers and Fords, weighed down by moneybags and jewellery. Over the last few years, the equestrian Al had taken a few dents but, ironically, the nearby stone statue of another former mayor, an obscurity named Daley, had been much more extensively vandalised. That must say something about the relative values of Chicagoans.

Chicago—not New York or Los Angeles or any other phoney, workshy, seaboard city—had been the seat of the Second American Revolution. And they never let you forget it. No matter what might be happening on Capitol Hill or the White House, this was the heart and guts of the USSA. The Windy City, he had been told endlessly, was where federal troops opened fire on Father O'Shaughnessy and his hunger marchers in the abortive uprising of 1905. Where Eugene V. Debs took control of the Union stockyard in 1912, as a prelude to launching the Revolution. In DeMille's famous 1926 film, the blood of the martyred strikers had mingled with that of the slaughtered cattle as the army stepped in, providing a single image that summed up the struggle to free the country from the Robber Barons. Actually, the fighting had been in the streets outside, not on the killing floor, but Americans always preferred a dramatic fiction to the dreary truth. Even now, official history accepted that Capone had got his scar in a knife-fight with William Randolph Hearst, though everyone knew he had really gashed his cheek on a garbage can lid falling over in a Brooklyn alley.

Even with the New Deal, slogans seemed to count more than policies. Researching a piece for *The Sun* on the etymology of what they were already calling Vonnegutspeak, he had discovered the First Secretary's team of advisors spent more time coming up with the catch phrases—Straight Talking, then Getting It Together—than in formulating the precise policies. He wondered if things could really change. Despite Vonnegut's efforts, the United Socialist States of America was as much under the shadow of Capone now as it had been under the Robber Barons in the '20s. After a yoke has been lifted, you have to get the ache out of your shoulders, rid yourself of the habit of being oppressed.

And if there were die-hard Caponists anywhere, this was the city for them. Back in '21, Chicago had been the power-base behind Mayor Al's bid for the highest office in the USSA. Now, with fifty-year-old crimes and massacres being raked over daily, Capone was constantly being labelled a monster, a mass murderer, a thief, a lecher, a pederast.

The Capone statue looked across the Plaza towards the Lexington Hotel, where Chairman Al once made his headquarters. Now, it was a national treasure and every fifteen minutes uniformed guides showed people around. Back in the '70s, they had opened a sealed room and found the leftovers of long-forgotten lights of the Party who had fallen out with Capone during one of the earliest purges. To the left of the Lexington was the Tomb of the Unknown Worker. A white marble temple, all pillars and steps and ecstatic muses, the Tomb was modelled on the National Monument in Rome and looked like a giant wedding cake left overnight in the rain. Atmospheric pollution had tarnished it, greying and blacking every niche and crevice. Opposite that was the People's Place of Culture, Lowe's nominal hosts for this trip. The PPC should have made him feel at home, since it was a replica of the Albert Hall. Actually, encountering it was as disorienting as, say, stumbling across London Bridge in the Arizona desert. And as if the statue and the buildings weren't enough, the Plaza was criss-crossed by the "El", giving the impression that the city had been invaded by giant locusts from a '50s Russian sci-fi film.

As he entered the People's Palace, Lowe imagined how it had all started. In the Oval Office, Aimee Semple McPherson, the Chairman's mistress-helpmeet, brings Scarface Al his morning mail. Included are a couple of postcards from Secretary of State Louis B. Mayer on his European travels. The First Comrade likes what he sees and calls in Secretary of the Interior Jimmy Hoffa. "Hey Jimmy, dat's whut I calls two real classy buildings. Get 'em built for me, in Chicago, by the Lexington, near dat statue of me lookin' like Napoleon on Trigger. Only build 'em bigger than dese, huh? We don't want no one sayin' we'se small guys. *Capisce?*"

The receptionist—a uniformed teenage girl with a pony tail—on the fifth floor smiled at him, asked him to wait, and returned her attention to a monochrome television perched near the ceiling. Connie Chung was on the border, watching the Texican wall come down. The return of the Lone Star State to the Union was front page news, and in the restaurant last night, Lowe had felt the excitement when the band played "The Eyes of Texas Are Upon Us" in honour of the reunification. Connie was saying that freedom of passage across the border would actually mean fewer Americans trying to sneak into Mexico to take advantage of higher wages. Lowe wasn't sure. The Mexican-American War of 1917 had never really been resolved, and he had noticed how deeply anti-Mex feeling still ran throughout the USSA. The partition of Texas, when the Tsars and Kaisers and Kings of the Old World had tried to stifle the Revolution at birth by supplying *Presidente* Villa with arms and advisors, was still a national open wound.

The people he was due to meet were only five minutes late. Hunt Thompson—a tall, thin, straight-looking man of about 50—emerged from the interior office, clip-board and itinerary under his arm. He wore the unofficial Party uniform, a suit that shone at all the leading edges. He gripped Lowe's hand a little too hard, a little too long. A Junior Secretary at the Ministry of Culture, Comrade Hunt was definitely not an undercover FBI man. He sweated too much for that.

"Comrade Lowe," the official began, "this is, uh…"

Lowe didn't need to be told. This was the man he had crossed an ocean and spent ten hours queuing at three airports to see.

"Charles Hardin Holley?"

Holley was skinny as a nurse's pay-packet and had thinning grey curly hair. He wore bottle-bottom spectacles, a loud checked suit a size too large and one of those Texican bootlace ties that all surly kids hanging around drugstores were wearing at the moment. But Holley had a huge, toothy grin that was a mixture of openness and conspiratorial leer. He was a slightly disreputable uncle who drops in unannounced to cadge money and cause mischief.

"Charlie," Holley said, "call me Charlie."

When Comrade Hunt produced a purse and asked them how they wanted their coffee, Holley arched an eyebrow towards the door. Lowe picked up the signal at once. Charlie wanted out of the PPC. Lowe could go along with that. He always preferred interviewing in the wild to visiting time at the zoo.

"Ah, wait here," Comrade Hunt said, as he headed into the communal cafeteria to get two cartons of California coffee.

Lowe stepped towards the lift. Holley shook his head.

"Never use an elevator unless a senior Party official is visiting the building, Mr. Lowe."

Holley smiled and blew a goodbye kiss to the receptionist. "Tell Hunt we went thataway," he said before she could protest, pointing up. "The limey wanted to see the view of Lake Michigan from the Director's office window."

He pushed the door, and held it opened for Lowe. The two men swiftly descended the stairs. Lowe, who smoked two packs of Strands a day, felt the strain in his chest, while the long-legged Holley, fifteen years older, jogged like one of the militia teenagers who skateboarded in Mother Jones Park.

They hit the streets, and Lowe took the time to cough some wind back into his lungs.

"You want to talk about music, right?," Holley said as they assumed a brisk pace along backstreets the sweepers hadn't visited for years.

"Yes, sure," he said. "There's a lot of interest in you in Europe."

They turned a corner. In minutes, they were away from the official Chicago, and back at the turn of the century. Sidewalk stalls, ready to shut up at the first gleam of a cop's shield, were open, selling chocolate, fruit and other expensive items.

A pretty, middle-aged woman who ran a clothing stall was looking Lowe up and down, with undisguised desire.

"Don't get excited," said Holley, "she's after your trousers."

Last night, in the hotel corridor, a young man had offered Lowe a large dollar sum for his fairly ordinary Burton's jacket. The mark of forbidden luxury here was an authentic London pinstripe suit. The flashiest of the street traders, who was offering Japanese videos and Russian gramophones, signalled his black market wealth by proudly wearing a Dunn & Co. bowler hat, and a carnation in the lapel of his Burberry raincoat.

"Where are we going?"

"A place I know. If you're interested in music, you've got to hear it in an authentic setting. You won't discover nothing chewing the fat up there with tightass Thompson offering 'advice' and 'cultural reference points' all the time."

"Won't Comrade Hunt be upset when he finds out we're bunking off?"

"Bunking off?" Holley grinned. "Oh, you mean playing hookey? Naaawww! Thompson's having a great time. So we take a little Mexican leave? What's he going to do about it? Rat on me to the Federal Bureau of Ideology? It's supposed to be a free country these days. Rave on, Mr. Lowe."

Lowe nodded, wondering which of the street traders was the informer.

"Here's the place," Holley said.

It was Texas John's Bar and Grill, a greasy, nicotine-stained diner down a back alley. A sign announced that the establishment was proud to sell near beer and took foodstamps. There were generous reductions for men and women in uniform.

There was a fat man in a worn topcoat huddled over a stove heater behind the counter, and a solitary diner with his nose in *Workboy*, otherwise the place was empty. On the wall there was a movie poster; Stallone and Chuck Norris defending the Alamo.

Holley waved at the fat man, and walked to the end of the room. He rapped his knuckles three times on the wall. A framed photo of President Vonnegut slid to one side, and a pair of eyes appeared. A concealed door opened, and Holley stepped into a smoke-smelly room. Lowe should have guessed that disreputable Uncle Charlie would be taking him to a speakeasy.

The room was large and simple, furnished with a random array of tables and chairs. Along one side ran a bar with a catholic and cosmopolitan array of beers and liquors. In a corner, a rock and roll band were tuning up. Customers of varying ages waved at Holley. A tall youth with a bootlace tie and a velvet-collared jacket slapped him on the back and asked whether he would be playing later.

"Sure," he said, "just as soon as I've finished talking with my buddy. This is Lowe, he's an English newspaperman."

The youth stuck out his hand, and Lowe shook.

"Comrade," the youth said. "Welcome to the real America."

Holley steered him to a quiet corner. A waiter brought a bottle of Matthews Southern Comfort and Lowe reached for his wallet. Holley waved his currency away.

"Let me pay, buddy. I'm flavour of the month, the government likes me all of a sudden, the government pays people it likes. The way I see it, I got to make the most of it, because it might not last."

Lowe took a drink, and felt it cosy up to his ulcers. He had a Fleet Street Stomach.

"Is this the interview then?" Holley asked.

"I suppose so."

"So what's the question? All the Europeans have questions? I'm big in France, you know. If I could get my foreign earnings, I'd be rich."

The lead guitarist of the group played a few chords, out of tune, grinning over at the dissenter and Holley laughed.

"Don't let Peggy Sue hear you do that to her song," he shouted. "That was my first real song, you know," he explained.

Lowe slipped some more liquor into his throat. "So, Charlie," he began, "why…?"

"Good question," Holley grinned. "A bit broad, but a good question."

"You know what I mean."

"Yeah, I suppose I do. You mean, why did I let myself in for a life of heartbreak and persecution?"

"If you like."

"You never think it'll be that bad, but then…well, like the man said, a socialist's gotta do what a socialist's gotta do…"

"You started when you were a teenager. Back in the '50s…"

Holley took a drink himself, and leaned back. His smile-lines turned into wrinkles, but he still looked like a gangling kid.

"Yeah, the '50s. Production drives, show trials, root beer and crinolines. I suppose when you get to my age, you tend to have a kind of misty picture of your young days, like with that fog around the frame you get in flashbacks in the movies. I always have to pull myself up and remember they were real hard times. Kids today don't know what it was like. Really, they don't…"

Lowe tried to remember his own experience of the '50s, but couldn't. There wasn't much to his memory before Telstar and Yeager's first spaceflight in the X-15. In Britain, that had been the fag-end of the Churchill Regime.

"It went sour before I was born, and my mama never let me forget. We were from Texas. We've been refugees all our lives. My grand-daddy stayed in Lubbock and got put up against a wall by Zapata. That gave me something against Chairman Al even before everyone else came out and said he was a sidewinder. When Capone muscled his way towards power off the back of the big labour unions, the first thing he did was cut Texas loose and make a deal with Villa."

Like all Americans over forty, Holley spoke as if he had known Al Capone personally.

"Scarface and his cronies just took over the whole ball game in the '20s. Long, Luciano, Hoffa and—of course—'Executioner' Hoover. They were no better than the Robber Barons. Everyone was afraid of the rat-tat-tat through the door. The I-Men always came to take people away at four in the morning. Some got a bullet in the head after a big circus trial, some didn't even get a trial. The lucky ones disappeared to Alaska.

"Just after the War, everything was rationed. Soldiers were coming back short a limb, if they came back at all. You know what casualties were like on the Japanese mainland. We didn't have it so bad because we lived in the country, but we went hungry a lot. We had to give up so much of our food quota to the Party. And one day every month was a

Day of Socialist Sacrifice when we didn't eat at all. But look at the newsreels, and see whether you think President Capone was losing any weight."

"What about music?"

"Music? I'll tell you what music was in those days: Mario fucking Lanza singing about agricultural machinery. And the movies weren't much better. All you'd get would be four-hour epics of the Revolution. They'd start by showing how bad things were under the Robber Barons, who were always played by Sydney Greenstreet or Oliver Hardy. Then the hero, usually played by Capone's pal George Raft, would make a half-hour speech and rouse the proletarian masses to a thrilling storming of somewhere or other choreographed by Busby Berkeley. Another speech, some opera, and that would be it. All us kids knew there was an I-Man in every theatre watching to see who didn't applaud loudly enough."

"Was this in Texas?"

"No. We were relocated during one of Capone's Reconstruction Drives. Just about the entire population of Lubbock was bussed North in '42, to work in munitions plants near Roseville, Kansas. Al was paranoid about putting anything strategically important near Mexico, just in case they threw in with the Axis. Dad worked on tanks for a while, and after the War, the plant turned over to tractors. We lived in a kind of ghetto, the Texan quarter. Texans took a lot of abuse. Everyone remembered the War of '17, and we were forever the State That Couldn't Defend Itself. As a pimply Texan kid with glasses, my early life wasn't exactly comfortable. Most of the other Texan boys were six-foot-wide football players, and I was a beanpole. That meant I was elected to be the butt of all the Texas jokes. At school, there was this one Kansas kid—Melvin Yandell, the son of the local Party Chairman—and he was always beating up on me, with his buddies Chick Willis and Philly Winspear."

"And that made you a rebel?"

"Hell no, that made me desperately want to make the team. I thought if I was a credit to the Revolution, all the crap would stop. I was kind of what these days they call a nerd. I became an enthusiastic member of the Pioneers of Socialist Youth of America. They'd be like your Boy Scouts, I guess, only tuned in to the Party. I was a real good little Communist. At the age of twelve, I was the youngest Section Leader in Kansas, and I was winning badges for everything. I had badges for basic, intermediate and advanced socialism, efficiency, personal hygiene, fieldcraft and Charles

H. Marx knows what else. My favourite was for Enemy Aircraft Identification. From silhouettes, I could tell a Sikorsky SI-51 jet fighter from a Supermarine Swift. If Churchill and the Tsar had ever decided to start World War Three, I was ready..."

Holley laughed.

"Let's put it this way, Mr. Lowe, I was a creep. I ate all the bullshit they fed us, then asked for seconds. The best thing about the Pioneers, though, was that I got to fly. I did my time in gliders and trainers at summer camp, and a corporal at Fort Baxter sometimes took me up in a spotter plane. Flying, yeah, that was the best. If I'd had better eyesight and didn't have music, I'd have been a pilot."

It was hard to imagine the stringbean troubadour as an Ace of the Skies. He couldn't talk about flying without stretching his arms out like a little kid playing aeroplane.

So, Lowe wondered, how did a good little communist turn into a semi-outlaw, a marginal who has spent most of his adult life damning the Party in song, keeping only one step ahead of the FBI?

"What happened, Charlie?"

Holley came in to land, and refilled their glasses.

"It's kind of complicated. Dad gave me a beat-up old guitar for my sixteenth birthday and that changed things. Remember your first kiss?"

Lowe did. Nicola Godsell. Churchill Day, 1968.

"That's what my first guitar was like for me."

His hands were strumming now, fingers moving fast.

"By then, I was kind of growing out of the Pioneers anyhow. There was a thing that started me to thinking real hard. Just before I was sixteen. It shook everything up. It's funny now I come to think about it, because that was about flying, too. I can even tell you exactly when it was. Labor Day in 1951. That would make it the weekend of the first Monday in September. You know how, when you were a kid, the Summers were longer. This one had gone on forever..."

"I'll settle your hash, you revisionist scum!" shouted Dick Tracy as he burst into the secret meeting of the Counter-Revolutionary Society for the Subjugation of the People. There was a gasp from Flabface, the last of the Robber Barons. Dick laughed his granite-jawed laugh as he surveyed the sorry crew.

Charlie tensed, willing the fearless FBI agent to pull his trusty Colt .45 and plug the bad guys.

"That's as far as you go, I-Man," said the smooth, sardonic voice of Bette Davis. "That prod you're feeling in your back is a pistol, and I'm not scared to use it. Finger some clouds…"

"Dick Tracy, Special Agent of the FBI is in a tight spot," said the announcer urgently as the staccato theme music rose. "Will Dick escape? And can he stop Flabface destroying New York with his death-ray? To find out, tune in to next week's thrilling episode of *Dick Tracy, Special Agent of the FBI.*"

"How do you like that, Dad?" said Charlie. "It just goes to show you can never trust a dame,"

"That's a fine thing to say," replied his father, as he plugged his corncob with Victory Virginia. He switched off the radio and pulled his chair across the wooden floorboards to be nearer Charlie. He lowered his voice, so that Ma wouldn't hear him from the kitchen.

"Listen, son, it's the big holiday weekend coming up, and you're getting about old enough to start finding out about, uh, dames for yourself. I got an idea…" He paused to put a match to the cheap tobacco, engulfing them in thick, stale-smelling smoke. "Your Dad may be dumb, but he ain't stupid, if that makes sense. I seen how young Peggy Sue next door's been looking at you these last few months."

Charlie shrank into his chair, partly to escape the bitter fumes, partly because he had an idea what was coming next.

He was scared. Not that a Pioneer would admit that to anyone.

"She's a nice girl, Charlie. From a good Texan family, too. She's just about your age. Why don't you go next door and ask her if she'll go to the movies with you. They've got *The Octopus* playing down at the People's Palace. Sounds like a real good picture, and I bet that your Captain in the Pioneers has recommended you all go see it."

That was true. Captain Rook said it was the duty of every Pioneer to catch *The Octopus.*

"It's got Sydney Greenstreet as the Railroad King," his father was saying. "And Julius Garfinkle plays the union leader. Of course, if everything goes right you won't be looking at the screen much. Might even have to go back to see the movie."

The kitchen door was shouldered open, and Mother came in, carrying Charlie's badge-festooned uniform jacket.

"What plots are you two hatching behind my back?" she asked.

Father grunted and retreated behind the *Roseville Echo* to read how his fellow worker-heroes had exceeded their annual targets.

"There you are, Charlie," said his mother. "I've sewed on your latest badge and ironed the jacket. Historical Perspective, whatever next. Don't you get this messed up before the parade tomorrow. What are you doing this evening?"

"I've got to go out," said Charlie. "The section is still a little rough on some of the drill. We've had a lot of young kids join in the last few weeks. I've got to practise them some more for the parade tomorrow."

"Don't be back too late. You'll need a good night's sleep."

His father put down the Echo and smiled. "Ella's right, Charlie. It'll be a big day tomorrow, with all those fliers coming to town. You know why they're coming? Because we exceeded all our production targets."

Charlie's father turned the radio on again. It was not a good idea to miss President Capone's Friday evening fireside chat.

The familiar, rough-edged voice, began. "Citizens, Workers, this is Chairman Al…"

"Fireside chat!" said mother. "It'd be a fine thing to have a proper fireside instead of a rickety old stove. And as for you, Charlie, I think you're getting a little old to be still playing with the Pioneers. It's about time you started seeing girls. Why don't you ask Peggy Sue out to a movie…And just what are you grinning at, Lawrence Holley?"

"I don't know how much you know about America, Mr. Lowe, but a Labor Day weekend is some big deal. Every town has its parades, and speeches and hoe-downs. It was an even bigger deal under Chairman Capone. Everyone I knew bought it outright. Except Mom, of course. She was a real old dissenter. She was taking the risks. She was First Aid officer at the tractor plant, and too good at it to be got rid of. Safety was kind of lax, and I had this idea that all kinds of gory accidents were happening that I wasn't being told about. They called my Mom a lifesaver, and cut her some slack. Dad respected Scarface Al, though. He was never a Party member, because Roseville couldn't have any Texan yellowstreaks on their team, but he eventually got to be a foreman at the plant. He kept his nose clean and half-believed all that bullstuff about the nobility of labour. And things like these famous fliers coming to town was proof to him that the Party cared about ordinary folks like us.

"After Al died, we had Goldwater and Nixon in the White House. Then came the three old farts nobody took seriously because they were senile. They were only alive because they were plugged into the direct current. That's when my mother really went to town. Back in '83, she was in a line at the Roseville General Store and cracked a joke about the shortages. Said what she wanted for her birthday was a pound of beefsteak wrapped in toilet paper. Someone squealed to the Sheriff and she ended up on charges of recidivism and aggravated hooliganism. She was eighty. All the neighbours clubbed together to pay her fine, then held a big party for her, and gave her a present of a pound of beefsteak wrapped in toilet paper.

"Now where the hell had we got to? Labor Day weekend, 1951. All righty.

"I couldn't sleep. When you're that age it's very important to appear real cool about everything. But I was bursting with excitement and pride. I was so wound up I could hardly pee. The Revolutionary Fraternity Squadron was coming to Roseville. I told you I wanted to be a pilot? Now, all my great heroes—every single one of them—were going to appear in my home town the following day. I'd been reading about this in the *Echo* and *Socialist Youth Magazine* for weeks and it still didn't sound true.

"The RFS was an elite cadre. Only the most famous names in American aviation need apply. If the Wright Brothers had been around, they might just have qualified to pull the chocks away. First, there was Lieutenant Lafayette R. Hubbard. He'd been a barnstormer before the War, flew for the Navy during it, had sunk more submarines than rust, and had personally killed Tojo in single combat with his bare hands. *Thrilling Air Battles* had a great cover of him strangling the Jap while leaping out of a burning Workers' Victory Twin-Engine Fighter. That's what the record said anyway, and the record ought to know, because Hubbard wrote most of it himself. I'd read his stuff in *Socialist Sky Aces*, *Blackhawk*, and a dozen other officially approved pulps. And Hubbard, Mr. Lowe, was just the ground crew.

"Then there was Major Joseph 'Bomber Joe' McCarthy. He had led the first carrier-borne attack on Japan with a squadron of B-25s. My favourite was Colonel Charles Lindbergh. He was famous as the first man to fly the Atlantic solo, but he had been a fighter pilot during the war, with 60 kills to his credit. I guess I liked him because he was something of a loner, like I was. The Lone Eagle, they called him. Who else? Oh yeah, General Mitch 'Duke' Morrison. He was the first American ashore at both Normandy and Iwo Jima and had also flown Warhawks with the Flying Tigers in China. A big Iowa farmboy with a grin that could crack pebbles, he was reputedly the toughest man in America, after J. Edgar Hoover.

"The leader was General Curtis LeMay. During the War, he was the great advocate of daylight precision bombing. At some point, he changed his opinion and took to snarling 'bomb 'em back into the Stone Age' and advocating a policy of wall-to-wall carpet bombing. Before the Invasion of Japan—you remember what a bloodbath that was—LeMay had supposedly disobeyed orders and personally lead a mission to drop incendiaries on a Black Dragon Cult suicide squad waiting to blow up the city, taking as many Yankee soldiers as possible with it. After his stylish flattening of Tokyo, Chairman Al presented the General with a pair of pearl-handled, silver-plated Wild West revolvers that he was rumoured to wear on all occasions."

The sun was already high as Charlie met the rest of his section at 08:00 hours on Main Street. On a nearby piece of waste ground, he ran them through some last-minute drill with their wooden rifles, and straightened out a few caps and scarves before he formed them up into line and marched them off towards the edge of town. He was satisfied, and confident.

They RV'd with Captain Rook and the three other sections out by the plant. None of the other sections were as well turned out as Charlie's boys. Pete Horowitz's section looked real sloppy: shorts not properly pressed, shoes and boots barely polished, unvarnished rifles held together with Utility Tape. Horowitz's Heroes couldn't dress a straight line if there was a year's ration of candy bars in it. For all that, it never seemed to bother Rook. Pete Horowitz, Kansas-born and good-looking, was the Captain's golden boy.

Rook ordered them to parade files, pushed his wire-rims back, and called out the register. All 108 boys in the Roseville Company of the Pioneers of Socialist Youth, First Brigade, the Frank Nitti (2nd Kansas) Guards Division, were present and correct. Rook, a bachelor who taught Gym and Political Education at Roseville High, pulled himself up to his full five-eight, heaved in his stomach so hard Charlie thought his shorts would fall down, and gave them the obligatory pep-talk. It was familiar stuff about representing their community, showing due respect towards the heroes, and striving in all ways to follow the example of the selfless socialist patriots. For good measure, he added his usual little warning on the dire dangers of sexual incontinence.

The Captain called come to attention, shoulder arms, right turn and march. Charlie expected that his section, since it was best turned-out, would take the point. But Rook ordered Pete Horowitz to lead off. Ah well, fuck you very much Comrade Captain Porky Rook. He led his section off second, pacing his long legs carefully so the younger kids could keep in step.

By now, everyone in town was also on the way to Baxter Field, the airstrip at the edge of Fort Baxter. Most people were on foot, some of the folk from the collective farms were coming in on donkey-carts or farm-wagons pulled by tractors. A group of Party officials from Tuttle Creek drove by slowly in a gleaming limousine.

Once, the section was forced to scatter into the dirt at the side of the road when an old Haynes Roadster, driven at speed, brushed by, the horn honking the first line of the "Internationale" at them. Charlie heard someone yell "Texas toy soldier" at him, and he recognised the driver as Melvin Yandell. He dressed and talked like a hoodlum, but his Daddy was Osgood Yandell, the local Party Chairman. Yandell's sidekicks Chick Willis and Philly Winspear leaned out of the car as they passed to make the usual cracks about "Texas faggots in short pants". Charlie saw Yandell taking a crafty pull on a bottle as he drove past.

Recently, the Yandell crowd hadn't been beating him up so often, but they had taken to cruising slowly through the Texan quarter on Summer evenings, calling out to the girls. According to the Thoughts of Chairman Junior Melvin, all Texan women were sex-starved because their men weren't capable, and he and his buddies were more than willing to step into the breach and do their duty for Kansas. Peggy Sue told Charlie that her older sister Patsy was staying in most nights, just to keep out of Melvin's way. One day, Yandell would cause some serious trouble...

But Charlie was determined that nothing was going to spoil his day. As he marched his guys through the bunting-festooned gates of Fort Baxter —"Home of the 194th Socialist Infantry Regiment, Comrade Col J.T. Hall Commanding"—he snapped a perfect salute. The guards smartly returned the gesture. He ordered his guys, his men, to eyes right as an additional though not strictly necessary courtesy. The Sergeant at the gate, a Tennessee Comrade with Texan sympathies, whistled admiration. Marching at the head of his section, perfectly in time with his comrades, Charlie felt like a hero himself.

The Pioneers formed up in front of a wooden grandstand erected for Party bosses, factory and collective farm representatives, and their families and hangers-on. To their right was the red carpet to the stand and to

Colonel Hall. Beyond the carpet was the regimental band, then the 194th itself. Already, it was getting hot, and Charlie's neck felt sweaty and gritty under his bandanna.

Charlie's folks weren't important enough to get into the grandstand. They were over in the bleachers at the far side of the runway, sitting with Peggy Sue and her parents. He didn't like that much. For all he knew, they could be discussing wedding arrangements...

"I hear them! They're coming!" someone shouted. Gradually, the field fell silent.

An aero-engine droned in the distance. Captain Rook yelled the Pioneers to attention and 108 pairs of feet slammed into the ground practically in unison. Even Pete Horowitz got in step for the occasion. Over on their right, the 194th did likewise. The regular army drilled a lot less smartly than the Pioneers.

The engine noise got louder. For Charlie, this was torture. He had to keep eyes front, but he wanted to watch the magnificent craft execute what would doubtless be a perfect landing.

The regimental band struck up Sousa's "Heroic Struggle of the Seventh Socialist Air Fleet". Charlie hated that march, because he had once taken a whipping in school for calling it "The Stars and Stripes Forever", the old title his mother still called it by.

Something was out of step. The plane sounded as if it needed a serious overhaul. And it was a small engine, a coughing insect almost lost under the music. Not nearly powerful enough for one of the big Curtiss Helldivers the RFS flew.

Tyres screeched like an abused seagull as they hit the tarmac, left it again, and definitely touched down. Spectators were gasping, chattering in surprise. Some were laughing.

It was time to disobey orders. He let his eyes wander right.

The aircraft bumping past was not a sleek Helldiver, but a biplane plainly held together by spit, gum and string. The landing was a disgrace. Pieces dropped off the smoke-belching machine as it limped down the runway, coming in like the song, On a Wing and an Oath of Loyalty to the Revolution. The engine burped its last, and a two-bladed wooden prop fluttered to a halt. If this was the RFS, everyone had been seriously misled. There were words painted down the side of the fuselage. HUGHES'S HELL'S ANGELS—BARN STORMING AND CROP SPRAYING (CHEAP). Charlie's Enemy Aircraft Recognition badge did not cover this flying freak.

Everyone else seemed just as confused, but it didn't pay to take risks; if these were the revolutionary heroes, it would cost someone a one-way trip to Alaska if they were insulted. So the military band struck up the latest national anthem, as two men climbed from the battered aircraft. Both wore torn leather flying jackets and oil-stained pants. The younger man reached into the forward cockpit and pulled out a guitar case. The older man, probably in his fifties, opened his jacket and, to the barely-suppressed shock of the spectators, struggled to pull a bottle from an inside pocket. Having succeeded, he uncorked it with his teeth, and took a lengthy, luxurious swig. Apart from Melvin Yandell, Charlie had never seen anyone drink alcohol—he knew the bottle had to be liquor—in public, although almost everyone violated the Prohibition Edict in private.

As the old pilot passed the bottle to the younger man, a girl in her late teens went forward along the red carpet to welcome the RFS on behalf of Roseville, and, in honour of General LeMay's achievements over Tokyo, present them with a bouquet of flowers in the shape of a bomb.

As the girl wobbled, on unfamiliar high heels, Melvin Yandell shouted out something crude about "Texas tootsies", and she blushed flag-red. It was Patsy, Peggy Sue's sister, and, Texan or not, the prettiest girl in town, which was why she was the Welcome Comrade. Patsy, who usually wore shorts or cheerleader skirts, was in a starched pink dress that stuck out three feet in any direction. Charlie wondered if, in three years time, Peggy Sue would be shaped like Patsy, and found himself a little hotter and grittier under the bandanna. He tried to think of Chairman Capone on the toilet, and hoped his mental incontinence wouldn't noticeably swell the front of his perfectly-pressed shorts. Actually, he realised later, he could have sprouted a boner the size of a B-29 and no one would have noticed.

As Patsy approached, a yellow-tooth grin split the older pilot's mask of flying grime. He unwound what had once been a white silk flying scarf to drape it over his plane's wing. He pulled off his flying helmet and goggles, and shook out a wild man's head of long, unkempt grey hair.

Patsy was so concerned with not falling off her heels and humiliating herself she didn't notice that the fliers hardly fit the description of the expected heroes. Charlie realised Patsy was not wearing her glasses this morning, and probably couldn't see the end of the carpet, let alone the air hobo she was giving a floral incendiary.

The drunk accepted the bouquet, laughed a little, tossed it over his shoulder and grabbed Patsy. He began dog-licking her face and sorting through her onion-layers of skirt in search of her backside. This was definitely not the way a socialist hero behaved. It was a prime example of sexual incontinence. Melvin was cheering, but his father shut him up.

Over to the right, a voice called for MPs. It was Colonel Hall, now scowling along the red carpet towards the plane. He reached the fliers as, at the prompting of his friend, the older man reluctantly released Patsy. She slipped off her shoes and ran back towards the grandstand, wiping her mouth on the back of her hand. She had probably had to get up at 04:00 hours to start painting her face, and was now badly smudged.

The Colonel was too far away for Charlie to hear everything being said. But he could catch the gist of it. Colonel Hall asked the fliers to identify themselves. Whatever their answer was, it had nothing to do with the RFS. Two MPs arrived and were told to take the pilots away. The younger began pleading apologetically with the Colonel. They had run out of gas and had needed somewhere to land. The Colonel, who just wanted this nuisance out of the way, relented, giving some kind of stern warning. All the soldiers said Colonel Hall was a pushover. The old guy cheered when he was let off, slapped the Colonel on the back so hard the officer's belly shook, and offered some of his liquor to the MPs.

The newcomers, Charlie gathered, were called Jack and Howie.

"In America, we set a great store on mobility, Mr. Lowe. That's one of the things Capone hated, but was never able to crush. Scarface wanted us to stay put on the farm or in the collective, but I guess we're just born with the urge to roam. It's such a goddamn big country. You travel enough, rack up enough good stories, and you become some kind of hero. Most of those wanderers were on the move all the time because they were fugitives from the state. Guess that's what happened to me. I wasn't the first to hit the road with a guitar, though. In the '30s, there was a guy named Guthrie, a wheel in his local collective who one day just plain had enough of Capone flushing the Revolution down the commode and set out to tell the country what he thought of the whole damn ball of wax. They caught him, and hanged him. That brings you up, doesn't it? They hanged a man for singing songs. Somehow, that's the worst thing Capone ever did. I know he had all those Navajos and blacks wiped out and used to shoot down his former friends like jackrabbits, but poor old Woody, hanging from a climbing frame in a schoolyard in Illinois, is like the

17

totem to me, the one victim who stands for all the others. Wrote a song about him, once.

"I wrote songs about Jack and Howie too, but you've never heard them. They were early things, and no good. And that's a shame, because those two bums in their beat-up ridiculous flying deathtrap turned my whole life around.

"Jack was French-Canadian, although I think he was born in the USSA. He was handsome in a comic strip way, like Smilin' Jack without the moustache. He started a lot more poems and stories than he finished, got drunk eight nights a week and threw in mornings too, and went after women as if he were trying to beat the record. He wrote a books that came out in Canada and France, and used to get smuggled in, distributed by dissenter groups. There might be official American editions of some of his novels, *In the Air*, *The Subterraneans* or *Lonesome Traveller*, real soon. Word is, he drank himself to death twenty years back, but I don't have to believe that if I don't want to. When I knew him, years of moonshine had given his voice an extra frog-croak, and he was in poetry the way some of the best guys are in music, because he didn't have a choice. The words were inside, and they just kept bursting out. I wish I could remember more of what he said, because I'd put tunes to it. He used to chew patent medicines like they were life savers, and tried to sleep as little as possible so he could get the most awake time out of his life.

"Howie is the real mystery. Some people say he was born rich and lost it all in the Revolution. This story also claims he gave Al his scar, smashing an ornamental pen-set into the Chairman's face during the storming of the Stock Exchange. Since that'd require Capone to be in the thick of some fighting I tend to discount it as a fanciful rumour. Other people say Howie was some kinda crazy wildcat oilman raised by Apaches, or coyotes. There's even a story that he made a living designing brassieres but that's just too ridiculous, although a job that required a lot of thinking about titties would have suited him fine. Another version is that he used to be a Hollywood movie director in the '30s, and fell foul of the Arbuckle Code while he was making a big aviation epic about aces flying south of the border to rescue POWs the Mexicans were holding after the war. Howie was in trouble because he kept leaving out the screenwriter's twelve-page political speeches so he could spend more time shooting airplanes, but he was actually fired for getting a Party Censor's daughter knocked up and using live ammunition to make a battle scene more realistic. That was considered wasteful and unsocialist. The Party brought in another director, but when they were doing one of these big aerial dogfights—with all the cameras rolling and a million dollars' worth of budget in the air, what with stunt men and old planes and special effects explosions and crashing dirigibles—Howie flies through in a biplane trailing a flag saying 'this movie is horseshit', heads off towards the sunset and is never seen again. Now I don't know if that's true or not, but it's the version you'd want to believe. Right?"

The low hum of powerful aero-engines came out of the East. This was the sound Charlie had been expecting, the fantasy-fuelled thrum of the machines that had made the USSA masters of the skies over Japan. Neither London nor Petrograd could match the glory of these masterpieces of precision combat engineering.

Captain Rook again ordered the Pioneers to attention, and a pair of Curtiss Helldivers roared out of the sun and overflew the field at 200 feet. The blue-painted aluminium dreams commanded the sky, gleaming in the morning. A banner began to trail from the second plane. THE RFS SALUTES THE GLORIOUS ACHIEVEMENT OF THE PEOPLE OF ROSEVILLE. The Kansans in the stands and the Texans in the bleachers rose as one to cheer, as if the Great Socialist Hero diMaggio had just belted another one out of the field.

The single-engined naval dive bombers circled and passed again, this time a little higher, each executing three perfect victory rolls revealing the red hammer and sickle within white star insignia painted on the port upper and starboard lower wings. The RFS were grandstanding, but it paid to play up to the crowd a little.

Charlie clamped the inside of his cheek with his back teeth, biting until he drew blood in an effort to keep tears from his eyes. On a day like this, he pitied anyone who wasn't a communist, who wasn't an American. For the millionth time he swore to be a pilot. He wouldn't let his eyes fail him; he would sneak a look at the doctor's wallchart and memorise it. To joust in the clouds with the beasts of capitalism and imperialism! That was the best the USSA could offer.

The Helldivers circled the field once more before touching down perfectly. They taxied up to the red carpet close to the biplane. The two deadbeats were watching the proceedings, sharing private jokes as they passed the bottle between them. Colonel Hall should have had these two and their revolting old stringbag taken well out of the way.

The fliers of the RFS clambered out of their long glass-canopied cockpits, and pulled off jackets and helmets to reveal full dress uniform. Applause greeted each hero as he showed his face. Charlie recognised them all from magazines and newsreels. Hubbard, with his shock of red hair; Duke Morrison, face like the sandy rock of Mount Rushmore; LeMay, jaunty cigar clamped in his teeth and a five-starred brass hat on his bullet-shaped head; and McCarthy, the chubby clown of the outfit. They stepped forward to take their bows. Then Lindbergh climbed out of his plane, dressed in a heated jumpsuit and shining helmet like a character from *Flash Gordon Liberates the Universe.* He took off his helmet, and showed himself, middle-aged but boyish.

When the bandmaster was satisfied all five were ready, he struck up the national anthem. The pilots slammed mechanically to attention, raising clenched fists in the salute of solidarity.

"Oh say can you see," a lone, clear voice sang, "by the dawn's early light, what so proudly we hailed at the twilight's last gleaming…"

More spectators joined the singer. Charlie felt the tug of the music, and opened his throat to join in…

"…whose red stripes and bright star…"

Charlie's voice was good, but they didn't like him to sing with the School Choral Society because, as his teacher said, "you can't leave a tune well enough alone…"

"…the rockets' red glare, the bombs bursting in air…"

There was something about music—any kind of music—that made him feel strange inside.

"Oh, say, does that star-spangled banner yet wave…"

The five heroes were deeply moved. Lindbergh and Morrison both had manly tears in their eyes. McCarthy was holding his hands over his mouth and nose as the emotion overcame him, shoulders shaking…

"…o'er the land of the true, and the home of the brave."

At the anthem's end, Howie loped over and presented LeMay with the floral bomb. The General looked uncertainly at the old man, but accepted the bouquet, holding it up for everyone to see. Someone screamed and the MPs drew their pistols. A tendril of smoke was curling up, as if the infernal device were about to go off, scattering shrapnel petals in the crowd. There was a crackle and flames popped out of tribute. LeMay dropped the gift in shocked dismay, spitting out his cigar, and drew one of his pearl-handled revolvers. On the carpet the flowers flared suddenly, as if doused in gasoline.

Howie made exaggeratedly sorry noises and stepped in to stamp on the burning flowers. Someone in the section tittered, and Charlie hissed shut up and stand to attention. His cheeks burned at the disgrace, and he hoped Rook hadn't noted the lapse of discipline. Moments later, Colonel Hall and two jeeploads of MPs, white bands around their helmets, were on the scene. Two soldiers grabbed the old man. A cigarette lighter fell from his grip.

Now, Charlie could hear exactly what was going on. LeMay said in a chill-making rasp that he'd never been so insulted, "not even Tojo tried to off me with a bunch of flowers dipped in aviation fuel. Not even that bastard Mountbatten. It's an insult to the Navy, the Air Force, First Secretary Capone, the Communist Party and the American People."

Colonel Hall apologised as though his career depended on it, which, come to think of it, it did. Jack, the younger pilot, pleaded on his friend's behalf, saying that the guy was a decorated war veteran, that whenever he saw a Helldiver it reminded him of the comrades he had lost in the Pacific and he broke down.

"Veritably, he's as good a communist as the next guy. He needs treatment not punishment." Jack spoke fast, with a singsong French flavour, and was persuasive, even if he was feeding everyone a bullshit salad with chives. LeMay was unimpressed and single-minded, demanding with icy authority that Hall have the recidivist shot right this instant.

Colonel Hall dithered. He wasn't sure if shooting strange civilians fell within his jurisdiction. "Goddamnit to Hell," LeMay swore, cocking his pistol, "I'll scrag the vermin myself."

"Uh, General, surely you wouldn't do that," said the Colonel, with a panic-tinged laugh, probably uttering the bravest sentence of his life.

"Hall you melonhead, I've killed cities! One tatterdemalian hooligan more or less will make no difference. Remember, we are already at War."

"Howie has a silver plate in his head from the War," said Jack. "The *boches* shot him down over Dresden, tortured him, burned his ranch..."

Jack was just talking, filling in the space between LeMay and the Colonel.

"Hold on, Comrade General," put in Colonel Lindbergh, "if the man's a veteran, we should make allowances. A man who fights for his country deserves to cut loose some time..."

"Goddamnit Lindy, this bastard tried to fry us. He's a dangerous arsonist!"

"Respectfully, calm down. We don't want to spoil this lovely reception."

"No, uh, sir," put in Colonel Hall, relieved at having the Lone Eagle back him up, "I'll have this malefactor slapped in the guardhouse at Fort Baxter pending a full investigation."

"Just keep him out of my flightpath, you hear," said LeMay, stabbing Colonel Hall in the chest with an unlit cigar.

LeMay lit up, and puffed angry smoke, while Lindbergh stood over him, willing him to settle his feathers. Hall had the MPs bundle Howie into one of the jeeps. He grinned and waved at the crowds as if he were sat next to the Homecoming Queen on the float at the Revolutionary Victory Parade. He exchanged a few words with his co-pilot and was unceremoniously driven off for a weekend's incarceration. Charlie heard they kept cattle prods and car batteries with crocodile clips and jump leads in the Fort Baxter guardhouse, and used them to re-educate political offenders. He guessed Howie's brains were too scrambled for the process to have much effect.

Everything calmed down again, and the reception was back on course.

It was time for the speeches to begin. He hoped the fliers might have something interesting to say, but he was experienced enough to realise the crowd was in for an hour or three of numbing boredom as various Party officials blew wind. Osgood Yandell was pulling twenty or thirty sheets of notes out of his briefcase. Charlie knew the Party Chairman would lecture the assembled multitudes on the Responsibilities of a Young Communist while Melvin, Philly and Chick sloped off to smoke cigarettes and play cards. Even after that, it was unlikely the fliers would treat them to anything more than the usual homilies about production targets and the Party. He hoped he would get a chance to talk to Colonel Lindbergh or one of the others later. The fliers would be presenting awards for achievement in the evening at the public reception. Since Charlie had a good shot at winning a medal, he hoped he'd meet Lindbergh on the dais as the award was pinned to his uniform. Then, he wouldn't mind how long the speeches had been.

Imagine: Charles Hardin Holley meets Lucky Lindy, the Lone Eagle. Only in America...

"If I think about all the time I wasted listening to speeches I just wanna break down and cry. No, I mean it. As a good little Pioneer, I reckon I listened to an average seven hours a week of speeches. More at summer camp. If I'd spent that seven hours practising the guitar I'd be Segovia. It's not as though these people were any good at making speeches. When I was studying for my public speaking badge, the manual said you should strive to convince an audience through logic and historical determinism—whatever the Sam Hill that is—rather than inflaming artificial passions. Passing through Tennessee years ago, I heard one of those black guys, a Baptist hedge-preacher. Strictly illegal back then. You could wind up in Alaska for hallelujahing a hellfire sermon. There was a guy who could make a speech. I went in there an atheist humanist and in half an hour I was looking behind me for a sheriff with horns waiting to drag my sinful soul to the Hot Place. Very nearly signed up to become a Baptist there and then. Wore off, though. Now, where were we? Yeah, speeches…

"First, Yandell made a speech welcoming the war heroes. He made lots of amusing references to 'flying forward for socialism' and was put out when only the Party juniors after his job even tried to laugh. Then Colonel Hall welcomed the war heroes. Then, plant director Hiram McGarrigle welcomed the war heroes. Then, union boss Bubby Cafferty, to everybody's surprise, welcomed the heroes. And Captain Rook, by way of a change, welcomed the heroes. It was obvious that welcoming the heroes was the keynote, and this went on until well into the afternoon. If any heroes ever got welcomed, the RFS were they. I'm sure McCarthy was cat-napping, but the rest of them sat there being awesome. Lindy just glowed. He was golden.

"The biplane was still parked a few yards away. With Howie safe, Jack was no longer interested in the reception. He told me later that he could think of about eighteen things to do with your lips that beat welcoming the heroes from here to sundown. He took a toolbag from the cockpit and was tinkering in a leisurely manner with the engine, scat-singing non-patriotic music to himself. A few disapproving looks got lobbed his way, but no one wanted to interrupt the speeches by telling him to clear out, so he was left to himself. Two and a half hours later when all the speeches were finished, Jack was still head-deep in his engine cowling.

"General LeMay made a mercifully brief address thanking the people of Roseville for their welcome—cue embarrassed smiles from Colonel Hall and company, and suppressed laughter, no doubt, among ideological backsliders out in the crowd—congratulating the workers on exceeding their targets and leaving it at that. The General promised that the RFS would have more to say at the award ceremony in the evening. "Just so long," he croaked with a threatening grin, "as no one else tries to welcome the heroes…"

"The thing I remember about LeMay is his eyes. He was a hero, but I got the impression he was also crazy. Looking back, I realise the Pentagon must have given him the RFS to keep him out of the way. Douglas MacArthur and George S. Patton must have been enough for the Joint Chiefs of Staff. LeMay, who had some big hate thing going on with your Lord Mountbatten, still occasionally suggested that dropping the Big Hot One on the lousy limeys would be a good idea, and might maybe convince them to lay off our ideological brothers in Malaya. He called it 'preventative war'.

"LeMay's address over, the good folk of Roseville let their hair down, at least as far as that was possible in Capone's America. The band played 'My Socialist Heart', which Sinatra had had a hit with that year. By the time they were a few bars in, the heroes were being mobbed by the crowd. Everyone wanted a piece of the famous fliers, to get an autograph, a lock of hair, or just to hear them say something. All the girls got in there, and most of the boys. The *Echo*'s photographer was popping flashbulbs, and the heroes were posing with lucky kids. Pete Horowitz, pushed forwards by Rook, was snapped next to the Duke, and Melvin Yandell, Junior Hoodlum of the Decade, got to be pictured shaking hands with the Lone Eagle. Me, I was at the back, and kind of getting the idea that injustice was being done. Porky Rook was too busy with his protegé and hadn't given the order to fall out, and when he finally remembered, there were far too many folk around the heroes for me to hope to get close. But I figured they'd be there all weekend, so I'd get my chance to kiss ass eventually.

"So I was hanging about on the edge of this huge crowd, craning my neck to see what was going on. A voice asks me if I know anything about aero-engines. Well, sure, of course I did. Next thing I know I'm helping Jack fix his engine. At first, I felt a bit embarrassed, because I didn't imagine it would go down well for a responsible little commie like me to be seen with a recidivist hooligan like Ti-Jack. After a while, though, it's okay, because it turned out I knew a lot more about planes than he did, and he seemed real impressed with the Texan kid. His fuel lead was leaking, and I patched it up neatly with first aid supplies. He introduced his plane to me as the H-1, more familiarly the Spruce Goose.

"She's a wonderful babe," he said, "but she's a woman jus' the same, and fickle. She likes to show temperament sometimes, likes to dump me and Howie on the ground, make us crawl a little. You have to love her for it."

"I liked him at once, because he treated me as an adult. That's important when you're that age. More than anything else you wanna be grown up, but people still insist you're a kid. The other thing, the unique thing, was that he wasn't guarded. He said what he thought, while everyone else saw a Pioneer uniform and started doling out their words like pennies, worrying that you'd spot an Anti-Al sentiment and turn them in.

"Jack was shooting the breeze, talking about the Spruce Goose and Howie, their adventures flying across the country and back again. They made a subsistence living as freelance crop-sprayers and barnstormers, with Jack doing a side act as a singer and poet. Jack wasn't worried about his buddy being thrown in the slammer for the weekend. He would be getting three hots and a cot without paying a red cent, which put him well ahead of his usual game. Everything was a poem with Jack. Some of the stories he told me were lies, but they were true all the same. One of Jack's lies was worth an afternoon of Yandell's targets and incentives. One way or another, they just about managed to keep the show in the air, and —he said—he had got some great material for his book, his 'make-the-grade, paid-and-laid, break-for-great, beat-to-the-street book', which was sort of true and sort of not and was about these two characters called Sal and Dean who weren't really Jack and Howie, but then again might be, and their lives in the currents above the USSA. "I want to write a book like Gaillard plays jazz, like Van Gogh paints harvests, you dig?"

"Now, part of young Charlie was finding it profoundly shocking that this kind of thing could possibly happen in a well-ordered socialist society. But another part was listening to the music. Another part of me was being seduced. I dug.

"After a while, I dug the most."

The afternoon's parade passed off without incident, but Charlie was still smarting. Again, Captain Rook gave the lead to Pete Horowitz's section. The Pioneers led the parade, symbolising the Great Socialist Hope of the nation's future. Charlie wondered if his rival was given preference because Rook had seen him consorting with Hooligan Jack. The Captain spoke of revisionism as if it were a communicable disease.

The Pioneer Lodge had posters up, warning the true socialist to Watch Your Neighbours.

In an empty field, a number of tents and a small stage had been erected. The formation broke, and Pioneers scattered in an orderly manner, heading for their families. Charlie found his parents and Peggy Sue's family by the lemonade stall. An ox was being roasted over a fire, a stocky chef from Fort Baxter sprinkling the revolving carcass with herbs and sauces. Charlie had never seen so much meat in one place before.

"Looks like some folks will be getting a good feed this evening," said his Mom, a little too loud. "Hero fliers and party officials, at least."

Dad gave him a glass of lemonade, which he got down in a gulp. It had been a long march in the sun.

Peggy Sue wore a pink-tinged white dress, and looked almost as pretty as Patsy, if a sight skinnier. Charlie saluted her, and she giggled like a six-year-old.

The chef got his hand too near the flame. He went "ooh ooh ooh" and hopped around while his base buddies laughed.

Osgood Yandell mounted the stage and, in a folksy voice Mom always said was "as phoney as a his wife's hair colour", asked for everyone to give the heroes a big hand. It was time for the year's awards. But first, everyone knew, there were more speeches.

First up was General LeMay. He did a familiar number about everyone all over the country pulling together in this time of crisis, increasing their production and striving to have more children to make the future secure for socialism. He called forward plant managers and union officials to congratulate them on the overrun. Each of the "heroes of tractor production" was given a small plaque.

"Funny how all them heroes just happen to be Kansas-born," said Peggy Sue's Dad. "Not a Texan among them."

Charlie's Dad shrugged and said they had no room for a plaque anyway.

"Nonsense," said Mom, "we could use it to plug up one of the holes in the wall that lets the wind in. What with all these heroes in town, I reckon there's going to be a lot more wind."

Next up was Duke Morrison, a big man who, according to the Party papers, embodied the virtues of the American worker. He told a thrilling story about how a buddy had died at Iwo Jima to save the rest of his platoon. His dying words had been "hell, Duke, I know any of the guys would have done exactly the same." This, Morrison explained, "embodied the socialist spirit in the hearts of the people of America." There was massive but vaguely mechanical applause. It was the first remotely exciting thing that anyone had said all day. Morrison called forward factory workers who had been commended by their managers for working especially hard that year, for showing good examples to their comrades. Each man came forward, cheered by family and friends, to shake Morrison's hand and be awarded the Hero of Socialist Labour medal.

"More Kansans," said Peggy Sue's Dad, who had lost an eye fighting Villa.

"Hi Charlie-cat," said a voice behind him. "Have I missed any major *gris-gris*? Oh, unprecedented! They're roasting a whole ox! Man, that smells beat! What chance do you think we hungry cats have of getting our feed-forks into that? I'd be grateful for a plateful."

"With every Party official in the state of Kansas here tonight," said Mom, "we'll be lucky to get a lick of one of the bones."

Jack laughed. Charlie reddened at the disrespectful crack, and hoped nobody outside the group of Texans had heard his mother.

Morrison left the stage to enthusiastic cheers, and McCarthy took his place. The Major grabbed the microphone off the stand, and it squealed feedback. He broke all the rules of socialist reasoning, launching into a fire-and-brimstone tirade about how the country was "in danger of being brought sobbing to its knees by the cancers of counter-revolution, capitalist subversion, foreign fifth-columnists and moral degeneracy." McCarthy was sweating, and the audience didn't know what to make of his shouting. Even his fellow heroes were trying not to look at him.

"It's the duty of every loyal American," he said, "to root out cap subversion wherever it rears its hideous, verminous head. On the farm, in the workplace, and, yes, even in your own family. It starts quiet. Maybe some schoolteacher wants to hold a meeting to yak about the problems of the community. Then, after your closet cap pal has started you thinking that maybe there *are* problems in the community, the hard stuff starts creepin' in, and you hear talk about maybe havin' elections, or questionin' the Party Line, or sayin' bad stuff about Comrade Capone. And it gets worse. Once cap subversion has set in, it's harder to get rid of than headlice. Remember, your ole grand-mamma could be a filthy cap, or maybe your General Store-keeper, the man next to you on the assembly line…Caps are everywhere, eatin' away the foundations of society."

He pulled a grimy piece of paper out of his jacket pocket. "I got me here a list off sixty-eight card-carrying caps in the Kansas Party Machine, legislature and Socialist Guard, and believe me, comrades, these rats are gonna regret the day they tried to cross Bomber Joe!"

He waved his list. There was a stunned silence from the crowd for a full ten seconds. Charlie heard Jack let out a low, admiring whistle. Then people applauded. Charlie couldn't understand it. The Major was obviously combat-shocked. People were applauding louder, spontaneously, energetically. He looked around. His own parents were clapping, and Peggy Sue's Dad was whistling as if the home team were celebrating a touchdown.

"Clap," Mom told him, "if you know what's good for you, clap..."

Charlie listlessly flapped his hands together, and McCarthy revelled in the acclaim. Jack was the only person not joining in. The poet shrugged and smiled. Charlie wondered if Jack's name were on any lists.

"Applause," Jack said, "applesauce..."

The applause continued as Lindbergh took the stage. In quiet, measured tones he endorsed the Capone's policy of isolationism. America, he said, could produce everything it needed without getting involved with other countries. He was plainly remembering by rote something someone else had written for him. He finished his brief speech by announcing more awards. Three townswomen who had borne more than five children were invited forward to receive Heroine of Socialist Motherhood medals.

Charlie knew what was coming next.

"And now, one of the most important awards any community can bestow," said the Lone Eagle, "the Young America medal for this year's most conscientious member of the Pioneers."

Charlie checked that his bandanna was tied properly, and his pants creases were aligned to the front. He knew he would win the Young America. Nobody had won more badges than him, and his section always scored the highest in the Socialist Debates.

"And the winner is..."

To receive the medal from Colonel Lindbergh himself, to shake the great man's hand...

"Section Leader Peter Horowitz."

Pete Horowitz went forward to climb up on to the stage, accompanied by applause. Charlie looked over and saw Captain Rook clapping, broad smile on his puffy face. Horowitz threw a ragged parody of a salute and accepted his medal.

"Well how do you like that!"

"What's the bring-down?" asked Jack.

"You tell me! You saw the parade this afternoon. Now tell me, Pioneer for Pioneer, badge for badge, section for section, who's the better man? Me or that sloppy, lame-assed, worthless Kansas goldbrick who's just shook hands with Colonel Lindbergh?"

"*Diable*, Charlie-cat, that's easy. I bet the brown-eyed handsome boy wouldn't know one end of an engine from another."

"Pete Horowitz's section would come third in the Circle Jerk. So how come he wins the goddamn medal, huh? I just don't understand it."

"Who decides who gets the medals?"

"Captain Comrade Rook."

"Uh-huh. That him over there? The fat cat in the army slouch hat and shorts, clapping and sweating?"

"Yeah. The bastard. What's he got against me?"

"I don't imagine he's got anything against you, Charlie-cat. It's what he's got for Pretty Petey."

"What are you talking about?" asked Charlie.

"I guess," said Jack quietly, "Captain Comrade Rook is victim of a particular variety of sexual incontinence."

"He's always talking about sexual incontinence. He wouldn't..."

"I didn't say he's done anything, the poor cold and old sister-sap, nor that he'd necessarily try anything. All I'm saying is that such thoughts prey upon him in his secret nights. He has the hots for the guy; in spades, but bad. Nothing amiss with that, Charlie-cat, so long as nobody gets hurt."

"Well I've ended up getting hurt. This isn't fair."

Charlie's eyes stung. Pioneers weren't supposed to feel hurt. Peggy Sue had walked over. If she had overheard, it would make it worse.

"Hi Charlie," she said brightly, "tough luck about not getting the medal. If you want my opinion, you should have got it. And everyone in town would agree with me..."

"Except that Horowitz cat," said Jack.

Charlie was relieved by the opportunity to change the subject and introduced the girl next door.

"Pleased to meet you, Mr. Kerouac," said Peggy Sue, "though I'm not sure I want to meet your partner after what he did to my sister."

"Yeah, well, I'm sorry about that, chicklet. I guess Howie doesn't always have the right etiquette for every social situation. He gets a little bit wigged-out sometimes, and goes uncool. Accept my sincerest..."

Peggy Sue warmed to Jack at once, and fluttered her eyelashes. Charlie didn't know how he felt about that.

Lieutenant Hubbard had taken the stage to make his speech, clearly the worse for something. Fruit punch and cider were not covered by the Prohibition Laws. Hubbard had a broad smile and a benign, avuncular manner and was talking about the duty of everyone to get married and have healthy communist children to keep America strong. He called forward a dozen couples who had announced their engagement in the last year. Each received a salute of solidarity from Hubbard and a radio for when they set up home. He made gruff jokes Charlie didn't quite get which usually made the prospective groom laugh uneasily while his fiancée blushed.

Charlie noticed that as each lucky pair went up to the stage, Peggy Sue was applauding and cheering loudly. "Gee, Mr. Kerouac," she spoke across Charlie, making him feel uncomfortable again, "don't you think it's wonderful? Are you married Mr. Kerouac?"

"No chicklet. I'm not married just now. No lady in her right mind would want a hipster like me. And I don't especially desire a radio that plays nothing but propaganda all the day and night, either."

"Are you a recidivist?" she asked, half-sternly, half-mockingly.

"Actually, like they say, I believe in freedom and fair shares. Cool stuff, you know. It's just that I also believe a radio should be for digging decent music. Jazz and jive, baby, bebop-ba-bop-bop."

Peggy Sue laughed.

LeMay returned to the microphone, also a drink past his best, by the look of him. His tie was skewed around his collar, his top shirt button was undone, and sweat was pouring out from under his helmet. He looked like a shifty cap subversive in one of the Hollywood movies J. Edgar Hoover liked to sponsor, *I Was a Capitalist for the FBI* or *I Married a Capitalist*. The characteristic half-smoked stogie poked from the corner of his mouth as he requested the presence of Osgood Yandell.

"I have here, Comrade Party Chief," he began, "a gift for the people of Roseville from Chairman Capone himself."

There were cheers from the audience as he tore brown wrapping paper from a rectangular object. The present was as a framed colour print, depicting a matronly woman in turn-of-the-century clothes standing at the rail of a ship, holding her baby up to see, looming in the distance, the Statue of Liberty. It was Norman Rockwell's famous impression of the arrival in the Land of the Free of the infant Capone. LeMay presented it to Yandell to be hung in the town hall. Yandell made a brief speech of startled gratitude and then announced that the party was to begin. On cue, the town band struck up a waltz.

"Come on, Charlie, and you too, Mr. Kerouac," said Peggy Sue, pulling both of them. "My mother's baked some of her special pies."

She dragged Charlie and Jack over towards a food-laden table where other members of the Roseville proletariat were congregating. In the opposite corner of the field, the roast ox was being devoured by Party officials and their families.

Charlie, Jack and Peggy Sue were sitting down to apple pie and cream as a shadow came up on them from behind.

"Whaddya hear, whaddya say, ace?" said the shadow's voice.

They turned. It was Howie.

"Howie, most esteemed cat. You busted out of the doghouse I see. I'm sore afraid I finished off all the hooch."

"Shit," said Howie, not noticing Peggy Sue's presence. "Suppose I'll just have to drink some of this godawful cider. Jeez, this'll be the ruination of my liver."

"So how'd you contrive to skip the joint, Howie?" asked Jack.

"Piece of cake. I was being guarded by this motor-pool sergeant and the crummiest bunch of GI Joes you ever saw. I won out in a poker game."

"Howie, I'd like to introduce *mes amis*. The chicklet is Peggy Sue. You encountered her big sister this morning, remember. And this is Charlie-cat, the coolest corn-fed Pioneer in Kansas."

"Pleased to meetcha, pilgrims. I'm gonna go requisition me a drink, and see if I can get me some of that cow on a stick they're burning over in the VIP area. Think I'll pass muster as a Party official?"

Howie grinned, showing his ravaged teeth. He stank of booze and aviation fuel. Close up, with his tall, skinny frame and filthy grey hair, the last thing he looked like was a Party official. He reminded Charlie of a scarecrow, only not so well dressed.

"Check, Squadron Leader," said Jack, "but take care how you go. LeMay is still out there, and I presume he still wants you refrigerated."

"LeMay? Fuck 'im—pardon my French ma'am."

Howie hawked and spat a stream of brown juice at the grass.

"Say kid," he said to Charlie, "you think these famous fly-boys are something special?"

"Of course," said Charlie, "they're the best pilots living in America today. Probably the world."

"Hogwash and flapdoodle. None of those old blowhards could fly for chickenfeed. Sure, they can *drive* an airplane, any damfool can drive an airplane. I wouldn't give you a torn lunch coupon for any of them. 'Cept maybe Lindbergh. He had it once, he had the stuff. But not any more."

"But what about their war records..." protested Charlie.

Howie grinned cynically. "Lindbergh, yeah, I'd believe his. But the rest of them are feeding you a line, kid. Specially Lafayette Hubbard...Listen, I gotta get me some chow and a drink..."

He sniggered to himself and turned to go.

"By the way," he added, "when I was on my way over here, I walked by that stage up there and tripped up. Clean put my boot through that picture of the broad showing the brat Miss Liberty. Big hole in the brat's face. I get the feeling the picture was important, so if anyone asks, it wasn't me, okay?"

"It's hard to remember exactly how I felt. You always look back on love affairs like they were songs—'True Love Ways', you know—and forget the pain. I liked Jack but he was scary, troubling. He was weird, but he meant what he said, unlike a lot of the non-weirds I knew. I even kind of liked being 'Charlie-cat'. It was better than being 'Pioneer Holley' and certainly beat 'Texas faggot'. But Howie was dangerous, crazy. If he wasn't on McCarthy's lists, then he ought to have been. I'm not saying he was a cap, but he sure was a subversive element. Remember Mr. Lowe, the things Howie was saying could have got him shot. And me and Peggy Sue shot too, or put in a work-camp, just for listening.

"Next, Patsy turned up. She kept out of Howie's way, but took a Texas shine to handsome Jack. Peggy Sue might be working up to her badge in eyelash-fluttering but Patsy was unchallenged tri-county champion. And as a ladies' man, Jack was faster on the draw than Wyatt Earp. Being around him when he was pitching woo was a complete education. A lot more useful than Enemy Aircraft Recognition. As Jack took Patsy out into the field to dance, I managed to nerve up to take Peggy Sue and follow them. I had my badge in dancing. After a few numbers, Jack left Patsy for a moment and went over to the band-leader, a coloured boy from Fort Baxter. There were more than a few negroes in his orchestra, but because there was still segregation in the army they had to sit apart. Jack and the band-leader had a short, intense conversation and parted with a slapping handshake. Jack came back smiling with half his mouth, and took Patsy by the waist while new orders were issued. A couple of whites with brass instruments stood down, and a black bassist lost his bow. Then, the band played the kind of music you didn't hear on the radio. Jack showed Patsy how to dance. The rest of the crowd couldn't fit their moves to the rhythm and stood around, not offended, while Jack showed them how. Then, everyone—including Peggy Sue and me—was dancing. It wasn't my stuff, exactly, but that jazz combo cum hootenanny sounded different. And it was exciting. The Young America medal didn't mean so much any more..."

Charlie was enjoying himself. And he knew Peggy Sue was enjoying herself. At the end of a dance while the musicians were wiping away sweat, he bowed with a flourish and kissed her hand just as Clark Gable had Tallulah Bankhead's in *Gone With the Wind*.

"Oh Charlie," giggled the girl, "you're getting mushy."

Charlie looked at Peggy Sue's pleasantly flushed throat as she fanned herself, trying not to stare. Was she beautiful? Check. Was he in love with her? Tricky. Was he on the slippery path into sexual incontinence? No. Well...

"Bay-aby!" grunted a voice. "Howsabout having a li'l fun with the air force. Let's get with this jungle bunny jive. Decadent cap crap, of course, but it gits the juices flowin'."

Peggy Sue turned around and cringed as Major McCarthy shoved his leering face at her. He grabbed her waist and puckered up his lips. Charlie was not sure what he should do. McCarthy's left hand was going for Peggy Sue's bottom, fingers splaying out to dig in violently.

"Charlie..." she cried as she tried to escape.

Charlie tapped McCarthy's shoulder politely. "Excuse me, sir..."

McCarthy turned, eyes red. "Bug off, kid! Can't you see I'm fuckin' engaged on official business."

"Pardon me, Comrade Major McCarthy, sir," Charlie stood his ground. "But I don't think the young lady wishes to do business with you. Further, sir, she is fifteen years old."

"Who asked your opinion, kid?" McCarthy let Peggy Sue go and pushed his booze-reeking face into Charlie's. "You look like a filthy cap..."

"Nobody asked my opinion, sir. But with respect, you did not ask the opinion of the young lady as to whether she wished to, ah, dance with you."

McCarthy began shaking, like a movie volcano about to explode.

"I'm a fuckin' war hero kid, I can do what I fuckin' please."

With no further warning, he swung his right fist in a long, fast arc, connecting with Charlie's face.

Charlie fell backwards, tasting blood, glasses flying. McCarthy shouted at him, calling him names. Charlie groped for his glasses as the crowd, then the band fell quiet. Peggy Sue was sobbing like a lost child.

"Come on then, revisionist kid. Fuckin' get up, fuckin' put yer mitts up. Mess with Bomber Joe and see what you get…"

Someone helped Charlie to his feet. His view of McCarthy was suddenly blocked by the shape of Jack.

Jack threw a series of short, powerful punches at the Major's face. McCarthy was powerless to stop or parry the blows. The hero's fists flailed about uselessly as he screamed abuse.

McCarthy slid to the ground, floored by a combination of punches and punch. Black blood fell in large drips from his nose.

Men in uniform pushed their way through the circle that had gathered. Hubbard and Morrison grabbed Jack, pinning his arms behind his back. He did not struggle. LeMay strode up, with Osgood Yandell a respectful three paces behind him.

"What the hell's going on here?" he asked quietly, removing the cigar butt from his mouth to spit away pieces of tobacco.

"I can explain, Comrade General, sir," volunteered Charlie. "Major McCarthy grabbed hold of the young lady. She didn't like it and I asked him to stop. Then he hit me. Then the comrade here…"

"Is that so, Comrade Major?" asked LeMay.

He was still sitting on the ground trying to staunch his nose. He had reached into a pocket for a handkerchief, but had come up with only his list of card-carrying capitalists. The list was thoroughly bled-on.

Before McCarthy could answer, there was another stirring in the crowd.

"Make way for a war veteran, war veteran coming through," said Howie, striding towards Jack, noticing nothing but his friend, "Hya ace, I got us some of that burned cow. Said I was an FBI agent in disguise on a special investigation. I got some booze from the VIP tent as well…Oh, shit. Good evening Comrade General LeMay, sir. Would you like a drink? Say, could you spare me one of them cigars?"

Instinctively, LeMay drew both his fancy revolvers, the ones Capone had given him. Howie grinned as the General levelled his weapons at him. Simultaneously, LeMay pulled the triggers, and, simultaneously, the pistols misfired, burping smoke. Howie laughed.

"Hubbard," LeMay snarled, his face bright red, "go and fetch some MPs. If you can't find any, then get me a gun. Any kind of gun. Understood?"

"Sir, yes sir!" snapped Hubbard, leaving Jack to Morrison.

"Hold up there a minute, Comrade General," said Howie, "I didn't escape or anything. I earned my freedom. Besides, if you want to have me shot, which I'm sure is entirely within your rights, ain't there certain due processes of the socialist law that have to be gone through first?"

"It may have escaped your attention," said LeMay, "but we *are* the socialist law. And just as soon as that moron gets back with a gun I'm going to shoot you without any further questions."

Charlie looked around, wondering where Lindbergh was, hoping he'd turn up to calm the General down.

Howie bit ferociously into a piece of meat. "In that case," he said, "you wouldn't wanna deny a man on death row one last request."

LeMay looked shiftily at the crowd around him, not sure how to take this. "Of course not," he said as loudly as he could manage, "let it never be said that the American Communist Party is inhumane. Name your request."

"I'd like a few minutes of everyone's time, that's all."

Charlie looked at Jack, whose face was a blank. Things had stopped being funny.

"You see, Comrade General sir, I'm a flier like you. I don't have any of these fancy birds from American Motors or Progress Dynamics. All I've got's a ship I made from the parts on up. I designed the H-1 myself, put it together with gum and prayer. I'm just a bum with wings, but I can out-fly any of you pilots any day of the week with a y in it."

"Yeah!" shouted Morrison, letting Jack go and squaring up massively to Howie. "That'll be the *day*!"

"Darn right it will, Duke," said Howie, looking the tall man in the eye. "You guys don't scare me. 'Cause at sundown, you're all shit and wind. Take you slobs out of your uniforms, and you'd be nothing. And your so-called war-records are nothing. I coulda been the best fighter jock in the Navy or the Air Force, but when the War came along they told me I was too old and 'not politically correct'. I told 'em that wasn't important, but no, they wouldn't have me. I ended up a bus-driver, flying Gooney Birds to Pacific Islands. Then, I did hop and skip runs behind our lines in Europe. But it was something, I was in the service..."

He raised his voice, talking not just to LeMay but to the whole crowd.

"Do you know something, ladies and gentlemen, I didn't hear about a single one of these aces all that time. I met all the real ones, the real heroes, Dick Bong, Jimmy Stewart, Doolittle. But they never talked about any of you. Except General LeMay, of course. You all know about him. He must have personally shortened the War by about six months when he hopped on that plane and flattened that Black Dragon Suicide Squad, getting there before his own troops, saving everybody from that horde of kill-crazed, fight-to-the-last-man Japs. I saw Stone Age Carpet here in '45 in Tinian Island. He spent a whole day behind the stick of the Boeing that dropped the incendiaries on Tokyo. He was being filmed for the newsreels. While this was going on, I talked to his crew. They were riled up that some gloryhound pushed in and took over from their regular pilot. Plus, it seems the General was more enthusiastic than accurate when it came to dropping the payload. Seems he just plain missed the fortifications he was supposed to be destroying and heroically blew up a hospital, a Buddhist shrine and a children's playground. Of course, them sick folks, priests and schoolkids could've put up a hell of a fight, lengthened the War some. That Black Dragon Division? Well, it seems there wasn't one. That was just a bit of left-over Jap propaganda, trying to discourage our boys."

LeMay just stared, jaw muscles working.

"So what about the rest of them?" continued Howie. "The way I hear it, McCarthy spent most of the War visiting his sick mother in Canada. Duke here was in all the main theatres of combat, with the newsreels long after the fighting had moved on to somewhere else. Lonesome Lafayette's record is a joke. The only thing he ever sunk was a tug. One of our own. He thought the Japs were invading Catalina and strafed it. After that, the only thing the Navy would let him do was write adventure stories for *Leatherneck*. That's the *Marines*' paper, by the way. The Navy didn't even trust him to write dime novels for their own pulp…"

"Comrade General, I've got a gun," came Hubbard's voice. He was pushing through, dragging Colonel Hall. "D'you want to shoot him now?"

"Lieutenant Hubbard," said Howie, "we were just talking about you."

"You can see the fix LeMay was in. If he had Howie shot now, it'd look like the bum had been telling the truth about their war records.

Also, he was mad as hell about losing face in front of people who were supposed to respect him. It ended with LeMay challenging Howie to a flying contest at sun-up the next day. I suppose he must have figured Howie for an old madman who'd be a pushover. The arrangement was that first they'd outfly Howie, then they'd take him out and shoot him. It suited Howie fine. So long as he got the chance to show Roseville what 'pudknockers' the RFS were, they could do what they liked to him. Then, Lindbergh arrived. Standing nearby, I heard McCarthy, who had sobered up fast, tell him what had happened. Lindbergh was floored. McCarthy was favour of the contest, telling him what a hoot it'd be, but Lindbergh said it was too risky. They all were in danger of losing their privileges, and if they screwed the pooch they'd end up drilling for oil in Alaska. He flatly refused to have anything to do with the deal. But the rest were gung ho to restore their reputations. So, Howie formally accepted the challenge…"

"Jack, is Howie crazy?" asked Charlie. Jack and Patsy and Peggy Sue and Charlie were sitting out back watching the moon and the stars.

"No idea, Charlie-cat. Why don't you ask him?"

"I would, but we don't know where he's got to."

"Do you think they've got him locked up somewhere?" asked Patsy.

"No, heartbeat. I don't think they'll dare do that."

Charlie's parents had seen everything that had happened earlier. Dad had come over when the shouting was finished and had ordered him home at once. Mom, on the scene shortly afterwards, had taken an immediate liking to Jack and had invited him, and Peggy Sue and Patsy, back home for supper, and had eagerly pumped Jack with questions about what was happening in other parts of America. Dad hadn't been too pleased about having the glamorous recidivist in their midst. It could get them into trouble. But he didn't call the shots in the Holley household.

"Jack, how come they won't dare to lock Howie up? Or you?"

"Because they'd like us to take a breeze before the big showdown. None of those squares is a natural flier the way Howie is. What they're hoping is that Howie'll be so piss-scared at the idea of being shot he'll skedaddle. That way they might not have the kick of killing him, but it'll save them the possible humiliation of losing the challenge. And it would also kinda prove to cats round here that Howie was talking moonshine all along. Thing is, I reckon Howie can outfly the best of them. Zoom, zoom."

"But you don't have to get in that plane tomorrow," said Patsy.

"Howie needs a bombardier. This is my trip as much as it is his."

"Aren't you frightened, Mr. Jack?" asked Peggy Sue.

"Sure I'm frightened. But I'm frightened every time I climb into the Spruce Goose with that old hipster. It's not a biplane, you know; it's a bop-plane. She has her own ways, and just goes along however she wants. Besides, what else could a no-account deadbeat like me do? Any ideas?"

"You could be a real writer," suggested Peggy Sue.

"Or a newspaperman. That's writing too," added Patsy.

Jack laughed. "Sure, I could write anything the Party lets me write. Or I could be a garbage collector, or a farm hand, or a short order cook, or a soldier...I could be lots of things, but, dig, the only thing that feels right is doing what I do now. Maybe I'll grow out of it. Most people spend their lives not really knowing what they should do."

"I know what I want to do," said Charlie, "I want to be a pilot."

"And end up like Howie?" giggled Patsy.

"I think I'd sooner be Lindbergh," smiled Charlie. "Even Howie reckons he's all right."

"The thing about Howie," said Jack, "is that he's a better cat than I am. He's crazy, but he's true to his heartbeat. Flying's about the only thing he's good at. Everything else he touches, he screws up. Flying's what he lives for. As long as he can fly it doesn't matter. That's his heartbeat. Everyone is born with a heartbeat, a rhythm inside that tells them what to do. Some have a heartbeat that says President of the USSA, some get a heartbeat that says hobo. It doesn't matter. Just so long as you follow your heartbeat."

"I'm going to follow mine," said Charlie, arms out like wings.

"But are you one hundred per cent sure it's what you're supposed to do?" asked Jack.

"Yeah, sure. That is, I guess so."

Jack picked up his guitar and played a few folk songs he'd learned on his travels. After a song about a hundred men losing their lives in a mine disaster, he decided to lighten the mood a little and began to improvise, strumming a few chords, making up words as he went along...

"Heartbeat," he said, looking at Patsy, "why do you miss when my baby kisses me?"

He tried to make up a tune, but wasn't very sure about it. "My thing is words," he said, "not chords."

"Heartbeat," Charlie said, hearing a tune.

"You know," said Peggy Sue, "there's a song for every girl in my class except me. Clementine Carter, Susannah Hickling, Genevieve Dieudonné, Adeline Williams, all of them. But no Peggy Sue song."

"My Darling Peggy Sue," said Patsy, laughing.

"Oh Peggy Sue, don't you cry for me," sang Jack, off-key.

"Peggy Sue," crooned Charlie to notes that came his way, "if you knew…"

Jack reached over, put a hand on Patsy's neck, and they were kissing.

Charlie ran out of words. Jack's mouth was working away, and Patsy wasn't resisting. He and Peggy Sue were surplus personnel.

Peggy Sue turned to Charlie, eyes a liquid in the dark. "I guess it's time I went home. Want to walk me back, Charlie?"

"Walk you back? You only live next door."

The girl's eyes narrowed, and Charlie decided to go along with her. Somehow, it took a long time to get next door.

As they walked slowly away from Jack and Patsy, towards the line of dimly-lit tin and weatherboard shacks, Peggy Sue slipped her hand into Charlie's. Her palm was already as rough as a cowboy's from hard work in the junior auxiliary at the tractor plant on Sunday mornings.

Charlie couldn't forget the music the band had played, and the tunes Jack had tried to wring out of his guitar.

Peggy Sue, Peggy Sue, if you knew…

"Well…" said Peggy Sue as they arrived at her gate.

"See you tomorrow?" said Charlie.

"Yes. Tomorrow. Yes, see you then," she said, looking him straight in the face, smiling.

Charlie felt nervous. He didn't want to leave her. Not just yet.

Next thing he knew, he was kissing her. Or she was kissing him. Not the sort of peck on the cheek his mother had made him perform in party games when he was a kid. This was the big-league thing. They were holding one another tight, and grinding their lips together, like people did in the kind of movies that Charlie didn't really enjoy, like Jack and Patsy back in the field. They said nothing. Just took time out every once in a while to look at each other before they got back to it again.

Finally. "Peggy Sue…uh, chicklet…there's something I'd like to ask you…"

Peggy Sue smiled, expecting. Then, they heard a girl, screaming. The moment was gone.

They ran to the back of Charlie's house and could see a number of moonlit figures moving around. The girl screamed again. It was Patsy.

"Stay here, Peggy Sue," said Charlie, running off towards the ruckus.

"That'll be the day," she shouted, running after him. "That's my sister they're hurting."

As Charlie got nearer the noise, he could see that it was not Patsy they were hurting at all. Three men with pickaxe handles or baseball bats were hitting a figure curled up on the ground. The victim had his arms over his head. It was Jack.

Charlie pulled his glasses off and handed them to Peggy Sue. "Look after these," he said, "and don't come an inch nearer."

Hell, Charlie though to himself as he ran towards the men. Three of them, pickaxe handles. I'm going to get killed. Still he ran on...

He couldn't see so well without his glasses, but he could tell who the thugs were. Chick Willis, Philly Winspear and Melvin Yandell. That was predictable. If anyone was going to be beating anyone else up in Roseville, Murderous Melvin and his buddies would elect themselves.

"Patsy!" he shouted, "get away before the bastards try and hurt you!"

Melvin turned from belabouring Jack. "Look what we got here, guys? It's Chocolate Soldier Charlie. Come to join in the fun, Texas limpdick?"

Charlie stopped. He knew he was going to get killed. He took a deep breath, tried to remember some of his Pioneer unarmed combat training, and charged straight at Melvin.

He wasn't moving.

With all that adrenalin pumping, it took him a moment to realise arms were holding him back. He struggled, but couldn't move forward. Melvin laughed, turned back to Jack, fetched him one final, savage swipe and started to walk away. Willis and Winspear also got in their last licks, and scurried after Melvin, hooting and laughing.

Still the arms held Charlie back as the sobbing Patsy was joined by Peggy Sue and the two women went over to Jack. He was on the ground, groaning, mumbling in French.

"*Pauvre Ti-Jack, pauvre...*"

Charlie tried to twist his head and see who was holding him. It was no good. He looked down at the arms. Uniformed arms. In the moonlight, three cuff-bars glinted in the moonlight. He knew who it was.

"What you so scared of, Colonel Lindbergh?" screamed Charlie. "That the Party brats you bought to beat up Jack are going to beat me up too?"

Lindbergh let go of him, and turned to walk in silence back towards town. Charlie watched the Lone Eagle go, and spat at his shadow.

"Chicken," he yelled.

Jack was groaning, and the girls were sniffling.

Someone else came out of the dark. Charlie waited for another attack, but it never came.

"So here the hell you all are," said Howie. "I wondered where you'd gotten to…Cheezis, what happened to my bombardier?"

"I had it all at once, Mr. Lowe, in two days. I met Jack and Howie, very deeply interesting people who were to be more of an influence on my life than I'd realise. Second, I kissed a girl for the first time. Third, I was starting to question the Pioneer ideal. Plus, I was starting to think about music. Yes sir, it was quite a weekend. Here, have another drink…

"We got Jack back to my place, and woke up my Mom, who dug out her First Aid stuff. She did a quick diagnosis, and told us he wasn't going to die. He was suffering from concussion, half a dozen cracked ribs, a couple of broken fingers and a fracture in his right arm. She spent almost two hours setting bones and taping on makeshift splints. Then, she went back to bed, leaving us all—Howie, Jack, me, Peggy Sue, Patsy—drinking coffee. That wasn't like her. She said Jack should rest up, but she didn't tell us to stop bothering him, she didn't kick the girls out, and, most particularly, she didn't tell me to get off to bed double-quick. Thinking about it, I guess she had a fair idea what we were going to discuss, and how it would turn out…"

"You're in no fit state to fly with me tomorrow," Howie said to Jack.

"Course I am. I can just about move my left hand."

"Howie's right," said Patsy, "you can't possibly fly. You'd be a danger to the pair of you."

"I'll take your place," said Charlie.

"What?!" said Jack. "*Non*, Charlie-cat, you don't dig how that plane works. You might get cooled. Even if you don't, the Party skulls will blacklist you for succouring a hooligan. They're going to shoot Howie tomorrow. Lord knows what the evils will do to you, but it won't be cool."

"I don't care," said Charlie. "Those people were my heroes. Now I realise what a bunch of yellow-bellied creeps they are. If Howie's going to take them down, I'd like to help."

"Hell, kid," said Howie, "look at me. I'm a burned out coot. I got nothing left to lose. You've got everything coming up ahead of you. Don't throw it away."

Charlie was unmoved. "You need a co-pilot. I've had 22 hours in planes, over 50 hours on gliders. I've got Pioneer badges in navigation and dive bombing. If you're going to show those pudknockers who's best tomorrow, I want to be part of it."

"Charlie-cat," sighed Jack. "It's your play. If you're going to do it, let me give you some advice. Hold tight, go to the crapper first and take a lump of leather to bite on."

"Fine, I'll remember that."

"Attaboy, Charlie," said Howie. "If you're so determined to put your ass on the line, then it's fine by me. Just don't let it be said that we didn't try to talk you out of it. I can't say what'll happen to you afterwards, but you've got no problems in the air. You're nearly 16, you must be a better pilot than Curtis LeMay. And I need someone to drop the bombs and watch my ass and light the cigars and pass the bottle."

"I didn't sleep too well, for the second night running. Early next morning, I followed Jack's advice and spent a good half an hour in the outhouse.

"I snuck out and found Peggy Sue waiting for me. She gave me a wet kiss and a rabbit's foot and asked me, somewhat unromantically I thought, if I'd been to the privy.

"Off we walked to Baxter Field. By now word had gotten round, and there were plenty of folks turning up to see the show. Most of town, in fact. About half an hour after I arrived, Mom and Dad showed. I kept my head low because I hadn't told them that I was going to be part of it. There were a lot of soldiers about, and the motor-pool sergeant was rumoured to be taking bets on the big contest, offering long odds on Crazy Howie and the Flying Deathtrap against the RFS.

"I got up to the Spruce Goose, and Howie was fooling around with the engine, drunk as a skunk of course. He even offered me a pull on the bottle. "Want some breakfast, kid?" he said. He also stated as Gospel that he'd never flown sober in his life and doubted he ever could.

"Scary stuff, huh? But the hand-on-heart truth is that I wasn't scared. This was my big chance to pay off Lindbergh and McCarthy and the others for letting me down, for destroying my illusions. I couldn't give the steam off a cow flop for the consequences. I suppose every sixteen-year-old thinks he's immortal. I wasn't worried about the flying, I wasn't worried what might happen to me afterward. Worst of all, I wasn't worried for what might happen to my parents, or Patsy or Peggy Sue. What can I say? I was a self-righteous little bastard."

The heroes of the RFS strode out across the tarmac. Hubbard and McCarthy looked hung-over. LeMay, who hadn't bothered to shave, tossed another cigar-butt to one side and started pulling on his flying-jacket. Morrison strode coolly along, bringing up the rear.

Lindbergh saw Charlie fitting Jack's flying-helmet over his head.

"Keep out of this, son. This isn't your fight."

"With respect, Comrade Colonel Lindbergh, sir," Charlie replied, "this is my fight. You used to be my hero. I wanted to grow up to be just like you. But last night I saw you acting like a sneaky two-faced yellow bastard. So even if the man you had beaten up wasn't a friend of mine, I have to take you on. I'm doing it on behalf of every kid in America who looks up to you without realising what an asshole you are. Sir."

"From cringing geek to pompous numbskull in one overnight step, eh?" said McCarthy. "Where's your ripe girlfriend?"

Lindbergh's face closed as McCarthy breathed fumes.

"We can call this off right now," said the Lone Eagle.

"Yes sir," replied Charlie. "We can...if you let Howie here go and promise not to harm him."

"Hell, no!" snapped LeMay. "Lindy, cut out the whining and fly."

LeMay proposed stunts, and Howie agreed to everything with a nod.

"Might as well put on a show for the folks who turned out to see this dogfight," said LeMay.

Lindbergh muttered something about Helldivers being built for killing Japs not barnstorming, and walked away to one of the huge blue craft to get into his flying jacket before climbing into the cockpit. He was joined by Morrison who took the back seat of the plane.

LeMay tossed Charlie two small wooden practise bombs and said "you know what to do with these, four-eyes?" Charlie nodded, and LeMay and McCarthy climbed into the other Helldiver.

Hubbard stayed behind as ground crew. He would, he had said, do as he usually did at RFS air displays and take the microphone on the grandstand and provide the public with a running commentary.

"Enough hot air for a Montgolfier balloon," Howie spat as Hubbard test-woofed into the mike.

The air-cooled engines of the powerful Navy planes coughed, then roared into life, spewing huge gobs of unhealthy black smoke from the engine-cowl exhausts.

Charlie climbed into the front cockpit of the Spruce Goose and belted himself in securely. From behind, Howie shouted "connnnnn-tacttt!!" and the engine turned over. It spluttered into action, shaking the plane so badly that Charlie was worried it would fall apart long before they got airborne.

The four-bladed props of the Helldivers, each as long as a full-grown man, spun smoothly. Charlie looked behind him at the stocky planes. The difference between them and the H-1 was like that between a healthy 20-year-old quarterback and an infirm, wheezing old man.

The Helldivers taxied out to the main part of the asphalt runway, pulled even more power from their engines and in an instant were airborne, just a few feet from the ground as they started retracting undercarriages.

Howie started moving the biplane out towards the runway. Charlie felt a tap on his shoulder. He looked behind to see Howie making a universal gesture at him. Charlie got the message, searched down by his feet, found a full bottle and passed it to the old man. Howie grinned and gave a thumbs-up sign, spat the cork away and drained half the bottle. At least he *acted* like a daredevil pilot.

The plane moved forward.

Above the howling of the engine, he could just about hear Howie whooping. Charlie joined in as the Spruce Goose left the ground. He stopped as it hit the ground again.

"Damn the torpedoes!" he yelled, for want of anything more appropriate or exuberant, as the plane left the ground decisively and the grey scar of the runway became highlighted against the green of Baxter Field below.

At the end of the runway, he could see three stick figures waving. Patsy and Peggy Sue had been joined by a third person, whose skull was swathed in greying bandage and whose left arm was stiff.

Charlie pulled the helmet's goggles down and fixed them over his glasses, feeling like Audie Murphy being catapulted off the aircraft carrier *Robert La Follette* to do battle with the Japanese in *Twelve O'Clock High*.

Ahead, he could see the Helldivers against the clouds. The planes circled the field at 500 feet, pulling a wide lazy arc as they went in for the first stunt.

LeMay's ship got in there impatiently. Charlie recognised it as LeMay's because he could just make out the yellow blur of the names of the Japanese and German cities the General was supposed to have bombed painted next to the cockpit. It executed three loops in succession without stalling. Charlie could imagine the people down below applauding.

LeMay's Helldiver made height to circle out of the way as Lindbergh's plane swooped down to repeat the trick. Again, Charlie felt Howie tapping his shoulder. He looked back to see a ferocious leer on the old man's face. "Strapped in boy?" shouted Howie. Charlie checked, and pulled the buckles tighter.

Lindbergh put his plane into an elegant descending arc, ready to loop a few loops. Charlie felt himself being pushed backwards in his seat as the Spruce Goose gathered speed and headed into a collision course for Lindbergh's port side.

Charlie tensed. The Helldiver seemed less than a hundred yards off. He could make out Morrison's face at the back of the cockpit, looking at them in what he was sure was horror. The Curtiss started pulling up at the beginning of its first loop. Something howled in Charlie's ear as they passed the plane. It was right above them. Then the world turned upside-down and the Helldiver was below them and the harness was straining on his shoulders.

The world turned again, and again, and again, and again.

Howie had flown his first loop through Lindbergh's first loop, and had gone on to execute four more loops himself.

Charlie was glad he'd been to the privy that morning.

The H-1 turned and swooped low towards Baxter Field. As it overflew the crowd at 80 feet, Howie put her through four victory rolls. As far as he was concerned, he had just won the first contest with flying colours.

At the side of the airfield, parallel to the runway, were a pair of large grain-silos. The Roseville Wheat Collective stored their produce there. Each was 150 feet tall and they were 95 feet apart. These were to be the site of the next stunt.

The three aircraft stacked, 200 feet apart, in a circle above the silos. The Spruce Goose was at the top, and Howie made a point of keeping directly above Lindbergh. Charlie fought the slipstream to lean over the side and make rude gestures at Morrison.

The first to try flying between the silos was LeMay. The plane took a long run in at the obstacles, but at the last moment, Stone Age Carpet's nerve must have gone, or he must have misjudged for, a good distance from them, the plane banked sharply to the right and upwards, rising in height to rejoin the stack for another go.

Charlie felt sure he could hear Howie jeering.

Next was Lindbergh. He broke out of the stack, curving upwards and turning gracefully half a mile away before beginning his run.

Below them, Lindbergh was down to 50 feet, skimming the flat Kansas countryside. Charlie knew that for a man experienced in flying off the pointy end of an aircraft carrier—and more difficult, landing on it again —this was no challenge at all.

He didn't hear the sound of Lindbergh's wingtip glancing off the side of one of the silos. Nor did he expect to be able to hear the sound of the grain pouring out of the corrugated iron tower like water. But he saw it, and he didn't believe it. He turned to Howie.

"Did that on purpose!" Howie mouthed.

Lindbergh's Curtiss wasn't seriously damaged. It had lost or dented perhaps two inches of wingtip, but he pulled up over Baxter Field, gained more height over Fort Baxter before curving round and coming in to land. Lindbergh had deliberately put himself out of the race.

"Cluck cluck," Charlie shouted. "There goes the Lone Chicken."

Now Howie broke the Spruce Goose out of its circling pattern and flew off over the fields before turning to face the silos.

Slowly, Howie let the plane lose height until Charlie felt as though he could put his hand out of his cockpit and touch the corn-stubble below. Howie was shouting.

"Hold on...*tight*..."

The twin towers of the silos loomed up ahead. Charlie tensed.

Suddenly, the world was thrown out of perspective again. The harnesses were cutting into his shoulders. His legs were trying to leave the floor and his centre of gravity was moving into his chest. The silos were still dead ahead. But they were upside down. The ground seemed only inches from the top of his head.

Charlie closed his eyes.

He could hear grains of corn, still spilling from the gash that Lindbergh's wing had made in the tower, spattering off the underside of the lower wing as they swooped through.

Howie pulled her up a little, gaining enough height to avoid crashing into Baxter Field's rudimentary control tower, and to do a few more victory rolls to acknowledge the admiration of the crowd, however muted it might be. Charlie wondered how this looked from the ground.

They ran up to 400 feet and watched LeMay go in for his second run. This time, he didn't refuse the jump, but went straight at the silos. From where he was, looking down from above, however, Charlie couldn't be sure if LeMay had actually flown between them. He may have just gone over the top of them. One thing was for sure: the steel-spined hero had not flown nearly as low between the things as he and Howie had just done.

It was time for the dive bombing contest.

A large cross of sheets and sacking, each axis fifty feet long, had been weighted down with stones on the grass to one side of the airfield. This was the target. The contestants simply had to drop their two bombs as close to the centre as possible. LeMay's Helldiver would be dropping its load from racks under the fuselage. The Spruce Goose's bombs would be dropped by Charlie. This was his main task as co-pilot. He'd done much the same from gliders.

The Helldivers were equipped with the very latest bombsight, and bombing was something the RFS demonstrated every time it visited somewhere. It was something Charlie expected LeMay's bombardier, Major McCarthy, to be quite good at. Presumably he didn't call himself "Bomber Joe" for nothing.

Charlie had an advantage that, as far as he was concerned, evened things up. He would be coming in over the target slower and lower. Besides, a fifty-foot cross was a trickier target than Berlin.

LeMay's ship went down first, dropping its practice bomb to spread a shock of blue dye about the grass a good fifteen feet too soon.

Charlie pulled the first of his bombs from the cockpit locker and sat it in his lap. The plane lowered itself in over the target, almost as leisurely as a hen sitting herself down on a clutch of eggs, then swooped, accelerating sharply.

Charlie leaned over the side, trying to get the right feel of the wind and slipstream, as he'd been taught at bombing classes at summer camp, and let go. The trick was to judge the exact speed of the plane, then calculate from the altitude just how soon before the plane was directly over the target to drop the bomb so it would follow a slanted trajectory towards the crux of the cross.

Howie pulled the plane gently upwards, riding parallel with the runway off to their left. Charlie strained backwards to see the effects of his work. There was a very satisfying splatter of red dye almost bang in the middle of the target.

On the edge of the field, he noticed three figures lounging in the grass by an old Haynes Roadster, passing a bottle between them. Melvin Yandell and his cronies. He was sorely tempted to drop his second bomb on them, but it wouldn't have been keeping in spirit with the contest.

They ambled about the sky, Howie finishing off the contents of his bottle as they watched LeMay go in for his second bomb run.

This time, Bomber Joe found his target, coming in fast at 100 feet and sloshing his blue paint right in the middle of the huge cross on the ground. It was an impressive achievement, but, Charlie reflected, as much a tribute to good old socialist know-how and repeated practice than any virtue on McCarthy's part.

The General's plane pulled up and away and it was Charlie's turn again. He was worried that Howie would try and outdo LeMay by trying more fancy aerobatics, but he just took her in steady as before.

Charlie dropped his bomb, and looked down and back to find it, too, had hit the target slap in the middle. He grinned back at Howie. Howie winked and handed him the bottle he had just emptied. Charlie was confused to see that the bottle was nearly full again, with a pale yellow liquid.

Howie pointed to Melvin's car and put his free thumb up, and Charlie caught on. Which was just as well, because he had been on the point of taking a celebratory drink. They had, after all, just won the contest.

Instead of taking the plane up to gain height, circle round and land, Howie kept her low as they swooped in over Melvin, Philly and Chick. Charlie, drawing on all his bombing expertise, emptied the bottle of urine over the choking thugs.

Howie banked to one side and Charlie noted with satisfaction that the hoods were shaking fists and brushing down their expensive clothes.

He turned back to Howie to give him the thumbs-up, but he noticed the huge blue shape of a Curtiss Helldiver swooping down from above, passing overhead at what must have been 300 mph.

The Spruce Goose shook and buffeted violently in the larger aircraft's slipstream. In the back of the Helldiver's long glazed cockpit he could see McCarthy drawing a bead on them with a tommy gun.

The gun quivered and small flames issued from its muzzle.

Charlie turned to Howie.

"Are those blanks?"

Howie pointed to the lower right hand wing. It was pockmarked with half a dozen holes, each surrounded by shreds of ripped canvas flapping in the wind like torn paper.

In the distance, the Helldiver was turning again for another run at them. Charlie knew that Curtiss Helldivers had six powerful wing-mounted 20 mm cannon. He hoped that they wouldn't be loaded since the plane was simply on a courtesy visit. If they were primed, he and Howie were finished. Using them against an old biplane would be like killing a butterfly with both barrels of a 16-gauge.

Howie turned the H-1 on a dime, keeping her low and running across Baxter Field. Keeping her low would stop LeMay from getting in underneath them where they were even more vulnerable. And perhaps Stone Age Carpet would be less willing to murder his opponents in full view of the people of Roseville. At the least, it would show them the bastard was a sore loser.

Even in the distance, and even over the rhythmic clatter of the Spruce Goose's engine, they could hear the Helldiver humming, the noise growing to a guttural roar as it came at them from behind.

Once again, the fragile biplane shook as the navy plane overflew them, slightly to the left. There was no damage done. Clearly, LeMay and McCarthy were wishing their wing guns were loaded.

Once again Charlie could see McCarthy squinting down the sights of the Thompson gun. It occurred to him that in combat, the Curtiss's rear-mounted weapon was normally a pair of .50 calibre machine guns. It was luck of a kind, though McCarthy's toy could kill them just as effectively if he got a bead on his target.

McCarthy's gun stuttered. Howie broke left to throw his aim.

It worked. By the time he realised what was going on, McCarthy was too far away to get an accurate shot. But it hadn't stopped him from trying anyway, and in following through, he had made the most dumb, elementary mistake imaginable.

If Charlie needed any more proof that the war record of Major Joseph McCarthy, at least, was somewhat exaggerated, here it was. He had just shot through his own tail.

He realised his mistake before it was too late. The Helldiver's huge sail-like tailplane was a little the worse for wear, but still intact. But McCarthy kept firing, even though the distance between the two planes was growing. Howie threw the H-1 all over the sky to evade fire.

They were overflying the edge of Baxter Field again, just where Charlie had earlier seen Peggy Sue, Patsy and Jack, and the Helldiver was still firing uselessly at them. Major McCarthy must be madder than hell, Charlie reflected, to be using up his ammunition in this way.

Howie turned the plane again, still keeping low, as the much faster naval aircraft disappeared into the distance. He brought the Spruce Goose over Baxter Field yet again, looping three loops and coming out into three victory rolls to prove to everyone that he and Charlie weren't harmed or scared.

Being thrown about the air like this was annoying Charlie a little. He was searching his brain for the vital statistics on Curtiss Helldivers, the rate of turn, rate of climb, stalling speed...

The Helldiver was coming up behind them again.

Once again, it took up position ahead of them to give McCarthy a shot at them. Once again, Bomber Joe took aim.

Nothing happened.

McCarthy's gun had either jammed or run out of ammunition.

The Helldiver swooped on into the wide blue yonder.

It was all over. Charlie could add another 45 minutes to his flying time.

Howie tapped him on the shoulder again, signalling for another bottle. Charlie leaned forwards and found one wedged at the back of the rudder bar.

"You...take...'er...in," yelled Howie, grabbing the bottle.

For a moment Charlie panicked. His 22 flying hours barely qualified him for a single-handed landing.

The Spruce Goose jinked lazily across open fields as Charlie realised that, without a bottle of rotgut jammed in front of it, the rudder bar in the front cockpit was operational and that his feet were on it.

For the first time, he grabbed the stick. Howie, singing in the back, had clearly decided to call it a day.

For all that she looked like a stringbag, the H-1 was light to the touch and very responsive. Charlie jerked her up and to the left and passed in a wide semicircle around the perimeter of Baxter Field to line her up on the runway.

There was no sign of the Curtiss Helldiver that had been trying to kill them. But down below, he noticed a growing knot of people away from the main area. An olive green army ambulance, painted at the top and sides with red crosses on white circles, was bumping across the field towards the group. There must have been some kind of accident.

Two minutes later, Charlie had the Spruce Goose pointing down the main runway. He took a deep breath and brought her in, easing down the throttle, hoping that Peggy Sue's rabbit's foot still had enough luck left in it.

It was a perfect landing. Tyres touched the tarmac and stayed there.

Suddenly, Charlie became aware that his shirt and trousers were soaking wet. He had shed more sweat in less than an hour than Porky Rook did in a year's worth of sexual incontinence lectures.

"Fuckin'-A-OK, Charlie boy," slurred Howie from the back. "Yer a born flier! Shit, I couldn't do a landing smooth as that, drunk or sober!"

Charlie taxied her to the area in front of the crowded grandstand before shutting off the engine.

Silence. Perfect silence.

He and Howie clambered out of the plane, pulling off gloves, goggles, helmets and jackets.

It was only then he realised that everyone was clapping and cheering.

Over the public address system someone was saying "ladies and gentlemen, comrades, I give you the heroes of the hour. That old barnstormer certainly showed the RFS a thing or two. The pilot of the H-1, as I was telling you, has a very distinguished war-record. I should know because I was Howie's squadron commander when we were escorting bombers over Germany and..."

With a start, Charlie realised the voice belonged to Lieutenant Lafayette R. Hubbard.

"Howie," he whispered urgently to his companion, "what's going on? Surely LeMay isn't going to approve of this?"

"Beats me, Charlie."

"And, comrades, I'm glad to tell you I've just had word from the doctor. Apparently the stray bullet that young Patsy caught in the leg only gave her a scratch. She's going to be fine ladies and gentlemen, just fine...You know, all this excitement we've had here this morning reminds me of the time I was flying Dauntlesses at the Battle of Midway. We were flying off the aircraft carrier *Matewan* and Admiral Nimitz came up to me and said..."

"Hubbard was what you'd call a pathological liar, I guess. Totally incapable of telling the truth. But he wasn't dumb. He'd seen that LeMay had flipped, and after Lindbergh and Morrison deliberately put themselves out of the running, the three of them had gotten together on the ground and decided to double-cross him and McCarthy. They all hated LeMay and McCarthy anyway, for being stone-crazy. And they'd just made several big mistakes.

"When McCarthy made that last run at us, squirting off all that ammo like it was water, he was firing downwards. And one of his stray shells caught Patsy. Just a scratch. If she'd caught it full, she'd have lost a leg. So when word got to Hubbard and Morrison and Lindbergh that LeMay's irresponsible behaviour had gotten someone hurt, it was an absolute godsend to them. They no longer had any qualms about ratting out on their buddies. So while we were in mortal danger up in the sky, Hubbard was giving a running commentary. Realising the crowd's sympathies would be with the underdogs—me and Howie—he played us up as socialist good guys, and stabbed Stone Age Carpet and Bomber Joe in the back.

"When they landed a few minutes later, everyone was jeering them, and Patsy's father—Peggy Sue's father—could walk up to McCarthy and punch him on the nose for shelling his daughter without any fear of reprisal. Way I heard it, LeMay and McCarthy ended up drilling for oil in Alaska, a pretty rough punishment in those days. And Lindbergh, Morrison and Hubbard carried on with the RFS as though nothing had happened. You can't really say everyone got what they deserved, but it was a kind of justice I guess.

"And they all lived happily ever after. Patsy got better a lot quicker than Jack did. Jack and Howie hung around Roseville a couple of days before disappearing over the very flat horizon of Kansas. After nearly getting killed, and after receiving the most almighty whopping for pulling such a stupid stunt, I gradually lost interest in planes. As a matter of fact, I sort of developed a phobia about them. I sometimes have dreams about how near to getting killed I was when McCarthy opened fire, and I've been travelling on the ground ever since. It was my sixteenth birthday a few days later. Same day that Jack and Howie flew off, I recall. My parents traded Jack a couple of home-grown squashes for his guitar, and, for my birthday, gave it to me. I wasn't too sure about the thing at first, but over the months I found myself fooling around with it more, and before I knew where I was I knew I'd found my heartbeat...

"Also, I got the girl, of course. At least for a year or two, but in the end, Peggy Sue got married to someone else. It could have been worse, I suppose. It could have been Melvin Yandell. He went to Washington a few years later and became one of the many people who make a good living doing nothing in particular down somewhere along the lines where the Party mixed with the Mafia. Shortly after Vonnegut came to power and he turned the FBI against organised crime, Yandell was one of the patsies thrown to the wolves by the wiseguys. Peggy Sue, I'm afraid, has the lousy taste to call herself Mrs. Pete Horowitz these days. Captain Porky Rook kept at the Pioneers until he was found doing something disgraceful with Melvin Yandell's little brother Fat Billy, and wound up in a re-education centre for the sexually incontinent out in Death Valley. Patsy took off one day a few months later, to get out of going to a dance with Chick Willis, and never came back. She was smart, so I reckon she found something somewhere. Osgood Yandell had a heart attack from overeating, and Colonel Hall was given the Order of Debs in 1961 for lifelong service to the USSA.

"Jack and Howie? They carried on their business for a while, I think. Jack eventually quit to write books. Howie? Who knows? I like to think he's still out there somewhere. Those guys were legends. They flew all over the country at a time when most folks never expected to go beyond ten or twenty miles outside their home-town in a lifetime. Me, I've been all over the place, and I always used to make a point of asking folks if Jack and Howie had been through back in the '40s or early '50s. And a lot of the time they had, putting on a show, spraying crops, getting drunk, falling foul of the Party or the local law. They didn't take any crap from anyone at a time when everyone had to take a lot of crap. And that's good enough for me..."

The crowd at Texas Jack's had been getting impatient with the second-rate band that had been grinding its way through three-chord covers all afternoon. So when they finished slaughtering Bruce Springsteen's "Born in the USSA", they got no encouragement at all to continue. They seemed to take it in good spirits. The place was full now, and Lowe knew people had been sneaking looks at him, envying his temporary monopoly on C.H. Holley, impatient for the musician to get on stage. The Crickets, Holley's backing band, were in the club already, setting up. This gig hadn't been announced, but everybody knew about it. Over the years, a finely-tuned grapevine had been cultivated all over America.

"Guess I have to go to work," said Holley, strumming his fingers on his chest.

C.H. Holley shook Lowe's hand, and got up onto the stage. He strapped his guitar on, and, without tuning up, hit a chord. He was perfectly in tune, calling up the music like an old friend. He played some of the old songs, and a lot of the new ones. Everything Lowe had heard about him was true.

"*Heart-beattt,*" Holley sang, "*why do you miss...*"

TEN DAYS THAT SHOOK
THE WORLD

1912-1917

Thursday, December 19th, 1912.
The Union Stockyard, Chicago, Illinois.

"Dash!"

Only Carter called him that. Sam heard his fellow Pinkerton's shout and turned, revolver drawn. He did not want to shoot anyone today, much less a starving Wobblie, but he was here to protect the President-Elect. And the Rough Riders, a mounted band of volunteer strike-breakers and gadabout gallants, were going to be in trouble if Teddy didn't back down.

Outside the gates of the Union Stockyard, the pickets had been reinforced. Among the ragged, desperate placard-wavers—meat-packers who had been laid off or who had had their wages cut—were a few cooler fish, tough-looking birds who looked a sight readier for a fight than the glory hounds trotting along behind Teddy, tall in their saddles, shotguns resting on their thighs, revolvers in buttoned-down chamois holsters on their hips.

Sam looked across the street, trying to see his partner. Nicholas Carter was half-way up a lamp-post, waving furiously, pointing at the President. Teddy must think he was back in Cuba two terms, three elections and one political party ago. Mounted on a splendid grey, he was ambling out of the ranks of the Rough Riders, easing his way through the cordon of Irish cops, entering alone the space of some twenty yards between the pickets and the law.

The President was either going to make a speech or call a charge. Sam wouldn't have advised either course. For the first time, he truly saw the face of the man whose life he was supposed to preserve. The famous grin was still there, and the round spectacles, but everything else was sagging, fading, flaking away. Sam had heard the newly-elected "Bull Moose" Progressive was not in the pink of health. He looked older than fifty-four.

The strikers' placards stopped waving, and the noise died. Sam could hear the clip-clop of the presidential horse's hooves. By the force of his legendary presence, Teddy had quelled, at least for a few moments, the fury of the crowd. Sam hoped the President would try appealing to reason. He would fail, but bloodshed might be put off.

You can't tell men whose wives and children have no food in their bellies to go home and be peaceable, to thank God for their blessings. Especially not if you intended to pot a few of them for sport and pose with the corpses for the rotogravure, then dine on pheasant under glass at a mayoral reception for the victor of poll and picket line. For the bulk of the people in this angry street, it was going to be a meagre Christmas.

Teddy surveyed the strikers, baring his teeth like an angry rat. Sam wished he had a shot of whisky in his hand.

This whole tour was getting nervier and nervier. Last night, Teddy had gorged himself in splendour with Colonel Cody at the Biltmore, after watching the show. Buffalo Bill's Wild West and Pawnee Bill's Far East. Teddy and the Colonel were old friends; the original Rough Riders had taken their name from Buffalo Bill's earlier show, the Wild West and Congress of the Rough Riders of the World. All through the spectacle, Sam had been on edge, unable to hear Frank Butler shoot a bauble without involuntarily reaching for his gun.

There had been pickets outside the arena. Teddy had mistaken them for well-wishers and insisted on taking a bow. Carter had nobly stepped in front of a rotten egg meant for the President. Next time it might not be an egg.

Sam was drinking again. This triumphal tour, "to sort out the local difficulties and see off this foulfart Debs", was wavering between farce and disaster. Whatever happened, his nerves would suffer. At the second reception last night, which Carter contemptuously called "the servants' ball", even the lesser performers in Cody's Cavalcade had been dubious about the situation. All over the country, he had been hearing similar sentiments.

It was hard to believe that Teddy had won his election only six weeks ago, beating the incumbent, his former Republican party-mate Taft, into third place after the Democrat Wilson. The first strikes had already begun while the polls were being counted. "One Big Union, One Big Strike," Eugene V. Debs had said, throwing what little weight the IWW had behind the stockyard employees. Debs's little weight was growing, Sam knew. At almost a million votes, the Socialist had come a long way behind even Taft in the election, but rushing about the country in his Red Special, he had been garnering increasing support. And if Teddy wanted to shoot a few thin-limbed meat-packers today, Debs would pick up more votes, more hearts, more guns...

"If that man's not careful," the small woman who shot so prettily in the arena had said, "he'll be carrying an ounce or two of lead under his well-filled waistcoat."

Teddy raised his arm, and Sam's heart spasmed. He was going to signal a charge! No. Sam breathed again as the President began to speak.

"Stand aside, and let these honest men through," he bellowed.

The pickets were in control of the Union Stockyard, inside and out. Sam heard Debs himself was sitting in the foreman's office, cronies Big Bill Haywood and Joe Hill with him, organising his campaign like a great general.

Teddy signalled for his Rough Riders to advance and they did, at a surprisingly disciplined trot. Half were society heroes, parading their elegant horses, but the rest were veterans of Teddy's campaigns, knuckle-heads who wanted a legal opportunity to shed some Red blood, and paid thugs. The cops, most of whom had relatives on the other side of the street and were here under threat of being fired, melted away to the sides of the advance. A few quivering, shabbily-dressed figures crept behind the horsemen.

"These honest men," Teddy said, indicating the creepers, "wish to work."

"Scabs," someone shouted.

The riot nearly started then. Everyone was shouting something. Sam saw Carter pulled down from his lamp-post by a cop, and wave his Pink badge as if he were brandishing the sword of God. The Agency had rank in anything to do with the President's safety.

He had to get near Teddy. Then, he could see what was coming. He pushed through the horses, ignoring the well-spoken and foully-spat oaths showered on him, holding up his badge and his gun like free passes to a ball-game.

There was scuffling at the gates, as strike-breakers with axe-handles and baseball bats got in there to clear a path for the "scabs" Teddy had sworn to shepherd right onto the killing floor. "One Big Union, One Big Strike," the pickets were chanting. More pickets were flowing out from somewhere, adding strength to the human defences. Sam knew Teddy had underestimated Debs. The "dreaming blowhard" was a better general than anyone gave him credit for.

Sam was close to the President now. Teddy's face was flushing red in spots, and the cold turned his breath to fog. If there had to be a fight, he was ready for it. He had his own gun out now. The man who was too tender-hearted to shoot a bear cub was about to gun down some of his fellow Americans. Their crime, as Cody's lady sharp-shooter had said, was "wanting to protect their families from cold, hunger and disease".

Sam was the only one close enough to hear Teddy's last word, "bully!" The shot neatly broke the President's spectacles. Sam saw a red trickle run down the side of Teddy's nose, and realised that the back of the man's head was blown away, his slouch hat with it.

As Teddy tumbled from his rearing horse, a barrel-shaped corpse, the Rough Riders met a hail of projectiles from the roof of the stockyards, and pickets laid into strike-breakers with ferocity. Sam was the only one who knew the President was dead.

He knew where the shot had come from. Taking his blows, he pushed through the fighting. Someone hit him in the side with a bludgeon, and he thought a few ribs were staved in. He forced himself on, teeth grit against the pain.

There were other shots now, from the Rough Riders. The scion of one wealthy family was pulled from his saddle, and soundly kicked, his gun passed to a picket.

Sam saw the small figure running away, and wondered if Teddy had been brought down by a child. There were plenty of hungry children in the IWW. Suddenly, a path was clear, and Sam ran through it, hurdling groaning bodies, escaping from the press of people.

"Halt," he shouted, a stab of pain in his lungs, icy wind in his face. Cold, salt tears filled his eyes.

The fleeing assassin did not stop. Sam was slow, though, wheezing. He was gaining on the killer. He could either stop, take a careful aim, and bring him down, risking a miss and the assassin's escape. Or he could keep running, and hope his injury didn't stop him before he caught up with the gunman.

He ran on, shouldering past a fat woman wearing a "READY FOR TEDDY" sash. The noise of the fighting was spreading, as was the riot itself. Sam outpaced the chaos, fixing his attention on the faltering figure in the long overcoat and big cap, scarf wrapped around his face.

The assassin stumbled. Sam covered the twenty yards between them, his lungs screaming. He threw himself on the killer, landing a blow with the butt of his revolver. The scarf came away, and Sam recognised the face. The small, bundled-up figure was not a child, but a woman.

He expected her to shout "long live the Revolution" or some Red slogan. Instead, she seemed relieved, and was trying to sit up, trying to get back her breath. His own heart was hammering, and he tasted blood in his mouth.

"Annie," he said, "why?"

"*Sic semper tyrannis*," she quoted.

He eased off her, and slumped against a wall, wondering how badly he was hurt inside. Her hands were on him, feeling for his wounds.

"Never was an Indian fighter," she said, "but I've seen enough falls and spills in the Wild West to know some bone-setting. Bite."

He sank his teeth in his coat cuff as she wound her scarf around his chest. The pain surged and peaked as his bones ground back together, and then faded. She walked away.

Later, Samuel Dashiell Hammett would tell himself he had let her go. But now he was too weak and too confused to do anything about the woman who had killed Theodore Roosevelt, the last democratically-elected President of the United States of America.

Tuesday, March 4, 1913.
The Capitol, Washington, D.C.

Reed was not the only one in the crowd with war wounds. He had picked up his bruises in Paterson, New Jersey, where he had been trying to organise a strike of silk-workers. One night a group of men in flour-sack hoods had come to his boarding house and burned it down. Reed and the other two Wobblies were lucky to get out alive. Since Roosevelt's fall, a lot of good union men had been killed. There were wars in the offing, and not just in Mexico or Europe.

He was at the Inauguration on his press ticket, although he didn't have a paper to write for any more. The police and the Pinkertons had closed down Max Eastman's *The Masses*, *Liberator* and any other organ of dissent they could sniff out. Even Hamilton Holt's liberal magazine *The Independent* had had its offices closed down and sealed. The assassin was still unknown, thus beyond even a rich man's justice. Therefore, the hawks of the House of Have were swooping down on anyone who raised voice against them. The 'plutes hadn't reacted so violently when President McKinley had been shot by a solitary, crazed anarchist. This was different, and everyone knew it. Everyone had to decide which side they were on in the coming war. The War of the Classes.

He could not bear to listen to the President's swearing-in or the inaugural address. The former he knew by heart and the latter he had already read in the *New York Inquirer*. In theory, Kane had given up his newspaper interests—to his teen-age son—when he consented to be Roosevelt's running mate, but in practice the President's papers were still his mouthpiece. In a sense, that was good news. At least you could guarantee the Pulitzer and Hearst press printed an approximation of the truth, out of enmity for the rival plutocrat if not devotion to the betterment of society.

Reed had felt he had to come, just to see the circus. He turned his coat collar up against the blast, and wandered among the crowds, keeping a wary eye out for policemen. Nothing had been announced yet, but he was sure he was on the Pinkertons' Red list. The celebrations were genuine, but muted. Even Taft—aptly the fattest President ever to squeeze into the White House—had rated more real enthusiasm.

In his speech, Kane was reassuring America that things were going to change but the old values would be preserved. Power and privilege would pass on intact to the next generation of Robber Barons. A whole raft of anti-trust laws—which, barely ten years before, Kane's papers had vigorously supported—were due to be revoked, and a friendly new family system was being readied.

Beside Kane was his silly wife Emily, bear-like in her shroud of furs. And next to the First Lady stood her spiritual adviser, the completely bald Englishman who styled himself the Great Beast and was rumoured to have put a curse on Roosevelt to bring his patron's husband to power. J.P. Morgan and Andrew Carnegie were not on the platform, content to stay in the warm and let their fellow club-man toss a few waves to the mobs while they drank brandy in their libraries.

Born in a Colorado boarding house, the new President was something of a joke to his peers.

The bunting looked surprisingly cheap for a man of solid financial standing, and a party who had fought and won an election with the backing of bankers and industrialists who treated dollars like footsoldiers, sending them out as cannon fodder to overwhelm the opposition. Short measure had always been a secret tenet of Carnegie's "Gospel of Wealth", Reed supposed.

"John," someone said, nearby. Reed turned, and saw a mask of grinning bandages.

"Jack?" he breathed.

The face nodded under his hat. Reed felt his own bruise, and was appalled at the extent of the injury his comrade must have suffered.

"No," London shook his head, reading Reed's thought, "it's a disguise."

Reed might have laughed.

"I'm hoping the Pinks won't think of looking for me here."

"Everyone's on the look-out for assassins."

London snorted through his bandages.

"Have you heard the rumour that it was me?"

Reed had, and had not been sure. There were people in the IWW, or affiliated to it, who would not hesitate to shoot a President or two. Jack London was certainly one of their number. If it came to the opportunity and he had a revolver rather than a notebook and pencil in his travelling case, so was John Reed.

"My favourite story," London said, "is that it was Jesse James, come back for another crack at the Pinks."

London steered him through the crowd, away from the very visible row of bodyguards and police.

"All the bars are shut," London complained, "I've heard they're thinking of making the country go dry. Brewers are mainly German, you know. The working men could better spend their dollars and cents on American goods."

"A mistake, I think. If a man is denied the opportunity of seeking oblivion in alcohol, he will need to hold his head high. And to do that, he needs to be free…"

London did not seem impressed with the argument. Reed knew his comrade was a drinker.

"Should we perhaps take the opportunity of visiting the Constitution?" London suggested. "To see if Ford or Cross are busy rewriting selected clauses."

"A slave-owners' charter," Reed said.

London shrugged. All around, white marble was lightly frosted with the persistent cold. There were uniformed police, ranks of soldiers in their dress blues and obvious Pinkerton men patrolling or on sentry duty in every street. The capital city was under military rule.

Eugene Debs was in South America, Reed knew. Theodore Dreiser, Emma Goldman and Elizabeth Gurley Flynn were in jail, thinking and debating; Big Bill Haywood, Joe Hill and canny old Daniel De Leon were on the run, agitating and organising. Every week, the Kane press gloated over the capture of a new "ring-leader", inevitably branding them as the man who pulled the trigger or the man who sold the gun or the man who gave the order. Two days ago, the Pinkertons had gone so far as to arrest eighty-two-year-old Mary Harris Jones and to charge her under the new Emergency Powers Acts. Mother Jones had been in West Virginia, at a coal strike, in the midst of a battle between armed miners and federal troops. She had been hand-cuffed and dragged away, her skirts raised and tied over her head.

"Look," London said, pointing.

They were by the Lincoln Memorial, and Jack London was looking upwards, at the massive white statue of Abraham Lincoln in repose.

Reed could not see it, but London told him something that would be repeated, at first as a whisper, then as a cry of rage.

While Charles Foster Kane was being inaugurated as President, the statue of Lincoln was weeping tears of ice.

Friday, October 9, 1914.
S.S. *Titanic*, North Atlantic.

They had only been out of Liverpool two days, but the orchestra in the First Class saloon had taken every available opportunity to defiantly play the liner's special anthem, "Sail on Great *Titanic*". Weiss was heartily sick of the tune, but it was not his part to complain. The crew knew their countrymen were fighting for the existence of their nation and probably saw any celebration of British achievements as a patriotic duty.

"Sail on Great *Titanic*," he hummed, "the ship that will never go down..."

The rest of the orchestra's repertoire was strictly jingo as well. Even Strauss waltzes had been struck from the card. There was, however, one patriotic song they wouldn't do. An hour ago, as the Captain was dining with some socialites who were fleeing to America to evade their duty, the band played a song Weiss had heard frequently in Britain before he left. He didn't know the title, but the refrain went "oh we don't want to lose you, but we think you ought to go…" It was a catchy melody, the words encouraging young men to sign up to fight for "your king and your country". For a moment, the room had fallen silent. The captain had flushed red and, it was rumoured, had to be dissuaded from clapping the bandleader in irons.

He stood on the deck, watching the full moon in the waters. His supple hands were feeling the cold. The great White Star liner was moving at full speed, trying to dash away from the British Isles, and away from the U-boats as quickly as possible. Of course, not even the Fiendish Hun would sink an unarmed passenger liner. Just to make sure they got the message, the master had ordered as much light be shown as possible and had forbidden any curtains to be closed until they were well into the North Atlantic.

Despite the chill, Weiss stayed outside, mainly to avoid the Colonel. The Colonel was in a perpetual rage, and Weiss knew better than most the reasons for his colourful choler. On the edge of bankruptcy, William Cody had been counting on "playing before the crowned heads of Europe" on one more tour before retiring. He resented the way his "close personal friend" Kaiser Wilhelm had invaded Belgium, dragging all the royal cousins and connections into a spat that was obviously going to rule out further engagements on the continent for the duration.

All the British hired hands had upped and enlisted, leaving the Colonel unable even to entertain the Crowned Head of England. Now, the great Indian Fighter and Frontier Scout was having to transport, out of his own shallow pocket, over 100 of his ropers, riders, shooters and showmen from war-ravaged Europe to the safety of America.

Weiss wished he had kept his act to himself, and refused to accept the Colonel's offer of a prominent position on the bill of the Wild West. The offer had been generous, because Cody had needed the Houdini name to revive flagging interest in his Wild West. He was especially irked by the great showman's current bugbear, his theory that the entire war was a conspiracy by Jews to undermine the strength of the white races. Everyone knew, he claimed, that it was a Jew who had shot Roosevelt.

Houdini sounded a lot less Jewish than Erich Weiss, but the eagle-eyed Colonel could surely not be stupid enough to be unaware of his race. In London, Weiss had been assailed twice by patriotic citizens who assumed from his real name that he was a German. Europe was one trap from which he was especially pleased to make an escape.

Looking at the dark waves, Weiss saw a white fleck of foam and the black snake-neck of the conning-tower. Then, the two fluffy trails of white in the water, catching the light as they neared the side of the great liner.

He looked around, but there was no one else on deck, no one to alert...He felt the explosions before he heard them.

Taking a deep breath, which he knew from experience he could hold longer than anyone alive, he was ready for the curtain of water.

Tuesday, May 9th, 1916.
Chemin des Dames, France.

"General Tom can't know about this," said Private Bartlett, face pale and sick under streaks of mud. "Else he'd do something to help us guys."

Sam wasn't sure about that. He'd had his doubts about General Tom ever since the Kane press started calling him "the American Alexander". The suspicion had always been that Black Jack Pershing was supposed to run the War while General Tom posed for all the photographs, made the speeches and kissed the babies. He was the handsomest officer Sam had ever seen, fond of his white ten-gallon hat and pithy guts and glory slogans. He had been with Roosevelt in Cuba, he said, and had been friends with the martyred Colonel Cody. He claimed he had a personal reason to get that rat, Kaiser Billy.

The story now was that Roosevelt had been struck down by a German bullet, the first of the Great War. Sergeant Hammett had never told what he knew, and had even been strangely pleased when he read in the accounts of the sinking of *Titanic* that Annie Oakley had survived, pulled out of the water by that funny little escapologist who had given his own life trying to save so many others in the freezing waters.

The shelling had been continuous for a week. Most of the men in the forward trenches were dead. The barbed wire forests were splintered into the mud. Sam thought he had an ear infection, and was on the point of going deaf.

With Eddie, Hemingway and Dobbs, he had drawn the worst detail imaginable in the U.S. Expeditionary Force. Digging out the dead, recovering personal effects and weapons. Between them, they were about all that was left of the 305th Machine Gun Battalion.

This was *Chemin des Dames* to the French, known in the U.S. Army as Ladies' Walk or, more poetically, the Road of the Damned. Officially a fortress, it was a muddy network of trenches, tunnels, artillery and gun positions, and huge underground galleries for use as living quarters, magazines and rudimentary hospitals. In summer, with a lot of work and without anyone throwing explosives at it, *Chemin des Dames* might have been a giant sandcastle, ideal for children playing soldiers. As it was, it was Sam's idea of Bloody Hell on Earth.

Eddie Bartlett, a cheerful mechanic back in Brooklyn, was still smiling. He had one of those faces that wouldn't work any other way, and his fixed grin was horribly contradicted by his shattered eyes. Hemingway, a kid who had lied about his age to get into the action, was taking it quietly, saying less, getting on with the work. Fred Dobbs—Fred *C.* Dobbs, as he insisted—was bitching and griping, malingering as usual.

Sam thought the privates were all near their breaking points. They had not slept since the shelling began. It was almost impossible.

There had been a trench here, but now it was just a packed-in heap of earth and bodies. Bartlett and Hemingway dug with their entrenching tools, scraping away clods from the ruins of men.

Weeks before last autumn's major offensive on the Somme, Pershing had been on a tour of the front lines. He had been standing next to a battery of field artillery during a practice, and a defective shell—like one in five of the shells supplied the army—had exploded in a breech, riddling him with steel splinters. Since then, Sam feared General Tom really had been in charge of the conduct of the War. That would explain the crazy, contradictory orders that occasionally filtered through to the front.

In the Somme, the Americans had exchanged half a million men for two hundred square miles of territory the enemy had intended to yield anyway when they pulled back to positions they had been preparing for months. Since then, it had been a question of dig in, and get shelled, gassed, shot at, diseased, maddened or bombed.

A large slab of earth fell away, disclosing the grinning, red-furred skull of a dead doughboy. Months ago, all four soldiers would have vomited instantly. Now, this was a commonplace. The skull still had staring blue eyes. He tried not to think this might have been someone he had known. With the rate of "replacements", it was unlikely. One infantry unit of seven hundred men could sustain such a high casualty rate that almost 7,000 soldiers might pass through it within a single year.

Dobbs was a long-haul veteran, but Bartlett and Hemingway were Cody Soldiers, part of the flood who enlisted after the Kaiser sank Buffalo Bill. A recruiting poster had shown the fierce-bearded American at the bottom of the sea, waving a vengeful fist at a retreating U-Boat. Kane had wanted the War because it was good for newspaper circulation, good for business, good for taking citizens' minds off rumoured abuses in Washington. Factories were turning out dud shells very profitably. The old world was taking a pounding, the titled aristocracy sinking into the mud of France, and the energetic young forces of American capital were cleaning up.

A month ago, ten soldiers of a unit posted in the front line between the Oise and Aisne rivers had been tried for mutiny and executed. Their mutinous act had consisted of being driven insane by the deaths of everyone around them.

A few, like Bartlett, still believed that General Tom was with them. Everyone else was sunk in a mud of despair. Sam knew murders were being committed every day by sullen, desperate, fed-up soldiers who knew they would be dead soon and had nothing to lose. An unpopular NCO could not expect to outlive the week. The officers were in a bad state, afraid of their own men as much as of the enemy. Back home, fortunes were being made. Here, death was like a black gas cloud enveloping them all.

Since the German offensive began, everything had been falling apart, and most of the supply services around *Chemin des Dames* had broken down. Positions had been lost through lack of ammunition, fighting men had collapsed from hunger and exhaustion for want of food provisions, wounded soldiers had died unnecessarily through lack of basic hygiene and medical supplies. The Germans, with saw-toothed bayonets and flamethrowers, might make it worse, but things were going to Hell quite nicely, thanks to American inefficiency and blundering.

"We should try to talk to the General," Bartlett said, hitching his shoulders nervously. "He's a regular guy, he'd try to help…"

Sam was coughing again, and Hemingway had to help him up. His lungs had been weak since his ribs were broken, and the climate around here was not good for his health. He thought he might have caught a whiff of gas somewhere along the line.

He could easily understand how the German commanders thought. The French would fight harder than the British because they were defending their country, and the British would fight harder than the Americans because if France fell, Britain would be next. Therefore, it was sound military sense to concentrate the offensive on the American lines. If they could break through between Noyon and Soissons, they might even have a chance to march on Paris.

"General Tom is in that chateau at that place, Crappy...?"

"Crépy-en-Valois," Hemingway said, quietly.

"Yeah, there. We could go see him, tell him how it really is, cut through all them staff officers telling him lies."

Sam coughed, painfully. "That'd be mutiny, Eddie," he said, his words not coming out properly.

"He should know about the rifles that fall apart," Bartlett said, "the shells that don't work, the orders that don't make sense."

Sam agreed. Hemingway nodded too. Tom Mix certainly ought to know about those things.

"A man alone ain't got no bloody fucking chance," Hemingway said, eyes old beyond his years. Sam guessed the kid was not yet seventeen. He was a reader, who carted Stephen Crane's *The Red Badge of Courage*, Jack London's *The Iron Heel* and Upton Sinclair's *The Jungle* in his duffel, even if they were mostly on the proscribed list drawn up by Kane's postmaster, Will H. Hays.

"Hem," Bartlett said, "you can write good. Let's get up a list of them complaint things."

"Grievances?"

"Yeah, a list of grievances. We could get all the men in the unit to sign. Then, we could go see General Tom. He'd probably be grateful to us for talking straight, telling him the true facts."

Sam was coughing so bad he had to sit down. Hemingway and Bartlett crowded around, concerned for their Sarge. Dobbs held back, leaning on his shovel, rat eyes glittering.

"Yeah," Bartlett said, wonder and belief rekindling in his face, "let's go see General Tom."

Saturday December 16th, 1916.
The Municipal Opera House, Chicago, Illinois.

Parker leaned against the poster, slumped so he was smaller than the female figure depicted on it, and brought up blood.

SUSAN ALEXANDER in *Thaïs*.

Red splattered across the young diva's face, soaking in, giving her a panicked look.

Everyone was in the auditorium, so the cavernous foyer was empty. Parker could hear the whining of the singers and the sawing of the orchestra. It was not what he would have picked to be the last thing he heard on this earth. A tiny voice struggled with the giant music.

In his ears, he could still hear the echoes of the shots. Not the ones he had taken earlier this evening, but all the others. Thirty years' of gunfire, from Wyoming to Bolivia and back. What the Kid had said was true; if you didn't die young, you outlived your time. Now, Parker guessed time was catching up. He had a couple in the gut, and a bastard of a bullet in his wrist, lodged between the bones.

A uniformed attendant saw him, and began limping across the acre of marble. One of his legs was tin, his young face was scarred. Since the War in Europe, America was left to cripples and relics.

He was sitting now, having slid down the poster. Blood was soaking through his starched shirtfront. At least he was dressed for the opera.

The President was in the auditorium, in a private box. Parker assumed that if what he had heard whispered about *la* Alexander were true, the First Lady and her cueball wizard would be otherwise engaged. Emily Kane must be annoyed by that, for she relished any chance to dress up. At the opening of the *Ballets Russes*, she had worn a gown that, according to the social column of the *Inquirer*, was made up of 100 square yards of French silk, imported from Europe despite U-boats and Zeppelins. Her diamonds were insured for a sum which would have fed an infantry division for a year.

Parker had tried to get into the army. After all, he had always made a living with his gun. But he was too old, too often-shot, too forgotten.

Still, he had served his President this evening.

The attendant was with him now, his mouth opening and closing. All Parker could hear were gunshots.

He had his gold. But now he needed more. He had done his job, and now he needed help.

"Cross," he said, "get Cross."

The attendant didn't understand.

Parker tried to stifle the pain in his gut, and said the name again, deliberately.

"Noah Cross."

Even this one-legged Cody soldier knew those were magic words.

They had met in South America, when Parker was guarding gold shipments. The Machiavelli from California had been part-owner of the mining company, walking tall in his white suit, handing out coins to fellow Americans down on their luck, puffing on cigars. Noah Cross saved people. He tucked them away until they could be useful. Parker had been tucked away for nearly twelve years, a weapon kept oiled and polished until needed.

The attendant was gone, and Parker relaxed his stomach, letting the pain grow and seep upwards.

Since the election, there had been a lot of shooting, a lot of work. Kane had won his re-election but, according to the handbills you saw on the streets if the cops were tardy about closing down trouble-making printers, he had only out-polled Wilson and Taft because of an almost unanimous support of the dead. Everyone in the Bronx Cemetery had voted Kane. There were other stories in the handbills, about the War, about the tins of army-issue beef that were offal swept from the slaughterhouse floor, explosives that were half-sawdust, gun barrels made from degraded materials that melted like wax. The Kane papers were full of victories and advances. Even after the troops rebelled, the *Inquirer* branded them as traitors in the pay of the Kaiser, not mutineers driven by appalling conditions.

There were more handbills now. Even here in the palace the President had built with federal funds for his "singer". Scraps of crudely-printed paper wafted across the floor like discarded programmes, drifting against Parker's legs. He had no sensation below his stomach.

Four years ago, the handbills would have reprinted speeches by Eugene Debs or Upton Sinclair. Now, they were reporting the opinions of Woodrow Wilson. WILSON ACCUSES, he read...

An act must have finished, or perhaps the whole show. Parker saw the trails of elegant gowns across the marble, and perfectly-pantsed legs.

Inside, some were applauding, their claps rifle-shots, but most of the audience were getting out before the curtain was even down.

This was society, he knew. With the President would be all his cronies, in and out of the administration. Vice President Bryan, Secretary of War Harding. Fords, Vanderbilts, Rockefellers, Dodsworths, Carnegies, Morgans. Underneath the shooting, Parker could hear the rustle of expensive material, the clink of jewellery, the snap of silver cigar cases. These, he knew, were the real sounds of murder.

A woman, not more than a girl, stared at him, eyes impossibly huge. She was the most beautiful thing Robert Leroy Parker had ever seen, and diamonds enough to fill a king's chest sparkled on her shallow decolletage. Her escort stepped in front of her, and knelt down.

It was Cross, a cigar in his hand.

"You were not to come here, Butch."

He slurped blood. Cross touched Parker's chest, and his fingers came away crimson-dipped. Smiling, he looked as if he wanted to lick his fingerprints clean.

A commotion was running through the crowd. Parker thought it was because of his impolite and bleeding presence, but it was the news, fresh from the street and spreading…

"Wilson's been shot, killed…"

Cross smiled wider, a skull in a silk hat.

"You did well," he said.

"There was a gunfight with the police. Six men dead or injured…"

"…but you weren't to come here."

Cross stood up, and, child-woman on his arm, walked away. He slipped the attendant a hundred dollar bill.

Parker saw the crowds making way for the President. Kane shambled like an old steer, surrounded by boiled-shirt bully boys. He had learned a lesson from Teddy Roosevelt, and no one was going to get close enough to plug him.

Kane received the news. Parker didn't need to hear it. He could still remember the candidate's look as the bullets went into his lungs, cutting short his call for a congressional inquiry into Kane's conduct of the War. The President nodded briefly, and made up a speech of tribute on the spot. Cross edged away from Kane long enough not to be in any of the pictures the newsman from the *Inquirer* was taking.

Everyone flowed out of the foyer, and left Parker behind, unnoticed. The gunshots got louder, then stopped…

Monday, February 5th, 1917.
Courtroom 1, Foley Square Courthouse, New York City.

The accused could not stop smiling, although Reed assumed he must be in a blue funk. If anyone was living on borrowed time, it was Private Edward Bartlett. He had come through the worst bloodbath of the War, and narrowly escaped summary execution without benefit of court martial —only a general mutiny, a strike-like downing-of-tools by his comrades had prevented the carrying-out of that order—and now, back in the States, he was having to be ferried to and from the court by armed guards lest some patriotic citizen try to cheat the firing squad. To Reed, and to many others, there was no greater hero in the United States Armed Forces than Eddie Bartlett.

Judge Royston Bean, past ninety and proud of his frontier reputation, looked like a bronzed cigar store Indian on the bench. The rumour was that he still wore guns under his robes. For the prosecution, Attorney General Ransom K. Stoddard had retained society lawyer Randolph Mason, usually the elegant ornament of libel suits and divorce actions. For the defence, Clarence Darrow was quietly magisterial, weighed down with the concerns of the case, but still sharply witty. If anyone could make anything of *l'affaire* Bartlett, it was Darrow, fresh from a three-month jail sentence for contempt of Congress, a crime Reed thought a man would have to be a blind and deaf half-wit not to commit in his heart every time he opened a newspaper and saw a troop ship unloading coffins from the hold while taking conscripts onto the deck.

Reed sat with the other reporters, making notes. His job was shaky at best—he had suffered four nuisance arrests in the past year—but he had noticed lately how the Iron Grip of the House of Have was less able to contain the boiling forces of the free in mind. Four million Americans, one-tenth of the adult male population, were in France, fighting and dying for muddy inches of Europe even as Villa's raiders massed on the Mexican borders, staking a claim to considerable spreads of Texas, Arizona and New Mexico. At the height of the mutiny, one quarter of the four million had expressed support for Bartlett. Back home, the Movement was gathering strength. Woodrow Wilson and dead-in-prison Mother Jones were martyrs of the Revolution, which must be causing considerable revolutions in Wilson's grave. The Kane press was a joke, and nobody bothered with it any more, even the most conservative recognising the truth of the handbills or folk songs no police force could stamp out. Joseph Pulitzer, a plutocrat cannily seeing a hole in the market to be profitably plugged, had been running accurate stories of the mismanagement of the War and the sufferings of "our boys at the front", a policy which even extended to hiring on John Reed, fresh from a spell as a foreign correspondent in Villa's Mexico, as a Washington commentator. The military censors had run out of blue pencils, and the muddy truth was starting to filter back to the mothers and sweethearts.

Sergeant Samuel Dashiell Hammett was giving evidence, retelling the now-familiar story of the petition of grievances Private Bartlett and his comrades had worked up, and of their month-long frustration as they tried through every legal and reasonable military channel to obtain an audience with General Mix. Darrow's questions drew out details to which Mason persistently objected as "not germane to the case", but which, by the weight of accretion, was giving the court a powerful, unpalatable depiction of the everyday lot of the American soldier in France.

Isabel Amberson Minafer—a society matron whose own son was an officer posthumously decorated for his gallantry—had come along on Mason's invitation to see the private whose treason shamed the memory of her boy. As Hammett spoke, Mrs. Minafer was shaking with deep sobs, tears flooding past her tiny handkerchief, realising at last how her country had betrayed its sons, betrayed her son.

Hammett concluded his evidence by confirming that he had been aware of Eddie Bartlett's intention to make his own way to the chateau at Crépy-en-Valois General Mix was using as a command post, to force his way through the obstructions placed around the General by ignorant staff officers and to explain, honest man to honest man, just how things were on the front line. "Eddie was convinced that General Mix was not being told the truth by those around him," Hammett said.

Mason began his cross-examination, probing Hammett for any memories he might have of statements on the part of Bartlett which revealed Red or anti-militarist sympathies.

Treachery was the by-word of the day. The Tsar of Russia, with his new "liberal" constitution and Prime Minister Kerensky to back him up, had slipped out of the War by the Treaty of Brest-Litovsk, deeding huge tracts of land to Germany and the remains of the Austro-Hungarian Empire. Russian factories were supplying munitions to both sides in the conflict, and Americans with "off" or "ovitch" or "ofsky" on their mailboxes were changing their names faster than Jim Thorpe with salt on his tail. In Europe, American lives were being freely spent by Great Britain and France, and there was a strong, popular feeling—expressed even by such unlikely personages as Henry Ford—to convince Kane and his ring to pull a "Tsar" and get out, leaving the old world to shed its own blood. After all, if Villa and the Kaiser ever ironed out their differences, America might face the opening-up of a front closer to home, and find itself underequipped to defend its own borders, all for the sake of the vanity of a few inbred crowned clowns.

Mason finished his dance around Hammett, and the witness left the stand. One or two people applauded, and Mrs. Minafer would not look the prosecuting lawyer in the eye. Reed could sense sympathy for the cause welling up in the hardest of hearts. The thing that gave him the most hope was the deep division the War was bringing out within the foundations of the House of Have. Thus weakened, it could fall, or be taken by a united proletariat.

This was a show trial, but Bean was strictly enforcing the number of spectators. A few interested parties, like Stoddard and Harding, were in the courtroom with a scattering of influential commentators and administration flunkies, but the sensation-seekers were mainly outside. At the opening, the guest list had been more distinguished—with Aleister Crowley, Noah Cross and Vice-President Bryan lending their presence to oversee the doing of justice—but now the society page names were staying away, uneasily aware perhaps of how the trial was going to pan out. Bean, a knotty old bruiser Kane had hauled out of retirement to whip the Supreme Court into line, knew as well as Reed that all America, all the world, had interests in this trial, and he was not going to go down in history as the judge who let the lawyers pass a black-cap verdict on him.

The witness now was the soldier who had been with Bartlett on his visit to Crépy-en-Valois, Ernest Hemingway. Darrow cannily established the young man's credentials by asking him to explain how he had come by his medal ribbons, whereupon Mason objected and Bean, who liked a good yarn, overruled. Hemingway modestly allowed Darrow to draw from him an account of his day and night crawl around no-man's-land under barbed wire and accurate fire, hauling home wounded soldiers. Hemingway impressed Reed, especially when his true age—sixteen—came out in court, and he had to admit he had lied to the enlistment board to get into the War. Mason sat impatiently through all this, finally objecting successfully when Darrow encouraged Hemingway to read out moving passages from the diary he had purportedly kept on the front—but which, according to newsroom rumour, he was actually busy writing as the trial went along—underlining everything Hammett had said about the inefficiency, brutality and insanity of the war effort. Hemingway used words like a sniper might use bullets.

There was a tense little pause, and Reed knew the question everyone had been waiting for was about to be asked. Hemingway looked at Bartlett, and made a fist over his heart. The accused fidgeted, clouds of memory passing over his face.

"Private Hemingway," Darrow began, "could you describe the situation you found at Crépy-en-Valois when you and Private Bartlett arrived on the morning of Sunday June 11th, 1916?"

Hemingway drew breath, then paused, then began, "we arrived at the chateau at about eleven o'clock. It was a warm day. There was a lull in the German shelling. There were two guards outside, and only a junior staff officer in the hall. The guards let us through when Eddie told them we had a message from the front for General Mix. We were so covered in mud they couldn't tell our rank. The junior staff officer, Lieutenant James Gatz, tried to stop us getting any further and I popped him one."

"You struck a superior officer?"

"I certainly did."

"And why did you do that?"

"I didn't care for his cologne. Cologne's a German perfume, ain't it?" Laughter rippled around.

"Was there any other reason?"

"He said General Mix was in the chateau's chapel and had given strict orders that he was not to be disturbed."

"Did anything strike you as unusual about the situation at Crépy-en-Valois?"

"Objection," said Mason, "counsel is calling for conjecture."

"Overruled," Bean said from one side of his mouth, as if spitting out a chew of tobacco.

"But..."

"That's m'rulin," Bean insisted, glaring. "Continue, Private Hemingway..."

"There was food, Mr. Darrow. Damn real food. Cakes and meat and bread. Potatoes and beans and coffee and wine and sugar. Eddie and me hadn't seen anything like that for months. The last meat we'd tasted was rat. I don't care for rat. It was left out on a table where there had been a dinner the night before. We couldn't understand it. They'd had all this food right there in front of them. They hadn't eaten everything. It was like finding out there were people who didn't deign to breathe air."

"And what did you do then?"

"We looked for the General in the chapel."

"And what did you find in the chapel?"

"Not General Mix. He wouldn't have been able to get in."

"Why is that?"

"It was stacked to the rafters with cases of champagne, sir."

"What did you do then?"

"We found the General's quarters. It was easy."

"How so?"

"We followed a trail."

"A trail?"

"Yes, sir."

"Of what?"

A pause. Hemingway cleared his throat. "Ladies' underthings. Lacy, perfume-smelling underthings."

Mason looked uncomfortable, and some of the spectators tittered.

"What did you find in the General's quarters?"

"General Mix. He was in a large sunken marble bath, wearing only his white ten-gallon-hat. He was leaning back, pouring champagne from the bottle into his mouth. Sir, he was drunk as a skunk."

Laughter, scowls, an objection, a ruling.

"Was there anyone else present?"

"Yes, there were three women in the bath with the General, one diving under the suds between his legs, hair floating on the surface of the water, bubbles foaming around her. She was French, I believe. The others were either side of him, working with their hands. It was plain they were drunk too. I believed from the sweet smell in the air that at least one of the bathers had been smoking opium."

"Did you recognise any of the three, let us say, *filles de joie?*"

"We had a different expression in the army, sir. One was Gertrud Zelle, a Dutch dancer I had seen perform in Paris. And one was an American adventuress, Miss Sadie Thompson. I don't know anything about the French lady."

"How did Private Bartlett react to this sight?"

"Eddie was overcome with emotion. All this time, he had insisted General Tom was a fine soldier who loved his men but was surrounded by incompetents. This display of excess sickened and revolted him. He was struck down."

"Struck down?"

"He was unable to express himself. He kept babbling about food and women and wine and mud and shells and gas."

"What happened then?"

"General Mix squirted champagne out of his mouth at Private Bartlett and told him to fu...to go away."

"Did Private Bartlett then, as legend has it, shoot the General?"

"No, sir."

Commotion, gavel-banging, quiet.

"Eddie said a bullet was too good for Traitor Tom. Besides, there was a chance of a dud blowing up in the barrel and taking his hand off. That was happening a lot. Eddie drew his bayonet. The women got out of the way quickly. They were a damn sight less drunk than the General."

"Did you try to stop Private Bartlett assaulting General Mix?"

"No, sir. I held the General down while Eddie cut him to pieces. The blood and the champagne and the perfumed bathwater soaked right through my sleeves."

Now, all Bean's gavelling could not stem the uproar in the court. Finally, he drew an antique revolver and fired a shot into the ceiling, calling for a recess. One of the raised letters of the motto behind him fell away. It now read IN GOD WE RUST.

Thursday, March 8th, 1917.
The Bramford, 1 West 72nd St, New York, N.Y.

From the window of Crowley's apartment, Nick Carraway could see the riots. It was dark, but there were flames even where the strikers had cut off the street-lights. There were mounted cops down there, creaky old-timers in blue uniforms while their sons and younger brothers were in khaki overseas. Many of the Reds were short a limb or otherwise scarred. It was a battle of the old and infirm, and it was turning bloody. Vance's face reflected in the dark mirror of the window, aloof and apparently unconcerned, his double slash of a moustache like a razor scar. He turned away, and Nick did too.

Tom was being hearty, talking too loud, bluff and nervous as he explained to the First Lady's astrological consultant that he was organising a volunteer force to take over the vital services in his district once the strikers were put down. It should only be a month or two before order was restored. According to Tom, the Reds were on the run.

Nick was not so sure. Also, Tom was no actor, and all his Rover Boys cheeriness could not but make the Great Beast suspicious. They said Crowley could read minds. They also said he had held a ceremony in the White House, with President and Mrs. Kane in attendance, promoting himself to the rank of Magus by baptising a frog as Jesus Christ and crucifying it.

Crowley stood in front of the fireplace, striking a Satanic pose. His bald head gleamed in the candle-light. This, Noah Cross had told Nick and Tom, was the dilettante whose ridiculous prophesies had prompted Kane to order the Vimy Ridge attack, exchanging 100,000 American casualties for not one foot of useless enemy territory. Early in the War, Crowley, an Englishman not welcome in his own country, had written Anti-British propaganda for pro-German press. After the *Titanic*, he had reused the same articles as anti-German propaganda for the Kane papers. Now, he was whimsically influencing the conduct of the War. This was the man they were here to kill.

Crowley had agreed to meet Tom Buchanan because Nick, a distant cousin of the First Lady, had intimated that his friend's influence might secure for the mystic an honourary doctorate at New Haven, Tom's school. Nick knew Cross had drawn his plans carefully here, selecting precisely the right people to appeal to the Englishman's snobbery, cruelty and self-interest. According to the canny financier, Aleister Crowley must die if the administration, if a whole class, were to have the chance to survive. Nick had almost got used to the notion of being doomed, of everyone he knew being doomed.

It was a peculiar feeling to be doing something about the doom, but Nick still didn't care to feel like a cog in Noah Cross's machine. They were all cogs in Cross's machine. Nick, Tom, Vance. And Crowley's secretary, Louella Parsons, who had helped them get this close with some discreet, well-paid manipulation of the appointments diary. Even Crowley's neighbour and fellow Magus Adrian Marcato, who had delicately suggested that Tom Buchanan was a young man the Great Beast should meet, was a component of the machine. Crowley and Marcato were unashamed to declare themselves Evil Incarnate, but Nick thought Noah Cross fit the Hornèd Goat mask a sight more comfortably.

They were discussing race now. Tom was hot on the Negro issue, and Crowley had prophesied a catastrophe in Texas if a single black face were found among the "army of the righteous" defending the state from Villa. Of course, the black regiments were about all the army had left over to hold the border, and their withdrawal had already allowed for a series of increasingly daring, insolent, German-advised raids against West Texas and Arizona. Nick guessed Cross was mainly annoyed that Crowley was better at influencing weak sister Kane than he was.

Tom suggested that Crowley and he drink a toast to Emily Kane. The Prohibition ordnance was in effect in New York, and Crowley couldn't offer them any of the brandy Nick knew he had stashed away. Philo Vance, who had effected the introduction between Crowley and Tom, produced a hip-flask from his inside pocket, and tossed it to Tom, who unscrewed the cap. This produced two small steel cups, one of which had been liberally smeared earlier with liquid potassium cyanide. Tom dextrously filled both cups, kept one, and gave Crowley the poisoned whisky.

The Englishman, eyes burning, knocked the liquor back, and grinned, almost in defiance. He should have been dead before the firewater hit his stomach, but he was asking for a refill.

Nick saw Tom spasming in panic, thinking he had got the cups mixed and poisoned himself. But he was alive too.

"I see you are making a mistake," Crowley said. He looked more alive than anyone Nick had ever seen.

Tom's nerve broke, and he pulled a revolver out from under his letter sweater. Crowley did not seem perturbed. Tom struggled to thumb-cock the gun.

Mrs. Parsons came into the room just as Tom shot her employer in the chest. She put her hands over her mouth, willing him to fall before he saw her treachery. Crowley kept smiling, a trickle of blood on his shirtfront. Tom shot Crowley again, low, blasting a hand resting just above the hip. One of his fingers came off. Vance had the poker in his hands, and brought it down upon the egg-like dome of the astrologer's head, denting it, striking him to the floor. They all stood back, standing over the man who was sprawled before his fire, his dressing gown twisted around him.

Slowly, Aleister Crowley stood up. His face showed no trace of pain. He examined his hand, a small spurt of blood fountaining from the stump of his missing finger.

With a cry of rage which Nick had heard on the football field, Tom tackled the astrologer, getting a bearhug around his chest and shoving him against the wall. Vance got in a few more blows with the poker, and Nick stepped back to the windows, elbowing out a pane of glass. They were ceiling-to-floor windows, opening onto a balcony six storeys from the street. Nick unfastened the windows, and the wind blew in. Outside, Reds were shouting slogans into the night.

Mrs. Parsons was frozen with horror. Tom was grappling with Crowley. There were shouts from the street, and the clip-clop of horses' hooves. Many people were being killed tonight in New York.

Vance and Nick helped Tom get Crowley onto the balcony, then stood back as he heaved him over the side. They all watched him fall, limbs loose, and smash against the sidewalk, red spilling into the gutter from his broken head.

"That's done," Vance said, brushing dust off his dinner jacket.

Tom looked as if he did not believe it. They left Mrs. Parsons peering over the balcony and went down to the lobby by the stairs. Vance bribed the doorman while Nick and Tom went out into the street. Crowley had crawled a few feet in the gutter. Tom kicked the Great Beast in the head until he wasn't moving any more. Breathing heavily, blood and tears on his face, the football hero stood away from the dead astrologer. A group of Reds ran past, wheezing police horses on their tails. A Red paused to fire a revolver at a cop, missing wildly, and ran off.

"Assassination has become our national sport," Vance said, shivering.

Nick had left his coat upstairs. For a young man of wealth and breeding, it was a cold night in the city.

Tuesday, May 1, 1917.
Union Station, Chicago, Illinois.

"The Red Special's a-comin'," shouted the coloured porter as he emerged from the telegraph office. The old black man was greeted with a cheer the like of which he had obviously never heard, and his face split with a grin like a slice of watermelon. To Reed, this was the face of the Movement.

Overnight, the fighting in the city had peaked and dwindled to mopping-up skirmishes, with mass defections from the police and army swelling the Red ranks. The Mayor had surrendered to Joe Hill, and was locked up in the drunk tank of the nearest police station. The city's plutocrats had fled, leaving empty mansions and bewildered servants. At some point, an overenthusiastic committee of workers had burned to the ground the Municipal Opera House, President Kane's gift to the city. A regrettable waste of revolutionary energy, Reed thought, but perhaps a necessary blowing-off of steam.

At lot of people, good and bad, had died in Chicago over the years. Father O'Shaughnessy, Roosevelt, Wilson. There would be more killing, Reed knew, but it would be over soon. Then, for the second time in its history, the United States would have to go through the painful, healthy process of Reconstruction.

"Out of my way, nigger," said a fat, scar-faced Italian youth as he pushed past the porter. Reed felt someone walk over his grave, but let it pass. The Movement was uniting so many creeds and colours, empowering the masses. The frictions would eventually ease: this, he believed with a fierce certainty. Reed had fought alongside black and white and yellow on picket lines for the last ten years, and he knew everyone bled the same colour. Red.

Still, he would watch the kid whose gang had been passing out firebrands all night. A lot of opportunists would be trying to board the Red Special without paying their fare.

The crowds here were excited, enthused, agitated. The Special had been coming for a long time. Many had given up hope of it ever arriving. Joe Hill was pacing the platform alone, looking older.

Reed had spent the night by the telegraph office, collating the words that came in from all over the country, turning terse dispatches into pointed articles. *The Masses* had managed three editions throughout the night, each the thickness of three handbills folded together. He had to catch the spirit of the moment in words, set them down for posterity. At Ossining, the Reds had taken over the prison, liberating Eddie Bartlett, the most befuddled hero of the Movement, from Death Row. In Texas, the Rangers and the last of the federal forces were fighting a scrappy guerilla war with Villa's raiders. In Europe, there was a downing-of-tools at the front, an unprecedented uprising of the Brothers of Eddie Bartlett.

In desperation, Vice-President Bryan had tried to deal with long-time "slowcialist" Samuel Gompers, asking the union moderate to form a provisional government, offering higher wages and shorter hours as a sop to strikers, immediate withdrawal from the War, and restitution of all property to the plutocrats. After two days of frantic activity, the Gompers Government fell apart before it was even established.

There was a pitched battle on the floor of the New York stock exchange. J.P. Morgan had been detained by patriots at the Canadian border, and clapped in chains. In Alabama, armed union men supported by black soldiers who had overthrown their officers, had routed the Ku Klux Klan outside Birmingham. Workers' Revolutionary Committees had sprung up like mushrooms in every city, in most small towns, in army bases, firehouses, prisons. Telegrams were coming in faster than the operators could hand them out. New York, San Francisco, New Orleans, Pittsburgh, Philadelphia, Minneapolis, Kansas City. The whole map of the country was dyeing itself Red.

For the man on the Special it must have been a gruelling journey in a sealed railroad carriage. From Nicaragua to Chicago, passing through a theoretical battlefield on the Tex-Mex border, Eugene Debs had been guarded every foot of the way by the comrades of the Railmen's Union. History would hail them as the finest of the Movement, socialist heroes who worked the points, engineered the locomotives, set the signals, provided fuel and water, evaded the Pinkertons. At every junction, men wearing the white ribbon of the Great Pullman Strike had put themselves at risk to speed Debs to the Windy City, each as dedicated as the members of the relay team carrying the Olympic torch. Only this flame, carefully fanned and preserved, was to be set to a powderkeg that would blow up a great nation.

Reed saw London in the crowds, the bandages off at last. The writer shouldered his way through celebrating men and women, and raised a clenched fist in a boxer's salute.

"Looks like we've given the Iron Heel a Hot Foot," he said, grinning.

Like a lot of the crowd, London was intoxicated. Many were drunk on the giddy exhilaration of change, but Reed guessed London had taken other stimulants, a supposition confirmed when he passed over a bottle.

"Go on, there'll never be another day like this." Reed tipped a mouthful of whisky into his throat. The fiery gulp made him cough and blink tears. London clapped his back. "We'll make a drinker of you yet, John."

Outside on the track, a piercing steam whistle let out a lengthy blast. Reed expected the crowds to cheer and throw their hats in the air, strangers to embrace and kiss, clapping to fill the cavernous interior of the station. But instead everyone fell as silent. The railroad terminal suddenly became a cathedral.

The train, an unimpressive black engine with a string of battered cattle-cars behind it, pulled in slowly, belching steam. Everyone looked at it. Reed realised he was holding his breath, the liquor burning in his stomach.

The Special nudged the buffers, and the steam died down. Armed men, some wearing red sashes or armbands, swarmed out of the cars.

A uniformed guard, clinging to the outside of one car, unloosed bolts, and a section of the side clanged down onto the platform like a drawbridge. People stood away as if the wooden slats, dyed brown with generations of hooves and trodden-in dung, were a red velvet carpet.

Debs emerged, shielding his eyes, chin stubbled, face tanned. He wore a soiled white tropical suit that ill-fit the climate, a blanket draped around him like a cloak. He was tall and thin, bald and forceful.

"Comrades," he said, small voice filling the vaulted arches of Union Station, ultimately filling the whole of the country, "it looks as if what we have here..."

Debs looked around, unable to contain his grin.

"...is a REVOLUTION!"

Then, the cheering began. Reed thought it would never end.

Tuesday, June 5th, 1917.
The Alamo, San Antonio, Republica de Mexico.

Presidente Villa was in his palace in Mexico City, poring over maps and ignoring his European advisers, and General Huerta was putting El Paso, the centre of the fiercest Texan resistance, to the sword. That left Emiliano Zapata for the purely symbolic retaking of the ruined mission in San Antonio, overrun eighty-one years earlier by Santa Anna, then taken back by the *Yanquis* in the First Mexican-American War. The one Mexico had lost, Zapata reminded himself.

He had hoped the Europeans would keep out of the way, and let him get this over without bloodshed. Of course, the die-hards of San Antonio were holed up in the mission with their grandfathers' guns, intent on being nobly massacred. A few smoke grenades would have been enough to flush them out, but the Flying Circus had to put on a show.

Faintly embarrassed at the comic opera melodrama of it all, Zapata crouched behind the low wall at the edge of the square, his detachment cradling their carbines, ready to fire. Up in the clear blue sky, the buzzing biplanes circled. Both the von Richthofen brothers were up there, jousting like the last of the Teutonic Knights, and so was their fat friend Göring. The brightly-painted airplanes swooped low over the Alamo, guns chattering, and dropped smoking incendiaries.

Zapata looked behind him, to the post office where Venustiano Carranza, the Europeans' liaison, was huddled with the Russian expert, Beria. Neither would want to be too near the scuffle, just in case one of the aspiring Davy Crocketts had a clear eye and a clean rifle. Carranza was a Huerta man, wagering his gold braid epaulettes that the Europeans would eventually prod his patron into Villa's presidential seat.

Gunshots crackled from inside the mission, and one wall was on fire. A bullet grooved across the stone top of the wall, and spanged into the shoulder of young Angel, drawing a blurt of blood and pain. The planes were up high now, executing showoff stunts, and doing something useful by drawing the meagre fire of the men inside the Alamo. The Flying Circus were playing a game of dare, seeing which man could get nearest to the range of the groundfire. For these Germans, war was a sport of landowners, not a way of keeping bellies filled and men free.

He judged that the defenders were being choosy about their shots, and gave the order. An armoured Model T Ford, formerly the pride of the late General Mapache's army, trundled into the square, the machine gun mounted on its steel windshield raking the walls of the mission, kicking out clouds of red dust. Grenades exploded against the make-shift barricade of the main doors, and Zapata could see into the roofless church. First over the wall, he was first at the gates, hurdling the fires with his men close behind him.

Nobody shot him.

Later, they found only seven dead men, all ancient and feeble. The soldiers who would have defended Texas were all dead in Europe, or fighting their own Revolution to the North. It was this Revolution the Europeans were so concerned with thwarting, concerned enough to send arms and advisors. With Russia out of the War in Europe and the new America on the point of withdrawal, an unacknowledged alliance existed between the Tsar, the Kaiser and the remnants of the former rulers of the United States. Their man in Mexico was Huerta, and Huerta had influenced Villa into pursuing the gnawing attack at the frayed Southern edges of the US.

Up in the bell-tower was a sniper who could barely get a grip on his antique Winchester .73, his arthritic knuckle too knotted to slip into the trigger guard. A couple of soldiers helped him down the ladder fairly gently, and presented him to Zapata.

The American saw Beria and Carranza coming, and commented to Zapata, "looks like you have friends willing to defend democracy in the States to the last Mexican."

"This man," Beria said, "we should have him shot."

Zapata looked at the young Russian's cold eyes. Lavrenti Beria's English was not good, and he had no Spanish at all, but he could order an execution in a terse sentence in any language in the world. Not a soldier, he was eager to shoot anyone who did not have the power of shooting back.

Zapata looked again at the American. "I know you," he said, finally, "you were at Chihuahua City in '15, when Madero and Villa made their pact. You are the writer, Bierce."

"Am I?" said the old man, spitting bitterly.

The Germans strode into the Alamo now, in their leather flying jackets and helmets, ignoring the dust on their white britches and polished boots. Theirs was a landowners' gait, somewhere between marching and sauntering. The Baron was at the head of his party, wearing the oily grime of battle on his cheeks like duelling scars. This von Richthofen was very like the men Zapata had spent his early life fighting.

A dog darted out from a nook in one collapsed wall, and yapped at the Baron's boots. It was a beagle, the pet of one of the defenders. The Baron took out his automatic pistol, and pumped a shot into the animal's head, kicking it dead in an instant.

"Absurd American dog," he said.

Fat Hermann laughed, and slapped his comrade on the back, raising a cloud of dust. "*Gut Essen für unsere Mexikanische Freunde, nicht wahr?*" he commented. A nice meal for our Mexican friends.

Beria and Carranza had maps out, and were scrawling their crosses and arrows.

Bierce, the old American, could hardly stand up. His leg was broken, Zapata realised, just below the knee, and he was hopping painfully, his last teeth grit into bare gums. Only anger was keeping him alive.

"How is your friend Mr. Reed? The one who was so amusing about our President."

Bierce glared. "Red Johnny's done well for himself. Picked the right side in the Revolution."

"Which Revolution? Yours or ours?"

Bierce smiled, an expression which, on him, suggested more wrath than an outright scowl.

"Of course, a revolution is merely an abrupt change in mismanagement. Even so, I don't think yours counts, General or Field Marshal or whatever. Red Johnny and his pack are doing their best to kick out men like my former employer, Mr. Hearst. Your crew said they'd reform the land, then threw in with...well, with these foreign gentlemen."

Bierce looked at the Russian and the Germans and at Carranza, a Mexican in a uniform a Hapsburg would have recognised.

"You know what a peasant is, General? A man with a bootprint for a face and a bullet in his back."

Von Richthofen and Göring were saluting each other with schnapps doled out from silver flasks, heels clicking smartly. The dead dog had exploded shit over the flagstones.

He gave orders for Bierce to be penned with the other resisters in the town jail. Zapata had had to shoot too many of these die-hards. He hoped the War would wind down like a clockwork toy, with no more unnecessary bloodshed.

Outside in the sun, the smoke was clearing away. The fires were out. Worried-looking Texan women and children had gathered in a crowd. Some of his men were trying to make time with the pretty girls. They had mutton-chop sleeves and pink ribbons in their strawberry blonde hair, and they were patriotically resisting, flinching away from smiles and snarling "greaser".

A photographer was setting up outside the Alamo. He had come with the Europeans. The Flying Circus came out, with Beria and Carranza, and they posed, guns brandished, moustaches fierce. The photographer insisted Zapata take his place in the centre. As he held still, a grin plastered to his face, he heard Manfred von Richthofen snarling in German to his brother. Zapata knew enough of the hawking and spitting language to realise that the Baron was complaining again, about the heat, the food, the filth and the smell. The Baron did what his Kaiser told him, but he disliked fighting alongside peasants.

Zapata could almost feel the German or Russian bullet in his back. And he had always had the bootprint on his face. Once, it had been the landowners and Porfirio Diaz wearing the boot. Now, it was his fellow peasant, Pancho Villa, and Diaz's pet killer, Victoriano Huerta, and the crowned heads Villa and Huerta chose for allies.

The flashpowder exploded, and Zapata felt his heart jump. The Baron made it a point of honour not to be fazed, but Zapata knew a true soldier couldn't hear an explosion and see a puff of smoke without trembling in his boots. A soldier without fear was a dangerous fool.

The ensemble broke up, and began discussing the situation in smaller groups, in too many languages.

A motorcycle rode into the square in a cloud of dust, and Sean Mallory dismounted. A man of many useful skills, Mallory had been running messages behind the front as it advanced across Texas, taking the occasional time out to dynamite a bridge or a bank building. Zapata liked the Irishman. He was another peasant, the British bootmark outlining his twinkling eyes. He didn't fuss with salutes or protocol, just handed over a despatch wrapped in oilskin. It had a wax seal Zapata recognised.

"From Villa?"

Mallory nodded, and he realised this was important news. How the rider knew what it was he carried was beyond Zapata, but the man was blessed with the luck of the Irish and a touch of the shining.

Zapata tore the packet open, and read quickly. He had always been a good reader, although the American papers called him an illiterate. As he read, his peasant heart filled with joyous blood.

Beria was talking to him, giving advice that sounded like an order, "...next, you should strike for Austin..."

Zapata shook his head, and folded up the despatch from Villa. Beria looked at him with a cold fury.

"We are at peace," Zapata said. "The frontier is here, under our feet, stretching from San Diego to Corpus Christi. We are in a no-man's-land. Behind us is the Republic of Mexico, ahead..." he tried to fit the new name into his mouth "...the United Socialist States of America."

He handed the paper to Beria, to whom it was useless.

"Villa has met with representatives of Mr. Debs, and North America is at peace. Your advice, Lavrenti, is no longer required. You must extend our thanks to your Tsar. By the way, General Huerta has been removed from his position, and I am now commander-in-chief of the armies of the Republic."

The Germans were listening too. Carranza looked as if he had just bitten a chilli pepper. Mallory was grinning broadly.

"Should your crowned heads still want someone to invade the USSA for them and overthrow its Revolution, I suggest they approach Canada. Gentlemen, good day and...*adios*."

Zapata walked away from the men in uniforms, past the canvas-winged airplanes and the battered tin lizzie. He would join Mallory in the cantina, and drink until he was insensible, then he would find a woman. It was a good day to be a peasant.

Wednesday, July 4th, 1917.
The White House, Washington, D.C.

The Red Special had arrived in the city over a week ago, bringing Debs, Hill, Sinclair, Elizabeth Flynn and the other leading lights of the Revolution. Sam had been in the crowd waiting at the station, a sergeant again in the militia of the Socialist Vanguard. The morning after the train had drawn up, and the fighting men of the SV had taken up positions around the city, linking up with the local Workers' Committee. Debs had walked up Capitol Hill, where both houses of Congress were still furiously in session, even if many Progressives and Republicans and not a few Democrats, were absent from their accustomed seats. The Speaker of the House of Representatives, at gunpoint, gave Debs the floor, and the new President, unanimously elected by the workers' committees, announced that the USSA was a reality.

Of course, Debs had put off the "storming of the White House" for six days, just to hit today's date. There was no sense in future generations having two holidays so close together. One Big Revolution, One Big Holiday! In the last days, the message had finally sunk in. Until Debs's arrival, the conventional life of Washington had been continuing as normal, even if a few of the legislators' wives were offended to be called "comrade" by streetcar conductors. When Debs addressed a meeting at City Hall, where the capital's sole battle had been fought a few days earlier between the militia and a handful of reactionaries, he had made one of his more inspirational speeches, concluding with "we shall now proceed to construct the Socialist order." Sam's ears still rung with the applause.

Now, the last palace of the robber barons was to fall. The masses were assembled, curiously quiet and orderly, on the White House lawn. Debs was there, and John Reed, Joe Hill, Upton Sinclair, Elizabeth Flynn, Frank Norris, Clarence Darrow, Helen Keller, Jack London. Big Bill Haywood and Theodore Dreiser were in California, but were there in spirit. Ernest Hemingway, now an officer in the SV, was leading

Sam's detachment, his red sash around his waist like a cummerbund. The summer sun bore down on them all.

Sam held his rifle with a sweaty grip. This was not like France. This meant something. The only casualty had been a railman killed by a comrade's dropped shotgun.

Reed was on the platform, reminiscing about Kane's inauguration, repeating the old wives' tale about Lincoln crying.

Then, it was time.

Sam knew this was a ceremony, not a battle. The robber barons were long fled. Noah Cross was already in Switzerland, railing against the man who had "to be smuggled into America in a sealed container like a bacillus". Many had preserved a portion of their fortunes in jewels or overseas holdings, and would henceforth be ornaments to the social seasons of London, Paris or Berlin. The crowned heads were still bogged down in their squabble, but that would not last. After all, they had a common cause in their enmity for the USSA. Even Kaiser Billy would throw in with the Tsar and the King to condemn the new regime across the Atlantic.

For the first time in living memory, this country felt like the New World again. Someone was running up the new flag on the White House lawn. Stars, stripes, hammer and scythe.

The lone figure strolled up to the White House, rifle in his hands. Sam knew Eddie Bartlett would be grinning, but with a genuine good humour this time. That was fit. This was a country for Eddie Bartlett and Jimmie Higgins now, not for John D. Rockefeller and Edward D. Stotesbury.

Hemingway gave the order, and the detachment marched across the lawn to support Eddie. Many of the unit were survivors of the bloody holocaust of France.

The doors were open, and Eddie pushed through, Sam and the men running after them, yelling. Their shouts echoed around the foyer. Outside, the masses were cheering again. Men and women flooded into the White House, and found it empty and abandoned. A few servants and guards surrendered immediately, and were absorbed instantly into the crowd.

Eddie was lifted high on his comrades' shoulders and was laughing, tears rolling down his face. The kid had done good, Sam thought. The crowds made way for Debs and the other leaders, and they began to make speeches no one could hear for the applause. Debs got a few sentences into his prepared address, then smiled and tore up his notes. He threw his hat in the air with the rest. Someone had found the White House's bootleg hoard and, although temperance was one of the planks of the SV, bottles were being passed around and cracked open.

Hemingway got close and tapped his shoulder, serious amid the gaiety.

"Sam," he said, "cut out a few of the sober men, and search the place. I won't feel secure until that's done."

Sam understood. There might still be die-hards lurking, waiting for a chance to put a bullet into Debs or Eddie or Reed or one of the others.

With a couple of tee-total Quakers, Sam started at the kitchens, and worked his way up. The White House had been abandoned in a hurry, and many offices were scattered with papers strewn at random. A few waste bins were full of ashes, and there were unfaded rectangles on the walls where paintings had been taken down. They found many of the paintings stacked at random on a landing, forgotten in the rush.

The President's family had left for Canada months ago. Nothing had been heard from Kane on Capitol Hill since the Red Special hit town. Debs had had to accept a formal surrender from Vice-President Bryan.

It was strange to prowl through these high-ceilinged rooms, to skim over the left-behind furniture, pictures, statues, files, clothes, fixtures, books, manuscripts. Presumably, Debs would move in within the month, and this would remain the centre of government. But to Sam, this was a haunted house, long-abandoned, inhabited only by unhealthy memories. The robber barons were gone, he told himself. Things had changed.

Opening a door into a drawing room, Sam saw a woman. She was hatless and in a plain dress, but there was a buckskin-fringed gunbelt around her hips, and she had a hogleg Colt in her hand. He recognised her, but she had forgotten him.

Following Annie's eyeline, he saw the broken man, hunched and huddled as he squatted on a low stool, staring at a bauble in his hands. Annie had her gun on the former President, Charles Foster Kane.

"So this was what we were fighting," he said.

Kane looked up, eyes empty, and mumbled something none of them caught.

"Hell," the sharpshooter said, putting her gun away, "there'll be a job for Charlie somewhere. He could be a gardener, or an usher at the opera house." She looked at Sam more closely. "The Pink, right?"

He nodded. A smile spread on her face.

"Funny how things come around," she said.

They left Kane, and were surrounded by the noise of the celebrating crowd. They were singing now, one-half "The Internationale", the other half "Polly-Wolly-Doodle". Grizzled old railmen were sobbing like children. John Reed and Ernest Hemingway were embracing like lovers. Eugene Debs was clinking bottles with a one-eyed militiamen.

Militia Sergeant Sam D. Hammett had done his duty. "Long live the Revolution," he shouted, "long live the USSA!"

TOM JOAD

1937

"I was out this way before," Purvis said as they waited for the waiter to come back. "With the Drive Against Superstition and Perversion."

Ness sipped on his coffee and decided not yet to allow himself one of his maximum daily allocation of three cigarettes. On the tiny table between them were the remains of Party Official dinners. His partner had wiped his plate clean enough to infringe the work rights of the train's dish-washer, but Ness had left half his steak and all his greasy potatoes. Purvis shook his head, remembering. "Bad business, the Drive," he commented. "Lot of folks vanished..."

He had been jumpy since Utah. He took things personally.

"Hell of a country," Purvis said, nodding through the window at the Red Star Special's jittering purple outline on the orange sands. The sun was so low the shadow elongated almost to the desert horizon.

Ness shrugged.

"It's right what they say about you, Eliot," Purvis said. "You're untouchable."

The Official Class salon, twice the length of the adjoining ordinary dining car, was almost empty. Two Agriculture Committee Inspectors gorged themselves at the other end. A silent bird presumably assigned to watch them ate frugally and alone, pretending to read a book.

Their waiter swayed along the car, a newspaper-wrapped package under his arm. He'd been impressed to learn the ugly little passenger in the oversized straw hat was Melvin Purvis, the Socialist Hero who took down People's Enemies like Dillinger and Floyd. He'd asked for Purvis's autograph, for his son who wanted to be an I-Man when he grew up.

With a modestly delighted grin, Purvis had scrawled his name to a good luck wish. The boy would need it: the only Negro in the FBI was the one who cleaned the Director's personal toilet. Purvis had whispered in the waiter's ear, pressing money—silver, not the paper reactionaries didn't trust—into the man's palm.

"All part of the Master Plan," his partner now explained. Ness won *his* Socialist Hero citation through months of meticulous paper-work with the Department of Parasite Regulation, and had stood unarmed in the background while Prohibition Officers made the arrests that broke up Boston Joe Kennedy's Chicago bootleg ring. He understood Purvis's usual Master Plan involved firing a gun at someone until they were incapable of surrender, then posing for photographs with smoking weapon and a cigar over the bullet-riddled corpses.

Purvis took the package. He skinned the paper away from a bottle-neck and held his purchase up to the light.

"I got a pal on the Buffalo run," the waiter explained. "He brings in stuff from Canada."

Purvis smiled. Ness didn't let his face show anything.

"Nothing's too good for the Man Who Shot John Dillinger," the Negro declared.

The agriculture officials and the poetry-lover eyed the hooch with fearful thirst. Sadly, Purvis handed the prize back.

"Sorry, comrade," he said, "this is too good. What I want is the rot-gut every other joe gets."

The waiter, plainly astonished, was disinclined to argue with the Man Who Shot John Dillinger.

"Give this to those comrades over there with the compliments of the comrade with the book."

Purvis grinned like a gnome as the Negro carried out his orders. One of the Agriculture Investigators coughed root-beer through his nose. The constant reader's eyes expanded like a fish's. Ness didn't laugh.

Purvis glanced at the attentive diner's book, *The White Ribbon*. "I believe Comrade Pound's celebration of the Great Pullman Strike the finest poetry in the American language," he said too loudly. "How do you think he compares with the insidious reactionary Thomas S. Eliot?"

The reader stuck his eyes to the page and stayed quiet. Purvis, having enjoyed his devilment, chuckled to himself.

"Who's going to inform on us?" he asked. "Remember, we're the Federal Bureau of Ideology."

The waiter returned from the next car with a bottle of honey-coloured liquor. Purvis unscrewed the top and the stench of strong boiler-cleaner caught in Ness's nostrils. It stank worse than the Kennedy warehouse on Thirty-Eighth and Shields after the vats were smashed.

"Ahh," Purvis said, wincing, "perfect."

"Elko!" yelled the conductor from somewhere outside. "Elko, Arizona! One-hour stop!"

The train slowed. Dying light fell on the shapes of a small town. A couple of horses, a moving jalopy, a line of wooden buildings, shabby-looking Indians, kids playing baseball.

"Come on," said Purvis, "let's take a stroll."

The train would take on fuel and water and change more rolling-stock. When they'd boarded in Chicago, thirty hours back, the Red Star had been a passenger-train, but few people had the permit to travel all the way to California. At every stop a passenger car was unhitched and replaced with freight wagons.

Purvis stood, picking up his sack and tucking it discreetly into his arm. From his DPR days, Ness recognised the gesture of a Habitual Violator of the Prohibition Laws.

They alighted on the platform. A poster by the ticket office showed the Chairman beaming, arm around a Girl Pioneer. "Forward for Socialist Youth." The artist, who'd omitted the jagged scar on his subject's cheek, somehow contrived to balance Capone's benevolence with a gleam suggestive of an unpaternal interest in the fresh-faced, clean-limbed blonde. Ness wouldn't be surprised to read soon that Norman Rockwell had been commissioned to provide a pictorial record of oil-drilling in Alaska.

In an intricate, clanking ballet, railmen hitched a couple of cattle trucks. Purvis sauntered off, hooking his finger to indicate that Ness should follow. Beyond the train, well away from what little artificial light Elko provided, Purvis pointed into the dark. Ness could see nothing. Purvis put a finger to his lips, then cupped a hand to his ear. Beneath the hiss of steam and the calling of the railmen, he made out the sounds of men waiting. Not talking, but breathing heavy, concentrating. Out in the dark beyond the rail yard and the town, men were gathered.

"Rail-rats," whispered Purvis. "Going our way."

The Labor Mobility laws were designed to maximise the efficiency of a planned socialist economy, but every railroad in the country was overrun with hoboes. Ness once spent a week with a smart engineer, redesigning freight-cars to make it impossible to bum rides. They'd received commendations, but the report wound up under a pile.

"When the train moves off, they'll come out and climb on," said Purvis. "We'll find ourselves a cosy cattle-wagon and have a drink with whoever turns up."

Purvis walked towards the first car that had been hooked up. "Take off your tie," he said. "Muss up your clothes. Imagine you've been on the bum for a month. Hoover won't know unless you report yourself."

"This isn't just a violation of FBI dress code. We're breaking laws it's our job to uphold."

"Untouchable, there are such things as lousy laws. Even in the United Socialist States of America."

Purvis slid over the door. An engineer walked past, swinging a lantern. Ness prepared to pull his badge to justify their trespass, but the railman smiled and bade them good journey.

"Guys like him made the Revolution," said Purvis, dumping his sack into the car. "They know the difference between law and justice."

He vaulted into the truck. Ness refused his offer of a hand up and climbed carefully. Inside, the car was filthy.

"Welcome aboard, 'bo," said Purvis.

Without thinking, Ness started to brush his knees. His partner chuckled. Getting the idea, Ness let his suit stay dusty.

Besides whiskey of dubious parentage, Purvis's grocery bag contained a length of candle, two packs of cigarettes, old apples and some jerky. He took a few empty crates he found in the corner of the wagon, laid one in its centre, put out a couple more as chairs and arranged his table with the precision of the Plutocrats' Feast in *Intolerance*.

"All aboaaard," shouted the conductor a hundred yards further up. The train shuddered into motion. Two men and a boy appeared inside the car, as though from nowhere. Ness wondered what the new smell was.

"Shut the door," said Purvis to the younger man, a skinny, clumsy-looking fellow. "We got vittles we can share, but there ain't enough for too many."

"I'll be dipped in dogshit!" exclaimed the man. "Gonna have us a rare old time, ain't we just?" Ness figured his accent for something Southern. Texan? "I thank you kindly, Mister."

The man dropped his haversack and bedroll and drew up a packing case. The boy, who wore a golf cap twice the size of his head, stared at the food. When the cap came off, a tangle of hair poured out and Ness realised "he" was a girl in her late teens. Purvis cut off a string of jerky with his pocket-knife and gave it to her. She bit in greedily and almost choked.

The other hobo was the new smell. He wore too-big baggy pants under a too-small jacket, and had a tiny bowler-hat and a silly little cane. With his sharp toothbrush moustache and wide, scary eyes, he looked oddly like *Reichskanzler* Hitler. Ness had met some low-life but never anyone who stank quite as foul as the bum now holding out his hand. His mouth smiled, but his eyes said pure hate.

Purvis handed him meat. He scuttled to the farthest corner to eat, picking fastidiously at the food with the tips of his fingers.

"You'll have to forgive mah friend's manners," said the Texan. "He's a queer old duck. He don't talk. Don't even know his right name. We call him the Tramp. Girl's named Thompson. Call her 'Boxcar Bertha' and she won't mind. Say thanks for the eatin', Bertha."

She nodded towards Purvis and carried on chewing. She might be pretty under the dirt, it was hard to tell.

"The name's Johnson," said the man, accepting jerky from Purvis, "L.B. Johnson, Texan born and bred, dispossessed by the Mexican Occupation."

"James Longford," said Purvis. "My buddy's Bill Brown. Where you headed?"

"Going to slip into California, get ourselves work on an out-of-the-way illegal orange ranch. Get a little sun on our backs. How about you?"

"Guy in San Francisco can get us papers. We can do construction work. Good money, good food stamps."

"A deal of people got on the train back there," said Ness. "They all on their way to California too?"

Bertha and the Tramp stopped chewing for a moment but Johnson blithely carried on. Ness knew he had been too pushy.

"Sure," said Johnson. "I guess a lot will be going by way of Nowhere. That's where the Kid here wants to go, but I ain't going near the place. No sir, no thank you."

"Nowhere?" said Purvis. "I don't understand."

This was what they were on the road for.

Johnson frowned. "How long you been on this train?"

"Since Illinois," said Purvis. "Hopped on round about Big Rock."

"Shoot," said Johnson. "You ain't spoken to nobody? Nowhere, Nevada, is where the squatter camp is."

"Squatter camp?" smiled Purvis, uncorking his bottle. "Why'd anyone want to squat in Nevada. It's all desert and mountains and snow."

Johnson helped himself to more jerky. "Trying to get over the state line, mostly. Folks wants to get into California. There's work in California. Good wages and fresh fruit and warm sun and cool mountains. Who wouldn't want to live in California?"

"Tom's at Nowhere," Boxcar Bertha cut in. "Tom's gonna lead us all to the Promised Land of Milk and Money."

"Like the kid says," shrugged Johnson, accepting the bottle, "Tom Joad's supposed to be there. I don't know if I believe that. If Tom Joad's real and at this camp, I figure there'll be I-Men all over like flies on fresh cowflop. A man like that's a threat to the Party. They call him an 'agitator.'"

Johnson took a long pull on the bottle.

"Cheezisfuckinchristawmighty!" he gasped. "Yes sir, that's J. Edgar's business. Mowin' down anyone says anythin' different from the CP. Bastard got the Amish, an' the nigra Baptists, an' the Mormons."

Ness shot a glance towards Purvis. He was fiddling distractedly with an unlit cigarette, neutral half-smile set on his face.

"Hey!" Johnson held the bottle out to the Tramp, "you want some of this kinkypoo joy juice you gotta get your cup. Ain't no way you can ask decent folk to drink outta this bottle after your diseased kisser's been round it."

"I heard about Tom Joad," said Purvis. "Ain't he supposed to've croaked a CP boss in Atlanta for screwing folks out of their land during Collectivisation?"

"Never heard that story," said Johnson. "Heard some others, though. Over Denver way he iced a buncha cops who gang-banged the only daughter of a widow-woman. Heard another how there was this shortage, people starving to death, good as, over in Iowa after Collectivisation. Joad and his sidekick Preacher Casey broke into the official stores and gave food to the folks. There's plenty of stories about Tom Joad feeding folks during the famines."

"The bird sure gets around," said Ness.

"Yeah," said Johnson. "I've even heard of him turning up in Texas. There's stories about how he's helped Texican folk—those of us still there, that is—against the Mexes."

"Tom'll win back the land the Reds gave to the Mexicans," said Bertha. "Comrade, can I have one of them smokes?"

Eugene Byrne & Kim Newman

Purvis threw pack to the girl. She chewed it open and pulled out a cigarette.

"One man can't be all these places at once," he said to Johnson. "Do you believe these stories?"

"I don't know," said Johnson. "Some of them sound real enough, but others are moondust. You hear the same stories about Jesse James, or Purty Boy Floyd."

Purvis's face was in darkness. Ness wondered if the Robin Hood tales about Floyd bothered him. No one said Boston Joe was anything but a parasite and a bourgeois counter-revolutionary, but plenty of saps rated some People's Enemies as heroes.

Bertha went into the shadows and took the bottle back from the Tramp. She handed it to Purvis, who unhesitatingly drank. He wasn't pretending, he really was drinking that rat-poison.

"Moondust?" said Purvis, encouraging Johnson.

"Sure. After all the Mormons got put into camps or shot down a few years back, the story is that Tom Joad walks out of the desert and leads some of them up into the mountains where nobody can get 'em and where they keep their crazy religion alive."

Purvis handed the bottle to Ness. He put it to his closed mouth. The booze stang against his clean-shaved upper lip.

Bertha sat next to Johnson, smoking like an old-timer. "Injuns say Tom Joad can turn bullets to water."

"Yeah!" laughed Johnson. "We were yakking with a 'bo the other day, a Navajo busted out of the reservation. He says Tom Joad is Navajo and he's given his people a heap powerful medicine that means nobody, not palefaces nor the Mexes, can steal their sheep again because if they try and shoot at a Navajo, the bullet turns to water."

Purvis laughed. "I'd sure like to meet Tom Joad. Even a glimpse of him would do me. You really think he's at this Nowhere?"

"I don't know what to think," said Johnson. "He's Moses, Santy Claus and Robin Hood all mixed up like my Mom's fruitcakes. If he's real, he's pretty much a regular guy. Not like in the stories."

"Course he's real," said Bertha. "Tom protects folks on the road. They'd be too scared to cross America if Tom wasn't there."

She took the bottle off Ness, and gulped at it as if it were mother's milk. Her big eyes watered. Ness wondered how she was getting by on the road.

"What's Joad doing at the camp?" he asked. "Is he there to protect people, or lead a rebellion?"

"Neither, the way I hear it," said Johnson. "Like Bertha says, he's gonna lead folks to the Promised Land, California. There are state troopers to stop people getting in because only Party Planners decide where people travel to. California's got a long border so it's easy to sneak past them, but folks're gathering at Lake Tahoe, which is a plum stupid place to try and get into California. Up in the mountains you're nowhere near decent roads or railroads. People are gathering because they think something's gonna happen."

"Maybe Tom Joad's going to part the waters lake and lead his people across," grinned Purvis, handing Johnson the bottle.

"With Pharoah Capone's troops and I-Men chasing, getting drownded," laughed Johnson. Suddenly, he was serious. "Friend, I can tell you're interested. But take my advice—it's all I can offer for your hospitality—don't go nowhere near Nowhere. About the state line, the railmen usually 'member they ain't supposed to give out rides and toss you off. No ill feeling, they just know they're being watched. Even so, you might be able to slip into California by staying on this freight."

In the light from Bertha's cigarette, L.B. Johnson looked old and sad, young face lined and battered.

"Know why they call it Nowhere? Chairman Al named it when he opened the Olympics in '32. He said, 'you'll find unhappy people nowhere in the USSA.' So now there's this place called Nowhere, and it's full of unhappy people. A gathering of the hopeless, all come together to chase moonbeams. The CP thugs in Debs D.C. ain't going to like it. Whether or not there's any such animal as Tom Joad, sooner or later the Reds're gonna break it up. It'll be the Farm Collectivisation or the war on the Mormons all over again. People will die. Stay well clear of Nowhere, friend."

"Untouchable," Purvis said, shaking him awake, "it's our stop."

As a FBI agent, he was supposed to snap to and become instantly alert. He assumed J. Edgar Hoover had never endured hours of L.B. Johnson's filthy jokes then tried to get his shut-eye on the filthier floor of a cattle car. He guessed Purvis hadn't been getting tight, but anaesthetizing himself. His partner's breath was sharp with bad booze.

"Reno, Nevada," Purvis explained.

The train was in a station. Thin dawnlight shone through the wooden slats. Purvis hauled the door open, the rasp cutting through Johnson's snoring but not waking the sozzled hobo. He jumped down and Ness followed. He tried to slide the door without waking their night companions. Looking back into the dark, he saw the glittering, alive eyes of the Little Tramp. Ness shivered, and shut away the icily piercing glare.

"The rummy made us, Purvis."

"Yeah, but he don't talk. LBJ and the broad, they've food in them. They wouldn't care if we were the Tsar of Russia and the King of England."

Ness still shivered. The desert was cold before sun-up. His back ached badly. He used to practise *ju-jitsu* three nights a week but had lost the habit. Some agents limped about with chunks of counter-revolutionary lead in them; his wound of honour came from years bent over a desk.

The porter had put off their cases in a heap. Standing by them was a cocky little fellow with a dandyish Western outfit, wide-brimmed stetson and bootlace tie. A star shone on his chest.

"Howdy, boys," the Sheriff said.

A toothless and enormously bearded deputy stood by, shotgun casually cradled. He wore patched overalls, only one shoulder-strap fastened.

Purvis took his crisp straw hat from the pile of luggage, and set it on his head. "Purvis," he said, extending a hand. "Bureau of Ideology."

"An I-Man, eh?" The Sheriff whistled tunelessly.

"You'll be Sheriff Autry."

Autry smiled like a mooncalf. The deputy spat a stream of tobacco juice that missed Purvis's shoes but not by much.

"This is my Deputy. We call him Gabby, on account of because he talks so much."

"Yessir, Sheriff Artery," said Gabby. "Sure do wonder how you-all kin stand my constant chatter and aggryvation."

"This is Eliot Ness," Purvis said. "You've heard of him."

Autry scratched his chin. "Nope," he said, "can't say as I have. You sir, Agent Purvis. Now you, I heard of. Got Dillinger, didn't you?"

Purvis grinned.

Sheriff Autry's coughing Tin Lizzie bumped along the road. Past Carson City was a wilderness. The Sierra Nevada rose ahead, a wall to keep trespassers out of California. Compared with the rail ride, the air was cooler, the country greener. Out of town, the car crawled uphill.

"No sign of this monkey at all," Autry yelled over ever-lowering gears. "These folks are all tetched. Camp's a regular barrel of worriment. Squatters feudin' with the locals. Going to be an outbreak of typhus or scarlet fever or something. On top of that, I got a warrant to arrest a guy who don't exist."

"Tom Joad exists," Purvis said. "He's the Okie."

The Population Index listed seven Joads with Tom or Thomas among their forenames. One too old, two still in grade school and one definitely dead last year in an works accident. Two more had been watched for months: they lead dull, blameless lives. Off to the People's Factory at eight every morning; home to wife and dinner at six every night. If the Index had every Tom Joad—under Minister of Manpower Resources Aimee Semple McPherson, a pretty reliable assumption—that left the Okie.

"I was out there," Purvis said. "Never found his place, but I could smell him. It was like that with Johnny Dillinger. Where he'd been, he left an invisible track."

Back in '31, the Oklahoma Tom Joad mashed a man's skull with a shovel in a dance-hall brawl. Sentenced to seven years State Service in the McAllister Pen, he'd kept his head down and got out in the summer of '35. After that, nothing was confirmed. Joad's prison file had disappeared. Before Ness was detailed to the case, Purvis had toured the county where Joad's family came from. Due to incompetence or corruption, it had been skipped in the '20s by former Secretary of Agriculture Long's Collectivisation drives.

"It was crazy," Purvis told Autry. Ness could tell his partner was about to mouth off. "The Kingfish left gaps all over the Mid-West. Frank Spellman is filling 'em in, sending federal troops to take over farms and turn them collective. Easy to plan, impossible to do. If the Okies could afford bullets for anything but hunting food, there'd be a shooting war. Spellman is beating them, but the dusters will beat him. No point in collectivising land that's blown away. The Joad family is supposed to have lit out West last fall, after Spellman sent in the cats to doze their homestead. That's about when we first started hearing stories."

The only element of physical description consistent between all the Tom Joad stories was that the agitator had a scar by his eye, where a comrade hit him with an axe-handle. Real or not, Tom Joad was the second most famous scarface in the USSA. Otherwise, he was a regular tall-short, fat-thin, handsome-ugly, black-white-yellow person.

The car was on the level again and he changed gear upwards. Ness caught a glimpse of water, Lake Tahoe.

"I gotta say this, guys," said Autry. "You seen bad stuff, I reckon, but Camp Nowhere is the worst. Most people here ain't human, not like you or me. A human man couldn't stand to be so miserable."

The Sheriff stopped his car behind a clump of trees. The I-Men got out: their plan was to walk into Nowhere, pick up the scuttlebutt on Tom Joad, then make a report. The camp stretched a quarter of a mile from the lake-shore, a mess of dull colours: mud shining in the sun; grey, brown and buff blankets raised as awnings and makeshift tents. It was strangely serene; no smoke from campfires, no sound of kids playing, no babies crying, no dogs barking, no machinery humming. There was no breeze, so not even the blankets moved. On Autry's reckoning, Nowhere had a population of 20,000 and growing, but it was silent in the middle of the day.

They were in among the tents and vehicles before they saw sign of life, a shawled old woman sitting on a heap of furniture, smoking a corncob. She spat in the dust as they walked past. As though the witch had made a signal, the place came alive. Ness and Purvis were mobbed by ragged kids. Little pot-bellies and big staring eyes accused accusing the I-Men for having eaten. They asked for food, money, work. Purvis held out his hands and shrugged. The kids faded away. No one had anything.

"This place doesn't have organisation," said Ness. "You'd think if there was leadership they'd get it tidied up, see to the sanitation."

"Yeah, Untouchable. Nowhere could do with a bureaucracy. A cadre of desk-jockeys would get it sorted."

The camp had no ground-plan. Tents were pitched at random, wagons and automobiles parked anywhere, most propping up "FOR SALE" signs. Every so often there was a garbage heap. On one a naked kid cleaned out already-spotless tin cans with his finger.

"Maybe Tom Joad has not arrived yet," said Purvis. "Maybe they're waiting for him."

Nobody did much of anything; one or two men moved around with fishing lines, but most sat or lay in the shade, staring into the middle distance. A man and dog tumbled in the dust in front of them, fighting over a pillow. The man, in vest and shirtsleeves, tried to tug the pillow from the dog's teeth. By the standards of Nowhere, the dog was well-fed. So was its adversary: in his fifties, stocky, with a bulbous drinker's nose. The cut of his clothes was good. A hip-flask stuck out from his back pants pocket. The pillow exploded, showering feathers. The man made things worse, shaking the pillowcase in exasperation while the dog retreated from the tip of his shoe. They all got covered in feathers. Purvis laughed.

"Harold," screeched a woman. "Those were my mother's feathers!"

"I didn't know your mother had feathers, dear," he drawled to himself.

The woman emerged from under a blanket-awning, tall and middle-aged, a touch too prosperous to be here. She snatched away the pillowcase.

"Harold, you're drunk!" she snapped, turning away.

"And you're a gooney bird, dear," said the man to himself, pulling his flask. "Tomorrow I'll be sober, you'll still be a gooney bird. Bringing us up here, when we could've been in California! Tom Joad, indeed!"

"Excuse me," began Purvis. The man jerked as if startled. "I couldn't help hearing you. We've just arrived and were wondering if the stories were true. Is Tom Joad here?"

"He is not, my friend," he intoned, lowering his voice, "if you want my opinion he never was, nor ever will be. I'd like to get out of here, but Amelia and the children are convinced they're going to meet him any day. Wanna snort?"

"Obliged," said Purvis, taking the flask and drinking.

"The name's Harold Bissonette," he said, brushing feathers from his clothes, "though Amelia prefers Bisson*ayyy*."

"What brings you to Nowhere?" asked Purvis.

Bissonnette looked around furtively. "We're out of Wappinger Falls, New Jersey. I'm going to manage a collective orange ranch in California. In Ogden, Utah about ten days ago, we heard tell of Nowhere, and how Tom Joad would be here. My lawful wedded gargoyle insisted we come this way."

"You must be the fastest typist in the West," Purvis commented. "Rat-tat-tat-tat-tat."

They were in Autry's tiny office. During the last five days, Purvis had talked. Now it was time for paper-work, Ness typed. They hadn't shown their badges. There was no point scaring information out of anyone when a crust of bread got them yarning up a storm. Starting with Bissonette, they'd logged 126 interviews spread evenly across Nowhere.

"Remember," Purvis said, imitating Bissonette's distinctive drawl, "Bissona*ayyy*."

Among the interviewees was Bertha Thompson, who had slipped off the freight and legged it to the camp. Ness felt sort of ashamed at having misrepresented himself to the girl but she was sunnily forgiving. "You're the first fellas in over a year willin' to put food in my mouth 'thout expectin' me to take anythin' else in there," she had explained. "This burg could purely do with a few more parasites shaped like her," Deputy Gabby had commented. Boxcar Bertha had even taken that in good part, although Ness had felt his skin redden at the clod's crudity.

Tom Joad wasn't in Nowhere, but everyone expected him to show. The squatters had made it to this hole in the Sierra Nevada, using up the last of their food and gas. Now they sat around and waited. Autry was going crazy because some stole food from the local collective farms and, worse, people's gardens. The Sheriff had a bum named Robert Elliot Burns, a run-away from a Southern Re-Education Camp, in jail, not so much for filching a scrawny chicken but to protect him from the Comrades' Vigilance Committee, who were shrieking to be deputised and turned loose.

They'd heard enough Tom Joad stories to fill a book. Everybody had at least one. Ness remembered Johnson's comment that stories told about the agitator were mostly refurbished tales about other characters. The most popular version of the fight in which Joad won his scar had him stepping in to defend his friend Casey from a Deputy who was about to bring him down from behind. Quite apart from the fact that this exact story, with Eugene V. Debs standing in for Casey, was one of many told about how Al Capone got his scar, it seemed obvious to Ness that this was a disguised Robin Hood story, with Friar Tuck turned into Preacher Casey.

This was not a job for I-Men but for collectors of folk-lore. Ness wondered how many times these tales had been dressed up. In the USSA, one face could do for Tom Joad, Abraham Lincoln, Frank James and Wyatt Earp.

Ness began typing the last page of the interview summaries.

"Sounds like a machine gun," Purvis said.

"I can do more damage with this than with a gun," he told his partner.

"Damn straight," Purvis said, sloshing whiskey into a paper cup from Autry's water-cooler. "How many did you put away in Chi with Parasite Regulation?"

"When Joseph Kennedy's ring was broken, there were 895 arrests, 763 convictions. Seventeen illegal breweries, five distilleries, and 105 outlets closed down. Over a hundred thousand cases of liquor seized."

"This is probably from that batch," Purvis said, raising his cup. Deputy Hayes had got him the bottle. "I hear most of the hooch went missing from the PR warehouse."

Ness said nothing. It was true: little of the goods impounded during the Kennedy raids had been destroyed under supervision of his old unit. He'd been transferred and his successors proved lax.

"You did a good job, Untouchable. Too good, right?"

Ness squared up the typed sheets on the desk.

"Like me," Purvis continued, swilling more whiskey. "I did a good job. Dillinger and Floyd, Baby Face Nelson. Ma Barker and Her Killer Sons: Floyd, Mad Dog, Ronnie and Clive. Rat-tat-tat-tat-tat. Got 'em all. Lined 'em up and gunned 'em down in the name of State, Party and Frigging Bureau."

"You shouldn't drink."

Purvis crumpled his empty cup and missed the waste-paper basket. He took another and filled it. The smell caught in Ness's nostrils. His partner had been drinking steadily.

"Why not? I've a trunk of Socialist Hero citations, and I'm still just outside Nowhere. Literally. Know Hoover's favourite commandment? 'Thou Shalt Have No Other Gods But Me'. The USSA's only got room for one Top Cop. I was reprimanded for 'encouraging bourgeois individualism' by walking around as a reminder of the way Hoover sets his fat ass in Debs, taking the credit for everything every field agent does. This is my punishment, Untouchable. The quest for the one People's Enemy there's no chance of me actually catching."

"You mean 'us.'"

"I was letting a tendency to encourage unproductive hero-worship cloud my mind. I mean us. Hoover loves you too."

"I regard this assignment as an honour."

Purvis laughed bitterly. "I saw your file, Untouchable. PR dumped you on Hoover and this is his way of getting you out of his hair. We're official heroes, but the USSA doesn't need any more heroes. Joe Hill was a hero, but he had to go to Bohemia. Even that wasn't far enough, as you'd have noticed if you paid attention to Canadian radio."

"Hill was murdered by a Russian. Despite the European press, it was nothing to do with the Party."

"Come on, Untouchable. Remember the date? Who is there apart from the Chairman who has people rubbed out on February the 14th?

Every year, regular as the Cannonball Express, there's a St Valentine's Day Purge."

Ness looked around. The Sheriff was off addressing a meeting, trying to cool the local lynch-lawyers. Ness wasn't sure the office wasn't rigged with a concealed wire-recorder.

He took out the last sheet from the typewriter. The report was complete. Now the agents had to add their own conclusions and suggestions.

"Are we agreed?" Ness asked. "We recommend supplies of food and gas be brought up to the camp along with state militia."

"Sounds jake," said Purvis.

"We help everyone get wherever they're legitimately headed. Any left over, we clear out with the militia. They can be returned to their point of departure."

"There's no case for letting them all into California," ventured Purvis, getting up to turn on the fan.

"These people got into this mess through their own stupidity."

"It's not good enough," sighed Purvis, sitting down and lighting a cigarette. "All we've said is, we can't find any Tom Joad here and we should use sticks and carrots to move these scarecrows along. Assistant Director Tolson's not going to buy that. We're not here to help people, remember. We're on a ghost hunt."

"I see that," agreed Ness. "We have to finish by saying who and what we think Tom Joad is."

"I'm all ears," said Purvis, head almost disappearing as he swung his feet up onto the desk.

"Tom Joad is a myth," said Ness. "Black propaganda to spread discontent and disrespect for the Party. It's so simple but so devious. My hunch is the British are behind it. Maybe Sidney Reilly himself."

"He was probably killed leading that cockamamie White Yank invasion from Canada in '24, but I like it otherwise. How's this play work?"

"In London, a council of Secret Service Agents and American exiles dream up Tom Joad stories. Like that guy Lovecraft the Brits paid to write horror tales about Re-Education Camps. Agents over here spread the stories. They probably start by telling 'em to hoboes like Johnson. After a while, people invent their own Tom Joad stories. It's cheap, it's clever. That's why I guess the Brits, not the Russkies."

"Untouchable, you're a genius," Purvis exclaimed. "It's so dumb they're sure to buy it in Debs. Fiendish Brits, a shadow-man, a counter-revolutionary conspiracy. I love it."

"You don't believe it?" said Ness.

"That doesn't matter. I'm smart, and we're reporting to stupid men. What's important is what Debs can be made to believe. Go on, write it up. Put Reilly in: you and Hoover are the only people ever to take that fraud seriously. Hell, put Lovecraft in; he's certainly International Grapefruit Number One. I'll gladly sign anything that means I go back somewhere where they have hot water on tap."

They stood by Autry's car on a road overlooking Nowhere. Ness scanned the camp with binoculars. In response to their report, Debs had cabled back this morning. The I-Men were to await reinforcements. The order had been signed by Tolson, but the reinforcements weren't FBI agents. Some special unit under the command of the Central Committee.

"Food, medicines and gas are on the way," Autry said. "I can get five hundred State Troopers to the Reno railhead in twenty four hours. I reckon we can clear the place in two days."

"Where's your authorization?" asked Ness.

"I'm authorization, Untouchable," said Purvis. "The camp is a threat to law and order. I'm anticipating orders so we can move 'em on out as fast as possible when we get the go-ahead."

"What in hell is that?" said Autry.

A dozen long black automobiles hummed up the road, followed by a fleet of olive drab military trucks. The air was quite damp, but the convoy gave the impression of raising a huge cloud of dust. Purvis groaned, holding his hung-over head. The leading car, a Plymouth with official plates, rolled to a halt beside Autry's heap, a shark next to a hound-dog.

A man got out, and adjusted his pearl-gray fedora. The sharp suit he wore was almost a uniform. All black, including the shirt, with a white silk tie. Even tailoring couldn't cover the way the suitcoat's armpit bulged. Ness recognised the man.

"Frank Nitti," the fedora announced.

Officially a Chicago Party Boss, Nitti was Capone's personal Enforcer. It was said that, if it came to it, he was the only man in the USSA with the power and the nerve to arrest J. Edgar Hoover.

The line of official cars pulled up next to Nitti. The trucks carried on. Ness counted twenty of them and they were still coming.

"Comrade, I'm Agent Ness. My partner is Agent Purvis, and this is Sheriff Autry. How can we help?"

"Follow us in, I-Man," said Nitti, standing on his running-board.

Still the army trucks came. Further up, some left the road. Men in full combat gear jumped out. Some carried rolls of barbed wire, which they pulled around the perimeter. Far from herding people away from Nowhere, they were keeping them in. As the last truck rumbled past, the Party cars started again. Autry followed. Nitti held his fedora to his head.

"He'd look funny if he didn't kill so many people," said Purvis. Autry flinched as if certain there were a microphone in his dashboard.

The black convoy drove straight into the middle of Nowhere, pulling up in a ring in a large and fairly clear area. Already panicked by the soldiers, children cried and screamed while women ran around desperately gathering families together. Ness noticed Bertha Thompson, cleaned-up and in a dress, helping with a tribe of loose kids. She looked like an underfed schoolmarm.

Inside the arena formed by the parked cars, soldiers with fixed bayonets pushed or kicked away a few wretched tents and shelters. After things had quieted down, Nitti got off his car. From each of the other cars emerged four or five men wearing exactly the same outfit as Nitti. They carried machine guns. Purvis groaned quietly. Ness tried to feel nothing. The black-clad men were highly-trained professionals, the paladins of socialism, America's best.

Nitti was given a megaphone. "Come on out," his amplified voice sounded. "We can't feed you all but we've got candy-bars for lucky children."

The previously-deserted area quickly filled. The most desperate came out first, the ones with least to lose. Nitti stood by his Plymouth, a no-man's-land of about ten feet between him and the scarecrow children.

Nitti motioned the three of them over. "Still no sign of Joad?"

"That's right," said Ness. "If you read the report we sent to Debs, you'll see we concluded Tom Joad is an apocryphal..."

"I don't need no poxyful report," said Nitti. He pulled out a candy bar. "Who would like this?"

If he expected a rush, he was wrong. These people were too weak to do anything fast. They were also surrounded by forty men with machine guns, not to mention a regiment of soldiers.

"Please comrade," said a skinny teen-ager, raising his hand and taking a tentative step forward. He had a mess of freckles and big wide, sad eyes. "I'd like that candy bar."

"If I gave it you," said Nitti, smiling. "What would you do?"

"Comrade, I'd share it with my family," said the kid, moving a little further forward. "There's a lot of us, and we haven't none of us eaten anything for days."

"What's your name, boy?"

"John."

"John," said Nitti, "I like the way you don't just think of yourself. I'll give you a candy bar for every one of your family you can bring here in the next five minutes. We got a deal?"

"I guess so, comrade," said John suspiciously. Then he made his mind up, turned round and ran, either to fetch his family or to hide.

"Why it's Little Mel," said Nitti, turning back to the I-Men. He held out his hand. Purvis hesitated, then went forward to shake. "I haven't seen you since when? Must've been the Superstition Drive in Utah. Boy, we had some good times there, didn't we just? All them God-bothered crazies with the extra wives?"

Purvis looked at the dirt.

"So what's going down," said Nitti. "We gonna find Tom Joad? You and me should have a wager on who gets to whack the jackass? We should've brought reporters. They'd love that: Little Mel versus the Enforcer. America's top lawmen race to nail People's Enemy Number One."

"He's not here, Frank," said Purvis. "Like Ness says, Tom Joad's a line, reactionary propaganda put about by the Whites and the limeys. He only exists in people's minds."

Nitti reached into his overcoat and pulled out a cigar. He sucked and puffed a while. "Won't do, Mel. Won't do at all. We've busted our asses to get here. The Chairman wants this business cleared up. You had your chance. Now let's try it my way."

John reappeared, along with three generations of his family. There were eight of them, and most looked worse than the kid. They all had freckles, and big glassy dog's eyes.

"Come forward," Nitti smiled to them. "Stand in a line."

The family hesitantly lined itself up ten feet from Nitti.

"Frank, for goodness' sake..." said Purvis.

"Hush, Mel. Don't annoy me."

"Okay," he addressed John's family, "can any of you good folks tell me where I'd find Comrade Tom Joad?"

The oldest man growled about having told them it was a trap. John stepped forward. "We don't know where Tom Joad is. We were told he might be coming here, but we've not seen him."

"You're lying, boy," said Nitti. He jammed his cigar into his mouth and reached backwards with his right arm. One of the men in black placed a machine gun into it, stock resting on his bicep, grip slotting into his hand. Nitti swung the tommy-gun down.

"I say again, you're lying. You must've been brought up wrong."

"Okay, I was lying," said John, holding up his arms. "Tom Joad passed through the other night. Came and spoke to us, lots of us. Said he'd get us all out in a few days."

"Now you're just trying to tell me what I want to hear."

"Frank," said Purvis, "what the hell else would you expect him to do?"

Nitti swung towards Purvis, pointing the gun. "I said it's my turn, Mel," he said evenly.

He turned back towards the family. The crowd standing behind them was thinning.

"Liar, liar, pants on fire..."

Nitti cocked the gun, and, aiming low to compensate for the recoil, directed a stream of fire across the line. He fired short, controlled bursts of four or five shots to keep his aim steady, not the continuous burst they show in the movies.

Ness flinched as a hot cartridge case hit his cheek. Autry shouted, but Ness's ears were too abused by the rat-tat-tat-tat-tat to make out what he was saying. Purvis looked away, hands over his ears. Bertha hugged children to her chest. The family danced, holes in their chests and heads gouting red.

Nitti used every shot in the fifty-round drum magazine, but one of the family still moved. It was John. After handing the empty gun to his assistant, like a surgeon returning a used scalpel to a nurse, Nitti took a .45 from inside his coat and stood over the teenager. He fired a bullet through his head.

"Good night, John-Boy," Nitti said.

Two days later, his cheek-bruise was gone but Ness could still hear the rat-tat-tat-tat.

"Getting to you, Untouchable?" Purvis had asked. "Try cotton in your ears."

Nine o'clock, and Nitti had been drinking since noon. So had the rest of his paladins. The finest America had, upholders of the law: including the one against the transportation and sale of alcoholic beverages.

"We offed about forty this morning," Nitti was saying. "This screwy preacher says 'I'm Tom Joad, the man you want' like he had a death-wish. C'mon Mel, have another drink, don't look so blue, you're spoiling the party."

Purvis didn't need a second invite. He took the one-third-full bottle and tipped it into his mouth until it was empty. They were in Saloon Bar of the Lake Hotel. The whole building, the only hotel in Carson City, had been taken over by Nitti.

"No way was he Joad. I noticed these weird tattoos on his knuckles. On one hand he had the 'love', and on the other 'hate'. I keep up with this psychology you read about in magazines, and I figure here is a guy so sick at himself that he wants to die. Since I couldn't give him the satisfaction of killing him, know what I did?"

"I can hardly wait," spat Purvis. The way he was sassing the Chairman's top torpedo you'd think he had a death-wish, too.

"I had 'Greasy Thumb' cut off his fingers."

Jake Guzik, the paladin they called "Greasy Thumb", chuckled at the happy memory, and waggled his own fingers like a cartoon character.

"You're a sadist, Frank," said Purvis.

"If that's a fancy way of saying I enjoy my work, you're right. But it's is the only language these folks understand. I'm going to keep going out to Nowhere every morning and shooting people until Tom Joad gives himself up."

"What if there isn't any Tom Joad?" Ness asked.

"We'll have had some fun," Nitti grinned. "And the USSA will be short a few parasites and reactionaries."

When Nitti's Family showed up, the I-Men had accepted Sheriff Autry's offer of alternative accommodation and moved out of the hotel into rooms in the house attached to the city jail. Burns, the chicken thief, had been let out on his own sufferance, and quite sensibly skedaddled. Ness realised Autry's interpretation of the federal law was about as strict as his Deputy's interpretation of the English language.

Four in the morning, Ness hadn't slept more than twenty minutes since turning in about midnight. The ringing in his ears kept him awake. He'd never seen anyone shot before. With the DPR, he carried a gun but it never come out of its holster. Usually, he hung it up with his coat to prevent the weighted leather chafing on his shirt as he paced from desk to filing cabinet and back. In the Kennedy case, his big win, the arrests had been quiet, clean.

Rat-tat-tat-tat-tat...

His partner had the experience. The Peoples' Enemies he'd brought down weren't like Boston Joe; they went out in storms of lead rather than be hauled in for a show trial and a long walk to the chair. Dillinger had been coming out of a movie house, where he'd just watched State Prosecutor William Powell purge childhood friend Clark Gable in *Manhattan Melodrama*, and Charles "Pretty Boy" Floyd was turned in by the collective farm he had tried to take over. Both chose to shoot it out and wound up riddled with I-Man bullets. It was expected, especially after George "Machine Gun" Kelly disgraced the outlaw breed by meekly surrendering and earning the new nickname, "Yellowjacket". Although Special Agent in Charge, Purvis never claimed personally to have fired the kill-shots, always taking care to give "credit" to other agents whose aim probably ended the criminal careers.

Rat-tat-tat-tat-tat...

Ness wondered what it was like to kill someone. Also, if Purvis had drunk quite so much before. Probably.

He sat up in bed, sweating and shivering at the same time. His robe, hanging on the back of the door, looked for a moment like someone standing in the dark, staring at him with accusing eyes. The eyes of the Little Tramp in the cattle car, the family Nitti wiped out, the dirty children in Camp Nowhere.

He remembered Bertha Thompson turning away after the killings, refusing to acknowledge him. People he had interviewed on a reasonably friendly basis were too scared to shun him now, but there was a coldness they couldn't keep out of their eyes. To them, he was no different from Frank Nitti.

He pulled on his robe and stepped into the hallway. There was a thin light under Purvis's door. Ness knocked and entered. The bed was rumpled, but empty. A bottle, a dried amber rind left at its bottom, stood up against the pillow.

"Bang," said someone.

Heart hammering, Ness wheeled. Purvis sat in a rocking chair, hand pointed out like a gun. He was still dressed but had his jacket off. His holster was empty. He held his real gun loosely in his left hand. An unopened bottle stuck up from his lap. His red-rimmed eyes were as scary as the eyes that kept Ness from sleeping.

"Do you know that more FBI men shoot themselves than are shot by enemies of the state?" Purvis asked.

"Tomorrow, I'll cable Debs. They have to know Nitti is exceeding his authority."

"A cable to Debs *brought* Nitti, Untouchable. Forget the law, forget authority. Frank Nitti is the law, in all its bloody, arbitrary, blind stupid glory. We don't live under socialism. This is the Rule of Rat-tat-tat-tat-tat."

Ness stood by the window and looked out at the silent streets. Now the Family were in town, no one came out at night. He suspected Autry had put out word, warning people to stay away. The Enforcer was a dark wind blowing through. Nothing could be done. People had to wait until the dust-storm was over and they could come out of their holes.

"Have you noticed what stupid assholes they are? They come back to the hotel at noon and get pie-eyed. Don't bother posting a guard..."

Ness kept quiet. Out on the street, something—not a cat—was moving.

"We could stop him. Crash a gas tanker through the front door and torch it."

Outside town, the sun rose over the Sierras, casting a pale light across the city. By the statue of Upton Sinclair, something definitely moved. Ness turned. Purvis had his revolver aimed, barrel pressed under his chin, hammer cocked.

"One wrong move," he said, "and the I-Man's brains are on the ceiling."

Ness waved away the foolishness. There was something going on.

"This place is surrounded," he told Purvis. "Some of them are inside."

"Hot damn," Purvis said, waving his gun.

They both looked at the door. It was the only way in. Ness's pistol was back in his room, hung over a chairback in a holster.

In the hall, a tiny creak signified the presence of someone trying to keep quiet. Ness hoped several bottles of hooch weren't enough to blunt Purvis's legendary cool under fire. There was a crash as someone kicked in Ness's door. Thanking Providence and Charlie Marx, Ness pulled open Purvis's door; his partner sprang from his chair, levelling his revolver to cover the corridor. A nice selection of backs clustered around Ness's doorway.

"Comrades," Purvis said, sounding sober. "Kindly put your guns on the floor and turn around."

If they all spun and shot, only one would go down. But nobody wanted to be the one. Three men turned. Two wore army uniform, the other was Sheriff Autry. They dropped guns, and their hands rose.

"Fellers," said Autry, "what can I say..."

"Make introductions," Purvis said, impatient.

"This is Major Smedley Darlington Butler," Autry explained, indicating a serious-faced officer. "*Commandante* of the soldier boys out at Nowhere."

Major Smed Butler and his aide were stiff-backed and ready to be tortured for days without saying a word, but Autry, more embarrassed than guilty, sang like a happy cowboy. Purvis asked questions, and drew out of the Sheriff an account of the group's intentions.

Evidently the Bureau's reputation was more fearsome than they knew. Butler and Autry had decided that they couldn't move against Nitti without first gunning the I-Men. Ness was flattered and alarmed they had tried to cool him first, assuming Purvis insensible.

"This is a nice little Counter-Revolution," Purvis commented. With a gun in his hand, he had a cockiness that was instantly impressive.

Butler snorted contempt. Despite his federal uniform, he seemed the epitome of White Yank. He'd be happier at a Klan meet than a union rally.

"C'mon, Mel," Autry said. "This ain't politics, this is killin'."

"Major Butler," began Ness, genuinely puzzled. "Why put your life at risk on account of a camp of scofflaws and reactionaries?"

The officer looked at Ness with something approaching pity.

"Call the squatters what you will," he said. "I daresay most are worthless hoboes. But it sits ill to be an accomplice to the murder of women and children. By holding the perimeter of that camp, we most surely are accomplices. This is no honourable man's conception of the profession of arms."

"Tell me, Major," sneered Purvis, "aren't there ideological officers in your outfit?"

"You'd be correct," said Butler. "We harbour three of the species, their main pastime being to spy on one another. Unfortunately, all have reported sick."

Purvis holstered his gun and looked thoughtful. Butler sat up at attention.

"You're going to kill Nitti and the rest?" Purvis asked. Butler nodded very slightly.

"We prefer to think of it as an execution."

Without thought, this honourable man would have killed them both, Ness knew. Somewhere, murder had become the main mode of political discourse in the USSA. It had started before the Revolution, with Roosevelt, Wilson, Mix, Crowley. In the last years, other names had been added. Hill, cut down by a "Russian disciple". John Reed, dead of "influenza" in Alaska. There were even whispers about the "chronic myocarditis" that put Eugene Debs into the tomb next to Lincoln's in 1926 and got the capital's name changed. Capone spent more on tributes than food programs. Perhaps that was why he'd purged his Chicago florist, Dion O'Banion.

"Autry," said Purvis "do you have a half-gallon of milk? I need to straighten out my head."

"Purvis," Ness protested. He could see how this was heading.

"Untouchable," he said, patting his gun. "Somewhere there's a line, and you have to step over it."

Would Purvis ever have left his gun in his room, no matter how safe he thought he was? Maybe he never thought he was safe. Maybe that was the smart way to be. Because Purvis had his gun and Ness didn't, he was deciding the Bureau's policy on Smed Butler and the six-gun Sheriff.

"So what are you going to do?" Purvis asked Butler, "go in there shooting?"

"No sir," said Butler. "Bravery has its place of honour, but a good soldier will not endanger his men through recklessness. We intend to dynamite the hotel."

Purvis whistled, and said "okay, I'm in."

Autry whooped silently, and waved his fancy hat.

"And you sir?" Butler turned to Ness.

"The Untouchable is with us," Purvis said, before Ness could protest. "He's my partner."

Butler had been working on this for days. The laundry room of the Lake Shore Hotel was stuffed with explosives. All the night-staff were warned to take an early morning walk between five and six. The plan had been to take out the I-Men, then proceed directly to the hotel, which was staked out by a hand-picked group of Butler's loyal officers, and toss a torch into the laundry room from a back window, then run like blazes. It was crude but serviceable, Ness supposed. Nitti hardly deserved more finesse. As Purvis had pointed out, he was so secure in the cloud of fear he spread about him that he hadn't bothered to have anyone on formal guard duty.

Opposite the hotel, Deputy Gabby stood under a statue, accompanied by a leather-faced lieutenant named Randy Scott. There was a drunk bundled behind the pedestal. He flopped forward and Ness recognised Phil D'Andrea, one of Nitti's button men, his neck broken.

"Varmint staggered out for a whiz," Gabby explained. "Don't take kindly to no city folks pissin' on a hero of the Revolution like Comrade Sinclair, nosirree-bob."

"We oughta put a blindfold on that statue," Autry said. "The order came in to take it down when ole Upton 'vanished', but we just plumb never got round to it. Made a speech in Carson, he did. Lot of folks was pretty inspired. We marched on Snob Hill, turfed them plutes into the streets."

Butler looked disgusted. Ness assumed he was not unacquainted with mansions on the right side of the tracks.

"Are the staff clear?" the Major asked Gabby.

The Deputy's face crinkled. "In a matter of speakin', yup, and, to a contrariwise way of lookin' at the sitchyation, nope."

"Explain yourself, man."

"It's like this: all them clerks and porters and waiters is well on their way to the bus depot, but them fedora fellers has them some feminine company in there. I guess they's all been practicin' their push-ups."

Purvis swore.

"Unfortunate," Butler declared, "but a few worthless drabs can hardly be allowed to stand in the way of our operation."

"They's only one ole gal. They brung her back from Nowhere last evening. She went in kickin' and screamin'."

"That settles it. She has doubtless suffered the proverbial 'fate worse than death' and would as like as not take her own life, if she has not already been murdered by her abductors."

Butler was brushing this fly off his map with the sort of casual ease Ness might have expected of Frank Nitti. The Major ordered Scott to fetch a torch.

Ness looked at the sky. The sun was up, but it was only five-thirty. The drink-sodden paladins would be sleeping a while yet.

"Give me fifteen minutes," he said. "I'm going in."

"Untouchable..."

Ness shook his head.

"Don't call me that, Mel."

The lights were on in the lobby. In an armchair by a potted palm, Jake "Greasy Thumb" Guzik, the finger-cutter, sat semi-conscious in his shirtsleeves. His tie was cinched around his arm and on an occasional table next to him was a syringe and an empty vial. It figured some of these monkeys would be addicts.

Ness took a deep breath and stood over the man. "Greasy Thumb," he murmured, "wake up."

Guzik groaned in a brutal, though not unpleasant, dream. Ness slapped him. He jumped three inches off the seat and pulled back his fist. Ness, unsure where he fit in Guzik's idea of how the world worked, stood back, the better to kick his face if he had to.

Guzik relaxed a little. "Whaddya want, I-Man?"

"The girl. I want the girl. Where is she?"

"What girl?" he said, shaking his head to clear it.

"Don't mess me around, Greasy Thumb. The boys brought a girl over here this evening. Maybe you had a piece yourself?"

"Oh her. The wild one. She's in one of the top rooms. You want a go, too? I thought you I-Men were clean-livers?"

"I want to get her out of here, Greasy Thumb. Her folks are worried."

Guzik shrugged. What a strange thing for anyone to want to do, he probably thought. "Big room, top front. I think the boys are finished with the gang-bang."

"Okay Greasy Thumb. You can go back to sleep."

Ness took the stairs as quietly as possible. The door he was looking for was ajar, the light on inside. There was no-one else on the landing so he stood, listening awhile.

Above the sound of snoring from some of the other rooms, he thought he heard two people breathing. He grasped Purvis's knife in his pocket and eased the door open. His partner had given him the knife, telling him to keep things quiet. Ness had plenty of motivation. One untoward sound and Smed Butler would blow the hotel to the moon and Eliot Ness with it.

The room, probably the biggest in the Hotel, was full of fussy, frilly feminine decoration - flowered wallpaper, fancy curtains, expensive-looking washstand and wardrobe. A naked woman was tied to the bed, and a man in his undershirt, fat buttocks wobbling, ground slowly down on top of her. The girl's face, eyes screwed shut, was turned to him.

The woman, he realised, was Bertha Thompson. The man was Frank Nitti. Bertha didn't register his presence.

It would have been easy to pull out his gun and put a bullet in the back of Nitti's head. Ness might even enjoy it.

Rat-tat-tat-tat-tat...

Instead, he slammed the hilt of the knife into Nitti's skull, hoping to make a sharp dent. Half-unconscious anyway, the Enforcer was put out of it completely. Blood greased Ness's hand. He hauled Nitti, heavy and bulgy out of his sharp suit, off Bertha, and rolled him onto the floor. To make sure he was out, Ness kicked Nitti in the head. To make extra sure, he kicked him again.

Shaking incipient fever from his brain, he turned to Bertha. Trying not to look at her body, blue bruises and red cuts on white skin, he sliced through the strips of sheet that bound her to the bedposts.

"Can you understand me?" he asked, urgently. She nodded non-commitally. "Do you know where your clothes are?"

She nodded again and sat up the way a woman of ninety would. She stood unsteadily and hobbled over to a small pile of clothing.

"Hurry," said Ness. "We have to get out quickly."

She looked at the clothes uncertainly.

"I need a bath," she said. "I'm not going until I've had a bath."

Her legs gave way. She fell and began to sob silently.

A terrible coldness spread through Ness's heart. He pocketed the knife and drew his gun, a .45 automatic. He released the safety and cocked it. He took two pillows from the bed and lay one over Nitti's head. He felt the man's boozy breath as he sandwiched the gun with the pillows. He made sure barrel was pressed into one of the Enforcer's eyes.

Bertha was starting to cry out loud now. Much more, and she would wake the house.

"Here, Bertha," he whispered, "look..."

He jerked the trigger. A bullet jammed into the floor through a pillow and Nitti's skull. There was a sound like a nail being slammed into floorboards. It wasn't quiet, but the hotel didn't explode.

Ness threw away the pillows and scorched feathers spurted. He tilted Nitti's head, one eye-socket a bloody crater, towards Bertha.

"Here, girl," he said. "Happy?"

Shocked silent, she wriggled into her dress and settled it around her grazed legs. Ness's hands were wrung out and bruised from the stifled recoil. Cold fire still burned in his head.

"Now," he said. "We leave."

His arm around her, he walked her firmly out of the room and down the stairs. Jake Guzik was still in the lobby, conscious this time.

"Have a fine time, Comrade?" said Jake. "You were mighty quick, and I heard a hell of a thump."

Guzik grinned. He had dirty teeth.

"This poor girl's had a terrible experience," said Ness sternly, playing the prissy I-Man. "You should be ashamed. I'll be making a full report to Debs."

Guzik shrugged, knowing anyone with Nitti was invincible. Ness pulled the girl towards the revolving door. He told her she'd be all right, they'd get her a doctor.

There was a noise upstairs. Bumping. Voices. Ness saw horror on Guzik's face, as if a ghost had appeared. From the doorway, he looked back at the lobby. The wind was taken out of him. On the stairs, his face half-red, naked from the waist down, a spasming animal keening escaping from his mouth, stood Frank "The Enforcer" Nitti. There were enough brains left in his smashed skull to keep him tottering. Ness pulled his .45 and got off another shot. Nitti's shoulder exploded, and he staggered back, belly and genitals bobbing. The shot sounded in the lobby like a drum-roll. Now, Butler would toss the torch.

Beside Nitti appeared a rabid little man with a tommy-gun. Vince Coll, one of the New York Party fedoras. Guzik's mouth was open. He must think he was overdosing. The Enforcer stumbled and fell—dead at last?—as Coll opened fire. Bullets ploughed through the carpets, raising wood-splinters in a line towards Ness and Bertha. Guzik yelped and danced back, a bullet in his ankle, his shoe full of blood.

Ness hit the revolving door, dragging Bertha with him. The door span on its spindle, then stopped. Bertha shrieked, her foot caught. She jiggled, trying to get free, and Ness turned in the confined space, looking through dusty glass at the lobby, which was filling with men.

They were nicely trapped in this triangular wedge. Coll ambled across the lobby, raising his tommy-gun and convulsively chewing. He aimed low, and fired a burst, jerking the barrel up.

The glass smashed as the first bullets struck, and Bertha's foot got loose. Ness pushed, and they were spat out of the hotel, stumbling down the front steps and away from the building. The door, pushed by the gunfire, span like a grinder, and a scatter of glass flew out of it. Taking Bertha's hand, Ness ran across the square.

Behind, the hotel lifted from its foundations and flew apart. A wave of heat and sound knocked them flat, and burning rocks fell all around.

Ness was in the dirt, his head hammered. Hands pulled at him. Bertha was babbling about a doctor.

"Come on, Eliot," said a voice through the noise. "Get up and dance."

Ness tried standing. It was surprisingly easy. None of his major bones were broken. He ran his fingers over his face, then looked at his hands. Blood smeared on his left palm, and he was aware of the throbbing in one side of his face.

"You'll have a scar," Purvis said. "Like..."

There was another explosion, smaller. Ness turned to where the hotel had been, and saw a clump of masonry falling in. The building didn't exist anymore. Dotted around the rubble were a number of medium-sized bonfires. The square was full of people, gawking.

"Where's the girl?" asked Ness.

"She ran off," said Purvis. "She's okay. Well, as okay as I guess she'll ever be. Autry called a doctor."

Butler waited with two of his men, handing out orders.

"A nice operation, Agent Ness," the Major said. "I salute you, sir."

Ness just nodded. He was tired, and wanted to go back to sleep.

"The job's not over," said Purvis. "We have to clear out Camp Nowhere before news reaches Debs and Capone orders reprisals. Butler's sent word to his men out there to give the squatters some good prods. It's cover-up time for us. In a minute, you and me are going to go running into the street as if we haven't a clue what the hell's happening. We'll organise the fire-fighting and rescue operation and generally pretend we care very deeply about what happened Nitti's nutsoes. We'll take it from there..."

"That Nitti, Mel. He wasn't human, he..."

"You're telling me."

Lieutenant Scott ran up to Butler and threw a salute. "Sir, Captain McCrea reports they're having trouble with the civilians out in Nowhere. They won't move out. Some say it's a trick to lure people into the open and kill them one by one."

It was a dumb idea, but given Nitti's behaviour, it was natural people wouldn't trust the army. Butler looked perplexed and shook his head in frustration. This wasn't in his line of work at all.

Ness wiped blood away from his face-wound. He was lucky not to have lost an eye.

"Let me try something," said Ness. "You stay here and see what you can do. I'll go over to the camp with Major Butler and try to get those people moving."

"Okay," said Purvis. "I'll see you back here as and when..."

"Mel, if Greasy Thumb Guzik is still alive, finish him off for me. He's a material witness."

"What are you going to do later, Major?" he asked as the staff car, driven by Lieutenant Scott, began the climb to Camp Nowhere. "No matter how innocent you can play it, they'll get you."

"I know that, Agent Ness. I've made arrangements to borrow those fast cars Nitti brought here. The day after tomorrow, my officers and I intend to apply for asylum at the British embassy in Mexico City."

"You're giving up everything."

"I give up nothing," said Butler, lighting a cheroot. "Everything has already been taken from me. I'm like these wretches here. My family lands were confiscated. All my tenant farmers, white and nigra, were expelled. Now the profession to which I was born has been stained. So as Charles Marx would have it, you take away everything a man has, you set him free once more."

Scott stopped the car outside the camp. Crowds parted to let the vehicle crawl to a halt. The only people talking were soldiers, mostly farmboys who'd joined up for three squares a day and now saw their own folks in the deluded suckers who'd bought the Tom Joad lie and used up the last of their food and gas to get to this mountain rat-hole. Butler's aide had been right. Nobody was making a move to leave. All the tents and makeshift shelters were all exactly in place. Men, women and children stood around under the climbing sun, still waiting for their deliverer.

Ness doubted the squatters could even be forced to go at bayonet-point. There must be twenty thousand individual souls here but they acted with one mind, one intention. To try and make any impression on them would be like putting your fist into a pool of water and hoping there'd be a hole when you took it out again.

The pain in Ness's face had settled down to a dull throb. He and Purvis could cover themselves, and Butler would make it over the border. That just left twenty thousand squatters to save.

He pulled up the collar of his overcoat and tipped the brim of his hat downwards over his eyes. He stepped out of the car, and looked around. The man he had been when the sun went down last night was a stranger to him, and he hoped he could walk into the camp clean and cold.

A thin figure stood up from where she had been lying. It was Bertha Thompson, her face scrubbed, her hair skinned back. She still wore her bloody, torn dress. Inside, she must be steel.

Ness still felt the kick in his hands as he shot under the pillow.

"Sister," he called to her.

She whimpered, but controlled herself. He tipped his hat, and showed her his marked face.

"Tell the people, sister."

She nodded.

"Tell the people Tom Joad is here."

He sat on the back of a flatbed truck, smoking a bent cigarette. When he flicked the butt and looked up, a solid ocean of people stretched before him. People all spoke to one another in low voices. The name "Tom Joad" emerged again and again from the shambling and hissing of the crowd. Kids were clustered around his feet, just looking up at him. If anyone recognised the man who had interviewed them days earlier and stood around while Frank Nitti murdered a family, no one said anything. Until that moment, he had been sure he could never pull this off, but he hadn't reckoned on the people's need for Tom Joad, their need to believe in their hero.

He stood up, and took off his hat, showing the new scar. People gasped. "Frank Nitti is dead," he said, projecting his best lecture-circuit voice. "I just dynamited his hotel."

There was a ragged cheer.

"When the Party find out, they'll want to track down every one of you and kill you. That's why you must get out of here right now. The Party will be after all of us. So don't waste any time. Pack up and get out. The road to California is that way. As soon as you're out of here, the safer you're going to be..."

"Tom," shouted a man who tossed his hat in the air. It was Harold Bissonette, Ness was astonished to realise. "Tom, will you be coming with us?"

Ness shrugged, and realised what he said next would decide it. If he sold them on Tom Joad, they would scatter and be saved. If not, this would be a killing field.

"You go on ahead of me, folks," he said, thrilled by the bright eyes all around him. "I've things to do back here."

The words came to him.

"I'll be all around in the dark. I will be everywhere wherever you look. Whenever there's a fight so hungry people can eat, whenever there's a cop beating up on a guy I'll be there. I'll be in the way guys yell when they're mad, I'll be in the way kids yell when they're hungry and they know their supper's ready. Wherever people are eating the stuff they raised and living in the houses they built, I'll be there too."

This hobo jungle was much like the last, although—being in Alabama —there were more blacks than whites grouped around the fire. Ness was used to these fringe gatherings now. In theory, Purvis and he were still being punished, but this assignment was being drawn out.

One thing about working for Hoover was that he put the Bureau ahead of everything, including Justice, Truth and Party. If anyone in Debs had an idea what had gone down in Nowhere, it had not been mentioned. Ness and Purvis picked up extra citations and were kicked back out into the field. The only casualty of the conspiracy was Sheriff Autry, who had resigned, ostensibly for letting the chicken-thief get away. Autry had quickly returned to state service as Carson City's best-loved singing dog-catcher, with Deputy Gabby as his assistant. Smed Butler was in Mexico, leading some jumped-up White Yank regiment with comic opera uniforms. Bertha Thompson was in California, somewhere. And Frank Nitti had more parks named after him than any other Hero of the Permanent Revolution.

As the sun went down, the hoboes had been telling Tom Joad stories. They were wilder, more extravagant now. One claimed Tom Joad was a ghost in a black cloak, and that he carved his initials on the cheeks of the Party goons he killed. Another, a scrawny Negro who called himself Fetchit, told of how, somewhere over Nevada way, Tom Joad dynamited that murdering sonofabitch Frank Nitti and how Nitti had staggered out, his fancy clothes in tatters, only to be confronted by the avenging Tom Joad, who strangled him with his bare hands. The tale-teller went through all the motions, popping his eyes out and calling on the Lord for forgiveness as he re-created Nitti's well-deserved end.

"That night," Fetchit said, "Marse Tom led a hundred thousand folks to California, into the promised land. An' he still out there..."

Which was true enough, in Debs's eyes. Which was why Ness and Purvis, as the Agents who had come closest to catching the phantom, where now headed South to investigate a report that he might be in Mobile, Alabama. They were well-placed to play their dangerous game, but they couldn't go on forever. There was a limit to the number of agitators they could ignore, the number of informants they could expose to their fellows.

Ness liked to think they were making a difference. One day they'd get caught, exposed and purged. Then they might be real heroes.

"That's some story," Purvis told Fetchit. The Negro grinned, and took a pull on the bottle.

"It weren't quite like that," said a skinny white guy with a cap pulled low over one eye. "I was there."

"You saw Tom Joad?" asked Purvis.

The hobo nodded, then qualified himself. "Missed the shootin', 'cause I showed up just as everyone else was fixin' to move out. Saw a feller who said he was Tom Joad. Said he'd killed the Enforcer and all troubles were ended. Might have been him, might not. Sure talked a fine speech, but unlike a lot of them talkers, he could do a deed or two on the side."

Ness shrank back into the shadows. The man looked familiar, but so did everyone they met on the road.

"Why ain't you in California still?" Purvis asked.

The hobo shrugged. He was a quiet, rangy man, and his voice was flat, the clipped tones of some mid-west farm.

"Didn't take to oranges, I guess."

The hobo rubbed his cap, and Ness saw the long-healed scar by his eye. It was like the red badge he had picked up in Carson City.

"That feller," Ness said. "The one who made the speech. What did you reckon? Was he Tom Joad?"

The hobo gave a sad smile. "Well, if he weren't then, he sure is now."

TEDDY BEARS' PICNIC

1965-1969

Bob splashed tap-water into his eyes, and tried to blink away the throbbing in his head. He wasn't supposed to be hung over til tomorrow, but everyone and his uncle was buying him drinks. In the Ladies' Lounge, he'd gone easy, knocking back only the sweet sherry his Mam and Thelma drank. He wished now he'd stuck to the Back Bar and brown ale.

Then again, Terry had just put a couple of gallons through his kidneys, on top of a fish and chip buttie tea, and he was in a worse state than Bob. Terry was in one of the stalls, hands jellyfish on the floor, chinning the porcelain rim as he spewed.

Bob went over and hooked his hands into Terry's armpits, lifting him up and aiming his mouth at the toilet bowl. He felt the racking of reverse peristalsis—a term remembered from school—run through Terry's ribs. The last of the chips and Mother's Pride came up as beery sludge.

"She let you tup her last night," Terry said. "Tight-drawers Thelma."

That was true.

"So thought you were going to die in foreign parts, so she dropped 'em for you."

That was arguable.

Yet more came up out of the bottom of Terry's stomach. It must be the last of it.

"She'll never understand, that one."

Bob hauled Terry upright and wiped his face with a rough paper towel, getting off the worst of the sick.

"You smell like a tramp's dustbin."

Terry touched a fist to his chest and lightly thumped Bob over the heart.

"She'll never get in here, Bob. Not bloody Thelma."

"I should hope not. It's the Gents."

"Ahh get on with you, you know what I mean."

Bob did.

"Come on, Bob. Back to the battlefront...King, country and Strongarm Ruby Red Bitter are calling."

Terry lurched out of the toilets. Bob followed, as he had been following his mate since St Godric's primary school.

Thelma had been furious when he volunteered. She'd screamed at him that he didn't have to go in the Army—he could have had a medical exemption from National Service for his flat feet—and that now he'd passed his City & Guilds he should make a career for himself, but oh no, he had to sign up just because his best pal Terry had...

The smell of piss was worse in the corridor outside the Gents. There was a sound, as if someone had left a tap running. Bob ran into Terry's back. By the stairs stood a fat bloke in a dark suit. It took a moment to realise he was piddling against the wall.

"I don't much like flock wallpaper either," said Terry, "but this is taking it a bit far."

The man turned and zipped the fly on immense trousers.

"It's me own fookin' club, y'daft get," he snorted in broad Mancunian. "I can take a burst where I fookin' like."

Bob recognised the fat man. The Comedian was chairman and secretary of the club. He was in with Jack Carter, and in this part of town, Jack Carter ran everything.

The Comedian looked at them. "I know you lads. It's your party tonight, in't it? Do or die, king and country?"

Somehow, Bob didn't want to admit it. But Terry took an unsteady bow.

"Daft bastards," the Comedian said, not without admiration. He pulled out a wad of notes. With pee-smelling fingers, he peeled off four blue fivers and shoved them into Bob's hankie pocket.

"Buy yourselves some slant-eyed scrubber in Saigon, lads."

Terry tried to thank him but spasmed again, bending double to drool thin bile on the already-stained carpet. Bob held him up.

"That's a fookin' pretty picture."

The Comedian's enormous mouth opened in a bark of laughter that shook all his mounds of fat. Terry coughed again, hawking stomach lining.

"Fare thee well, lads," said the Comedian. "And when you get to the Bloody 'Chine, kill some fookin' treens for the Wheeltappers and Shunters Social Club. Bring us back a necklace of ears we can hang on the darts trophy."

He put his hand round the full glass and left it there. He told Bet Lynch to have one herself.

"Don't mind if I do, Bob," said the barmaid, looking him up and down. He'd lost a lot of weight. "A vodka-tonic. That'll be four and ninepence please."

1965 seemed a long time ago. Prices had doubled in two years. Everything in Indo or the NAAFI was dirt cheap. It was as well he had a wedge of back-pay from the months when he couldn't spend it.

Bet gave him change, peering at him from under vast false eyelashes like hideous jungle insects. He could hear her thinking "poor love, the things you've been through..."

At quarter to two on a wet Sunday in February, the Club was almost empty. The few customers were old lads, men with no missus at home to do them Sunday dinner. They looked up from the *News of the World* and eyed him. Word of his adventures had obviously come home ahead of him.

He'd sent a telegram saying he'd be back Monday, but had made it a day earlier. The taxi had dropped him off at the house an hour ago, but there was no-one in and he didn't have a key. Mam and Dad must have gone to Auntie Glad's in Hartlepool. He went over to Thelma's and found she'd gone on the bus to visit a schoolfriend in Thornley. Walking by Terry's parents' house, he noticed a boarded-over window. There was a red paint splash like blood on the front door.

He looked at the beer. Foam ran down the sides of the glass. He strained to hear the fizz. Hundreds of tiny bubbles burst. A pint of Whitbread Trophy Bitter! The pint that thinks it's a quart! He'd liked the IPA in the NAAFI and Tiger Beer in Saigon, but Trophy was the taste of home, the taste of before.

Maybe because he was a sort of hero or someone further up the chain of contempt thought he was cute, or maybe it was just procedure, but they'd decided to Blighty him fast. After a few days' checkup at a base hospital at Cam Ranh Bay, he was on the gozome bird.

The RAF had a few ancient, hideously noisy, Sunderland flying boats to shuttle quacks and Blighty Ones from Cam Ranh Bay to whatever troopship was nearest home. In a few days T for Tommy flew him from Indo to Rangoon, Calcutta, Karachi and Aden. He was dropped him off at Port Said to join the SS *Uganda*. Nobody from his unit was on board, but some of the blokes had heard about him. Before they passed Malta he'd been awarded honourary extra stripes and invited to join the Sergeants' messdeck.

The door opened with a blast of damp air, chilling him to the bone. An old man with a toothbrush moustache, flat cap and stained overcoat ambled in, shouting to Bet that he'd have "just the usual 'alf." Further down, a man and a woman had an animated argument about whether someone's car was blue or green.

On the boat, a Welsh Sergeant-Major called Williams took a sort of shine to him. Old as the hills, he'd even been out in Burma during the Real War. Now, he was coming home from his third tour in Indo.

"You get 'ome, it's a lot smaller than it used to be," he'd said. "Not just the size of the 'ouses. Things people are worried about are smaller, too. You'll be dying for a pint of the local brew. I bet you've been dreaming about this foaming glass of Newcastle Brown or whatever muck it is you drink up there. For two years you've imagined that dirty great 'andful of beer you'll down in one the minute you get off the train. Queer stuff, beer. Wherever you go, the first pint's no bloody good. Especially at 'ome. The last pint you 'ave is always the best one."

The top of the pint had almost gone flat. Only a thin line of white foam ringed the brown liquid's surface.

He patted the pockets of his battledress trying to find a cigarette. One thing about the Army was they gave you plenty of pockets. Not like the tight bell-bottoms the younger blokes were wearing these days. The fashion came from Russia, like most daft things. He found a battered pack of Guards in the Penguin Pocket on his trousers. He took it out, along with the paperback Williams had given him, *The Edge of the Sword* by Anthony Farrar-Hockley. The author had been captured in Korea and been tortured. Farrar-Hockley had guts, but his book was very stiff upper lip, officerly and British and matter of fact. If Bob wrote up his story, he wouldn't be nearly so polite.

They had docked at Avonmouth late last night. Troopships never landed at Southampton, Pompey, London or even Liverpool any more because it was "bad for morale". Indo hands returned furtively to a dock miles from anywhere, preferably in the middle of the night. It was not a heroes' welcome: no Lord Mayors, no military bands. They were greeted by glaring yellow sodium lamps, cranes, a knot of dock-workers huddling in grimy, glistening oilskins, a few MPs glowering from under the peaks of their red caps and a couple of dozen Queen Alexandra nurses in khaki cloaks…No anthems or hymns were sung, there was only the hiss of the rain on concrete, the clanking of chains, the occasional shout. There were no cigars, only the smell of bunker-oil and damp clothes, and the diesel fumes from the Deltic loco hauling the hospital train waiting on the quay for *Uganda's* less fortunate passengers.

The tab burned his throat, reminding him he'd not had anything to drink since a mug of tea at the WRVS caravan on the docks. Sod it, he thought. He lifted the glass and necked the lot in one go.

"Worth waiting for, was it?" asked Bet.

"To be perfectly honest, no. It tastes of nowt much, doesn't have enough alcohol in, and is full of gas."

He theatrically placed the empty glass by the pump-handle in front of her.

"But it is nonetheless what we drink round here, and here is home. So I'll have another pint please, Bet, love."

Off the boat, Williams saw to it that Bob was marched through demob on the double. Everyone was frightened of Sergeant-Majors, especially officers. He'd sorted Bob's pay and made sure he didn't have to bother with the nonsense of giving up his uniform and kitbag and signing for every little bloody thing. He even wangled first-class express rail warrants.

They travelled together as far as Bristol Temple Meads, then Williams had to get off to change for Swansea. He was going to spend a few weeks with his sister, then he'd be back in the Army again.

"Listen to me, lovely boy," he'd said. "Going 'ome is hard work, but you got to stick it out, see."

The next pint was a little better.

"What are you going to do, Bob?" asked Bet.

"Reckon I'll hang around 'til you close, then find a caff that's open and read the Sunday papers 'til me Mam and Dad get back home."

She looked at him, knowing he was kidding her.

"I'll go back to accountancy I suppose," he admitted. "I can count with both sets of fingers and me toes, you know."

Aye, so it's just as well you didn't get any of them shot off, isn't it? Sorry to butt in like this, man, but I had to introduce meself sooner or later. Me name's Survivor-Guilt. You and me, we're about to get to know one another right canny well, young Robert.

"You are a card Bob," said Bet. "And after everything you've been through and all."

Obviously there were stories going around town: how he'd suffered, how heroic he'd been. Maybe he should write a book so everyone would know the truth. He was lucky. He'd come back in one piece. The firm had even taken the trouble to find his BFPO address and write him that his old job was waiting. He was all right. Better than most.

Awright, Bob, whatever you say, marra.

"And what about Terry, eh?" Bet said. "Who'd have thought he'd be that big a bastard? Pardon my French. If he come in here, the only pint he'd get'd be flung in his bloody rotten face."

"*Do I look like a fanny?*" yelled Sergeant Grimshaw, face up close against Terry's. "I repeat, do I look like a fanny?"

"No, sergeant," Terry said, wide-eyed.

"Then *why* are *you* trying to *fuck* me? You 'orrible Northern bollockbrain scum-filth snot-gobbling shit-faced granny-shagger."

Bob, backbone rigid, swivelled his eyes. Terry seemed to be blasted by the sergeant's breath.

"And what are *you* looking at, tart?"

Grimshaw loomed up against Bob, eyes huge.

"Are you his girlfriend? Are you two nancy-boys homos of the botty-banging jessie persuasion? I'll have no unauthorised buggery in my barracks."

There were thirty or so young men on the parade ground, still in civvies, suitcases beside them. They were almost all National Servicemen, barely willing to heed the call of their country. Someone sniggered.

A weight was lifted from Bob and Terry, as the sergeant wheeled off to shout at someone else.

"Let me make myself perfectly clear, ladies. These two poove puddings may be lower than the shreds of toe-cheese I scrape out of my socks, but you are all equally worthless in my eyes. You are all, I repeat all, less than nothing. You are merely the fanny-discharge of your miserable whores of mothers. After nine weeks, you may, and I underline may, be elevated from the mud to the position of Private Soldier in the service of His Majesty, the King. You, do you love His Majesty, the King?"

The sergeant addressed a London lad called Butler, whose permanent grin could not be wiped away. Bob and Terry had met him at the station, on route to Basic Training Depot No. 9, which was near Walmington-on-Sea, a small town on the south coast.

"Yes, sergeant, I love His Majesty the King."

"If His Majesty the King needed to wipe his bottom after a royal shit, would you rip the tongue out of your head and humbly offer it to him as toilet paper? If His Majesty the King needed a holder for his candle-stick would you bend double from the waist and open your arsehole? If His Majesty the King required you to gob in your father's face, tit-fuck your mother and run a lawn mower over your virgin sister, would you reply 'at once Your Majesty, anything you say Your Majesty'?"

"Is that a rhetorical question, sergeant?"

The sergeant's hand latched onto Butler's crotch like a vice. Butler's eyes went red.

"Sing soprano, you spunk-eating splash of spew. Sing 'The Happy Wanderer'."

Butler screeched, tears pouring down his cheeks. Grimshaw literally squeezed the tune out of him, wringing his balls as if they were a musical instrument.

"I love to go a-wandering..." Butler yelped, stumbling through the song, "...with my knapsack on my back...fol-de-ree, fol-de-rah, fol-de-rah-hah-hah-hah-*aaarrgh*!"

Grimshaw gripped, white-knuckled, protracting the final note.

"Above us all is Lord God Almighty, who takes no interest in our affairs. Directly below God is His Majesty the King. Loyal to His Majesty the King are His Majesty's Armed Forces. His Majesty's Armed Forces have bestowed upon me absolute power of life and death over you, Butler. When I speak, it is not merely myself, Sergeant Grimshaw, speaking, but it is the voice of God, transmitted through His Majesty the King and down through every honoured echelon of His Majesty's Armed Services direct to your pustulant earholes. Can you hear me, Butler?"

The Londoner nodded through agony. Grimshaw eased his grip, then kissed him full on the lips.

"I love you, Butler. You are the best, the only, man in this whole squad. You are promoted to honourary Corporal for the duration of your basic. In my eyes, you are still the drippings from a syphilitic rat's knob-end. But, in comparison with them, you are a demi-god. You walk with giants, and you carry a Bren gun."

The sergeant stood back to survey the recruits, who stood like trees next to their suitcases and duffel bags. Bob realised the man had managed in five minutes to make a cohesive unit of young men who were mostly still strangers to each other. They were united in their utter hatred of Sergeant Grimshaw.

"In a moment, you will all get a cheap thrill," Grimshaw shouted. "Corporal Butler here will order you to strip naked. The last man out of his kit will be cleaning the bogs with his toothbrush for the next month. Then, you will be examined for hideous diseases and disgusting parasites, be given a proper haircut with scissors the size of sheep-shears, and be issued with uniforms, boots and other essential kit. You will be required to care for these with your worthless lives. Remember, these are not presents. These are lent to you for the duration of your service. Each and every bootlace and jockstrap is the personal property of His Majesty the King. If an item is damaged or lost, the rules of war require me to inflict merciless and disproportionate punishment. Butler, give the order to disrobe, now."

"Men," Butler squeak-shouted, then dropping his voice an octave, "at the double, kit *off!*"

Bob unlaced his shoes first, and began neatly to get out of his civvies, folding and piling every garment as his Mam had taught him.

Some of the others were stark naked before he had his shirt and trousers off.

Buttons pattered on the asphalt. Terry was ripping off his clothes as if invited in for late night coffee with Sabrina. It began softly to rain.

Grimshaw wove in and out of struggling lines. It was not easy to undress standing-up. Men hopped from foot to foot as they fought with socks and shoes.

Bob knew he would be last. He tried to hurry, but he could not break the habit of neatness. At last, he folded his underpants and put them on the pile. He supposed he would have to learn how to clean toilets.

Grimshaw walked past and looked down, first at his shrivelled genitals, then at his perfectly-folded square of clothes.

"Very neat, Nancy."

Bob was astonished and relieved. There were other men still trying to undress.

Finally, there was only Frank Spencer, the squeaky-voiced semi-imbecile who had been at the station with Butler. He had started undressing with his cap and worked down, and got his trousers stuck on his shoes.

Spencer fell over, sobbing silently.

"Butler, over here," Grimshaw shouted. "Piss in this man's eyes."

Bob saw Butler pause, realise how precarious his position was, and trot over to his friend. He pointed his knob, but couldn't get a flow going.

The rain was pissing down for him. Finally, he managed a pathetic dribble. He missed Spencer's face. Bob would have liked to think that was deliberate.

Spencer was crying out loud, scrabbling round like a crab, ripping his trousers apart at the seams in a last, desperate attempt to get them off.

"Rest of you, line up," Grimshaw shouted.

The rain was stinging cold, with a January wind pelting it against bare skins. Bob felt needles of ice against his back and buttocks. Like everyone, he was shaking, dripping rain droplets with every shiver.

"Best bath you've 'ad in years, you dirty beggars."

They huddled in a line, hugging themselves. Their clothes were forgotten, soaked through by the rain.

"Nobody gets a towel or a uniform until Spencer has well and truly been pissed on. And I mean by every man here."

Dread closed on Bob's heart. He had never been able to use a public urinal. He would point and feel pressure in his bladder, but it just didn't happen. He always waited for a sit-down to be free and pissed in private.

And now he didn't even need to take a slash.

Grimshaw, this elemental force of malign nature, would skip to Bob as quixotically as he had from Terry to Butler to Spencer. When he failed to produce the thinnest squirt of piss, Bob would be on the ground where Spencer was. The sergeant would probably order the rest to shit on him.

This was a nightmare that would never end. Nothing could be worse than this.

And it was only his first day in the Army.

"Sod this for a game of soldiers," Terry said through chattering teeth.

William Casper, who claimed to be eighteen but looked four years younger, was in line after Butler. He was the only other "volunteer" in the squad. He hardly had hair on his pubes. And he couldn't manage a piddle.

Bob thanked His Majesty the King and God. The wrath of Grim would not descend next on him.

"Pathetic, the lot of you."

The Sergeant picked up Spencer, who was now at last free of all clothes but his socks and shoes.

"You all right, lad?" he asked, tenderly, smiling. "Could do with a cuppa rosie lee, I'll bet."

Spencer cried out and nodded.

"You'd love to be inside, warm. Wrapped up. Jam bun. Bourbon biscuits. *Sing Something Simple* on the wireless."

Spencer looked wistful, cracked an idiotic longing smile, and sagged, almost leaning on the sergeant, a cat cuddling up to a loving owner.

"Well, you can forget that, Private Piss-Stain Spencer!" Grimshaw yelled, raping the moment to bleeding bits. "You've not earned a uniform yet. None of you human-shaped lumps of shit have. Fall in formation, and start running."

Naked and delirious, Bob collided with Terry as they tried to stand in an orderly group. Grimshaw took his swagger-stick to shins, then started whipping buttocks.

The Sergeant jogged, and Bob tried to run along after him. His feet bled on the rough asphalt, and his ankles jarred with every step. The rain was bucketing down on them.

After half an hour, Grimshaw called enough and directed them to the baths where, he delighted in telling them, they could get the filth off their feet with a nice cold shower.

Bob thought it was a wonder no one had died. He and Terry leaned against each other and limped, moaning, towards the bath-house.

Inside, immaculately uniformed, plumply pink and comfortable, was an officer. He took a look at the stumbling men, who must have seemed like survivors of some war atrocity, and his look of composure vanished. He pantomimed appalled sympathy and wheeled on Grimshaw, red-faced.

"It looks like these men have been tortured," he shouted.

"That is correct, *sah*!"

All anger vanished and the officer smiled indulgently.

"Well done," he said. "Carry on, sergeant."

Grimshaw looked at the men and shouted "into the showers, girls. And be sure to scrub behind your ears."

Bob read it over again.

Some will tell you the greatest hero the British Armed Forces have ever produced was Admiral Nelson, some will put up Monty, some General Gordon.

But to any National Serviceman who went through Basic Training Depot No. 9, the only real hero is Private Arthur Seaton. They didn't give Seaton the Victoria Cross. In fact, they hanged him and buried him in an unmarked grave. If I knew where it was, I'd smother the plot in wreaths, and so would a hundred others. Seaton, you see, was the soldier who killed Sergeant Grimshaw. Grim would have been proud of him. One shot, straight to the head, just the way he liked it. Sometimes, when I wake up thinking I'm back in Walmington-on-Sea or Khe Sanh, I sob at the injustice. Seaton wasn't in our mob. He came along months after we'd shipped out. There's not a man who trained at Walmington who wouldn't swap tickets for the Cup Final for the chance to see Sergeant Grimshaw's brains shot out. It's a tragedy it wasn't captured on film. I hope they buried Grim at a crossroads with a bayonet through his heart and a tin of bully beef rammed up his arse.

He handed the page to Thelma. Frown-lines crinkled her forehead, and she was unable not to look as if she smelled something bad.

"What do you think?"

Thelma struggled to find words. "It's a bit…hard. Really nasty."

"I can't write a soft book, love. Not about the Army, not about the war."

"It's so bitter, Bob. This poor man Grimshaw was just trying to…well, to toughen you up, make men of you. You can't still hate him."

"Thelma, Frank Spencer had eleven thumbs. He was a walking disaster. He couldn't cross the road without causing an accident. He couldn't boil a kettle without burning the water. When he got through his basic, Grimshaw wrote up a report on him and got him assigned to the REME, recommended him for *bomb-disposal*. How long do you think he lasted? There are bits of him they still haven't found."

"Have you noticed," Terry said, "how Grim fixes everything according to the weather? We get PT or beasting or cross-country runs or assault-courses only if it's cold and wet."

"Right," Bob agreed. "If the weather outside is halfway decent, we're indoors, learning how to use Blanco and Brasso, or how to clean a rifle, or how to break someone's neck with our bare hands."

"'olds and rolls and throws and breakfalls," Butler snapped, getting the sergeant's voice perfectly. "I'd like to try some 'olds on Grimmy."

"He's not such a bad bloke underneath," Casper put in.

Everyone looked at him as if he'd just admitted he fancied Hitler.

Casper was a strange one. The grand obsession of his life was bird-watching. Birds of prey.

"He's a bleedin' monster, birdy-boy," Butler said. "I tell you, when I'm out of this, back behind the wheel of a bus where the Lord intended I should be, I'll be dreaming of the day Grim steps out on that zebra crossing in front of my double-decker. Bump! Oh! Have I killed you Grim? Bloody shame! Never mind, eh?"

"But he likes you, Corporal Cockney Get," said Terry.

"Sing 'The Happy Sodding Wanderer', Geordie Shite."

"Fol-de-reeeee, fol-de-*raaaarrgh-my-bollocks!*" sang Terry.

Butler smiled. Bob couldn't get used to the way Butler and Terry tossed unforgivable insults at each other, yet had become friends for life within days.

Bob wondered if he wasn't getting a bit jealous. He was starting to feel Butler getting in the way of Bob and Terry, just as Terry always resented Thelma.

"Cheer up," Bob said. "It's a half-holiday tomorrow."

After two months, they were finally getting leave to visit the town for Saturday night. Apparently, there wasn't much to do besides visit the pier that almost got blown up in the Real War and hang around Walker's Palais de Danse. Walker's was where the local girls would be. Butler had been talking about it all week. South Coast Girls were legendary in London. Butler was full of stories about knickers lost under the pier.

Bob wondered if he'd be better for Thelma if he were more experienced. He could imagine what she'd think, especially if he caught something. Still, he'd be away for two years.

"You'll never get any birds again, Butler," said Terry. "Not after they've had some proper Northern cock. Me and Bob'll run through 'em like a dose of salts."

"I jus' want to see somewhere that's not this bloody cage," said Casper.

There were moans of assent from up and down the hut.

"Snap inspection," someone shouted.

Grimshaw burst in like the Federal Bureau of Inquisition, flanked by hard-faced corporals, pace-stick under his arm.

Everyone stood to attention by their lockers. Grimshaw started examining gear, passing brusque comments on the state of socks and confiscating copies of *Health and Efficiency* and *Tit-Bits*.

Two lockers down from Bob was Frank Spencer, a ticking bomb. His mother, one of those smothering, protective sorts, was always sending him parcels of things like vests, hot-water-bottles, and tracts on the evils of drink. She also sent tins of corned beef. He told them

136

he'd always liked it, and that his Mum must have assumed they didn't have it in the Army.

Grimshaw opened Spencer's locker, and two tins of Fray Bentos fell out.

"What's this, cuntface?"

"Two tins of c-corned beef, sergeant. From my mother."

"His Majesty's rations not good enough for you, spastic? These foreign objects are an insult to the crown. You are aware of the regulation that says you can only eat Army bully beef?"

"My Mum…"

"I'm not interested in the pox-rotted slag who birthed you between Saturday night shag sessions with Sheffield Wednesday's second team."

Irrepressible anger sparked in Spencer's eyes.

"Don't you pick on my Mum," he squeaked.

In the silence, Bob's spirit shrank. Spencer, the cringing reed, had snapped and talked back. Grimshaw would show no mercy.

"So you're missing your Mum's cooking? Have to do something about that, won't we? How'd you like a 48-hour pass so's you can visit your Mum for a slap-up feed?"

Spencer was as surprised as anyone but still mistrustful. This must be a prelude to a punishment so ghastly it would go in the record books.

Bob prayed Spencer would turn down the offer.

"Nice," Spencer said.

Bob knew the abyss had just opened up,

"Very well, Spencer, your wish shall be granted. Fairy Godmother Grimshaw will see to it that you spend this weekend in the bosom of your family. However, to compensate, all other leave is withdrawn."

Twenty-nine hearts turned to stone. Even Butler's smile vanished.

"While you, Spencer, are eating home cooking, we shall endeavour to change the situation here, so the grub comes up to your high standard of cuisine. The rest of you slags will spend the weekend peeling spuds."

Spencer could still get out of it, and turn down the leave, but he was too addle-headed to see ahead more than a few minutes. Bob knew even Frank Spencer would hardly enjoy his time at home, knowing what was waiting when he got back.

They spent Saturday in a freezing shed next to the cookhouse peeling an Everest of potatoes. Grimshaw insisted each be peeled like an apple, in a single stroke that produced a perfect spiral of peel and a completely skinless potato. Bob's fingers were cut ragged. They were so chilled and shrivelled that he couldn't feel them, but he knew agony would set in over the next few days.

Throughout it all, they talked about Frank Spencer. Terry kept up a bitter running commentary, about the warm tea and hot food he was eating.

"That Betty of his'll be giving him one right now," he said. "I bet she has to put the rubber johnny on for him, or he'd get it over his head."

There were grumbles.

Just now, much as Bob hated Grim, he hated Frank Spencer worse.

"How about a song to cheer us up?" Casper suggested, feebly. "'Boiled Beef and Carrots'?"

He was pelted with potatoes.

Finally, it was done. To one side was a heap of peelings as high as a man's waist. To the other tubs of naked potatoes, streaked with blood.

They sat in the hut, too exhausted to move.

Grimshaw arrived, fresh from the mess, and examined the work.

"A job well done, men."

He picked up a potato and tossed it into the air, catching it again like a cricket-ball. Then, he picked up a peeling and delicately wrapped it around the potato. It didn't quite fit.

"While you've been working, I've given some thought to the matter of your diet. Choosy types like your friend Spencer have made me wonder if the staple fare in our cookhouse is fine enough for your poor delicate tummies. After consideration, I've decided to take potatoes off the menu for a month. Tighten your bellies. Give you variety."

Bob was numbed. He couldn't follow Grimshaw.

"So," the sergeant continued, "we shan't need the fruits of your labours. This mess must be tidied away. Butler, get some flour and some buckets and make up paste. The rest of you, pay attention. By morning, you will have glued the peelings back in place. All neat and tidy. Tomorrow, we shall do the decent thing and bury the spuds with full military honours."

The next night, Butler and Terry held Frank Spencer down while the rest of the squad lined up, raw potatoes in their frostbitten fingers. They forced him to eat the cold, hard spuds. Frank sobbed, mouth bleeding, as he chewed. His teeth cracked on the stringy potato mulch.

Bob held Spencer's chin and forced him to swallow. He felt nothing.

"Come in, come in, dear boy. We meet at last!"

The Bloomsbury office was just as he had imagined a literary agent's would be: thick carpet, heavy mahogany furniture, a few cardboard boxes (manuscripts, no doubt), an occasional table with a bottle of sherry. The only things out of place were framed pictures, messy collages made of pictures scissored from books and magazines.

Kenneth Halliwell looked the part, too, wearing a silk dressing gown, smoking a pink Sobranje in a cigarette-holder.

He pressed a desk buzzer, "Joseph, could you delight us a moment with your presence."

A man popped in. Joseph wore Russian-style bell-bottoms and a white vest. In his thirties, he was trying to look younger. His glossy hair was down over the tops of his ears.

"Bob and I are in need of some refreshment. Would you procure some tea?"

"Earl Grey, Lapsang Souchong or Ty-Phoo?"

Halliwell's assistant had a thin voice, with a little Leicester in it somewhere. Bob chose Earl Grey. It wasn't Ty-Phoo and was easier to pronounce than Lapsang Souchong. Joseph flounced out.

"I am sorry about the boy," said Halliwell. "Sometimes I think, 'if only I had a hammer...' It's so hard to get the help. Poor Joe fancies himself a writer, but he just hasn't got it. He keeps turning out silly little plays, daft experimental stuff full of obscenities. How does he imagine he'd ever get by the Lord Chamberlain?"

Halliwell picked up what Bob realised was his manuscript.

"This, on the other hand, is good. Needs a polish, but I think we have something very saleable. It's raw, it's immediate, direct. Above all it's angry, without being unpatriotic. I shouldn't think we'll have too much trouble with the censors, though I hope to Heaven we have a little."

"Why do you want trouble with the censors?"

Even a publishing novice like Bob knew how heavily the Lord Chamberlain could come down on a book. The *Lady Chatterley* trial had all but bankrupted Penguin, and the upholding of the Obscenity verdict by Lord Chief Justice Goddard had forced everyone to play safe.

"Because, dear boy, every time the papers report that a book worries the censors, it means an extra ten thousand copies."

Ten thousand copies! An *extra* ten thousand copies! But only if they weren't pulped by the Post Office.

"I also took the liberty of getting a Roneo of your manuscript sent to Gelbfisch."

"Schmuel Gelbfisch? The Russian film producer?"

"He's Polish actually. Well, Jewish really. Gelbfisch won't read your book himself. He has people to do that for him. Sam dodders into London every year to buy books and plays. I know he's desperate to do a film about the Indo-China War. The Russkies are just as mired in it as we are, and the right story could be terrific box-office."

He knew he was being a prat, but Bob couldn't help but imagine Albert Finney playing him, and Larushka Skikne as Terry, with Michael Caine maybe as Stan Butler. Julie Christie as Thelma, William Pratt as Grimshaw, Jack Hawkins as Molesworth, Peter O'Toole as Fotherington-Thomas. A Royal Film Premiere, with the King and the Tsarina. Queues outside the Regal, with his name up in lights.

"We're going to have to think of a title. Joseph suggested *It Ain't Half Hot, Mum*. I quite like it. Conjures the insolent cheeriness of the ordinary soldier, but also suggests sentimentality and yearning for home. What do you think?"

"Actually, Mr. Halliwell…"

"Kenneth, please…"

"Actually, er, Kenneth, I don't like that at all. It's the sort of thing a Londoner would say. I'm from the North-East."

"Oh. Pity."

"Mortar!" yelled Bob "Hit the deck!"

A second shell fell with an ill-tempered crump into a paddy field. A ten-foot tall column of water rose.

Everyone yelled at everyone else to take cover. Bob threw himself at the dirt next to a wooden hut. He took the safety off his SLR and chanced a peep over a low wall of baked mud. Lieutenant Gurney paced up and down about thirty yards away, right out in the open, scanning the treeline with binoculars.

"Bloody toff," said Terry, crawling up beside Bob.

"He's trying to draw their fire so's we can get some idea where they are."

"He's showing off is what he's doing," said Terry. "He's a belted earl. He has to prove he's got more guts than us proles."

A ball of oily flame engulfed the lieutenant.

"Christ in Heaven," said Terry. "I didn't mean *that*!"

Burning pieces of Jack Gurney filled the air. They were breathing him, choking on him.

Casper squirmed up next to them.

"See any small-arms?"

"Nowt yet. Only mortars. They just hit Lieutenant Gurney."

"That was no mortar. He trod on a mine."

Bob's stomach clenched. This wasn't a chance encounter with the treens. The platoon had been drawn into a trap.

He flinched as a machine gun opened up from the treeline about three hundred yards away. Tracers churned up the ground a comfortable distance beyond the wall. Earth pattered on them.

"Aye, this spot'll do," said Casper.

He unslung a long leather case from his back and drew out a lovingly-oiled Lee-Enfield. From one of his ammunition-pouches, he took a telescopic sight wrapped in oilcloth. Neatly, he fixed the sight to the rifle.

Casper was the platoon sniper. He'd been in Indo ten days when he took the brigade trophy for skill-at-arms.

Butler came over.

"Snudge says we're to set up along here with whatever cover we can. He's put one of the Brens over to our right. He says you're to set up here too, Casper. If you clock anything wearing pyjamas, slot it and pray it's Ho Chi Mekon himself."

"Willco," Casper breathed. His mind was already miles away, willing victims to wander into his cross-hairs.

Bob was starting to be afraid of little William Casper, with his hawk-eyes and ever-mounting kill score. He was an ancient child, more bird of prey than man.

Bob, Terry and Butler sat with backs to the wall and heads well down. If Vic tried to come at them across open rice paddies, they'd hear about it soon enough.

"What are we in for?" asked Terry.

"Dunno," said Butler. "Snudge is dialling 999."

A shell burst very close to the wall. Bob's ears hurt. Nobody said anything for a while.

At the morning briefing, Captain Fisher, the battalion intelligence officer, had said this would be a routine Bryant and May raid. Everyone home in time for tea and the football results on the Forces Broadcasting Service. It was only as the platoon was rattling along a dirt road in a couple of old Matadors that Butler told Bob why the old sweats groaned when Captain Fisher walked into the tent.

Bob had liked Fisher. He had a soft West Yorkshire accent, not a wireless announcer drawl like Gurney. He seemed an ordinary bloke. But behind his back, he was called Billy Liar. The Indo-China War in his head was long over and he was mopping up before the Victory Parade. Nothing he said bore any relationship with the truth. The way Fisher told it, all they had to do was come out here and burn down this village.

The civilians and their livestock had already been moved to a protected compound (which was what Fisher insisted they call concentration camps). This was in keeping with the policy in the British sector of depriving the Viet-Cong or any NVA infiltrators of help from the civil population.

The tactic had worked in Malaya in the 1950s, prompting Anthony Eden, the Saviour of Suez, to commit himself to the Relief of Indo-China. Eden hoped to replay World War II, with himself as Churchill and Ho Chi Minh, "that little Indo-Chinese Upstart", cast as Hitler. When France went communist after the War, they pulled out of their former colonies, leaving a few idealogues—Red Jesuits, they called them—behind. A "democratic" regime sprouted, puppeteered by French colonial die-hards who refused to follow the Paris line, but that collapsed after the humiliation visited on all those battle-hardened Maurices at Dien Bien Phu. It fell to Britain and her Empire and Commonwealth to disinfect Indo on behalf of the free world. Naturally, Russia couldn't let that happen, so Premier Kissinger got up in the Duma and pledged to match the Brits man for man and gun for gun. Eden and Kissinger both claimed to have made the first commitment to South-East Asia. The British and Russian armies each referred to their allies as "reinforcements".

It had been bloodless enough to start with, merely a matter of sending a few technicians and instructors to help the regimes in the Republic of South Vietnam. Now the commies were on the march again, with the support of plenty of folk fed up with the corrupt and incompetent succession of governments in Saigon. What had started as a "limited police action" with a few Gurkhas had in seven years become so popular it was keeping 100,000 British and 20,000 Anzac troops in work, not to mention the 150,000 Russians (and rising) who'd come along, too. Enoch Powell, Eden's successor as Prime Minister, would gladly give the whole bloody shooting-match to the Ivans, *anyone dammit!*, and get Britain out. But a British Government's word was its bond, and the Russians couldn't be allowed win the war on their own.

The British were supposed to be fighting American-backed communists, but strategists spent more time jockeying for position with the Russians. A *Punch* cartoon showed King Edward VIII and Tsarina Tatiana in full state uniforms standing over a map of Indo-China, squabbling about who would administer which regions "when the victory was won", while a tiny, ragged Ho said "what do you mean 'when'?"

The treens found their range. One of the eggs landed somewhere behind them, in the village. Someone yelled "first aid!"

It all happened in slow motion. Bob reckoned he should have been deafened by the racket from the explosions. Somehow, he wasn't. He was in mortal danger here and realised he was enjoying it, savouring it. It was something to write home about. This was making a man of him.

"The condemned men are entitled to a last smoke," said Terry, offering round Capstans.

They all lit up. Someone scurried over at a low crouch.

"Put those fuckers out you stupid fucks!" shouted Sergeant Snudge. "Fucking treens can see your fucking smoke a fucking mile away. Then you fuckers'll be fucking fucked."

Bob stubbed the cigarette. He knew Snudge—bloody silly name—didn't like him. None of the old lags did. They were new bugs, the sprogs, and as such bad joss. Regulars despised National Servicemen, claiming that they tended to get themselves and others killed, but the one time Bob snapped and declared himself as a volunteer, he was scorned even more openly.

"The Mekon's got us pinned," said Snudge. "We can't rush him because we don't know where he is or how strong he is, and it's over nearly-open ground. We can't do a runner because the little bastards have cut the fucking road as well. I've radioed for help, but we've to wait here until Billy Liar finds the bottle to tell Lieutenant-Colonel Windrush he's fucked up afuckinggain. Then we have to wait until Windrush finishes dithering and gets Brigade's permission to call for assistance. Just pray it's the dropshorts and not the fucking Raf. If you see any aircraft, then for fuck's sake, fucking hide. Now get dug in. If a firework comes your way before you've got a hole, flatten yourself on the dirt face-down. And keep your gob open. It'll stop you going deaf. Butler, report to Popeye, collect some spare ammo, and a crate of gold-tops and pineapples. Get yourselves nice and fucking comfy. It's going to be a fucking long day."

Bob wasn't enjoying this anymore.

Terry had the spade, a crummy little thing with a handle no longer than his forearm. Eighteen inches down and he hit water. Not surprising, with a paddy field not close by.

"Bollocks!" said Terry.

Two shells landed in front of them in rapid succession, spattering loose change against the wall.

Bob's ears were ringing.

"They're comin'," said Casper quietly, from behind his rifle-sight. "Usin' t'mud banks in t'paddy for cover. I see at least five. Can't get a bead on any yet."

"I'll tell Snudge and get the ammo," said Butler, crawling at speed towards the middle of the village.

Moments later, a vast cage of hot metal enveloped them. Mortar shells exploded all around, machine-gun bullets hammered the dirt wall. Any more and the wall would simply disintegrate.

Bloody Yanks.

The Mekon's Communist Allies, the United Socialist States of America, were pledged to support North Vietnam and the Viet Cong to the hilt. Except there were no actual Yanks in Indo. They'd learned a lesson invading Japan in '45 and liked to get others to do their fighting in the Pacific Rim. There was a supply route—the Casey Jones Trail—running through the warring statelets that used to be China, all the way down to Cambodia. By the feel of it, all that Yank ordnance was being delivered right here.

Casper fired, smoothly slid his rifle-bolt back, then forward, and bit his lower lip. He'd got one.

Butler came back, dragging two wooden boxes behind him. "Help yourselves," he said. One box contained smooth, round phosphorus grenades—gold-tops. In the other were the Mills bombs—pineapples—beloved of the Commando comics Bob and Terry had read as kids.

They spaced out behind the wall, laying out grenades and spare magazines. They'd lost interest in digging in.

There was a bigger than usual explosion behind them. Black smoke. Popping and zipping noises. The Mekon's mortars had brewed up one of the lorries, and plenty of spare ammunition by the sound of it.

Bob was breathing too fast. Was this what a panic attack felt like?

"Terry?" he shouted.

"Kiddo?" said Terry, tightening the chinstrap on his helmet.

"Nothing," said Bob.

"Aye, mate," said Terry, smiling. "Me too."

At the far end of the wall, the Bren opened up. Short, intense bursts hammered like a pneumatic drill. Casper fired over and over, working his rifle-bolt like the pistons of the Flying Scotsman.

Bob peered over the wall, saw the top of a head—a shock of black hair—over a little mud-bank a hundred yards off. He aimed, squeezed the trigger—almighty bang!—and missed. The Bren tore up water and mud. Bob jammed himself against the wall, head well down, and held the rifle over his head with both hands, working the trigger with his thumb, trying to stop the thing flying out of his hands, firing in the general direction of the enemy.

A gold-top exploded like some pure white blossom, sending thin trails zipping out in every direction, searing squiggles into his eyeballs. Gleaming aluminium roared overhead. Trees burned like a Guy Fawkes bonfire.

"Canberras!" shouted Butler.

"*English Electric* Canberras," said Bob.

The napalm and the heat of the engines made the air look like the clear, freezing water of a brook in the Yorkshire Dales.

The Main Humanities Lecture Hall of the University of Sussex was packed to capacity. Students even sat cross-legged in the aisles. There were nearly a thousand of them out there, all impossibly young and fresh. Bob had only a couple of years on the older ones, but they looked like they came from another world. Clean-cut girls in college scarves and duffel-coats; Beetniki aping Russian style in goatee beards, bell-bottoms and Afghan coats; clever, angry lads from pit villages and factory towns; ironic, waspish waifs who had failed Oxbridge entrance and were going the plateglass route.

"Settle down, please," said Dr. Dixon from the podium.

Bob hadn't wanted to come, but Kenneth had pleaded. It would get into the papers, it would sell more of books.

He glanced across the stage at the men with whom he would debate. Francis Urquhart, the local MP, was talking down to the bewildered Jim Hacker, a former Eden protégé serving his time as a Junior Minister. The government spokesmen sat unsubtly to the right, while Bob was next to Howard Kirk, reader in Sociology, who took the extreme left. Author of *The Russians Can Bloody Have Constantinople*, a book about radical opposition to British imperialism, the long-haired academic smoked a roll-up with casual arrogance.

"I suppose this is as quiet as it's going to be," said Dixon, nervously, "perhaps we can get started."

There was a uproar and cheering as a group of students unfurled a long banner. They wore American-style broad-brimmed hats and sleeveless leather jackets with red tin sheriff star badges. Dixon attempted an apologetic smile that came out as a grimace. The thirty-foot-long banner declared WORKERS AND INTELLECTUELS UNITE AGAINST ANGLO-RUSSIAN IMPERIALISM IN INDO-CHINA.

Urquhart sneered at the misspelling. Hacker asked to have it pointed out, then laughed loudly at "intellectuels". Men with cameras—press?—took pictures of the banner.

His book had been out for five weeks and garnered good reviews. Bernard Levin, Malcolm Muggeridge and Christopher Booker praised him in the *Times*, *Punch* and the *Statesman*. Even a blimp called Brigadier Alistair Lethbridge-Stewart, drafted by the *Daily Telegraph* to pass comment, acknowledged Bob had "seen a thing or two," though he finally dismissed the book as "a rather insolent eructation from the ranks".

Dixon introduced the panel. The politicians were hissed, which upset Hacker but steeled Urquhart's contempt for young people. Kirk grinned and waved at the regimented clapping which greeted him. This was not an impartial crowd.

"And finally," said Dixon, "an Indo-China veteran who, as author of *It Ain't Half Hot, Mum*, has done much to bring into the public arena questions about British involvement in the war."

Students cheered and whistled. For *him*! They kept on cheering. Kirk was a bit put out. Bob was puzzled, but thrilled. At last, he had his hero's welcome, from people who had looked down at him all his life.

"Perhaps we could begin," said Dixon, "by asking Bob for an assessment of the feelings of the ordinary soldier about service in Indo-China. Do the troops feel as though they don't belong there?"

Over and again, Captain Vinh had asked the same question, between punches, slaps, and blows from rifle-butts. Bob never did have an answer. For Vimto or anyone else.

"To be honest," he said, "most squaddies have no strong opinion on whether they should be there or not. They've been called up..."

"What I think Bob's trying to say," interrupted Kirk, "is that our soldiers have been lied to by the British and Russian governments. Well over ninety percent of our servicemen in Indo-China are conscripts..."

"What I think Bob's trying to say," interrupted Urquhart, "is that our splendid lads are doing their duty like honest, loyal patriots..."

"What I think Bob is saying is..." interrupted Hacker.

He never got the chance to finish. The hall erupted. Some students jeered and whistled, the others chanted "*Heavens no, we won't go!*"

Most boys here would have National Service deferred so they could complete their education. Then they'd be called up. At least half would end up in Indo during their two years. Bob wasn't sure how he felt about the politics, but he honestly couldn't blame them for not wanting to go. He'd been stupid enough to volunteer.

"This war is none of our business," shouted Kirk above the din, to huge cheers. Urquhart tried to say something about an international duty to save the world from the evils of American Communism. Hacker looked queasy.

Over to the side of the stage, a tall, muscular middle-aged bloke in a suit, short hair, thin lips, definitely ex-military—Hacker's bodyguard?—spoke into a walkie-talkie.

A knot of men in brown corduroy trousers and polo-neck sweaters moved rapidly down the left hand edge of the hall towards the stage. Bob knew at once these were serious people, not like the rich poseurs wearing Red Chic slouch hats and tin stars.

He reached for the commando-knife taped as always to his ankle. Then he remembered he was the hero here. They'd be after the MPs.

Objects flew.

Bob's entire body flinched, and he fought the urge to throw himself flat on the stage. He heard explosions and gunfire, but it was just the slamming of spring-hinged wooden seat-bottoms as kids stood up.

He looked at Hacker and Urquhart, who were cringing behind a human wall. The bodyguard's broad back was splattered with egg-yolks.

Bob shook, uncontrollably.

With a straight face, Captain Fisher assured us our action had been an outstanding success. We had killed fifteen Viet-Cong, wounded another twenty and captured two machine guns and 42 assorted small-arms, all American-made. We listened in astonishment. There was only our platoon involved and as soon as the Raf pounded what may or may not have been enemy positions, the treens just faded away. I only saw a single dead enemy—the one Casper hit—and we certainly didn't carry off any weapons. Our score was one dead lieutenant—posthumous VC, of course, for the 14th Earl—and three men wounded. Nonetheless "Billy Liar" wrote it up as a victory. I don't know if anybody higher up the chain of command really believes him, but my impression is that we are sinking further into the mire of Indo because "Fisher" is too soft-hearted to tell his superiors how badly we're doing. In turn, they are too timid to tell the generals, who keep the worst of it from Enoch Powell, who tells the King we won the War in 1964. The only people who realise we're losing are sergeants, and they're as inscrutable as hateful buddhas. If they had any opinions of their own, they'd die rather than let them out. Believe me, I've seen that happen.

In the senior common room Bob drank whisky with Dixon, Kirk and a few others. After the Minister and the MP fled, Kirk had turned the meeting into an anti-war rally, hijacking Bob's book for his political ends. Bob flustered and turned red at first, but part of him enjoyed the hero-worship of a thousand passionate and intelligent young people. And it was hard to argue with Kirk's line that Britain had no business in Indo-China.

Dixon came over, evidently half-cut. "You know, old man, we tried to get your pal to come along."

"Terry?"

The name was a stone in Bob's mouth.

"He's controversial, isn't he? Does he mean it?"

He was vaguely surprised Terry hadn't come up earlier.

"Yes, Dr. Dixon."

"Jim, please."

"Yes, Jim. Terry means what he says."

Bob hadn't seen Terry since coming back, and Terry had made no attempt to contact him. Most people thought what Terry had done was treasonable, but Bob hadn't written it that way. The least he could do was give his oldest friend the benefit of a doubt.

Would Terry have got three cheers from the students? Yes, he probably would.

"Hello," said a woman. Bob looked into startling eyes. She was in her late teens or early twenties and slim, with long straight hair and an elfin face. She wore blue corduroy bell-bottoms and an embroidered *Afghantsy* coat.

"Bob, this is Diana. Diana Scott."

"I'm a drama student," she said. "I'm with Howard. Dr. Kirk."

Bob guessed what that meant. Lucky bastard.

A woman in early middle aged bustled into the room, all smiles and theatrical kisses.

"Who's that?" said Bob.

"Howard's wife," admitted Diana. "Probably come to collect him. It's her birthday. They're going to the theatre. The latest Rattigan. Howard's looking forward to shredding it."

He looked funny at her, trying to work it out. She sighed and smiled indulgently. Bob must seem amazingly provincial to her. He was painfully conscious of his accent.

"It's an open marriage. They're well-known for it. They regard wedlock as patriarchal and exploitative."

Bob had read about this kind of thing in the *Observer*. Him and Thelma would be in bed together of a Sunday morning, with the papers. He'd make fun of it, but secretly be envious; she'd be disgusted, but be secretly threatened.

That was back when they were still sharing a bed. Recently, Thelma was losing interest in sex, and objected to him screaming in his sleep. Then there was the business of keeping the commando-knife under the pillow. Just in case burglars came in when they were asleep, he said.

Everybody nagged them both about having kids.

"Come on, Bob," said Diana. "I don't want to spend the rest of the evening drowning in sherry with these tweedy codgers. There's a wine bar just opened in town. From there we can go on to a discotheque."

They had 72 hours' leave. Lieutenant Noote, the padre, had tried to muster a team for "a game of footer against our ARVN friends." Bob was deputed to tell him that the platoon would rather spend time in Saigon.

It was hard to explain without mentioning whores. Bob knew Noote understood the situation exactly, but still felt guilty for disappointing the poor man. The padre was okay.

He tried not to think about Thelma.

During awkward pauses in the conversation, Noote's office rattled with skiffle from his wireless. Mostly, the Forces Broadcasting Service played ballads and big band, but there was one anarchic announcer— Simon Dee—who played Lonnie Donegan, Chas McDevitt and Ray Ellington, and was starting to give needle-time to radical new music coming out of Russia and Ireland and even Great Britain.

You never heard Lulu or Cilla Black, who sang as if they were desperate for a shag, on *Two-Way Family Favourites*, and certainly you never heard

Alan Price or the Quarrymen, or Newcastle's own People's Balladeer, Alan Hull. Those songs made Bob feel things he'd couldn't say out loud. Angry, joyous, sexual, Northern things. He couldn't hear Price's "Kalinka" without wanting to explode, and there was something dreadful in the Quarrymen's "gallant cossack horsemen in their thousands dying" he couldn't get out of his mind.

Saigon would have been wonderful if there wasn't a war on. All the mystery of the orient combined with the chic of France, the former colonial power. Many of the buildings are elegant, the food—if you can be bothered to wander beyond the NAAFI—is a marvellous mixture of French and oriental, the streets are full of bustle and life. Whole families riding on Russian motorbikes, street traders selling cigarettes and souvenirs, kids asking for buckshee...and the women. But before a squaddy could find himself a nice girl and exchange ten shillings for three or four minutes of true love, he had to get tanked up. That was easy in Saigon, if dangerous. Walking into a bar where the Anzacs were drinking was asking to be duffed up. When Aussies get more than two "tubes" of Fosters in them, they start wondering what they are doing in Indo. Then they reason Britain got them in the war. Their next impulse is to find a Pom and knock his teeth out.

The air was thick with the screeches: "*I want you give me one, Tommy.*" "*Bet you fancy me, Brian.*" "*Sucky-fucky, ten-bob note!*"

As Terry negotiated with some fifteen-year-old street angel, her younger sister was draping herself around Bob, fingers fluttering against his fly.

"I love you long-time, Tommy," she cooed in his ear. "Do you fine knee-trembler."

Butler came along and unpeeled the girl.

Bob wanted to deck the cockney bastard. But he was also grateful. The longer he was in Indo, the harder he found it to be unfaithful to Thelma. At first, like everyone, he had been on holiday; all arrangements were suspended, all bets were off. Sex was affordable and available all the time, and no one thought less of you for whoring.

Every time, he thought more about Thelma and disappointed himself. The funny thing was that sometimes he couldn't even remember what Thelma looked like.

All around him were tiny, pretty faces. Almond eyes dark as night, tiny teeth sharp as pins.

"Watch the door, our kid," Terry said, as he and Bob went upstairs. Bob nodded.

Often, soldiers were interrupted *in flagrante* by chopper-waving young men claiming to be brothers or fiancés of supposedly nice girls. It took a lot more than ten bob to square them.

Down the street, a radio was playing. "A Mouse Lived in a Windmill in Old Amsterdam" by Ronnie Hilton. All signs were in faded French and Vietnamese, battered English and new-painted cyrillic. Everywhere, there were posters for Vimto. Some of the whores believed douching with the stuff prevented conception and VD.

The Russians were taking over in Indo-China, relieving the British in the south, particularly the Mekong and the Piedmont areas. The Brits ran the show on the coastal plains and the highlands, where most guerilla activity was. HM Forces had more practice at dealing with that than Ivan. Popeye Popplewell said the year before you could get "sucky-fucky" in Saigon for half a crown. The Russkies drove prices up, and wore girls out. They did everything to excess. Including, so dark rumour had it, commit war crimes.

A staff car cruised by, scattering children. In the back, an ARVN officer sat bolt upright, with more braid on his uniform than a cinema usher. With him sat a veiled Dragon Lady, one of the daughters of Fu Manchu.

An ox-cart got in the way and the car stopped. The officer stood up to shriek at a peasant, who shrugged. The officer ordered his driver to reverse. The Dragon Lady leaned forward to whisper in the driver's ear and something flashed. The driver's head tilted back, a red yawn opening in his throat. Bob saw, but the officer didn't.

A tiny gun went off, and the top of the officer's head came off in his hat. He tumbled out of the car like an unstrung Muffin the Mule.

The Dragon Lady vaulted out of the car, *ao dai* riding up to reveal bare and boyish calves. She paused, pointing a gloved hand at Bob. Her ladylike gun was almost swallowed by her velvet fist.

His guts were ice. The sound was turned way down.

A breeze lifted the veil and he saw a man's face. A European face. The world wasn't making sense.

Then he was gone and noise fell in on Bob. Ronnie Hilton was still singing that a windmill with mice in was hardly surprising. The staff car's engine was still turning over.

Terry and Butler came down, buttoning up, big grins on their stupid faces. Bob was still shivering.

Whistles sounded. Bob looked at faces in the street. No one had made any more attempt than he had to detain the assassin. No one seemed even to notice anything unusual.

Terry took charge and got them out of there before the police arrived. "Blimey, Bob," said Butler. "Can't leave you alone for a minute."

On our last evening in Pay-Gone there was an ENSA concert hosted by Simon Dee in an aircraft-hangar on the edge of town. The comedian was supposed to be Terry Milligan, but he was cancelled by the Ministry of Defence because he'd thrown a batter pudding at 10 Downing Street in protest at the war. Instead, we got Arthur Askey dressed as a bumble-bee. Cliff Richard came on and brought the house down with "I've Got Sixpence", Britain's Eurovision entry that year. I think even he was surprised at the way everyone sang along, but he probably wasn't aware of the superstition among troops in Indo. On the exact date when you have just six months' service left you start a "chuff chart". Thereafter, you tick off each day as it passes. This gave rise to a song popular in camps and barracks throughout South-East Asia:

I've got six months, lousy ****ing six months,
Six months to hang on to my life,
I've got two months to whore, two months to be sore,
And two months to get cured for my wife.

You won't have read in the papers about what happened next. The censors like you to think our troops are wholesome chaps who suspend their sexual desire for the duration of hostilities until they can go home and get married. That night, as a troupe of go-go dancers called Pan's People kicked into their routine, two thousand battle-scarred squaddies rushed the stage. Vietnamese girls are beautiful, but they don't look like the girls back home. We'd none of us seen a girl from back home for quite a while. In their spangled union jack shorts and halters, with long white legs and bulging breasts, Pan's People were the girls from home we had all been imagining every night. Any man in the audience would have raped the pack of them —seeing on each the faces of his fiancée, girlfriend, some shopgirl, a meter maid—while the rest of us cheered him on.

Redcaps came in with firehoses and doused our ardour. I understand two blokes were crushed in the chaos. I wonder what they told the families.

Diana had a rich father and a Triumph Spitfire. It made getting to Avening a lot simpler. All morning they'd driven through the Cotswold countryside, stopping for a pub lunch of cheese, beer and fresh bread.

No scampi and chips in a basket here. This was England as everyone wanted it to be. With the aid of the AA map, they'd finally found Avening and asked a man at the local garage for directions to the Powell place.

In the back garden, next to a heap of uncut firewood, was a battered Land Rover. The cottage was tiny, cut into the side of a hill at the top of a country lane. It seemed unusually modest for the home of the director of *A Matter of Life and Death*.

Bob knocked. Somewhere a dog barked. The door opened. A small man in his sixties answered. He wore a cardigan and frayed carpet-slippers. He had a small, meticulously-groomed moustache, a large, bony, bald head and huge, bright eyes.

For a moment, he said nothing. Then he noticed Diana. He smiled at her.

"Who's your agent, then?"

Diana giggled. "Haven't got one."

"But you are an actress?"

"How did you guess?"

"With your looks it would be a sin not to be an actress, or perhaps a King's mistress."

Bob cleared his throat.

"In you come then," said Powell to Diana. "You as well," to Bob. "I suppose you're the chap who had the memorable adventures in Indo-China."

"That's right," said Bob. "Have you been sent my book?"

"Unfortunately, yes," said the old man, leading them into a small, cosy living room. "Earl Grey or Lapsang Souchong?"

"Lapsang Souchong," said Bob.

"And you, my dear? You remind me of a pre-Raphaelite model. Cup of tea?"

"PG Tips'll do me fine," said Diana, taking off her coat and flopping onto a sofa.

"Good girl. I'm all out of the posh teas anyway. Temporary financial embarrassment. Haven't made a movie for three years. And that was a nudist flick for a Greek friend."

Powell went off to busy himself with the kettle. Bob took off his crombie and sat next to Diana. She had never heard of Michael Powell and barely recollected the films he had made with his Hungarian partner, Imre Pressburger. But she was an actress and a movie director was a movie director. No wonder the cunning little vixen had insisted on driving him down here.

Until two weeks ago, Bob hadn't heard of Michael Powell either. Him and Terry had gone to the pictures twice a week for fifteen years and knew all the actors and actresses, but couldn't imagine why anybody would read credits. Kenneth had to explain to him the difference between a producer and a director. However, when given a list of Powell's films, Bob realised he had seen most of them back when they were kids, though Terry had insisted they not go to see *The Red Shoes*, which Thelma had been interested in, because it was a girlies' film, about ballet.

When the Gelbfisch corporation bought the rights to *It Ain't Half Hot, Mum*, Bob had gone to London to meet one of Gelbfisch's producers, a hyperactive young Italian (actually he insisted he was Sicilian), Martino Scorsese. Through the producer's excited discourse Bob gathered Gelbfisch thought it best to have a British director for this subject, and he, Scorsese, had just the man in mind.

A man who hadn't worked for three years, had been rude about his book within moments of meeting him, and was now trying to seduce his girlfriend.

"Sugar, anyone?" shouted Powell from the kitchen.

"No thanks," said Diana.

"Three for me please," said Bob.

"Only joking" said Powell. "I'm afraid I don't have any."

In a tiny cinema at an advertising agency's offices in Soho, Scorsese had shown him *The Red Shoes*. It was about a young ballerina and a ruthless White Yank impresario played by John Barrymore who told her she could be happy in love or be a great artist but not both. Scorsese sighed with pleasure every time Barrymore appeared. Terry had been right about it being a daft girlie film, but Bob found himself in tears at the end when the company perform the ballet without Moira Shearer, who had just killed herself. Maybe it was Scorsese's enthusiasm, but Bob was moved—perhaps even upset—by the film. He couldn't forget it, even if he didn't like it.

Thelma said something similar about Bob's book.

Powell's career stalled in 1960, when his *Peeping Tom* was refused a certificate by the Lord Chamberlain's Office and the negative impounded by the police. It was allegedly the most disgusting picture ever made in Britain, but of course no one would ever know. Since then, he had only shot "glamour" films—silent strip-off shorts lasting one reel or, more bluntly, the length of the average wank—and *Nakeder Than Nude*. Scorsese desperately wanted to get Powell working again.

Powell came back with the tea.

"Didn't bring any Scotch, did you?"

"No, I'm sorry," said Bob.

"Pity," said Powell. "I asked Gelbfisch's representative on earth to get you to bring me a bottle. It's the least I deserve for having waded through your book."

Bob was burning at this persistent rudeness.

"I noticed a pub in the village," said Diana. "They won't have called time yet. I'll go and get a bottle."

"There's no need."

"It won't take a minute. I insist."

She pulled on her coat and disappeared.

"Sit at the table," said Powell, "and I'll explain what I'm going to do."

Bob did as he was told, and accepted a cup of sugarless tea.

"I'll make this movie," said Powell, fixing him with inquisitor's eyes. "Not because of your wretched book. I'll do it for the money, but mainly I'll do it for little Scorsese. He's watched all my films, dozens of times. He was quoting great lumps of dialogue to me over the phone the other day. I've been here for years. The phone wouldn't ring for weeks at a time. Then this crazy Sicilian calls."

On the table was the figure of a winged lion, painted gold. Powell picked it up and fidgeted with it for a moment, drifting off into a personal reverie.

"Look," Bob started

"You didn't come all the way down here to be insulted?"

"If you don't like the book, why don't we just forget it?"

"Should never have put it between hard covers, Bob. It's a penny-dreadful, a poorly-written compendium of cliches. Some nice yarns in it, I admit, but there are two reasons I dislike it. First, there's no magic, no poetry. Second, and this is far more important, there's a great dishonesty at the heart of it. Haven't got a fag on you, have you?"

Bob fished a packet of Strands and his new Dunhill lighter from his pocket and flung them onto the table. Powell put a cigarette in his mouth and offered one to Bob. Bob refused. Powell lit his cigarette, passed the lighter back, and stuffed the packet into the pocket of his cardigan.

"Now," said Powell, "you're feeling hard-done-by. You're probably trying to think of a way of saying how dare I insult you after all you've been through that won't sound petulant."

Bob shook his head. "I don't care whether you like the book or not."

"Of course you do!" he smiled. "You're being dishonest again. Now, what we need is a shopping list."

Powell took an envelope from a letter-rack and produced a stub of pencil.

"Unpaid rates bill. Should be big enough to make the list of the things we're going to have to change."

"That's enough!" said Bob, standing up. "I'm a frigging war-hero, me. I don't have to put up with this."

"Sit down!" snapped Powell. "Have one of your cigarettes."

Do as the man says, Bobby, or thee and me'll have a major falling-out.

Survivor-Guilt, again.

There was plenty in the book that was dishonest, Bob knew. He couldn't go on too much about the whores with Thelma reading over his shoulder as he typed. Not that that mattered anymore. She'd found out about him carrying on with Diana. All the train-trips to London and overnight stays, pretending he was on business to do with the book. The marriage had been in trouble anyhow. Compared to his new friends, Thelma was just so trivial in her concerns, so boring. They wanted to change the world, she wanted to change the curtains.

Bob took a Strand without lighting it.

I wasn't talking about Thelma, Bobby lad. This rude old get here has tumbled the Other Thing, hasn't he? The unfinished business.

"As it happens, I had another offer yesterday. The reputation, no matter how unearned, of having made the most shocking film ever shot in Britain can sometimes be helpful. So, either I film your book, or I make *Confessions of a Radiogram Repair Man*, a sex-comedy which has precious little sex and isn't funny. But it's British, and our cinemas are swamped with Russian police films, Australian musicals and German horror movies. I do have yet another choice, to starve, but I don't much fancy that.

"Bob, you rightly believe you've had hard times and have earned certain rights. So you have. Fair enough. But you can't expect medals from an audience. They don't automatically care about your suffering. They'll buy their tickets and want something in return. Two hours of magic, wonder, terror, laughter and tears. Gelbfisch bought your book, and Martino, bless him, is giving it to me. You now forfeit any rights you have in this work, and gracefully pass them on to the experts. It'll be an exploration. We'll find out things you don't know about yourself. Maybe things you don't want to know."

Bob was afraid, but couldn't let it show. He sighed, smiled and shook his head in resignation.

"Whatever you say, Mr. P."

"Call me Micky."

Diana returned with a bottle of Johnnie Walker.

"Just the ticket, my dear," said Powell, patting the chair next to him. "Come sit. Bob, are we on exes?"

"Eh?"

"Expenses. Did Martino float you any of Sam Gelbfisch's wonga for development?"

"Couple of hundred quid."

Powell's eyes twinkled.

"Excellent. We must adjourn to somewhere more amenable. Bob, be a good fellow and toddle into the village and get a jerrican of three-star. Then we can take the Land Rover. Harvey's in Bristol, I think. Imre tells me great things about the new chef."

As Bob left, he noticed Powell patting Diana's knee. There was no resemblance, physical or vocal, but Micky Powell reminded him of Terry.

"You lot, get out to the mortar pits and piss on them."

"Come again, Sarge?"

"Water's low and the mortar tubes are overheating. Your piddle'll cool them down for a while. Get cracking."

"Why-nor," said Terry, "me grandbairns'll never believe I passed water for King and Country."

Bob and Butler laughed a little too loud, a little too long. They pulled on helmets and their new Russian-made flak-jackets and ran out of the bunker at a crouch to the battalion mortar-pits.

This was Day 67 or 68 of the siege of Khe Sanh, depending on which reckoning you used. By chuff-chart, it was Day 42, exactly six weeks before Bob was due to ship home. And Terry, Butler and Casper. If they got out of this place. There wasn't an airstrip anymore. The Viet-Cong and the NVA had pushed the perimeter in that close. It was ten days since the last transport, a Blackburn Beverley, had attempted a landing. It lay in a blackened, twisted heap inside what had become enemy territory two days ago.

Behind the mortar pits, a small queue of men lay on their bellies. A corporal ushered them in, one at a time, to have a burst on the tubes. Bob had got over being piss-shy after about two minutes in Indo-China.

As the perimeter shrank, eight thousand men and 60 artillery pieces were noosed into a smaller and smaller area of rocky, messed-up orange soil. Every enemy shell had been carried over the mountains on the back of a peasant, but now every shell was pulling its weight. There were dozens of casualties each day and they could only be evacuated by helicopter. The Army and Air Force were overstretched and the Navy was pressed into service, taking the wounded out to HMS *Bulwark* somewhere out off the coast.

The brass were getting edgy about sending the wokkas. You could tell when they were coming, not by the sound of their engines or rotors, but by the enemy machine-guns and ack-ack opening up on them all along the valley. Now they only flew in in the thick fog that covered everything until the late morning, but the treens had the range of the landing-strip, and threw everything they had at it anyway.

"You next," said the corporal. Bob scuttled into the sandbagged pit where half a dozen men, stripped to the waist, worked the mortars.

"Over here," said a squat little bloke with fair hair and a black beard. Everyone had beards now. If there'd been water for shaving they wouldn't have to Jimmy Riddle on the artillery. "Try to give it a hosing from the middle down to the bottom. If you've not got enough, concentrate on the bottom."

They'd been here more than two months. At first, they'd been on "offensive patrols" but found nothing. In the dense elephant grass and bamboo thickets, you couldn't see anyone not holding a gun to your nose. Mostly, they'd been holding a shrinking perimeter, living in holes in the ground covered in sandbags and oil-drums and empty shell-casings full of dirt, trying to ignore the rats, being shelled and shot at by snipers every hour of the day, wondering if they'd ever be able to sleep again.

Bob undid his fly and pissed. The mortar-tube hissed and a cloud of toxic steam billowed up from it. The little bloke studied his work with interest. The poor sod was only doing his job.

It was bad enough that the wokkas couldn't get casualties out, much worse that they couldn't get supplies in. Food and ammo were low. Three divisions were supposed to be fighting their way up to break the siege, but no sign of them yet. The Raf dropped HE and napalm all over the jungle to no effect. The treens moved their big guns to new positions every night.

"Nice one, son," said the blonde bloke. "Cover your ears."

A round was dropped into the tube. Bob put his hands to his ears and turned away with his cock still hanging out. The shell went away with a nasty, loud "boink!"

"I'd put that away if I was you," said the blonde bloke. "Send in the next one, would yer?"

Bob buttoned up and scrambled out of the pit. "You're in, Butler…Ha-ha! You're in—urine—get it?"

Captain Fisher had given a compulsory lecture, which was supposed to convince the men that there was no comparison between the British position at Khe Sanh and the Free French debacle at Dien Bien Phu. No, Captain Fisher said, this was more like the British at Kohima-Imphal, where General Slim lured the Japs into wearing themselves out by attacking a strong position, then defeated them. That night, someone finally settled Billy Liar's hash. Person or persons unknown sneaked into Fisher's billet and cooked off a gold-top in his sleeping-bag. "White-saucing" was by no means an uncommon fate for unpopular officers and NCOs. Lieutenant-Colonel Windrush didn't even bother to start an enquiry. The bush telegraph had it that the CO was crackers or hitting the bottle, or simply just as pleased as everyone else that his intelligence officer had vaporised.

Crackers or not, Windrush had more important things to worry about.

Crouching behind the sandbags of the mortar-pit, Bob wondered whether or not to make a run for the billet. Along with food, water and ammo, cover was in short supply.

Khe Sanh was, in Army parlance, a super-sangar, a fort and artillery base on a plateau deep in the Annamite mountains, surrounded by other mountains, near the border with North Vietnam and Laos. Its artillery covered the main NVA infiltration route into South Vietnam. Billy Liar aside, the Viet-Cong and the NVA—and their friends in Debs DC—certainly saw it as Britain's Dien Bien Phu. Its loss could finally force the British to pull out of Indo-China. That would prompt the Australians and New Zealanders to leave too. The Russians might be unwilling to stay on by themselves. Potentially, the future of communism in South East Asia hung on this rat-infested, rust-coloured shit-hole on top of a mountain in the middle of a load of bigger mountains.

The big NVA guns, 155mms, opened up from their positions on the Co Roc Ridge about four miles away. In Laos. In another country.

"Best stay put for a bit, eh?," Butler sniggered. "Bloomin' marvellous, innit? I've been taking diarrhoea pills for the last month so's I can get good and constipated and keep the number of bog-trips I have to make at an absolute minimum. Now we get orders to evacuate bodily wastes. I'm going to write to my MP about this."

"Well stick me in the envelope along with the letter. I've had enough of this now, I want to go home," said Terry.

Three 155mm shells crashed onto the airstrip in rapid succession.

"Hell's bells," said Terry. "Anyone got a tab?"

"Only these," said Bob, fishing a packet of Players No 6 from a pocket at the side of his flak-jacket. "I was reading in the *Mirror* the other week that the fag company makes these specially as going-to-work gaspers. You have your nasty cheap little Number 6s at the factory or the office. Then, when you go out in the evening, to the pub or club, like, you have your proper king-sized fags."

"Wouldn't mind being down the club this evening. What day is it?"

"Saturday, man."

"Never mind!" said Butler. "That means there'll be a film show in the parish hall tonight. Wonder what it'll be?"

"Same as it's been for the last five weeks," said Terry. "The Reverend Noote will run *The Browning Version*, a travelogue called *This is Belgium* and Cliff Richard in *Summer Holiday*."

"'spect you're right," said Butler. "Never thought I'd get sick of the sight of a bus."

"You think you've got problems?" said Terry. "I'm having strange erotic fantasies about shoving a Mills Bomb up Melvin Hayes's jacksie."

Casper emerged from the mortar pit.

"Getting a bit crowded this side," said Butler. "Shall we make a run for it?"

Casper gazed at the sky, thought for a moment, then nodded. He hadn't said anything in two weeks. People dealt with the strain of the constant shelling in different ways. Casper was no crazier than anyone else. To Butler, Bob and Terry, he was becoming something of a lucky charm. There was no logical reason, just that everyone was getting superstitious.

Before he stopped talking, Casper explained that if he looked at the jungle down a rifle-sight, his spirit soared like a kestrel over the trees, enabling him to see treens hidden from ordinary men's eyes. He popped off shots regularly, but there was no way of knowing if he scored any kills. Casper was satisfied that each bullet told.

Casper led off and the rest followed, separated by a couple of paces, making for the big underground bunker known as the Parish Hall. It was the battalion briefing-room, storage-space and place of entertainment. The flicks would be starting in an hour or so, and there was no sense in going back to their billet only to have to run over here again later. They'd just have to be early.

"Ah fuck! Ah fuck, fuck, fuck!" said Terry as they scurried through the bunker's entrance.

"What's up, our kid?" asked Bob.

Terry pointed to a blackboard. TONIGHT'S LECTURE. ESCAPE AND EVASION TECHNIQUES. ALL ATTEND. Terry took a piece of greying paper from his bum pocket. His chuff-chart. He tore it to confetti.

"I'm going to be played by *Rodney Bewes*?"

Bob had sort of been hoping for someone like Albert Finney. Rodney Bewes was the star of *Wish You Were Here*, a television series set in a Morecambe guest-house run by Thora Hird (his mother-in-law) and wife Rita Tushingham, dreaming of a better life than cooking miserly fried breakfasts and rationing the toilet-paper.

"Yes," said Powell. "He was recommended by the screenwriters, Clement and La Frenais. Ideally I'd have wanted Imre, but our relationship is still a little, ah, encumbered by the past. You should know about that. Still, Clement and La Frenais have done an excellent job."

They sat in a bare office at Pinewood Studios. Rusting, metal-framed window, several layers of bland, green paint over the brickwork of the walls and flaking off a big, barely-warm radiator.

"For Terry, we have a young man named James Bolam. Also an actor from the television, I believe."

Powell was no longer the rude, shabby old man in the Cotswold cottage. In a sharp suit, he was as abrasive as ever, but every discourtesy seemed part of a relentless drive towards some distant but attainable goal. He was just like John Barrymore in *The Red Shoes*.

"Aye, I think I know him," said Bob. "Little bloke. Terry is big and coarse. This fellow has the right accent, mind. I suppose he'll do at a push. Is it too late to get rid of Rodney Bewes? There's Albert..."

Powell smiled. "Now, for Thelma, we've got Brigit Forsyth."

"*Thelma*! You can't put her in the film! I only mentioned her a few times in the book. It doesn't seem decent, bringing personal business in like that."

If Powell put Thelma in his bloody film, her Dad would probably belt him. Bob would lose the house in the divorce settlement.

"How is that charming girlfriend of yours, by the way?"

"You mean Diana? I'd've thought you could tell me, Micky. It's a while since I've seen her."

"Oh," said Powell, wistfully. "I took her to a press do in Wardour Street a couple of weeks ago. Last I saw of her she was talking to a trendy young director with mutton-chop whiskers and a spotty hankie tied round his neck."

Bob had been at the same party. Diana had wandered over to say hello, given him a peck on the cheek and ran off with her director, who wanted to put her in something called *Devil Bride of Dracula*. He couldn't honestly say he was too upset; he'd been out with four women (an actress, a painter and two models) in the last month.

"Now we've got Reg Varney to play Butler," said Powell. "He's a little on the old side, but he can put a lot of cheek into it. Hartnell's a little long in the tooth as well, but I have to have him for Sergeant Grimshaw."

"You've cast *Dr. Who* as Grim! Micky, that man was a monster, a bloody psychopath with stripes. Not some doddering old eccentric."

"Padre Noote will be played by Derek Nimmo."

Bob smiled. "Now that's good. Nimmo for Noote is spot-on, Micky."

Oh he is now, is he?

"But, err..."

"But what, Bob?"

Tell him, kidder. Tell him how that chinless clown of a sky-pilot turned out to be the best man in the battalion.

"Noote wasn't just a caricature. He was a very courageous man."

"Don't worry," said Powell shuffling through sheets of paper, scribbling his initials on some.

He was at Pinewood as a technical advisor. He'd been there two days showing the extras how a British soldier wore his kit and how to slouch the right way. For this, he was getting an exorbitant £150 per week, with £15 of that to Kenneth. He'd been shocked to find the jungle sequences would all be shot in the studio.

A knock at the door. "Come!" snapped Powell. A woman came in, dressed from neck to toe in an immense fur costume. She held more fur under her arm.

"Want to see this now?"

Powell nodded. She put the fur thing under her arm and onto her head. She was a giant teddy-bear.

"Jump up and down a bit," said Powell.

The teddy-bear did as it was bid.

"Good," said Powell. The woman took off her bear's head. "Is it easy to move around in?"

"I'll use nylon for the fur," she said. "Cheapest and lightest. It'll be uncomfortable under the lights. You'll need to damp everyone down between takes."

Powell sniggered. "Let 'em suffer for their art. Run off two dozen. All different styles and sizes. Make some of them quite battered. Miss out the odd ear and eye. They should look like they've been loved for a long time."

"All in shades of brown?"

Powell gave her the thumbs-up. She left.

Bob didn't know quite what to say. "The Viet-Cong dress in black pyjamas, generally, Micky."

Bob had long since given up asking to see the script. Powell kept making excuses.

"I said your book had no magic in it," said Powell. "Well I may have been mistaken. I managed to find some."

"I still don't get it. Why teddy bears?"

"You will."

Another knock at the door. A bespectacled woman clutching a clipboard popped her head in.

"Just thought I'd let you know, Micky, that the young man from the Lord Chamberlain's office is still waiting outside. You've kept him for seven hours, now."

"Poor little lamb," he said. "What's his name?"

She consulted her clipboard. "Puttnam."

"Puttman. Good."

"No, I said Putt-Nam."

"And I said Putt-Man. Make sure it gets spelled that way on all correspondence. Shall we let him in?"

The woman shrugged.

"Go on then."

She left.

"Bob, for the next ten to twelve weeks I'm going to be doing one of the most stressful jobs in the world. If I get more than four hours' sleep a night, I'll be lucky. The reason I'm not going to show you a script is that I don't want to have any more arguments than are strictly necessary."

"I understand, Micky, but…"

Powell stared him in the face. The intense stare of an angry headmaster.

"Good. Now I need a big favour from you. The usual drill with the Lord Chamberlain's office is that you show them a completed film. If they want anything cut, they ask for it. Things are a bit different with me. Ever since I made *Peeping Tom*, I've been on the blacklist. I get my own personal censor for the duration of principal photography. You don't have a huge amount to do on the set all day. I'll get someone to let you know which days you'll be needed. For the rest of the time, I'd be greatly indebted if you were to keep young Puttman as far out of the way as possible. Give him *la vie Bohéme*, take him to parties, introduce him to loose women. Bloody hell, try and get him addicted to black bombers or the white mischief. Only thing is, there's a restaurant near here called *Les Oiseaux*. For God's sake, don't ever take him there. I promise you, Bob, by all I hold dear: the more you keep this cretin out of my hair, the better our film will be."

His shoulders started to shake. It was a moment before it became clear he was laughing.

"Not that I've got a lot of hair anymore. Ah, young Mr. Puttman from the Lord Chamberlain's Office! Come in! Come in! I want you to meet Bob…"

The official version is that fourteen hundred men surrendered at Khe Sanh. Actually, on the day Major Lampton, the highest-ranking surviving officer, ran up the white flag, I'd say that there were about two thousand us left, though a lot of them were stretcher-cases. Of the original garrison of eight thousand I've no idea how many were killed or wounded, but it was a lot.

When the situation became hopeless, we took advantage of three mornings of exceptionally heavy fog to try and scuttle the place. The Raf, the Army and the Navy threw in every aircraft they could. While the bombers and fighter-bombers tried to keep the enemy artillery busy, helicopters and light aircraft zoomed in, filled up as fast as possible and got out again. Regular

Dunkirk, it was. Orders were to abandon everything but helmets and flak-jackets and just get aboard.

The Loamshires—us—were to hold the perimeter, along with a West African Commonwealth unit and a few companies of Gurkhas. We were bitter about this. Three Para had been got out, as had the Greenjackets, the Somerset Light Infantry, Princess Wallis's Own Royal Borsetshires and most of the gunners and engineers. The powers-that-be decided a mixed bag of non-Brits were expendable. And us? One of the blokes in the platoon, Eddie Booth, put into words what we were all thinking: "We've been tossed in so's the f***ing government isn't seen to be saving the white cream and just leaving the wogs."

"Well, they've bloody left me, white honky," said Eddie's best mate Bill Reynolds, who came from Jamaica. Strange pair, Bill and Eddie. They used to insult one another's skin-colour all the time, but they were inseparable.

It was our bad luck to be in an unfashionable foot-and-mouth regiment that didn't have anyone fighting its corner in Whitehall.

We wondered where the ARVN were. It was their bloody country we were fighting for, after all. The word was that most of them were so useless top brass didn't want them in the way. But the big question is where were the Russians? The Russian Air Force would have been big enough to provide plenty of cover and helicopter more of us out. It seems HM government was too proud to ask for help, but we heard a whisper they actually refused a Russian offer of help. Was a little national humiliation too much to ask to save hundreds of lives and hundreds of men from the horrors of captivity?

Day four of the evacuation dawned bright and sunny. A few wokkas tried to come in, but without cover it was hopeless. Three were shot down and only two made it out again. The next day was the same, only I got promoted to lance-corporal. The day after the enemy were on top of us anyway. We surrendered.

Captain Vinh was tall for a treen—five foot ten, maybe six foot. He wore a spotless olive-green uniform, unembellished by insignia. Only the red star on his pith-helmet broke the anonymity. And the livid purple scars on the left side of his face.

Vinh noticed Bob was trying not to stare.

"Does my face offend you? My unit was attacked by your British Air Force two years ago, just North of the Demilitarised Zone. I lost a lot of comrades."

"I'm sorry," said Bob. A mistake: rule one of interrogation was to keep it polite, but neutral. Give away no information, no emotions, no nothing.

Vinh looked him in the face, nodded slightly and offered a cigarette from a red and white packet. There were three other men in the room, guards with American-made Garand rifles. No cameras. Bob accepted the cigarette and a light.

Noote warned against pictures of the NVA being nice to their captives. One tab might make Bob a propaganda snapshot: see how nice we are to the European imperialists?

The interrogation room was half the interior of a wooden hut on bamboo stilts. They weren't in a prison-camp as such, but an ordinary village the NVA had taken over and fenced in with barbed wire for the temporary storage of prisoners. They'd been split into smaller groups. Just two companies of the Loamshires were billeted here. He was still with Terry, Butler and Casper. And Noote, who was the CO.

The cigarette tasted surprisingly good. American Virginia tobacco. Two draws on it and Bob felt quite light-headed. It'd been a week since he'd last had a smoke.

Vinh consulted a buff folder on his desk. There was a single sheet of paper in it.

They'd all been kicked around by the guards, and by civilians when they were being marched here. They were fed more or less regularly— rice and bits of vegetables. Everyone had the shits of course.

"Lance Corporal, Second Battalion, Loamshire Regiment," said Vinh. His English had a heavy American accent. A lot of NVA officers had studied at American universities.

Bob said nothing. Name, rank, serial number, date of birth. That was all you had to give them.

"I understand everybody calls you 'Bob'?"

Bob tensed. How had he found that out? Probably no big deal. Captain Vinh was "interviewing" everyone. Someone probably dropped his name in an unguarded moment. Or had it beaten out of him, more like.

"You come from an industrial area of England? Many people work in factories, often in unhealthy and unpleasant conditions."

Bob tried to look pleasant and accommodating without saying anything.

"Your government conscripts its working men and sends them to the other side of the world to burn the homes of peasants, to bomb women and kids. Bob, you have studied at night-school to better yourself. You are, I am sure, an intelligent man. Have you ever asked what in tarnation you and your, ah, mates, are doing here?"

Aye, you're right enough there, Captain Vinh. How the hell do you know all this about me, Captain Vinh? Who's been blabbing?

Vinh turned suddenly and banged his fist on the table.

"Why are you in Indo-China?"

Bob shrugged.

"Let me level with you, Bob," said Vinh, sounding all reasonable again. "You can't give me any military intelligence. The entire active strength of the second Loamshires was captured. I'm not interested in what platoon or company you belong to, or your tactics or weapons or operating procedures, or any of that shit. All I want is the answer to that one question. It's not for my superiors, it's just something I cannot understand, something that keeps me awake. Why the hell are working men from Britain oppressing working men in Indo-China?"

Terry would have said "that's the British working man all over, Captain Vinh. Can't resist a scrap." But Terry always had to be carried away from interrogations.

Bob shrugged.

"Bob, do you want to go home?"

Bob nodded. No point in lying.

"Here's some literature."

He pushed leaflets across the desk. Pictures of British PoWs getting off a plane in Switzerland. The catch was that they had to sign a statement condemning British imperialism in South East Asia. And embrace international socialism, and convince the treens you meant it.

"Thank you," said Bob. He'd wipe his arse with them.

"You have a good think about it, huh?" said Vinh. "I know some of your comrades are certainly considering this offer very carefully."

Though he walked with the aid of a stick since "Vimto" Vinh broke his ankle, Lieutenant Noote lead the morning stroll around the camp. I fell in with Terry, beside the padre, ambling along. Butler—just out of the cage after a week's punishment—leaned on Casper, who hadn't spoken to anyone in months. Whistling through cracked lips, we made a racket out of "Colonel Bogey". Behind us, Eddie Booth and Bill Reynolds had suspended their colour-prejudiced bickering to poke fun at our yellow captors. "Ugly little treen f***ers," they muttered in agreement. Water dripped from the thatch of the huts, and gushed out of the nearby trees. There had been a hell of a storm the night before.

Noote greeted each guard personally, calling him by the nicknames that had been agreed on.

"Good morning, Herman. Good morning, Prof. Good morning, Gertie. Lovely weather we're having. Lovely for ducks, that is."

The guards grinned humourlessly at the absurd Englishman, hobbling with pride as if he ran the camp.

It was Noote's idea to give all the guards nicknames to rob them of their dignity. It made us less afraid of them. He organised a series of meetings to democratically elect names for all the goons, and to establish routines.

Noote, of course, was Escape Officer. Early on, he had gathered us all and announced "I'm asking each hut to appoint a representative to the Escape Committee. We also need an adjutant, an intelligence officer and a quartermaster. You're QM, Butler. I've got you marked as a scrounger who can rustle up larcenous miracles. We have to take a crack at getting some men over the wire soon, because the longer we wait the more beaten-up and malnourished we're going to get. We can't be more than five or six days' march from the Demilitarized Zone. With the Lord on our side, we stand a fair chance of making a home run. What we need to do is pool our resources. Think about what kit you have, and about what you know, what skills you have, what information you might possess. It's all for one, here."

I wasn't entirely sure about Noote's optimism. This wasn't Colditz, with tunnels and Red Cross parcels and forged papers. But it was true that we had a fair bit of equipment; with a few days' warning that we might be captured, every man had concealed something useful. Razor-blades were sewn into trouser turn-ups; rat-packs, maps and water purification tablets stuffed into jacket-linings; compasses hidden in boot-heels; groundsheets tucked away in waistbands; cigarette lighters, pencils and pocket-knives shoved up where the sun don't shine.

This morning, the padre was chipper. The storm had knocked down several stretches of wire in the night, and none of the guards were making any effort to repair the perimeter. It was clearly time to put *Plan Wooden Horse* into action. It involved no subtle deception. Simply put, the plan was to break through the wire and walk to safety. The only clever part was that Noote would spend hours running the remaining prisoners around the village so energetically that a head-count was impossible.

The observation tower leaned on three bamboo stilts, battered by the storm. There was no one manning it and the machine gun had fallen down and been carried away.

Terry and me had drawn lots and were ready for the go. Butler had scrounged the compass out of a broken penknife, and we were kitted out with a hand-drawn map on the back of one of Vinh's propaganda-leaflets, a lighter and six cigarettes (for burning off leeches), a groundsheet, two sachets of vegetable soup and four Durexes.

"A, err, prophylactic appliance in a sock makes a very serviceable water-canteen," Noote had explained. "In the jungle, you can't risk drinking river or stream water if you can avoid it. Collect rain from the plants."

"They never taught us about rubber Johnnies in the Scouts," said Terry.

Now, with everything sopping wet, there was a rare surfeit of potable water.

"The Lord is conspiring," Noote commented.

It was nearly time for the break. With double rations in my belly to build my strength, I felt stuffed rather than nervous. Terry was eager, dancing a little like a boxer.

Butler sat down, exhausted, unsupported.

I saw Billy Casper wheeling around, arms outstretched and flapping, tweeting scratchily. The kid had been acting like that for a while, turning his head like a bird, squatting everywhere as if perching.

"Good man," Noote said, assuming this was a diversion.

Casper climbed the rickety tower. Guards gathered around, shouting up at the prisoner, their language as birdlike as his screeches. Rifles were raised.

Terry and me drifted towards the wire.

Casper spread his arms in an "I can fly" gesture, and the tower collapsed under him. He pulled himself into the air, stretching. For a moment, it was as if he really could fly. He would soar above the village and flap lazily over the jungle, migrating to freedom.

Gertie the guard shot Billy. He fell to Earth like Icarus, broken.

Terry was ready to go, but I froze, staring at Billy's dead face. He was just a kid. A crazy kid.

"Come on, kidder," Terry said.

I couldn't move. My nerve was shot.

Captain Vinh marched up. Noote said, "Captain, I wish to protest most strongly at this atrocious…" Vinh swatted the padre to the ground with a backhand. Then, he drew his revolver and shot Noote in the head, twice.

"There will be no escape this morning," he announced. "Bob, Terry, bury your dead."

Vinh's adjutant had brought shovels.

He couldn't stand up straight, couldn't lie down properly. All he could do was crouch. Any attempt at stretching brought him up against bamboo and barbed wire. Bob had been in this little cage, roasting by day, freezing by night, for half a week. The pain wasn't usually physical apart from the times you got cramps. But it was still agony. He wanted to scream, give Vimto whatever he wanted. Terry was in the other cage, within sight.

"Times like this I wish you were a woman," said Terry, making calf-eyes through the wire.

"I wish I was a bloody woman," said Bob, "then I wouldn't bloody be here."

When every scrap of him wanted to chuck it, Bob would think that if Terry was taking it, so could he. They recited Newcastle United squads from all the years they'd been following the team. They sang songs together, always the filthiest versions.

"My old man said go to Viet-Nam,
I said 'fuck off, bollocks, you're a cunt'."

In the dead of night when the guards were asleep, Bob and Terry talked about those shovels Vinh had brought for them to bury Casper and the Lieutenant. Vimto had known about Plan Wooden Horse. Someone was being talkative.

When fear and pain and despair set in, there was always hate. Only their hut had known more than half an hour before that Wooden Horse was a goer.

They had a traitor among them. Someone had grassed them up.

If it wasn't Bob or Terry—and, since Bob froze, he was petrified Terry would think it was him—and it couldn't have been poor Billy Casper because he was no longer able to talk, which left only be one man.

Bob and Terry realised at exactly the same moment who the traitor was.

"I hate you, Butler," Terry breathed.

Terry (James Bolam) was being interrogated by Captain Rambo (Raymond Massey), the American Communist agent who ran the camp, issuing orders to the NVA and Vietcong.

"Absurd Englishman," Rambo said, in close-up. "You force us to such things. But then, the British have always been the world's fools. You are like children who will never leave the nursery, who still have rules about telling tales, who want to cry but can't be seen with tears on their faces. Oh no, mustn't show emotion, mustn't 'let the side down'."

White leader ran across the screen, flashing scribbles and blips. Lights came up in the projection room.

"Ray is spot-on, isn't he?" said Powell, cheerfully. "It was difficult to get a sufficiently eagle-faced Yank. In the old days, Imre and I would have used Barrymore, but poor John's drunk dead."

Three weeks into filming, these rushes were the first Bob had seen of *It Ain't Half Hot, Mum*. He'd been busy keeping the man from the Lord Chamberlain's Office out of the way. This evening, Puttnam was off at the ICA, watching a fashionable new movie from America, *Seven Brides for Seven Comrades*. Bob had tried hard to appreciate these left-wing art movies, but still preferred British comedies or Italian police thrillers.

"Do I have to tell you I never saw any Americans in Indo," said Bob. "Plenty of American guns and shells, but no actual Americans."

"I know, I know," said Powell, "but it's an article of faith among our political masters that the enemy war effort is directed from Debs DC. This is horse-trading. Little Puttman appreciates a splash of transatlantic evil. It's funny: he's supposed to be the guardian of good taste and morality, but he came over all excited yesterday and insisted we shoot a scene where Rambo forces Butler to play Russian Roulette. My Rambo would never do that."

"Did you have to give Rambo all the best lines? He's obviously your favourite character in the film."

"Balance, Bob. You have to make your villains a little heroic and your heroes a little villainous. It adds spice."

Bob felt out-manoeuvred.

Everyone else in the projection-room left their seats. About half of them clustered around Powell wanting decisions, signatures, orders.

"Have you eaten?" Powell asked Bob. "Hang around and we'll go to *Les Oiseaux*. Restaurant near here, run by a chap who used to make films before the War. Kept falling foul of the censors and had to pack it in. I want to talk about the scene we're doing tomorrow, where Terry murders the traitor."

Bob was aghast. "That's not in the book."

Powell smiled, eyes hard. "Ah, but it should have been, shouldn't it?"

Butler cradled the broken Billy Casper in his arms, tears pouring down his cheeks, sobbing.

"You don't 'ave to do that," he said to Vinh. "Billy was just a kid. Poor little sod had gone soft in the 'ead."

I couldn't see which of the guards shot Stan. He fell backwards, a look of peace on his face.

Terry and I crawled close.

I remembered Butler from Walmington-on-Sea, a million years ago. The spivvy lad who could always get fags and sweets, who could recite bus routes like scripture, who laughed like Sid James.

That lad was dying.

Terry held his hand. Vimto stood over us, sneering contemptuously.

"Don't cry, lads," Butler said, "I'm goin' 'ome. I'm driving the number 42 straight to the Cemetery Gates."

He died smiling.

Butler squirmed against the wall of the hut, tears pouring down his cheeks, sobbing.

Terry and Bob crawled close.

Butler didn't try to deny or explain or justify himself. Most likely, he'd sold them out because he couldn't stand the idea of being put back in the cage. Maybe he did it for chocolate or extra ciggies.

"I never did like cockney cunts," said Terry.

Butler snivelled.

Terry held his throat. Bob concentrated his hatred, focusing, willing Terry's fingers to be strong.

There was a loud crack as Butler's neck snapped. Inside the hut, it sounded like a gunshot.

"That's done the bastard," Terry said.

"Ey, look here," muttered Bob. "He's got three packs of tabs and a bar of chocolate stowed in his corner."

Terry spat in Butler's dead face.

INT. HUT. NIGHT.

BUTLER sits, waiting, dead inside. Monsoon rains pour down, rattling in the thatch. The door opens. TERRY and BOB stand in the doorway, water pouring off their coats. BUTLER has been expecting them, he is almost relieved.

TERRY

You know why we're here, Stan. You know what we have to do.

BUTLER

In your shoes, I'd do the same. I'm just so sorry. For everything.

BOB watches as TERRY steps towards BUTLER. He doesn't understand the bond between the two men. BUTLER opens his arms in a cruciform pose. Water and moonlight makes his face beautiful. TERRY gently places his hands around BUTLER's neck.

TERRY

(with love)

I hate you, Butler.

BOB shuts his eyes. We hear the rain pouring down. BUTLER doesn't struggle. TERRY lays him out on his cot, at peace. TERRY wipes BUTLER's face.

BOB

(v.o.)

In the end, everyone wanted Butler dead, himself most of all. The prisoners, the guards, his mates, his enemies. Even the jungle wanted him dead. There'd be no medals for Terry, but he was a hero all the same.

Through the noise of the storm, we hear helicopters. And music: "Teddy Bears' Picnic".

"Good eeee-vening," said the restaurateur. He was an immense, jowly man with a deep, rich London voice. "If it isn't Micky Powell!"

"Alfred, you old devil," said Powell. "How are you?"

Alfred shrugged. "Come and have the best table, chum."

In the taxi, Powell had explained that Alfred had also been a director, rising from "quota quickies" at about the time Powell had done. Bob remembered many of the films he had done: *The Thirty-Nine Steps, Fanny By Gaslight, The Trouble With Harry, The Third Man*. Like Powell, Alfred was blacklisted on the strength of a single picture. *Nutter* cast the Lithuanian star Larushka Skikne as a young man who keeps the mummified corpse of his mother (Margaret Rutherford) in the attic of his boarding-house in Skegness. "They never forgave him for the scene where Sylvia Sims is murdered in the bathing machine," Powell said. Crucified by critics, bishops and politicians, Alfred quit the business.

"This restaurant is my way of getting my own back," Alfred said as he showed them to their table. "To my certain knowledge, I've killed two MPs and three clergymen, not to mention that dreadful woman. Let me get you a wine list."

Bob sat down. As befitted a restaurant near a studio, the walls were covered with framed film stills. It took him a while to realise Alfred was in all the pictures, often peeping out from behind the scenery.

Powell chuckled. "The queer thing is, I don't think he's joking..."

"Sorry?"

"About killing people. Alfred was ruined by do-gooders and God-botherers. No-one's ever proved anything, of course. He was questioned by the police a few years ago. This ghastly suburban woman —Whitewash? Whitewall?—started a campaign to get piano-legs covered, that sort of thing. Wanted to clean up smutty movies. Said *Brief Encounter* was immoral and undermined the family. J. Arthur tried to calm her down by inviting her to the studios, giving her the VIP treatment. He made the mistake of getting *Les Oiseaux* to do the catering. Three days later, she was dead of a 'mystery stomach bug'. I hope you like poultry and game-birds. That's Alfred's speciality. Shall we order?"

After three excellent courses, during which Powell had astounded Bob with funny stories about famous actresses he had slept with, the coffee arrived and Powell's eyes turned to neons again.

"Now, about Terry and Butler," he began.

Bob writhed in his seat, coffee gritty in his mouth.

"You can't show Terry killing Butler. They've both got families."

Powell smiled, sharp teeth showing.

"Every time you see an extra with his kit slung incorrectly, you whine. Whenever we combine or manufacture characters to distil a greater truth from the morass of reality, you complain. And yet, you lie throughout your book. And you feel threatened when we diverge from your lies to tell the truth."

"You weren't there, you don't understand."

"No, Bob, I wasn't and I don't. But you were there, and you don't understand. You have no excuse."

"Thelma was reading the manuscript over my shoulder as I was typing it. There were things I couldn't put in the book."

"Did you write the book for Thelma?"

"It's dedicated to her."

"Why not to Terry?"

"You know…what he did afterward…the terrible thing. Some say he's no better than a traitor himself."

"Some? Do you?"

Bob took another swallow of coffee. It wasn't helping.

He had scuppered Plan Wooden Horse, by freezing up. He hadn't killed Butler, but let Terry do it for him. And, in Fotherington-Thomas's compound, where severed heads were kicked about like footballs, he had lost it again.

"When you came to visit me in Avening, I told you there was a great dishonesty in the book. What I'm trying to do is squeeze that out of the film. Sometimes, that involves making up things that didn't happen. Sometimes, it involves showing things that will upset Thelma and people's families and the bloody Church of England. Now, Bob, are you with me or against me? Can I count on you for the rest of the shoot, or do I have to ask Alfred to whip up one of his special cream desserts for you?"

Bob didn't know.

"I have no time for politics," said Powell, running a huge cigar under his nose. "But the way I see it, your friend Terry is being the honest one. Fancy a brandy?"

"I haven't seen him since. I called on his parents. His Dad's disowned him. Yes please."

"He could have changed his name, gone to earth, maybe moved to another country."

"But your film, Micky, is going to make it worse for him. He'll never be able to get on a bus again without worrying that one of Stan Butler's mates will recognise him."

Powell shook his head. "Your unfinished business with your friend is between you and him, Bob. Nobody else."

He was right, of course. Even in rare moments when he was being civil, Micky Powell had a way of making Bob feel a total wanker. He was like a combination of Captain Vinh and Terry.

There was a commotion at the door. A small man in an immaculately-cut overcoat stormed in like a raging bull.

"Mee-keey!" he yelled through a jet-black beard, "Mee-key Powell! Wonderful news!"

Powell rose and engulfed the little Sicilian in a hug.

"I am so happy," said Scorsese. "I have been to see Gelbfisch," he crossed himself, "he like rushes. He say you get extra twenty thou for the, you know…" He made circular motions with both hands.

"Helicopters?" suggested Powell.

"Helicopters! *Si!* All helicopters you need! Is great news, no?"

Vinh was incandescent with fury. All the prisoners were lined up as if for inspection. His reasoning was that since the head-count was one short and he knew no-one had breached the perimeter, someone was playing hide-and-seek.

"Very well. If Butler does not show himself within ten minutes, I shall have one of you executed."

Bob and Terry looked at each other.

All night, they had scrabbled at the soft earth under the floor of the hut, digging not a tunnel but a grave. The idea had been that Vimto would assume Stan—strengthened by that extra chocolate and driven insane by guilt—had escaped into the jungle.

Vinh was waving his Colt .45.

Minutes passed. Some of the weaker prisoners sagged. Others got fidgety.

"Stan Butler, come out, come out," yelled Vimto. "Olly-olly-ox-in-free!"

"He'll be half-way to Saigon, by now," Terry said.

Vinh marched over, furious, pistol cocked.

"Or Hanoi," Terry allowed. "He was a bus driver. Terrible sense of direction."

"Escape is not possible."

"Captain, do you really think one of your guards would put it in his report if he fell asleep at his post?"

Vimto obviously had thought of that, but couldn't afford to lose face. Only the prisoners would suffer now. Later, he was quite capable of having some sixteen-year-old NVA peasant shot as well. The Captain put the muzzle of the gun to Terry's nose, and grinned.

"Not so uppity, eh?"

Terry stared the treen down.

Bob heard something. A boom, off away in the distance, like far-off thunder. He thought it was panicked blood pounding in his ears, but he realised Terry and Vinh heard it too, and were distracted from their face-off.

It was a thrumm, now. Like a gramophone played too loud three doors down, rattling ornaments on the mantelpiece, but too distorted to make out the tune. There was just a throbbing bass line.

Vinh, strangely, was struck afraid. He backed away from Terry and looked up into the sky, clutching his gun as if it were a lucky charm.

Dum-dum-dum-dum-dum-dum-dummm-dum...

It was music. Ominous oom-pahs. Someone laughed in surprise. Vimto shot him in the knee.

Bob recognised the tune as the words cut in.

"*If you go down in the woods today,*" sang Henry Hall...

"It's the bloody 'Teddy Bears' Picnic'," said Terry.

Accompanying the song was the slicing of helicopter rotors. Vimto was issuing orders in rapid Vietnamese to scurrying guards. Bob's stomach sank. Anything that scared Vinh's boys was not necessarily good for the prisoners.

The music filled the air like a hailstorm. Bob felt it in his teeth.

Tum-te-tum-te-tum-te-tum-te-tum-te...

"Look!" said Terry, pointed.

Above the treeline were ten helicopters, in a loose vee formation. Westland Wessexes and Scouts. The music came from loudspeakers mounted over their cargo doors.

Some of the prisoners started waving their arms and dancing for joy. Rescue was at hand.

Vinh shouted orders up to the observation tower. For a moment, Bob was certain he'd have the machine gun rake the exercise ground and massacre the prisoners. Instead, the gun was pointed at the sky.

Some of the men were singing along.

Bob found himself humming, *dit-dit-de-de, dit-dit-de-dum...*

Something flared from the lead wokka, burning a trail across the sky, imprinting a neon squiggle on Bob's eyeballs.

"Everybody down," Terry yelled.

Henry Hall—mainstay of *Children's Favourites*, hosted on the BBC Light Programme by Uncle Mac throughout the halcyon decade of Bob's childhood—whispered thunderously, as the delicate sounds of his band drowned out explosions and gunfire.

The rocket detonated in the observation tower. Guards and the gun exploded out of the fireball and rained around in flaming chunks.

Today was the bloody day, the day those sodding teddy bears finally had their fucking picnic!

This was not a day anybody wanted to be in the woods!

The guards started shooting the prisoners. A bullet spanged in the dirt between Bob and Terry. They rolled backwards, towards a hut.

Machine guns opened up from the helicopters, stitching across the village at random, killing as many prisoners as guards. Bob realised this was not a rescue mission. The men in the helicopters probably didn't realise they were attacking a prison camp. Everyone who died was a treen. That was how you knew one Indo-Chinese from another. The ones you killed were the enemy.

Eddie Booth and Bill Reynolds jumped up and down and waved in the middle of the carnage, trying to signal the wokkas. The machines circled the village, machine-gunning and firing missiles.

Everything was on fire.

Terry had swiped a rifle from a dead guard. Bob knew he was looking for Vimto. But this was Indo-China. You didn't kill who you wanted to, you killed who you could.

Terry shot a jabbering guard.

Bob felt burning thatch fall on his legs. Terry dragged him out of the fire.

"I owe you, our kid."

"I'm paying you back for that Stanley Matthews cigarette card."

There was an explosion, very near. Eddie Booth was tossed up in the air and came down in flames. It was no use. The wokkas were going to blitzkrieg everyone and everything. They were going to die.

"Terry?"

"Aye?"

"When you went out with Thelma, you know, for those two weeks."

"Forget it."

"But did you..."

"Yes."

Bastard, Bob thought. "I forgive you," he said.

"So do I."

Then the shooting stopped. A xylophone sounded in the song's middle-eight. Crackling fires spread. A few people were moaning.

Bob and Terry were still alive.

The helicopters touched down, rotors slowing. The music faded.

A rotund officer, wearing a panama hat over earphones and cricket-pads over khaki drills, jumped out, accompanied by a small mongrel dog and juniors with guns. He strode straight under the whipping scythes of the rotors, towering over men who bent double. Pausing, he took a deep breath, and said, "I love the smell of burning flesh in the morning. It tastes like…*cooked breakfast.*"

We soon realised the man who had stepped out of the sky was Major Nigel "Mad Nye" Molesworth of the Long Range Jungle Patrol Group. Terry was greatly dischuffed to discover the LURP hadn't made a special raid to rescue us.

What they'd seen from the air was a couple of hundred yards square of empty jungle—our exercise ground—that was the nearest thing they'd find to a cricket pitch this far up the Ulu. They even parked two of their helicopters at either end to act as sight-screens for the bowlers. Apparently, it was Sunday, and Molesworth always played cricket on Sunday. He wasn't going to let a little thing like the Indo-China War break that habit. He even insisted on breaking for tea at four sharp, and served cucumber sandwiches with the crusts cut off. He had a standing order with Fortnum and Mason's Hong Kong branch.

Terry and I were too exhausted to complain. We weren't the only survivors; of the 200 or so of us there, perhaps 50 had been killed or injured, and a few of the guards had disappeared into the jungle to chance the snakes and their own punji *traps.*

So we sat there and watched the cricket. Molesworth ordered two of the helicopters to ferry survivors back to our lines south of the DMZ, starting with the most urgent casualties.

Molesworth quickly fixed on the tall and athletic Bill Reynolds, reckoning that any West Indian must be a born cricketer. He was right. Bill was a demon bowler and a handy batsman. Terry and me had always reckoned cricket was for nancies—not a proper game like football—though we both kept quiet about that. Molesworth's Gurkha wicket keeper had a necklace of human fingerbones.

Lieutenant Darbishire, the bespectacled medical officer and the nearest thing to a sane man in the unit, got us to help him out collecting identity discs from the dead.

"This Noote sounds VC material," he commented.

Late that afternoon, with Captain Jennings at the bat, an enemy patrol found us. Some of the guards must have got through to make a report. The treens could hardly miss a load of helicopters and two-dozen white-clad Ruperts hitting a ball around the jungle. They opened up with small arms and grenades. Molesworth ordered the machine-gunners to keep them at bay while the last few overs were played. I revised my opinion of cricket. Or decided that nancies were a lot harder than we had thought.

Jennings was bowled out and, since his side needed thirty off two overs to draw level with Molesworth, gracefully conceded. Molesworth considered it and accepted. I knew damn well he'd have liked to play it out to the end.

We realised that all the other survivors had been ferried out by now. Terry, Bill Reynolds and me were the last Loamshires left. We had no choice but to go along with the LURP.

Molesworth was the last aboard the bus. He strolled over to the machine Terry and me were in, bat slung over his shoulder, stumps under his other arm, pads flapping in the downdraft from the rotors. He sat down next to me and unbuckled his pads. Over the racket of the engine, the door-gunner pumping tracers into the jungle below. This time, the loudspeakers were playing "Nellie the Elephant".

"The Mekon don't play cricket," he shouted to me, "chiz chiz."

Bob had realised within moments of setting foot on the sound stage that he came at the absolute bottom of the pecking order. Having written "the original book" made him of considerably less interest to grips and extras than, say, being the lad from the canteen who brought down the tea-urn and biscuits.

After two months of shooting, he had learned to blend in with the many busily-employed people whose jobs were hard to define. Sometimes, he would be called on for an opinion that would, likely as not, be ignored or overruled by Powell. Very occasionally, he was palmed off on some journalist or television interviewer down to do a story on the film.

Puttnam had gone native and joined the effects crew. He was merrily sloshing buckets of kensington gore over people. Powell was sneakily getting shots of the man from the censors with blood up to his elbows. He was shooting ridiculously violent scenes that he would willingly sacrifice during the inevitable arguments over final cut, just so he could get away with the things he really wanted to keep.

They really did use tomato ketchup. Every time Powell shot a battle scene, the set smelled like a chip shop.

I love the smell of burning flesh in the morning…

Bob shuddered.

At first, he had worried that he wouldn't be able to stand watching the filming. He still wore his commando knife and had nightmares. Everything had associations that took him back: noises, sights, smells, phrases.

Though the actors had real-looking guns, they made only the feeblest of pops when they were fired off. Bob understood that the rat-tat-tat sounds were added later by Dino DiCampo, the foley artist. As Rodney Bewes and James Bolam ran across the stage for the dozenth time, stepping between pre-set firework charges, firing their toy guns into the air, Bob was taken back not to Indo but to the Waste Ground where he and Terry played War as kids. The actors were doing the same thing.

He felt an almost physical ache for what was lost. They had played British and Germans. Or, during the War of 1956, British and Egyptians. Then, after they had both seen Jack Warner as the secret agent in *I Was a Communist for MI6*, they had been parachuted into America to ferret out atom secrets. Thelma had been briefly impressed into service as the Yankee temptress played by Patricia Roc.

If Bob ever had a son, and caught him playing War, he would belt him black and blue. If, as it seemed sometimes, the Indo-China War dragged on long enough for a son of Bob's to grow up and be conscripted into it, Bob would put the lad on the Paddy Boat himself, and send him off to Ireland with all the other beetniki and conchies.

His family had done its bit.

"Again," drawled Powell, who treated actors worse than he treated anyone else, which was quite an achievement. "Try to look more terrified, fellows. The treens are trying to kill you, after all."

In the back of the helicopter, as "I am a Mole and I Live in a Hole" played on a reel-to-reel tape recorder, Bob and Terry clung to the webbing and listened to Darbishire's modest war stories. The lieutenant clearly didn't like recounting his own exploits and played everything down if he had been involved. With Captain Jennings, he had actually been to Hanoi undercover, and blown up two American oil-tankers in Haiphong Harbour. Darbishire was keener on regaling them with anecdotes about his comrades.

Molesworth and his band of merry cut-throats specialised in rescuing downed pilots, carrying out daring acts of sabotage along the Casey Jones Trail or having hairsbreadth escapes. They were supposed to be executing covert reconnaissance missions deep inside enemy territory but spent most of their time on high-profile japes and wheezes. These public schoolboys seemed to be in a different war. Bob couldn't imagine them experiencing the terror, discomfort, misery and doubt that had been his lot ever since Sergeant Grimshaw first called him a tart. In peacetime they'd all be Arctic explorers, mountaineers or in prison.

"Winker" Watson, who had been captured by the enemy five times and on each occasion had escaped in the same way most people would nip out for a packet of tabs, was the door-gunner on this ship. He periodically raked the jungle with fire, claiming to be tiger-hunting.

"Do you know," said Darbishire, "I think Winker's just popped someone."

They looked out of the open door and saw two bodies sprawled in a clearing. Among them were the half-assembled parts of what looked like an American-made rocket-launcher.

"A boundary," said Winker.

The helicopters were playing "pub cricket", scoring runs on the number of legs possessed by their kills. It was considered bad form to take pot shots at innocent goats to get ahead.

Darbishire, trusted to keep the score, made a note.

"You're all bloody doolally," Terry said.

Darbishire shrugged, embarrassed.

"If you think we're mad, wait until you meet the chap at the end of our little Sunday jaunt."

They were proceeding north-west into Laos, over mountainous country. The jungle below was thicker, more remote from the War, but primordially dangerous. Bob half-expected a long-necked brontosaurus to poke its head out of the trees, roaring at the flying machines.

Darbishire flipped open a file folder marked "MOST SECRET" and showed them a photograph. It showed a smooth-faced chinless youth with a mop of curly locks in the uniform of the Coldstream Guards, sheathed sword in one hand, bearskin in the other. He stood erect, but had a big, open smile. He looked about fourteen.

"This is Major Basil Fotherington-Thomas. Major Molesworth was at school with him."

"Looks harmless," Terry said.

Darbishire wiped his specs.

"Looks can be deceiving, old man. Fotherington-Thomas has more medal ribbons than Lord Emsworth's prize pig. Mountbatten called him 'the finest jungle fighter of his generation', said he was the new Wingate.

He's been out here since '63. We haven't had official word from him in 18 months, but intelligence suggests he is running his own show from some stone age settlement way, way up the Ulu. He's got his own war going, and has been upsetting top brass by popping off some people who are supposed to be our allies. He issues statements, claiming responsibility for assassinations, always branding the dead as traitors or corrupt. He's had a few ARVN Generals killed."

"And were they traitors or corrupt?" Bob asked.

"Well, in all probability, yes. But it still doesn't do just to top them in the street, you know. Due process of law, and all that."

"You've let this go on for a year and a half?" said Terry.

"This isn't the first attempt to, um, re-establish contact with Major Fotherington-Thomas. Have you ever heard of 'Just William'?"

"The tunnel fighter?"

"That's the fellow. Captain William Brown, the solo man. Once sat in one of those enemy tunnels on his own for twenty days awaiting business, then scragged eighteen treens, armed with only a Sykes-Fairburn knife and a torch."

Darbishire dug out another photograph.

"Brown was sent in alone to talk sense to Fotherington-Thomas. Hasn't been seen since."

Bob looked at the photograph.

"Yes, he bloody has," he said. "I saw this bloke dragged up as a tart in Saigon. He assassinated an ARVN officer. One shot to the head."

"I'm not surprised. Seems 'Just William' has joined the other team. Frightful bad show, really."

Though he must have been pushing eighty, Schmuel Gelbfisch wore a violently orange kaftan over his swollen belly and a leopard-spotted fur hat on his bald head. He was propped up by a nineteen-year-old "secretary" with the shortest skirt Bob had ever seen and soft leather thigh-boots. He had to be arranged in his seat in the screening room like a sultan being lowered into a bath of pillows.

Born in Warsaw, Gelbfisch was the first film producer to relocate from Berlin and establish his studio in the Ukraine, which became the global centre of the entertainment industry in the teens and was only now surrendering its pre-eminence to international co-productions shot with the cheap labour of Spain and the Philippines. The growling bear of Metropolis-Gelbfisch-Mayer, the company Gelbfisch founded with the

Czech writer Carl Mayer in 1919 to make the silent classic *The Blood Lust of Dr. Caligari*, was still the most familiar trademark in the world. He had stayed in power longer than any president or monarch.

Martino Scorsese, Gelbfisch's grand vizier, sat immediately to his left and a little below. Michael Powell, a supplicant for once, had dressed up a bit with a beret, and was seated within swatting distance of the mogul.

Bob was jammed in down at the front with the "talent". Rodney Bewes apologetically introduced himself.

"I'm doing my best to be you, mate. Honest."

Bob thanked him. From what he had seen, Bewes was a fine actor, even if he wouldn't last ten minutes in the Wheeltappers much less Indo-China. He'd still have preferred Albert Finney, who had just made *King and Country*, a film about the man who shot Sergeant Grimshaw, with Leo McKern as John Mortimer, the QC whose argument failed to save Arthur Seaton from the gallows. In *King and Country*, Grim was being played by a much more sinister actor than William Hartnell, the black-browed and scowling Patrick Troughton.

Powell got up and coughed for silence. Bob had expected him to moderate his manner in the Royal Presence, but he drawled as confidently as usual, explaining that they were about to see a fine assembly of the attack on the prison camp. It would be the last scene before the intermission.

The lights went down.

Over black leader, the first ominous thrums of "Teddy Bears' Picnic" played. Dread clutched Bob's heart. The scene faded up on the jungle treeline, shot by Jack Cardiff's second unit in Queensland, as bombs exploded, turning everything into a big bonfire. Helicopter blades sliced on the soundtrack. Bob's hand crept unbidden to the knife at his ankle. His heart pounded in synch with the wokkas.

Then came a shot of the twelve helicopters in flight, music pouring out of them. Scorsese sighed in contentment. The money was on the screen. The shot pulled back, and the wokkas overflew rolling green fields. Intercut were flashes of the second-unit jungle and the elaborate studio set. Powell had explained that he wanted the artificial jungle to look like a Douanier Rousseau, and dozens of art students had been set to work painting each leaf a bright colour.

The helicopters flew over what was very recognisably Canterbury Cathedral. A family of Indo-Chinese peasants trying to repair a stalled ox-cart looked up from the main street of a small Kentish market town as the LURP passed overhead. An explosion filled the screen.

There was a close-up of Dirk Bogarde, elegantly inexpressive. He looked nothing like "Mad Nye" Molesworth, but managed that spark in the eyes.

The green fields of England were intercut, faster and faster, with the jungles. Fires raged in both landscapes, overlapping in the editing.

Bob was covered with a jungle sweat.

He couldn't watch the actual attack scenes and turned to look at the audience. Scorsese was rapt, Powell critical. The secretary covered her eyes. The actors, who knew it was only play, were mostly shattered. Rodney Bewes breathed "good God".

The lights went up.

"So," said Powell to Gelbfisch, "how much did you love it?"

The mogul tilted his head to one side, as if deciding which way up a painting should be hung, and thought about it.

"Micky," he croaked. "One thing I understand not. The War is in Indo-China. Why you let us see you film it in England?"

"This isn't a film about Indo-China, Sam. It's about England."

Gelbfisch thought some more.

We put down in a clearing, which turned out to be a graveyard. There were giant granite heads, with thick lips and lazy eyes, stuck all around, staring blindly at the helicopters.

"Welcome to beautiful Laos," said Terry.

"Looks like more bloody jungle to me," I replied.

The humid, steaming heat was almost unbearable. You could choke just by trying to breathe in a place like this.

Molesworth ordered Jennings and some others to stay with the wokkas, then organised the rest to march the short distance to the camp they had overflown. He led us all in singing "They're Changing Guards at Buckingham Palace" to keep us in step.

As we entered the village, the locals came out from the huts to look at us. They were savages, naked except for grey mud-streaks, though some spear-carrying men had rank insignia tattooed on their arms.

The 20th Century was a long way away.

A crazy little Englishman darted out from somewhere and introduced himself as David Bailey, a news photographer on an assignment for the Observer. *He ranted about Fotherington-Thomas, making the Major sound like a cross between Florence Nightingale and Jack the Ripper.*

Molesworth had Darbishire take a look at the malarial civilian. Bailey begged us for a place on the helicopter home. He seemed concerned that he had missed his deadline by a few years.

At last, we stood in the village square. Flies buzzed all around. More dead eyes stared at us. Even some of Molesworth's Marauders were horrified.

From the largest hut, he came. A golden youth with ringlets half-way down his back, he had a tattered paperback of A.A. Milne's Now We Are Six *in one hand and a flint axe in the other. He looked up at the world, then around at the village, then down at us.*

"Hullo clouds, hullo sky, hullo pile of severed human heads," said Major Basil Fotherington-Thomas.

Bob realised that this was what they whispered about as an XPD mission—meaning "expedient demise". A murder raid. But, though Fotherington-Thomas was armed only with a sharp rock and his men seemed mostly to rely on spears, Molesworth didn't unholster his Webley and shoot the blighter. Instead, the Major stuck out his paw and joked, "Dr. Livingstone, I presume."

The heat was worse than ever and the stench was indescribably ghastly. Bob and Terry huddled together for safety, instinctively recognising that they alone in this place were as yet not completely insane. The pile of heads Fotherington-Thomas mentioned was jumbled on a dais in the village square. Bob had a nasty feeling that the Major viewed his visitors as the potential raw material for another such monument.

Something snakelike and black stirred. It had been camouflaged against one of the giant heads. Bob realised it was a white man, face and clothes striped black and dark green. He smiled, showing a red tongue and white teeth against the primal background. His eyes glittered.

It was "Just William".

No one else had seen him. Bob nudged Terry, but Brown had blended into the scenery again. Bob looked around. How many shadow men, armed with more than spears, were there around the village?

"Hullo, Molesworth," said Fotherington-Thomas gaily. "You're just in time for tea. Did you bring any tuck?"

Outside the Empire Cinema, Leicester Square was thronged. There were rival groups of beetniki peace protesters and Young Conservative patriots, both claiming the film was an insult to their causes and threatening to disrupt the performance. There was also a rumour that some mad royalist who still thought the King had been seduced away from righteousness by his White Yank wife intended to throw glue into Princess Consort Wallis's hair-do, gumming her tiara to her beehive. The word was that the King's sister-in-law, the Dowager Duchess of York, had agreed to turn up tonight on the offchance that the glueman would strike and she could pretend to be sympathetic.

A discreet row of well-dressed but dangerous men were doubtless ready to step in if trouble started. They were under the direction of a calm chap with a bowler hat, an umbrella and a carnation in his frogged lapel, and a startlingly beautiful woman with auburn hair who wore a leather jump-suit. Bob would have fancied his chances with the security lady, but apparently she was married.

For Bob, the worst of it was the pathetic gaggle of men in wheelchairs or on crutches, with shaggily grown-out Army cuts and the remains of combat gear, holding a candle-lit vigil for the Ex-Servicemen's Peace Campaign. He had wanted to give them a donation, but the security chief discreetly hooked him with his umbrella, saving him from the fate of being photographed by the *Daily Mirror* consorting with men who were regarded as no better than conchies. He heard that Terry was one of the underground leaders of the ESPC. That made sense.

It Ain't Half Hot, Mum was the Royal Film Performance. It was a controversial choice, but Lord Mountbatten, who liked a good war film, had seen it and advised King Edward he would enjoy the battle scenes. And the Duke of Cornwall (next in line to the throne), who had served in Indo-China and won the respect of a surprising number of cynical soldiers, was on record as saying that this was the first film to give the truth of the conflict. Bob heard the King would rather see something with an X-certificate featuring Sarah Miles or Glenda Jackson with no clothes on, but that Princess Consort Wallis overruled him. Powell was obviously delighted at the honour, but still professed indifference. When reporters asked him about it, he responded with stories they could never print about the King's nieces.

In his new-fitted tail-coat, Bob felt like a prat, but his Mam and Dad were beaming, truly happy with him for the first time since he went away. They were chatting with Rodney Bewes, clucking over him as if they had adoption papers in their back pocket. Malcolm McDowell, hotly tipped to win a Best Supporting Actor BAFTA for his mad-eyed performance as Fotherington-Thomas, was being interviewed by McDonald Hobley for BBC-TV. Kenneth Halliwell trotted about with Joan Bakewell, loudly crediting himself with the discovery of Bob. Joseph, in a violently white two-piece that left his midriff bare, attracted photographers. He poked his tongue out at Bob. Diana swanned through, cleavage down to her navel and hair like a termite hill, accompanied by the film's production designer, Ken Russell.

Standing on the velvet carpet, alone for a moment, Bob looked over the ropes, at the pressing crowds. Most of them were here to see the Royals and the stars. But some were here to make a point, to be seen, to make trouble. Banners were waving across the square as a group of students, under the direction of the snakelike Howard Kirk, protested against the War. Two weeks ago, riot police had been sent onto the campus at Sussex, and a girl was in a coma after taking a truncheon blow to the head during a "sit-in". Even the most patriotic papers seemed to think there was something wrong with bashing a pretty middle-class girl's brains in just because she was silly enough to have let her boyfriend persuade her to go to an anti-war demo. If she'd been ugly, it would probably have been all right.

Rather embarrassingly, Bob was button-holed by Noote's widow, who thanked him profusely for what he had said in his book. He didn't think she'd enjoy the film—after much back and forth argument, the censors had left in the bullet-hole in Derek Nimmo's head but taken out the blood and brains on the ground—and didn't know what to say to her. Among the showfolk, there were quite a few other VIPs. Dennis Potter, the Labour party leader, was here, along with Clement Freud, the Liberal chairman, but the Prime Minister would not be coming until later, making his entrance shortly before the Royal Party.

Everyone he met asked him what he thought of the film. Rather than admit he still didn't understand why Micky shot half the jungle scenes in Kent, he claimed not to have seen it yet. After the performance, he'd have to stay out of the way.

Bob looked around the crowd, passing over famous faces, and sensed acutely who was missing. Thelma must be fuming at home. Despite the divorce, he'd asked her to come, but she had seen a photograph of him with Britt Ekland in the Sunday papers and drawn unwarranted conclusions.

He thought for a moment that he saw Terry. But it was only James Bolam in a blue tuxedo, sporting the Fu Manchu moustache he had grown for his next picture.

188

Fotherington-Thomas sat cross-legged in the square, shaded by his pyramid of severed heads, and read aloud, his clear voice transporting them all to the Thousand Acre Wood where a boy would always be playing with his bear. Bob felt his mind stretching around the craziness of it all. Terry was laughing and crying silently at the same time. Bailey took photographs, though there was no film in his camera. The villagers gathered, lulled by Fotherington-Thomas's voice, and even chimed in with well-loved phrases and sentences.

Every time Bob felt fear crawl down his spine like a many-legged insect, he found that William Brown was looking at him. The tunnel fighter always stood in the shadows, rarely getting more than a few yards away from the jungle. In this, the worst place in the world, the worst thing was Captain Brown. Worse than Vinh, worse than Grimshaw, worse than the Devil. Because Brown was touched by an angel. His eyes burned with a pure white light of purpose.

With a dozen men like Brown, Fotherington-Thomas could win the War. But then, which war would they find next? These men were not taking orders from Saigon, much less London. This was a whole new country.

"Fotherington-Thomas," Molesworth announced, "as any fool knows, you're utterly wet and a weed."

Tears started in the eyes of the Boy Monster God. He spread his white arms, and bared his chest. Molesworth drove a sharpened cricket wicket through Fotherington-Thomas's heart. Without a sound, he died. His face was almost beatific. He tumbled from his position and sprawled at the Major's feet.

The tribesmen looked at the murderer of their god. Bob didn't know if they'd bow down or rise up.

Brown had disappeared. Bob felt a spasm of panic. Just because he couldn't see Brown didn't mean Brown couldn't see him. In fact, that was when "Just William" was at his most dangerous. And Bob was a left-over witness, unfinished business.

Molesworth picked up *The House at Pooh Corner*, and wiped blood off its cover. The natives, filed teeth bared, hissed at the sacrilege.

"'In which Tigger is unbounced'," he announced.

As he read, Molesworth was accepted.

There was a tug at Bob's sleeve. He expected a stab at his heart, but it was Darbishire not Brown.

"I've called Captain Jennings on the wireless. He'll bring the helicopters over and get us out. Then we'll *flambé* this whole place, burn it to the ground."

"Best news I've heard all week," said Terry.

"What about him?" Bob nodded, indicating Molesworth.

"The Major? We've lost him, I fear," sighed Darbishire, shaking his head. "It happens sometimes. He's lived too much, seen too much. He can't take any more."

"Too right, son."

The helicopters were coming. A missile streaked out of the sky, burning white, and exploded.

"I thought the plan was for an air strike *after* we were evacuated," said Terry.

"Do you chaps ever do anything but complain?" snapped Darbishire.

A hut exploded. More fire fell from above. Through the heat-haze, Bob saw one helicopter hovering low. Jennings had fired at the outskirts of the camp to provide a distraction.

People were running all over the place. Molesworth stood still and tall, still reading aloud about Owl and Tigger and Eeyore.

Some of the natives had guns. Watson went down on one knee, with a hideous leg wound that he shrugged off.

A shroud of flame enveloped the pile of heads. They must be preserved in something flammable. Faces shrank to skulls. Eyes boiled to angry points.

A rope ladder unrolled, conking Darbishire, who clutched his head and looked irritated. Terry grabbed and secured the ladder with his weight, nodding through the din. Darbishire was first up. Bob made it second.

A few other men scrambled up, climbing past Terry and into the cabin. Watson pulled himself up with his hands.

Tribesmen gathered, jabbing with spears, in a circle, closing on Terry. Bill Reynolds got half-way up the ladder, and took a round between the shoulder-blades. He fell backwards, boots clumping Terry, who let go of the ladder and staggered.

The helicopter lifted up.

Bob shouted at Jennings.

"There's still a man on the ground."

The ladder dangled out of Terry's reach.

"Can't stay here forever," Jennings yelled over the noise.

There were explosions all around as the other wokkas poured tracers into the village. Bob, choking on hot fumes, flung himself out of the cabin door, and crawled head-first down the ladder, hooking his boots into the rungs, swaying in the wind, bullets whistling past his head.

He was caught up in the rope and couldn't go any lower. But he could reach out. He stretched his arm, popping his shoulder-joint, and held out a hand for Terry.

Terry was holding his head, bewildered. Tribesmen were within stabbing distance.

"Terry," Bob shouted. "Take my hand!"

His fingers brushed mine, but suddenly there was a yard of space between us. It might as well have been a million miles. I shall never forget the look of horror on Terry's face. I shall never forgive myself for not doing more.

His fingers brushed Terry's hair. Then the helicopter rose three feet. Terry looked up and saw the opportunity. He jumped, but missed his grasp. A native swung a spear at him, and he jumped again...

Hanging upside-down, Bob saw a black-and-green face in the native crowd, its eyes fixed malevolently on his. "Just William" would not let him go so easily. Reflexively, he made a fist...

Terry's hand closed around Bob's, and the helicopter lifted upwards. But Terry's fingers slipped on Bob's fist. Their eyes met and Bob saw blame in Terry's surprised glare.

It was too late to open his fist and interlock his fingers with Terry's.

In huge close-up, a hundred feet across, on the screen of the Empire, Leicester Square, James Bolam failed to get a grip on Rodney Bewes's fist. It was the first time Bob had seen the scene cut together.

How had Micky Powell known? In his book, he'd been unable to put it down. He'd taken all the blame, but not given the details.

Only two other people alive could have known.

Bob, soaked with sweat, looked around the darkness. Which of them had it been? Who was here, tonight?

Terry? Or "Just William"?

The helicopter was twenty feet from the ground. Bob was slung underneath it like an anchor. Terry sprawled among the natives, who looked up at the departing war machine. Bob saw the dark shape of William Brown closing on the writhing Terry.

He screamed and screamed, eyes shut tight, unable to watch the inevitable play out.

"It's this passage," Halliwell had said. "You can't let it stand and expect to be published. It's tantamount to treason."

Bob remembered what he had written.

Somehow, Terry got out of the camp—I think Brown might have rescued him, and dumped him in the jungle—and wandered around for days in the jungle, delirious and fever-struck. He was recaptured by the treens and wound up in another prison camp, where another officer presented him with the deal Vinh had offered. I have a cutting from the Straits Times, *an English language newspaper from Hong Kong, with a photograph of Terry getting off an airliner in Zurich and the story of the press conference he gave to denounce the War as Anglo-Russian imperialism. Now, he travels around Britain, almost a fugitive in his own country, addressing anti-War meetings, and saying that Britain has no business in Indo-China, that the peoples of the country should be left to work out their destiny for themselves. He also campaigns for the government to do more to secure the release of prisoners of war. In his place, I would have done the same thing in Indo, and be doing the same thing at home.*

Halliwell had made him change the last sentence to "*some things can be understood but not forgiven*". He always told himself that he meant his own moment of cowardice, but he knew everyone else who read the book thought he meant Terry's "treason".

The film ended with another scene Bob had not seen before. The fires engulfed Fotherington-Thomas's camp and faded into a blood-red banner. There was a pan down to Rodney Bewes, with long hair and fashionable clothes, sitting in a bookshop, signing copies of Bob's book.

Filing past, with books to be autographed, were all the characters from the film. Those who had died were hideously mangled. Intermingled were life-sized teddy bears. At the end of the line, making eye contact with Rodney Bewes as he neared him, was James Bolam, still in uniform.

On the soundtrack, a ragged chorus of soldiers sung "Teddy Bears' Picnic".

The film ended with Rodney Bewes and James Bolam—no, damn it, Bob and Terry—looking at each other, not saying anything out loud.

Haunted faces.

The applause was still continuing, and Micky Powell was taking bows, smiling broadly at the small but significant section of the audience who were booing as loud as the others were cheering, as Bob made it to the

Gents. He was a wreck. The film had brought everything back. Now here he was in his silk shirts and his MG sports car and his poncey £2 haircut swanning around with shallow pseuds and arty-farty types who didn't care nearly as much as they pretended they did.

Who was he trying to kid?

He knelt over a toilet bowl and puked up the smoked salmon he had eaten at the reception. He had been presented to the King and now he was throwing up like a teenage drinker. He was sick until he was empty.

How could he ever face anyone? Now that everyone knew?

He staggered out of the stall and shoved his head under a running tap. Cold water stabbed his hackles.

He looked up, rubbing paper towels into his neck. Water had seeped down into the back of his shirt.

He looked into the mirror. Eyes glittered from behind him. He wasn't afraid.

He turned.

A shape came out of one of the stalls. Bob knew it was Brown, somehow come from out the jungle hells of the other side of the world, still intent on settling accounts, silencing the witness.

This was the best. At least he would die as he was supposed to have died.

It wasn't Brown.

"Hello, our kid. This time, you're the one spewing."

Terry was thinner than he had been. In the photographs Bob had seen, he wore his hair long and beard shaggy, but now he was clean-shaven and had a severe short back and sides.

He wore a navy uniform.

"I'm not enlisted in me own name," he explained.

"Terry, I'm..."

Terry shrugged. "Aye, I know."

They looked at each other, just as the actors had in the film. Bob wondered if Powell were directing them.

"For a while, in the jungle, I thought you'd done it because of Thelma," Terry said.

Bob laughed.

"I know, I know," said Terry. "I went daft. That's a good picture, you know. I don't know what all those English fields and teddy bears were for, but it brings it back. A lot of people are going to have their minds changed. You've done well."

"It's not my picture."

Terry smiled.

"How've you been, kidder?" Bob asked.

"Busy. But I can't take it any more. The speeches, the meetings, the organising. I can't do that. I'm just a Geordie piss-head in way over my depth. You're the clever one. I'm going to sea because I can't be a hero any more. That's your job, Bobby. Know what I mean?"

Bob did, but shook his head.

"It's bloody funny when you think about it, Bob. Living through it all, from Grimshaw through Khe Sanh to Fotherington-Thomas counted for nothing. Your book made people sit up, but it's only this film that will get through. From now on, the film and our lives are mixed up in a jumble. People will ask you about things in the film they made up, and you'll start to wonder whether they happened. Eventually, the film will seem more real than the life. In the meantime, you know what you have to do."

Bob left his tailcoat in the toilet, and joined the crowd piling out into the square. The mood was strange. He wondered what the King had thought.

A reedy young bloke shook his hand and congratulated him. Bob realised that had been Charles, Duke of Cornwall. He fancied the Prime Minister looked at him with hatred. He couldn't get within twenty yards of Powell, who was beaming between Scorsese and a small man Bob took to be Imre Pressburger. He allowed himself to be washed out of the foyer with the surge of people.

Terry had vanished. Bob was no longer looking around for the mad eyes of William Brown.

Bob fought his way to the stand of the Ex-Servicemen's Peace Campaign. A couple of Young Conservatives were jeering at the bearded men, some of whom were in wheelchairs.

"Excuse me," he said to a man holding a placard, "but how do I join up with you?"

CITIZEN ED

1945-84

Now Ed's gone and died, they're going to put up a memorial in the park. Order of Debs, First Class. Two-Time Hero of the United Socialist States of America. Loyal Servant of the Party Agricultural Committee for Waushara County. Saviour of Plainfield, Wisconsin. A bronze of his head, topped off with that plaid hat half-sideways like he always wore it. It'll be sited by the bench where he used to sit. It's a bus stop, but I never saw him ride the bus.

Ed would wait for someone—a middle-aged or elderly woman, for preference—to sit by him, and just yap at them. Bore 'em stiff, mostly.

Sometimes, he'd kill 'em.

He had his little set phrases, all starting with that "ayup" sound that announced he was going to say something. "Ayup," he'd go, "life's like a joint of meat. You can carve it any which way you like, but you'll never know how bloody it is 'til you cut to the bone."

No, I don't know what he meant either. I have some ideas. None pleasant.

You want to hear the story of Edward Gein, Socialist Hero? Ask around and all you'll get is what's in the pamphlet. It'll tell you how he won the Medal for Marksmanship, how he got everyone through the Big Freeze of '56 with his "cured meats", how he took the state prize for American Craftsmanship with leatherwork, how he was always *soooo* nice and polite to his old ladies.

Ask me, and I'll fill in the footnotes: he was a degenerate, murdering, corpse-fucking piece of filth.

That doesn't mean he doesn't deserve his damn statue.

For me, it started in the War. I know, I know. You want to hear about Plainfield, but you're getting my story. My angle on it. It was in the War that I was set on the course that ran me smack into Mama Gein's Best-Loved Boy. So I have to tell you about it. Bear with me, and it'll come straight.

I was in Yurrup. Battle of the Bulge. We raise ten-foot snowdrifts in these parts, but that was the worst winter I ever spent. Somehow the prospect of getting killed or coming home minus a testicle made it seem a lot colder. Not a one of my unit came back with all his fingers and toes. I'm missing my left little toe. It still itches like little ants are swarming all over it. Phantom pain.

The Allies were all mixed in at the Bulge. Normally, we stuck our own sectors of the line to stop us killing each other by mistake (or not), but when Adolf's last desperate push came through in December of '44, Brits, Yanks and Russkies all got thrown into it together. Tommies, Ivans and American officers all had boots and gloves fit for high-ranking Party officials. They damn well hung onto their frozen digits. And their ears. That's what started a lot of the complaining you heard in the '50s. Boots and gloves.

Before the War, Capone came on the radio and said, in decadent capitalist countries, only plutocrats got decent food and clothing. In Yurrup, a lot of us saw that wasn't the way it was. The lowest latrine-scraper in His Majesty's Forces was as well equipped as an American officer, and a damn sight better than any GI south of a Second Lieutenant. We came back with the feeling we'd been lied to, and didn't much like it.

So there we were, a single company of the 83rd (Edward Bartlett) Infantry Brigade. Charles H. Marx only knows where the rest of the battalion got to in all the confusion, but our orders were to stand and fight. We were lined up along a big clearing somewhere in the Ardennes forest with a road running through the middle, a road along which, we were assured, a Panzer division would be coming before too long.

Problems, problems. Like digging yourself a foxhole in frozen ground with army-issue entrenching tools that fold up like sheet lead if you actually try and use them for entrenching. There's a battalion of Brits to the right of us so we asked them to extend some fraternal assistance, but they just told us to "fack orff" and not disturb them while they were busy drinking tea and bellyaching. So then one of the guys went over to the Ivans on our left flank and, in fluent sign language, requested the loan of some spades. They didn't say much, they just came on over with picks and shovels and helped us dig in, gave us some vodka and a bag of rice and smiled a little. They were just kids, sixteen-eighteen years old, like my brother Jim, who was just dead in the Pacific Theatre. Nice kids.

All the while, we could hear artillery and small arms in the distance, but we didn't get out own sniff of Kraut for another six hours or so.

Trying to guess the big picture, I assume we were up against an infantry unit that had gotten itself lost. They just settled themselves at the other side of the clearing and popped off at us with mortars and small arms. They didn't have any tanks or anything. In the big picture, it was chickenshit, but that's not how it felt at the time.

There was a stone building in the middle of the clearing and the Brits, who had the highest ranking officer in the area, had volunteered some of the Ivans to occupy it with a couple of their heavy machine guns. The Krauts softened it up with mortars then tried to rush it with grenades and all the supporting fire they could muster. Ten minutes later, the building was half a building, but the Krauts ran off leaving half a dozen of their comrades lying roundabout, groaning or screaming. The poor Ivans inside were doing the same.

I'd seen it once before when we were slogging through Normandy. A kind of paralysis sets in on both sides. They just stand in their foxholes, half-heartedly shooting each other's shadows, kinda disgusted by what they're doing and kinda terrified to do anything that'll make it worse. So they just wait for a superior officer, or some tanks or airplanes or bad weather—anything at all, really—to come along and change the situation without them actually having to make any decisions. That's how it was in the forest that afternoon.

We none of us gave a hang about the wounded Germans, but those poor Russian kids who'd given us vodka and dug our nice safe holes for us, well…We could hear them shouting. The army-issue phrase book was full of helpful sentences like "I am not interested in your black market goods" or "the matter must be referred to a superior officer". None of us knew what "help, my leg has been minced up by a stick-grenade" sounded like in Russian.

Then, someone did decide to do something. Captain Cooney, our political officer, told me to get over there and check them out. His Old

Man was one of Capone's beer buddies, and he had been promised a position well away from the fighting, but there was a SNAFU and he found himself stuck in the field with a bunch of half-frozen, all-the-way-shit-scared GIs who, given the choice, would sooner have shot him than Hitler. Our radio was out and Cooney wanted to requisition theirs so he could squeal for Daddy to haul him out of dangerville. So, I was volunteered to squirrel across open ground, ice chunks crawling into my clothes, bullets spanging around my ass. Turned out the Ivans didn't have a radio. What they had was shrapnel wounds, bullet wounds and limbs crushed by fallen masonry.

So, with a little supporting fire from my buddies and from the Russians next to us—and none from the Brits, who I think were taking a tea-break —I hauled the four Ivans who were still alive out of the house. The third time out, I took a Schmeisser slug in the shoulder but didn't feel it 'til a while after I'd gone in again to haul the fourth. My whole body was like a side of frozen beef. The bullet just thumped into solid meat. Later, it hurt like hell.

I don't want to make myself out a hero. I did what I did because I was too scared not to. Lot of guys got killed because they couldn't bear for their comrades to see how chicken they were. Lots more because the habit of taking orders, especially from assholes like Cooney, was ingrained too deeply. When I unfroze, it turned out I had a wound which would mean pain 85 out of every 100 days for the rest of my life.

Two of the Ivan kids made it. One sent me Easter cards for years, when they got through the censors. I had to write and ask him to stop: back in the '50s, mail from Russia marked you down as a counter-revolutionary and got you on the shitlist. Easter cards got you marked as a superstitious reactionary, which was another shitlist. Naturally, the two were rigorously cross-referenced. That was what the USSA's first computers were invented for.

I also received some Russki medal that got my name on the master-shitlist underlined in neon. Cooney got a commendation for Fraternal Gesture Heroism, and a transfer to the General Staff, where he spent the rest of the War trotting around behind Patton with a Zippo lighter. Inside track for advancement within the Party, you understand.

My red badge of stupidity was enough, when I was shipped home, to win me a sympathy appointment. Plainfield made me Deputy Sheriff Joe Costa. Might not sound much, but it was better than the six-foot

Victory Plots a bunch of my friends and relations wound up in. It came with a cabin on the edge of the woods; not much more than a stove and a cot in a shack, but I wasn't sharing with five others like most people.

If I had known Ed Gein was waiting for me, I'd have jumped ship and swam back to the War.

They had a parade for me. High schoolers in Junior Pioneer uniforms, coonskin caps and all, marching past, holding banner-sized tapestries of a heroic Capone, scar turned away from the weavers.

I still had shellfire ringing in my ears.

I was twenty-four years old, and sole survivor of my male graduating class. One thing Capone said that wasn't a lie was that the King and the Tsarina had been determined to fight the Axis until there wasn't an American left standing. Yurrup was bad enough, but the Pacific was the Big Betrayal. Remember, Russia had the Bomb in mid-'45 but didn't drop it until Fall. By then, 75,000 USS invasion troops had been killed fighting ditch-to-ditch, town-to-town on the Japanese mainland. 6,000 Americans died in Hiroshima and Nagasaki, along with no Russians and no Englishmen. I've never been much of a goodthinkful socialist, but when the Limeys and the Ivans got their asses whipped in Indochina, I cheered for the North Vietnamese and Vietcong. Only Party-minded thing I ever did was go door-to-door raising Fraternal Funds for the Indochinese.

Ed wasn't at the parade, but his Mom was. Augusta Gein was still alive. It was in '45, just before the Total Victory. She didn't last out the year. She was a Lutheran and thought we should have been on the Germans' side. But she saw her duty and baked me a cake, cried and gave me a leaflet about the perils of sexual incontinence and masturbation. I don't believe Augusta remembered which of the kids I had been. Very few did. My Old Man sometimes called me "Jimmy" and promised to take me out after deer come spring.

After the Bulge, I never wanted to hold a rifle ever again. Even before the War, it was Jimmy who had dreamed of an eighteen-point buck on the wall in his half of the bedroom. I was never sold on the idea of shooting things dead for no particular reason. But in these parts, that's like publically espousing the cause of counter-revolution.

Augusta Gein was cracked, but no more so than half the biddies in town. She and Ed's Pop ran a collective farm out in the boonies. When Gein Senior pegged out, she ran it with her son, Eddie. Thanks to Frank Spellman's "agricultural reforms", the place nearly came apart in the 1930s.

But the War put land at a premium, and the collective almost thrived for a while. Raised hogs, mostly.

But the Gein Place was basically the Waushara County Slaughterhouse.

In the USSA, outside the cities, the dollar is a worthless piece of paper. Currency is something you can eat. Out here, they still use the old name for the Communist Party. The Farmer-Labor Party.

In the 1930s, before they purged Spellman, the collectivised farm system all but collapsed. In the mid-West, everything turned to dust. That dragged down the rest of the set-up all over the place. Kids like me were raised on short rations. I grew up on a dairy farm, but didn't taste butter for ten years until a Tommy swapped me a "bully beef" sandwich for my steel helmet at a field hospital in Bastogne.

When the time came, we were supposed to take our animals out to the Gein Place. After his Old Man died, Ed did the slaughtering, and Augusta—a Party member, naturally—decided how meat resources be allocated, which meant keeping the prime cuts for her family and cronies, and shipping the rest off to the cities where other Party officials served them to their friends. In return, we were given scrip redeemable at the Party store in town.

Once, when Jim let off a cherry bomb in the outhouse, the Old Man threatened to haul him out to the Gein Place and turn him over to Ed and his sledge-hammer and cleavers. By rights, Jimmy should have got a whipping, but Pop was so appalled by what he had said but not meant to that the kid was let off. I wonder now if Pop hadn't had some idea. He died in '49 of the tuberculosis, so I can't ask him.

If the business of America is butchery, then Ed Gein was Our Killer. Our Greatest Killer.

Everyone hereabouts had to kiss up to Augusta Gein, hoping for scraps. Occasionally, she would allow a few chickens to escape the coop around Thanksgiving, Revolution Day or Christmas. You know, that made folks hate her more. She was showing them the power she had.

The whole town turned out for her funeral. The Party Committee, in full uniform, arranged for a Junior Pioneer Corps team to fire a salute over the grave. Ed insisted he be among their number; some say he brought down a duck with his shot, and gave it to a poor family.

I was there, in my new Deputy's uniform with the shirt that almost fit and the tin star. When the volley was fired, I threw myself behind a couple of grave-markers and had to be restrained. I was trying to pull my piece and return fire. The rifle-cracks took me back to Yurrup.

I was embarrassed, but Ed gave out a grin that was creepily friendly. His whole world had died with Augusta, but he didn't seem upset by my foolishness at the funeral. Though I was having my own fit, or maybe because I was off my mind, I saw then that he was a crazy person. I could have sworn that he was still with Augusta, looking around for her approval. Maybe he was nice to me because he saw and heard things that weren't there too.

After the funeral, he laid on a barbecue and everyone in town had at least a taste of meat. For some of the kids, it was the first time. He talked about Ma as though she was just inside the house and would be out in a minute. She was, he said, "a good person", and always came to chat with him in the evening as he was going to sleep. He went around playing up to his Mama's cronies on the Party Ladies' Committee, insisting that they eat up, have second helpings.

"Ayup," he kept saying, "put some meat on your bones."

The desecrations started in 1947. They were never a mystery. Every time some grave was dug up and bits of a corpse went missing, Ed Gein had just been visiting his mother. He always had a shovel with him in his pick-up.

Sheriff Truman and I went out to the cemetery a couple of times, mostly at the request of grieving relatives. The caretaker knew better than to call the Sheriff's office.

The job almost never called for what you might think of as detective work. You know, if there was a fight in a shebeen and someone got stabbed, it was a question of finding out which one of the brawlers was a Party member and letting him off for defending himself against an unprovoked attack or nailing the other guy for hooliganism. In the case of missing foodstuffs from the Party store, Harry Truman always assumed someone who needed to eat pretty badly was doing so and shifted reports around until the matter was dropped. If an official really put pepper on his ass, he'd throw Elmer, the town parasite, into the pokey for a few weeks and write him up as the pilferer. Elmer kinda liked getting two square meals a day for nothing, so everyone was happy.

Out at the cemetery, we didn't need Sherlock Holmes. There were the dug-up graves. There were the empty coffins. And there were the tire-tracks.

Several times, we had this conversation with angry relatives.

"Mama," or "Grandma" sometimes, "she's gone. Someone took her."

"There's evidence of grave-tampering, certainly. And there are tire tracks."

That would bring them up short.

"Yes," Sheriff Truman would say, slowly in case they were too preoccupied to think it through, "whoever did this certainly had a truck."

Back then, most folks got around by horse and buggy. Gasoline was harder to come by than Pope's piss. Anybody who had a car on the road was connected. And anybody who had a truck was a made man!

Usually, about then, the complaint would be dropped.

After a couple of years, and some really bad ones—just-dead folks missing, or worse still, found with holes in them, holes full of semen—it got so my shoulder nagged me so badly that I had to do something. The worse things got, the worse my wound played up.

One day Harry Truman just upped and disappeared.

Since he had not officially been discharged from office and no one wanted to ask where he had gone, Truman had to remain Sheriff. But I had to do his job.

About this time, someone dug up the corpse of my Great Aunt Effie, put a ballgown on it and wired it to the statue of Plainfield's lone Socialist Hero like the pair of them were dancing. The monument was our sole civic ornament, to a local boy named Jim Boon who'd been wounded in the Spanish war of 1898 and who'd been sweet on Effie. One day, he shot the no-good son of one of the local plutocrats for bothering Effie. He was hanged for it. When the town was looking around for a Revolutionary hero, someone remembered Jim Boon and the local party committee bought the statue from a monument dealer over Madison way. The statue was actually a representation of Joe Hill, but that line was discontinued after Hill was purged, so they got it for a couple of dozen eggs and the price of the rail freight.

I don't recall as any of this bothered Aunt Effie, who remained a spinster all her life, but now here she was doing the fandango with Jim/Joe, and she was family, dammit.

My shoulder hurt so badly I had to grip my belt for two hours to keep from screaming. People thought I was about to pull my gun.

I knew I had to pay a call on Comrade Gein, Butcher.

The other deputy, Lou Ford, was a Party snitch, so I went out to the Gein Place on my own. The gas ration had run low, so I couldn't use the Sheriff's vehicle, but I had a horse handy. I always figured Champion would be a lot more use in a crisis than Lou Ford.

Out in the woods, alone on a horse, occasionally startling a deer, your breath frosting the air, you can sometimes forget the shitpit. That's why you still find so many people living alone in log-cabins all over the boonies. America could be a hell of a country if enough people were shot dead.

I could sense Champion didn't want to go near the Gein Place. He dragged hooves for the last two miles, ankle-dredging through the fallen leaves. I guess animals talk to each other, and Champ knew that very few things of the four-footed persuasion ever got to come back from Eddie Gein's back-barn.

Usually, you can tell if a farmer is high in the Party. Their places are newly-painted and have shining machinery, like you see in the movies, around the yard, with the lesser members of the "collective" there to do all the work. The Gein Place wasn't like that. When you first came on it, you thought "well, this is where the Gein Dump is, but where does he keep the farm?" And he worked alone, getting bloody all by himself. This was a collective of one.

He could have used his position to second workers from the other collectives, and sat back on the porch getting fat on jerky, fiddling his quotas. Instead, he spent so much time on his slaughter that he didn't bother much with tidying up.

Of course, the place stank like a week-old battlefield in August. There were bones—mostly animal—all over the place, like a crunchy carpet, and hides nailed up on the walls. Everything was streaked with dried blood. There was a pile of cow skulls on the porch, heaped around a cheap concrete statue of Eugene V. Debs. A side of rotting meat was arranged before it, like an offering at an altar. First, my stomach heaved, but then I was thinking, "what a waste!"

Champion whinnied and reared as I hitched him to the rail on the porch. Somewhere, a mechanical saw was hacking through something. It wasn't the high whine of a buzz-saw through timber. I figured it for one of those newfangled chain affairs, and it was encountering different levels of resistance all the time. Something hard here, something sinewy there, something soft further along...

My shoulder jolted like I'd been shot.

I called out for Ed. The sawing continued. I thought about taking out my gun and executing the bastard child there and then. If he hadn't been Farmer-Labor, I might have been able to cover it. Blamed counter-revolutionary elements. But fat folks in Chicago would miss their Sunday joints, and the goddamn Federal Bureau of Ideology would be all over the show.

I walked over the bones to Ed's barn.

It hadn't been a barn for decades. But people didn't like to call it by its right name. It was the Killing House.

Inside, something screamed as a saw cut into guts.

Mama Gein was dressing a live deer with a chainsaw. Charlie Marx only knows how Ed had roped a fourteen-point buck, hog-tied it and hauled it up on a meathook. Now, his dead mother was standing under the screeching beast, scraping at its sides with a chainsaw like a Mexican child battering a piñata. If you've never heard a deer screech, you don't want to. Instead of candies, the deer was dropping apple-sized gobbets of flesh and arcing squirts of blood.

Augusta Gein, you will recall, was dead. But here she was. I recognised the dress she was buried in, under the red sunflowers of drying deer blood, and her leathery face was unmistakable, despite the heavy stitches holding it together where the cheeks had split. Her hair was unbound and hung down her back.

I drew my Colt and shot the ceiling. I wasn't firing a warning; I was trying to get the dead woman's attention.

She turned away from the deer and let the saw choke down.

Her cheeks cracked again and she tried to smile.

My gun was poked up in the air. My shoulder was on fire. My phantom toe, the one that had been frozen off in Europe, was a white-hot knot of pain.

Augusta's face broke across like a mask. The underside of her skin was raw and red.

Under Mrs. Gein's face was her son, Ed.

It wouldn't have been so bad if it was just the face and dress, but Ed was wearing more of his Mama. He had skinned her, and fit himself inside. She had been a big woman, so he fit easily. There was rough stitchwork down the backs of her legs like stocking seams, and down her arms.

He had turned his mother into an all-over suit.

"Ed," I said. "I think we've got a problem here."

The deer kicked and died, a gush of blood bursting from its throat, pouring onto Ed's jubilant, radiant face like gentle rain. His teeth gleamed red.

He stepped towards me, and I tried to level my gun. The pain was too much. I stood like a fool, gun aimed at the sky, as the man-woman-thing advanced, revving the chainsaw in smoky bursts.

It occurred to me that, as a Party member, Ed Gein would have no trouble getting gasoline to run his chainsaw.

Almost with reverence, he hung the chainsaw up on hooks, and considered an array of butcher knives, hooks, cleavers and choppers. Bloodied blades chinked against each other as he ran his humanskin-gloved fingers over them.

"Ayup," he said, "gotta have the right tools for the job."

I was backing away. I tripped on something I figured was a hay bale and reached out to grab something. I found myself hanging onto a dangling, greasy chain. I had dropped my gun.

Looking down, I saw that under a thin heaping of straw was Sheriff Truman. His face had been ripped off and put back upside-down, so his bloody nose-bone poked out through an open mouth and his eyeholes showed glints of jawbone.

Obviously, Harry had finally decided to do something.

"Ed," I said, trying to find the guts that had got those Ivans out of the crushed house, "I'm going to have to take you in."

"Ayup, Deputy Costa," he agreed.

In his hand, he held something small and shiny. It was Truman's tin star, filed to a razor-edge.

Ed just flicked the star at me, like those things the Japanese kids used to throw at the GIs in the army of occupation after the War. I felt as if I'd been punched in the eye. The shiny edge lodged in my socket like a sliver of ice. Hot blood exploded out of my face.

I didn't panic. The combat-instinct took over. I levelled my pistol and took aim. I had one good eye, and could still sort of see out of the injured one. Ed was too quick, though. He hitched up his skirts and came at me. There was a blur of petticoats, a glimpse of an enormous pair of flower-patterned drawers and the gun the been kicked from my hand. He jabbed a vicious rabbit-pinch to my throat and I fell backwards.

I must have hit my head on something hard as I fell and passed out briefly, because the next thing I knew, Ed was standing over me, trying to start up his chainsaw.

"Ayup," he said to himself, "just finish this critter and it'll be time for lunch."

That's when Lou Ford, bless his snitching little heart, showed up.

To recap, by this date, Ed Gein had committed wholesale grave-robbery, compounded by necrophilia and mutilation of corpses. On top of that, he had murdered the Sheriff and committed a felonious assault on a Deputy, to wit, me, resulting in said Deputy losing the sight of one of his eyes. That's not even considering exhuming, skinning and wearing his mother. Or unauthorised use of government-issue gasoline and countless violations of slaughterhouse hygiene regulations.

You would think that there was some possibility of him facing criminal prosecution. But Ed Gein was a Party member in Good Standing. He had just been commended for increasing slaughter production by 20% per annum for three years running, and awarded the Meritorious Order of Debs.

As soon as I got fitted with an eye-patch, I was determined to do something. This time, we couldn't let it slide.

I made a full report to the Waushara County Party Committee. The Committee was composed of Martha and Abby Brewster, two members of Augusta Gein's sewing circle; Norm Bates, Ed's twice-removed cousin; Bruno Anthony, a time-server from the state capitol who never set foot inside the county; Randall Flagg, the local ideologue; and Kaspar Gutman, manager of the Party Stores. Gutman had the fattest belly in town, closely followed by the bellies of his wife and kids, because Ed kept his table well-supplied with choice cuts.

Naturally, Lou Ford failed to corroborate my story in public. Without supporting evidence, the Committee were reluctant to pursue any action against a valued servant of the state like Edward Gein.

"But he's a homicidal maniac," I protested.

"Under socialism, there is no serious mental illness," explained the ideologue. "Only in the capitalist countries do such conditions exist. Homicidal or psychotic behaviour results from injustice or from alienation in a society which treats the individual as a mere machine for the enrichment of plutocrats. It is a well-known fact that alienation from the means of production can also lead to schizophrenic tendencies. These conditions do not exist in Waushara County, or anywhere else in the USSA, Comrade Deputy."

That was the Party Line. Hannibal Lecter, the USSA's leading psychiatric theorist, had won a Frank Norris prize for his book-length argument on the subject, *It Doesn't Happen Here.*

"That's as may be, Mr. Flagg. But Gein killed Sheriff Truman. That has to suggest something is wrong."

"Deputy Costa, did you see Eddie actually commit this dreadful crime?" asked Martha Brewster.

I had to admit that I did not.

"Well, it seems likely to me the Sheriff was assassinated by counter-revolutionary elements operating in the area."

"Martha, you're so right," put in Abby, without dropping a stitch. She was knitting what looked like a noose, and I had an itchy sensation in my neck. "There are counter-revolutionaries everywhere. I do believe they hide under my bed some nights. I can hear them plotting."

"What this town needs is a Drive to Rid Ourselves of Counter-Revolutionary Elements," declared Gutman. He had gravy stains on his shirt and tie. "I propose that Sheriff Costa be put in charge of the Drive. I do so like a man who can take firm action against counter-revolutionaries."

It was news to me that I was the new Sheriff. I later learned Lou Ford had turned it down. He didn't want to be in a position where he could publicly foul up.

I tried to bring up the fact that Ed Gein, Socialist Hero, was prancing about his farm dressed up in his Mama's desiccated skin, but they were all so excited about their Drive Against Counter-Revolution that they didn't listen.

"Round up all the subversives," I was told, "and we'll have the Federal Bureau of Ideology down here. No one kills our Sheriff and gets away with it."

When I got back to the office, Lou Ford had already worked up a list of subversives. It included a nine-year-old boy Abby Brewster had reported was given to loitering outside her house and whom she suspected of pelting her cat with stones. Otherwise, the best our fearless defender of state socialism could come up with were a few citizens who had been overheard complaining about shortages or voicing criticism of the Party. Oh, and Elmer, the town parasite.

"Okay, genius," I said. "Which of these killed Harry?"

Lou Ford thought about it, and suggested Elmer.

"Do you happen to remember Ed Gein dressed up in his Mama's bloody carcass fishing out my eye with Harry Truman's sharpened badge? Or him standing over me pulling at the starter on his chainsaw?"

"That's not how it looked to me, Joe," Lou Ford mumbled. "Could be you got hurt discoverin' the old Sheriff's body, and Ed was just tryin' to help out."

"Yeah, he's real helpful."

"Maybe we should put him in for a commendation."

I looked hard at Lou Ford. So far as I could tell, he was serious.

The pain in my shoulder bugged me really bad over the next few days, and the eye-injury added a terrible headache. Only thing I could do to deaden the pain was drink. On the morning of the third hangover I'd come up with a strategy.

I went and told Lou Ford that if anyone asked, he and I had spent the day in my office catching up on the paperwork. If he ever told anyone any different, I said, I'd see to it he didn't live another year. I'd written to a few old Army buddies saying that if anything happened to me, they were to waste him. It was all moonshine, of course, but it got me my alibi.

Next, me, Champion and my M1 went out to the Gein Place with a few sticks of dynamite in the saddlebags to carry out a little Counter-Revolutionary action of our own. I tethered the horse in the woods a good way off and snuck over.

I found Ed in the barn wearing his Mom and butchering a hog with his chainsaw. He never heard the hiss of the fuse, or the clink of the top being flipped back on my lighter, or the thump of the bundle of dynamite on the blood-soaked dirt floor behind him, or the patter of my feet vamoosing to behind a nice big tree two hundred yards away. And he certainly wouldn't have heard the sound of my hands covering my ears. Nope, sound didn't come into it.

Later, he told me he'd smelled the burning fuse, though. Just in time for him to get himself behind a bale of hides.

With my good eye, I watched the barn turn to a ball of flame and matchwood.

Moments later, Ed emerged in a daze. The explosion had stripped Ma of every last stitch of clothing, but like a motorcyclist's leather jacket, the old lady's tanned and toughened hide had protected Ed from the worst of the explosion. I caught myself admiring the intricate stitchwork and thinking what a shame it was that such a well-made garment was now covered in burn-marks. Then I unslung my rifle.

I cocked the gun. Little wisps of smoke rose from Ma's frizzled hair. I aimed for between the eyes, blinking inside the slightly too-large holes in the mask. I squeezed the trigger.

Nothing.

The goddamn rifle was jammed.

Desperately, I tried to clear the breech, but a round had stuck fast in there and there was no way my fingers were going to remove it. I should have known. Plenty of boys had died in the War because of dud ammunition.

Ed was coming towards me, still trying to shake the grogginess from his head.

I didn't have a sidearm, and given the nature of my last experience at the Gein Place, I figured it best to make myself scarce.

I hadn't gotten rid of him, but one of the first things you learn when you set out to work with lethal weapons, is that you don't just need a plan, you need a fall-back plan, too, and I had one.

As soon as I got back to town I got Lou Ford to run around and call a posse together. While out riding, I said, I'd heard an explosion from the Gein Place. A dozen of us drove and rode out as fast as possible.

Ed was wandering in a daze around the remains of his barn. He was still wearing his mother's hide and cradled the chainsaw in his arms like it was his baby. I made sure everyone got a good look before setting Lou to work on him with the First Aid box. Then I told the others to search the place thoroughly for any "evidence" as to who might have done this terrible deed. I wanted our townsfolk to stare Citizen Ed's calling in the face.

I also made sure we took a good look around the house. Just a regular timber house, it was. Only in the parlour, instead of cushions, there were masks made from human faces. Upholstered chairs were backed with human skin; you could still make out strips of fat on the undersides. There were lampshades and a waste-paper basket, made of human leather, too; all painstakingly sewed and tooled with pretty flower patterns.

Up in Ed's room, the four-poster bed had a human skull at each corner. Slung on a chair next to his Sunday-best pants was a belt studded with what appeared to be nipples. On the nightstand was a bowl of dried flower petals made from the top of a skull. In the wardrobe, someone found a shoebox full of strange shrivelled objects covered in salt. Nine of them. I believe the medical term is "vulvas".

Then we came to a room that had been nailed shut. Most of the guys had already taken one or two trips outside to throw up, so there was only three of us set about battering the door down. Surely nothing in there could be any worse than what we'd already seen.

It was Ma's room, left just as it was when she was alive. Just a regular old lady's room—bed, chair, closet, nice old cedar chest—all covered in a thick layer of dust.

Back outside, I called everyone together and announced that since Counter-Revolutionary elements were obviously at work in the area, it would be for the best to take Ed into "Indefinite Protective Custody" for his own safety until the miscreants were rounded up. Having had a good look around, everyone agreed. We gently helped Ed out of Ma's skin, and one or two of our number—the ones who'd maybe found bits of their relatives among Ed's trophies—took a mind to making his case for protection more convincing by kicking the shit out of him.

And that's how I got to keep Citizen Ed in the slammer for three glorious years. The posse told their families and neighbours in hushed tones about what they'd seen out there and we all happily connived in telling one another the big lie that we had to protect Ed the Socialist Hero from the great White Yank conspiracy or recidivist conspiracy or Counter-Revolutionary Plutocrat conspiracy that was out to get him. Truth is, we didn't get TV round our way until the mid-'60s, so cooking up conspiracies became one of Plainfield's favourite ways of passing the evening.

Ed was a model prisoner. He'd sit in his cell all day talking flapdoodle at anyone who'd listen. Once or twice a week, more in winter, three or four armed men would accompany him out to his place, where the barn had been re-built with Party money, and watch over him as the did the butchering. For three years, no corpses got dug up and no old ladies disappeared.

The only people who weren't happy with the arrangement were the local Party hacks. For the simple reason that their meat supplies weren't as good as they used to be. More seriously, Ed's production figures were falling, and the higher-ups wanted to know what was going on. Gutman leaned on me some to find the phantom Counter-Revolutionaries and let Ed go home, but try as I might, I just couldn't find any of the varmints anywhere. The best I could do was run Elmer the town parasite in and out of jail. Elmer didn't like this as much as he used to. Said that being in a cell next to Ed gave him the wim-wams.

Finally, in the Spring of '56, I was told that the FBI were despatching an expert to take over the Drive. I was ordered by Gutman to co-operate in every way with the big city hotshot.

"We'll get some results, my boy," he said. "Now that the professionals are on the job. We'll get some real action."

What we got was Special Agent Erskine Cooney.

I reckon Cooney was about as pleased to see me after 12 years as I was to see him. My shoulder still hurt whenever I thought of the Bulge, though it had a bit of competition from my burst eye and missing toe.

The Captain had come home from the War and landed a cushy job as one of J. Edgar Hoover's brightest and bushiest purge-meisters. He'd been compiling lists of names, cross-referencing the testimony of thousands of informers, and just plain making up stuff to fill in the gaps. He probably killed more people than Ed, and never had to leave his office before Hoover got so sick of his face that he sent him out to Wisconsin to do some honest-to-Marx field work.

He turned up in his Party car, with papers that meant he could get unlimited gas; wearing his sharp-shouldered city suit, which came with two pair of pants; and lots of stationery and folders with which to compile his lists of subversive elements. Gutman turfed me out of my office to make room for him. He spent near on an afternoon watching Lou Ford shift his goods into the office.

After that, he was so exhausted he had to go to his motel room and sleep off the work.

The next morning, at the crack of eleven, he showed up and called me and Lou Ford in for a conference, "to get the lie of the land." I was reminded of those Hollywood movies indicting British imperialism: Cooney wanted to treat me and Lou like those colonial exploiters treated native bearers…

"So, to sum up your efforts to date, you've done nothing. The subversion has continued unchecked, and no real progress has been made."

I looked at Lou Ford and decided I'd have to take pity on the Special Agent and tell him what was really going on.

"There is no subversion, comrade. Nothing bad has happened here for three years. The only problem we've got in Plainfield is Ed Gein, but we've got him under control at the moment."

Cooney looked in one of his files. "I have a string of Party commendations for Gein. He appears to me to be an asset to this community and an ideologically-sound citizen."

"Cooney, he's killed at least five people. You can come out to his place and see the evidence. Ed Gein is a mass-murderer That's the only fact that means any damn thing."

"Director Hoover has proved mass murder does not exist in the USSA. It's a societal impossibility."

"Impossible or not, there's a farmer in the cells and I've got him marked down as connected with at least five homicides and several more grave robberies."

Cooney smiled at me. "I see your error, Costa. As ever, you allow your admirable emotions to blind you to the larger situation."

Not for the first time, I regretted omitting accidentally to roll a grenade into Erskine Cooney's foxhole when I had the chance.

He ordered me to release Ed at once.

"What has obviously happened here," says Cooney, "is that the subversives have recognised Edward Gein as a loyal servant of the Party, as one of those rare paragons who embodies entirely the ideal of American state socialism, and have orchestrated a cunning and fiendish campaign to blacken his name. I detect the involvement of insidious foreign powers, and it would take at least a dozen home-grown traitors to manufacture the mass of evidence you've stumbled over. I'm ashamed, Joe, that you've failed to see through such obvious deception, and have allowed a good man to suffer unjust accusations rather than pursuing the real traitorous elements."

Cooney, tired out by all his reasoning, decided he should go home and lie down. Meanwhile, I was to get on the job of tracing all these conspirators.

Cooney had a parting shot, though. "You know, Joe, if it weren't for the fact that I know you from the War, I'd have thought you swallowed the Gein frame-up too easily and been forced to conclude you were yourself one of the counter-revolutionary elements involved. Now, let Comrade Gein go home and let's see you get some results for once."

It occurred to me that I could compile a list consisting of the entire Party Committee for Waushara County, bulked out with a couple of now-grown-up kids who had beaten up on me in High School and a few girls who had laughed in my face when I asked them out. If I turned that list over to Cooney, he probably wouldn't do any checking before having them all rounded up and put on a train for an Alaskan rehabilitation centre.

"Ayup, Sheriff Costa, Deputy Ford," said Ed as we sent him on his way. "Mighty obliged to you for your hospitality. I'd better be getting back to Ma."

Sure, I could give Cooney a list of anyone I wanted, but the problem was that Ed Gein would continue doing what he did, and eventually we'd be back where we started, with a bunch of major atrocities and the need to pin them on someone. Eventually, I knew it'd be me.

To this day, I don't know if Cooney was stupid enough to believe what he said or just going along with policy. I can't decide which would be the worst.

A week after he hit town, and once he'd had the chance to get bored, Cooney hit on Elmer's file.

Every place has a town parasite. Physically awkward and a bit slow, always half-drunk on moonshine from some backwoods still, sitting around on porches shooting the gab, occasionally doing odd jobs badly, cadging scraps of food and tobacco. Elmer was exactly like that. It was sort of comforting to have him about the place. Not a one of us doesn't occasionally think Elmer might have the smart idea, just taking life as it comes and not being beholden to Party or person.

Cooney had Lou Ford haul Elmer out of the cell where we usually let him sleep in the Winter, march him round the back of the jailhouse, and blow his brains out with a shotgun.

"Don't clean the wall," he said. "That red patch is a stop light for subversives."

Elmer's brains were a scatter on the wall. They spread on the snow about five feet all around the slumped corpse.

I saw other red patches. Other slumped corpses. On the snow of the Bulge. Another notch for Killer Cooney.

"We ought to leave the scum there," Cooney said. "As a warning. Of course, he'd go off."

"I believe Ed Gein has some experience in taxidermy," I said.

Cooney was on the point of taking the suggestion seriously when he worked it out. Scowling, he went home to have some more sleep.

When the Special Agent was out of sight, I took off my gloves and beat Lou Ford senseless. I broke all the knuckles of my left hand on his chin, and had to shove them into the snow to deaden the pain. I got frostbite. My fingers still don't unbend properly, and they got arthritic a few years later. I've got a permanent, useless fist. But I broke Lou Ford's jaw, and he can't inform clearly to this day.

Killing Elmer satisfied Cooney for a while. The whole town turned out for a meeting, and took turns getting up to accuse Elmer of all manner of posthumous crimes. A lot of petty stuff—some of which Elmer might even have been guilty of, who knows?—got shifted off the books.

Cooney sat on the stage beside Gutman and Flagg, modestly accepting all the fulsomely-worded tributes to his daring and cunning. I hung back and tried to keep my stomach settled. Lou Ford was still excused from duty while his jaw knit back together.

Cooney read out a message of congratulations from Director Hoover, commending the whole community for its valiant achievement in ridding itself of the last traces of poisonous subversion. Everyone applauded warmly.

Afterwards, they all tucked into a buffet of Ed's famous smoked meats. I went outside and puked.

I straightened up after emptying my stomach into the snow, and saw people spilling out of the Party meeting hall.

Ed, wearing his check cap and his mama's house dress over dungarees, smiled thinly at me as he walked past. I never knew what went on inside his head. Whether he was Ed or thought he was his Mom. It's a mystery.

Even Cooney, a newcomer, could look at Ed and not see anything odd about him. It got so he was a kind of blur, looked at sideways. When he was wearing his human skin face-mask and women's clothing, people thought there might be something a bit odd about Ed today but could never put their finger on it.

It was just the same as the way we could go without food for three days and listen to Walter Winchell praising Wisconsin for its food surpluses, and then turn round and give each other pats on the back because it was us Walter was talking about. Our bellies told us one thing, but we believed the radio.

I almost got to the point where I gave in. If everyone in the world tells you snow is red, you start to question your eyes. Maybe you've got some rare condition that makes you see red as white. Maybe the white you see is the same thing everyone else sees as red.

The day after Cooney lit out back to Debs D.C., the freshest grave in town was emptied. Ed was back in business.

If you weren't around back when Capone was running the show, I guess you'll find it hard to understand why the townsfolk, who all knew perfectly well what was going on, didn't just get together and march on the Gein Place with burning brands and a noose and just hang him from the tallest tree. Put simply, it was because Ed had friends in very high places. Agent Cooney was rumoured to be one of Hoover's personal bed-warmers, which is about as high as you could get in Capone's United Socialist States of America. If anything bad happened to Ed, something super-bad would happen to Plainfield. That's why we all of us wilfully ignored what he got up to.

I have another theory, too. A lot of people still believed in socialism back then. Some of the older, poorer folks would tell you how things really were better now than they had been before the Revolution. Younger people tended to think that while the regime in Debs D.C. might be corrupt, socialism was still the best route to a perfect society. Lot of people believed—hell, I still believe—that guys like Joe Hill and Eugene V. Debs really were heroes. And the point about socialism is that it rejects superstition, meaning that when you die, that's it. So people weren't as worried about their relatives' corpses disappearing as you might think. Leastways, not worried enough to risk their own living hides by stiffing Ed Gein. Fact is, if you don't believe in the Resurrection, you've got no need of your cadaver, have you?

"Course it wasn't just cadavers he was taking. He was still killing people, too. Not many, but enough.

One winter night, I woke up with an itch in my right foot. I reached down to scratch it, and touched a wet, jagged end where my foot should have been.

I realised I had been woken up by a thudding sound.

Ed Gein, grinning through his mother's shrivelled lips, stood at the end of the bed, holding a bloody cleaver in one hand and my right foot in the other.

Then the wave of pain crashed over me.

"Ayup," said Ed, "better hop to it, Sheriff Joe."

Screaming, I crawled across my cabin and jammed my ragged ankle against the stove.

By the time I'd unclenched my teeth from my tongue, my midnight visitor had departed.

I never saw my foot again. If you ask me, I think Ed ate it. Productivity went up and up. No one ever asked how come Ed slaughtered more animals than were taken out to his place.

I got used to my new tin foot a lot quicker than I'd anticipated. Only thing was, every time I saw Ed Gein, or even just thought about him, it hurt like there was a nine-inch nail being hammered through it. More phantom pain.

The disappearances of corpses and people continued through the rest of the 1950s. And a hell of a lot of animals just upped and vanished, too, or showed up dead and mutilated. There was a lot of noise from the Gein Place, but that was what you had to expect when production records were being set. Weirdly, it was the animals people noticed: from the purges of the '30s, everyone was used to people suddenly not being there any more, leaving behind houses with kicked-in doors; however, even at the worst, Al Capone never had the FBI pounce on hog-pens or cattle ranges and hustle pigs and beeves into a four-door saloon to be taken to a cellar and tenderised with rubber hoses.

There was some muttering, especially from those who lost relatives, but that ended when Gein stood up to the local Committee and insisted that from now on he would take on his mother's old role and decide who got the products of his slaughterhouse. He came to town, in a dress and his mummified mask, and made a speech at a meeting, saying that from now on the people of Plainfield would get to live off the food they produced, not pass it on to fatcats in the cities. People got over the shock and cheered him. From then on, Ed personally ensured that every family in town got their share of his meats.

I became a vegetarian.

I think it was 1960 when I read in a magazine how some of the bigger cities were having problems because their cemeteries were full up. The solution was clean, it was efficient, it fitted the sharp new technological image that Nixon's government was trying to project. Yes, I know the history books say Goldwater was Party Chairman, First Secretary and President, but, as we now know, Nixon was working the levers.

I clanked over to Gutman's place to tell him about my idea.

"A crematorium, here in Waushara County?" he said, astonished.

"Sure," I said, "why not? It'd show them city slickers that we're not hicks and hayseeds. It'd be a big feather in Plainfield's cap, too. It'd be the first crematorium in the whole state."

"But wouldn't it be expensive? The budgets for the coming year are..."

"Got it covered," I said, handing him the cyclostyled price-list from the Acme Crematorium and Blast-Furnace Collective of Pittsburgh.

Gutman took out his spectacles and examined the paper closely. He was definitely a little thinner than he'd been before Ed had decreed he'd be allocating the meat supplies. "It would mean making sacrifices on certain of our budgets."

"You can have twenty percent of mine, Comrade," I volunteered. "If we burn our dead instead of burying 'em it'll solve a lot of my problems."

He looked at me over the top of his glasses. I could almost hear the cogs creaking inside his head. Suddenly he smiled. "Yes, Comrade Sheriff, I understand. I do like a man who can make sacrifices."

The day that the first crematorium in the state of Wisconsin was opened was a gala occasion. Everyone in Plainfield was there in their best clothes, genuinely happy that the next members of their families to die would be safe from Ed Gein. Half the party brass in the state showed up, too, partly for the free feed (naturally, Ed saw to the catering), and partly because they hoped something would foul up and they could laugh at Gutman.

Nothing did go wrong. I saw to that. I'd worked late with the engineers from Acme to see that everything was okay. The only thing missing was a corpse. At a Committee meeting we'd discussed all the possibilities. Maybe doing a trial run with a cow or hog (we'd decided that city folks might joke about us. Besides, unless it was carrying bubonic plague or something, everyone'd rather eat it). We thought about asking the State Pen if they were hanging anyone, but to make our first customer a criminal didn't seem worthy somehow.

Finally, Jimmy Worden had the good grace to have a fatal heart attack three days before the Grand Opening. Jimmy used to run Plainfield's Post & Telegram Office and so he was a Party Member in Good Standing. Short of roasting Kaspar Gutman himself, Jimmy was the perfect candidate. Just to make sure that Ed didn't spoil the party, I moved Jimmy's mortal remains into the jail. We put him in a bathtub and covered him in crushed ice. Me and Jimmy's son Frank took turns at keeping watch round the clock. Frank was a good boy and I later took him on as a Deputy. I still had Lou Ford, but Frank I knew wouldn't snitch on me.

So Jimmy got sent on his way, everyone applauded when they saw the smoke coming out of the chimney and everyone agreed that the new crematorium was just dandy. In the months after, people came from all over the county, and even from further afield, to have their relatives burned, or to just look at this amazing new technological wonder. Despite the best efforts of the local Committee, the crematorium had the indecency to make a profit, all of which found its way into the pockets of Gutman and his cronies.

Everyone in Plainfield now had their loved ones cremated. I'd won this round with Ed. I knew he'd be back, though.

In the months after that, Ed's production figures didn't fall. He redoubled his efforts at livestock-rustling and his production figures actually went up. He won a Hero of Socialist Labor Citation (first class) signed by Chairman Goldwater himself. They had a big presentation in town; Ed accepted it. Since there were photographers from some out of town papers Gutman had persuaded him not to show up in his Ma get-up. He wore a suit and tie, and the pains in my hand, shoulder, head and missing foot became almost unbearable.

Late that evening, Ed came up to me in the street. He'd been wearing this same fixed smile all day. He had a hunting rifle with him. He unslung it as he looked into my eyes, seeing that my pain was getting in his way, saving me from him.

In a way, I guess he respected me. I guess he saw the world much the way I see it. Through a magnifying glass of pain.

Ed shot me in the chest.

I lost the use of a lung, and half my face—the half with the eye that works, of course—froze immobile. Nerve damage. After that, I couldn't breathe so easily, especially in the cold, but some of the pain was dulled. Losing a couple of those nerves might just have kept me going.

Ed claimed he'd mistaken me in the near-dark for the counter-revolutionary who'd dynamited his barn years back. I got removed from office, for inefficiency. This time, Lou Ford had to become Sheriff. He was the hero who had shot it out with Elmer the Capitalist Mastermind in a pitched Wild West gun battle.

For a while, I considered becoming town parasite. But, as a veteran, I was entitled to work. There's no unemployment in the USSA. Just redeployed manpower.

Gutman appointed me to the post of dog-catcher and pest control officer. With my one lung and tin foot, I could hobble after most critters with an even chance of catching up, and my monocular, non-stereoscopic vision flattened everything into a picture book puzzle. How many animals are hiding in this forest? I couldn't tell you.

In twenty years, I've never caught anything. Round here, stray dogs disappear.

And stray middle-aged-to-elderly ladies.

It came as a shock when Ed shot Frank Worden's mother and roped her to the hood of his pick-up. He hauled her out to his place and apparently played his chainsaw piñata act on her, showering himself with fresh guts.

Frank tried to get Sheriff Ford to do something. Then he hanged himself. That was convenient, because Lou Ford was then able to construct convincing proof that the Wordens had been secret subversives, nestling close to the heart of the Party, sapping our precious socialist strengths. Bernice Worden was a dangerous ringleader and, without her diabolical cunning, Frank was lost and unable to live with the self-loathing and guilt.

Gutman left the bullet-hole in the wall of the Party Store, and put up a plaque commemorating Ed Gein's swift-thinking, fast-draw defence of his community and his ideals.

Erskine Cooney was appointed Assistant Director of the Federal Bureau of Ideology. He orchestrated nationwide Drives Against Counter-Revolution, modelled on the Plainfield Operation, in '64 and '72. He wrote a book about "flying cigars", claiming that those glowing things people saw in the skies in the '50s were a Russian secret weapon, and that comrades abducted by the unidentified flying objects were replaced with exact doubles skilled in subversion and sabotage. That got made into a movie and a TV series.

Sheriff Lou Ford stayed in office until 1964, though he avoided making speeches at town meetings. One night, he vanished and I figured Ed had got him. Ten years later, he came back from Alaska and it turned out Cooney had got him sent to an oil-drilling camp just in case he ever decided to tell the truth about Elmer. By then, Andy Taylor was Sheriff, but Lou Ford got his old Deputy's star back. He's hanging on until retirement, and doesn't like to talk about anything much. If it weren't for his wonky jaw, you wouldn't recognise him as the same man who disappeared in 1964.

Things in Plainfield changed a bit after Goldwater died. When Nixon took over in person he worked hard and buddying up to the Ivans and the Brits who were having problems of their own in Indochina. Nixon got some military production re-deployed to consumer goods, and if you worked hard and kept your nose clean you could eventually get on the waiting-list for a refrigerator, washing-machine or an automobile. Everyone got televisions because the TV could spend a lot of time telling us what a great guy Trickydick was. People still disappeared of course, plenty of 'em in the first couple of years after Roy Cohn elbowed Hoover out and took over the FBI, but they were mostly city types and almost all Party members.

Kaspar Gutman had a heart attack through being too damned fat and was forced off the Committee, but his fat son took over and is still running the county, eating as much as he can.

Ed, he was still around of course, just getting a bit older, that's all. Ed was born in 1909 and jumping people or steers in a lonely place late at night started getting a bit more than he could handle.

That's when he discovered modern agricultural methods.

When Nixon set his mind on turning the country into a consumer paradise, he directed that a lot of money and know-how be spent on scientific breeding of livestock.

I'd always figured Ed for semi-literate at best, but when I discovered him spending more and more time in the county library I was more than a little curious.

Turned out he was reading government booklets about growth-hormones and steroids and stuff like that. Next thing I know, he's taking shipment of these chemicals.

Shortly after, he started asking old ladies over to tea. He'd serve 'em tea and coffee and applejack and sandwiches and dainty little cakes he made himself. But always, one of 'em would get extra-special treatment.

Got so's it became a kind of joke around town. An elderly widow or spinster would suddenly start putting on weight and folks'd say to each other, "looks like old Mrs. or Miss so-and-so ain't gonna be with us much longer." Sure enough, after six to nine months, the lady in question would just disappear.

'Course all the ladies who showed up to his little parties—and the big one he held every second Sunday in May (Socialist Motherhood Day— used to be known as Mothering Sunday before the Revolution)—knew perfectly well what was happening. A lot of women turned down his invitations flat, but a few went along because he was such a nice boy, so polite, so attentive, so happy to chat with them about their aches and pains and how their worthless kids didn't visit them often enough. I don't think any of these biddies consciously made the connection between tea at Ed's and their ultimate fate, but they still knew. I guess some of 'em were just so tired, or so lonely, or just reckoned they weren't going to be around for much longer, that they figured Ed's dishonourable intentions were a price worth paying for having a part-share in a perfect son.

My job gave me an excuse to prowl around, after Ed. When he sat in the park, making up to old ladies, or trying to seem like an old lady, I would look for strays to round up. As near as I could, I saw to it that he never hurt a fly. When he was out at his place with his power tools, I was in the woods, tracking wildcats. I kept children away from him.

Of course, people kept children away from me. I guess I look pretty frightening.

I've got more parts missing: Doc Cook misdiagnosed my stomach ulcers in 1965 and hauled out a couple of yards of large intestine, someone lopped off my right thumb while I was flat-out drunk one night after the invasion of Cuba in '68 and all my teeth fell out in the early '70s thanks to that sugar-laced party-issue orange juice.

I couldn't stop Ed altogether. In fact, I might not have done anything much. He slowed down in the late '60s. In the last fifteen years, I don't reckon he killed more than five or six folks. Most of them old women not long for the world. In '75, he carried off Abby and Martha Brewster in a tender double-embrace. As a joke, when he was finished with them, he chopped off their heads and swapped them around.

Here we are in 1984—the year in which George Orwell predicted the world would be run by tyrannical capitalists, and citizens would all be the slaves of big Russian and British corporations—and they're burying Ed with full honours. He just keeled over of natural causes, struck down while in the act of sexual congress with a week-dead pig. It would be a proper tribute to him if they cooked and ate that pig at Ed Gein's wake. I trooped past the coffin with all the others. By popular demand, he lay in the Party Hall for a few days, so folks could pay their last respects.

I made my way through crowds who were respectfully remembering the great man and took a look into the open coffin. I guess I wanted to make sure he was dead. As I stood over him, a fly crawled over one of his open eyes. I shooed it away. I'd thought there might be some satisfaction in seeing with my one good eye that the corpse-maker was a corpse himself. I was wrong.

Looking down on that thin old man with his thin satisfied smile, lying in his mother's best dress and with his favourite cap, I realised that he had escaped. Wherever he was, he was as happy as a pig in shit; and whatever his life had been like out there on the Gein Place with his power tools and dead bodies, it had been as fulfilled and delightful as any man's who had ever lived.

ABDICATION STREET

1972

"Perfect place to plot," commented Isaac Judaiovich as they were admitted into the Happy Guys Club, "this nest of parasites, old guard, nouveau money, witless younger sons, yankee Reds, perfumed exquisites and mad Jews. We Russians love to plot, Cinzia. I scry this was where they plotted to sack poor Georgi."

Though it was early, the function room was athrong with fashionably-dressed writers, actresses, poets, and wireless and televisniks. Cinzia Davidovna Bronstein saw a lot of silver lipstick mouths and silver foil mini-dresses. All the men had hair down to their bums, Tartar plaits threaded with ceramic beads.

Half the people at the party were drunk. Customarily first to the bar, the guest of honour was very drunk. Three quarters of an hour ago, on the early news, Georgi Sanders was noticeably squiffy as he quoted Duma leader Kissinger's latest denials.

1972 had not so far been a good year for Old Russia. Maybe '73 would be better. She should ask Isaac. He was supposed to be the seer.

"It's a marvel ITV were satisfied with giving the old soak his cards," Isaac muttered to her through a long-range rictus of ingratiation directed at program planners across the room. The grin disturbed his fiercely generous sideburns and set payesses jiggling under the rim of his conical cabbalist cap. "Something permanent with poison would be more in the style of our new masters."

Georgi, news anchor for as long as she could remember, was staggering, unable to coordinate his long body, dark vodka spots on his electric blue velvet evening jacket. In the centre of the room, he held court for the last time. After tonight, it was off to Siberia or into the library with a bottle and a bullet.

"I'm wrong," said Isaac. "The decision to axe Georgi would have been taken at a much higher level."

"At a board meeting?" said Cinzia.

"No my dear, at the highest level. *Batiushka.*"

"The Tsar?" she whispered.

"He's majority shareholder in ITV. There was a time when politicos could have stopped him, but the Duma are tearing themselves to bits over Indo-China and the scandals."

Isaac arranged fingers against his forehead and fluttered his eyes shut, as he did on tele before uttering his popular predictions.

"I foresee that Nicholas III will wrestle the Duma. He dreams of winning back the power Nicholas Alexandrovich had to give up in 1916."

A young man in a white polo neck kaftan and sparkly smoked glasses wound through the revellers towards them. Before he could speak, Isaac flung out a hand to fend him off.

"This is Harlan," he said. "He's supposed to be a cultural attaché, but everybody knows he's a spy."

The American was devastated by Isaac's perception.

"Just because I'm from the USSA doesn't mean I can't be a swinger, Ike."

"'Ike'" Isaac spat, delighted with disgust. "'*Ike!*' Harlan is a godless communist barbarian for all his democratic hipster threads. Admit it, you come here for the secrets."

"All the best *girlchiks* are here, comrade citizen."

Harlan was looking at Cinzia over his silly spectacles.

"Are you a model, sister?"

She didn't have to have cabbalist powers of insight to recognise that for flannel.

"Make-up girl, actually. With this lighting, I'd use Number 5."

"Cinzia has no secrets, Harlan."

"*Nichevo,*" the American mispronounced. He was distracted, eyes pulled to one side.

Cinzia turned. A ballerina was walking by in a backless dress, a face painted in red on her elegant shoulderblades, blind eyes rolling over taut back muscles.

Harlan was off in pursuit.

"Is he really a spy?"

Isaac smiled mystically, losing his hands in the sleeves of his symbol-spotted robe.

"The United Socialist States of America doesn't have a culture, so what would be the point of a cultural attaché?"

"He doesn't seem like one of those ascetic Caponists."

"He's been corrupted. That's Petrograd for you. Varoomshka is the mistress of Admiral Beria. Bound to be with SMERSH."

Harlan tried to French kiss the small of the ballerina's back. She turned in his drunken embrace, showing predatory teeth, and dragged him onto the tiny dance-floor. They spasmed about in an attempt at the new French dance, *le Bompe*.

"Interesting people you meet in this business."

Television was not her first choice career. She had wanted to be a doctor, but abandoned college for a clarinet player. Now, at 23, she was a paint-slapper for Imperial Television. She had not stopped telling herself it was temporary.

Applause exploded from the main door. Someone special must have entered to make the glamorous people of Petrograd's closed little world of tele abandon their normal collective pose of languid boredom.

It was Brynner, striding in baggy trousers, soft leather boots and immaculately-cut *moujik* smock. Though it was spring, he had a heavy military coat draped over his shoulders. Nobody knew quite how much the coat was an affectation; the star wanted to fight in Indo-China, and had volunteered to take the place of a conscript soldier. The army turned him down as too old, but he continued to wear the coat.

"I predict Yul will have a shock at the next script meeting."

"Why's that?" Cinzia asked.

Brynner carried himself like a king. There was authority in everything he did. Now he held out his hand, never looking away from Sanders, and someone placed a glass in it. He was famous as Prince Bolkonsky in *The Rostovs*, ITV's most successful beet opera.

"Because Natasha's going to go by August."

"Mother will be devastated. She always says Natasha's not really a bitch, just misunderstood."

"That's as may be, but the board just looked at Talia Gurdin's demand for a pay hike and have decided 'Tasha Rostova is going to be kidnapped by a flying samovar and returned to Earth as a disfigured hag. A chin-dimpled plastic surgeon played by Issur Demsky will reconstruct her in the likeness of a more affordable actress who happens to be mistress of the Head of Quality Drama."

"But that's ridiculous!"

"Cinzia Davidovna, it's no more ridiculous than anything else that happens in *The Rostovs*. Remember when everyone was assassinated by anarchists but it turned out to be Natasha's dream? Nothing in tele is real. The more unreal it is, the more the people like it."

Issac Judaiovch was difficult: always complaining, usually patronising, probably a lech. But it wasn't all charlatanry: he really could see the future. In cabbalist robes, he was presenter of ITV's top-rated gruel-time show, *It's Your Fate*. He began with a mystic weather forecast, ran through everyone's horoscopes and read tarot for guest celebrities to whom he was spectacularly rude ("I see you in the future," he had told Peter Ustinov, "entering your *anecdotage*"). He used means occult and mathematical to try to predict the kind of people who would win this week's lottery. He had never yet been right, but millions believed in his powers. His strongest suit was predicting the career reversals of politicians and the romantic down-turns of film stars. Much of it came from sitting in the Happy Guys Club and listening. If you needed gossip, Isaac Judaiovich had it.

"What will Brynner do?" she asked.

"Go back to the *kinos*. He's signed up for a cossack picture in which he leads a band of mercenaries in saving a poor village from a band of marauding Chechens."

At the far end of the room, by the tall windows, gathered a drunken mainly male group. Illya Kuriakin, the game show host, was at its centre. A scar-faced lad hauled a revolver out of his kaftan.

"*Bozhe moi!*" exclaimed Isaac, foreseeing trouble.

The gun-owner spun the chamber and handed it over. Kuriakin drunkenly waved the revolver around, an extremely effective way of getting elbow-room. He sat on a velvet-upholstered chair, and, gripping the weapon with both hands, held the barrel against his rainbow-pattern left boot about where his big toe would be. The room fell silent as Kuriakin squinted down, tongue sticking out as he tried to focus through vodka fog. The hammer clicked against an empty chamber. Everyone cheered. Kuriakin bowed, spun the chamber and handed the gun to another man.

Kuriakin was another tele personality, presenter of *Russian Roulette*. Ordinary people came on and spun a giant mock-up revolver. If they got an "empty chamber" they won a fortune. If they got the "bullet", they had to give all they owned, down to their children's toys, to charity.

Bloody silly, really.

"Cinzia, you look troubled," Isaac said.

"Nothing's wrong," she said.

Apart from the fact that she had no chance of getting back into medical school unless Mother won the lottery or her brother got a job. The odds of winning the lottery were eighteen million to one. A better bet than Vladimir getting a job.

"Nothing's wrong, child," Isaac pronounced, "but nothing's right either."

"*Nichevo,*" she shrugged. Lousy job, few prospects. She was off men, too.

The seer took an empty ashtray and scooped melt-water from an ice-bucket. Sacramentally, he put the ashtray on the table.

"Take my hands," said the seer, "and we'll penetrate the veil of the future."

Yeah, sure, she thought, giving him her hands anyway.

"Now look into the water. What do you see?"

An ashtray full of water.

Isaac stared intently. His face reddened and veins in his temples throbbed as though he were suffering from constipation, yet his hands grasped hers gently.

"You will marry a prince," he said, matter-of-factly. "I know you don't believe me and I don't blame you. But sometimes, just sometimes, I see things so clearly I could almost be watching tele. Cinzia Davidovna, before this year's leaves have fallen, you will be married to a man who is wealthy, kind, dignified and courageous beyond words. And a Prince."

She laughed. He laughed. She leaned over and kissed him. "You are too kind, Isaac Judaiovich."

He shrugged. "You'll see."

Cologne stung her nostrils as someone oozed into a free space by their table. A hand settled on her shoulder.

"Prince Yussupov, what a pleasure," lied Isaac as the new newscaster sat next to them. The Prince didn't take his hand off her shoulder.

"You dirty old dog, Asimov," said Prince Felix Dimitrovich Yussupov, looking at her as if she were a plate of strawberries in honey. "Who's your charming young friend?"

"Prince Yussupov, may I introduce Cinzia Davidovna Bronstein."

"Are you a good little Jewish girl, Cinzia Davidovna, or might we be fortunate enough to assume you consort with *goyim*?"

The Prince was in his late twenties, six-feet-something tall, built like an Olympic athlete. His blonde hair was permed, his flared jeans and jacket were of fashionably-distressed *fabric de Nimes*, and his cheesecloth shirt was open at the chest to reveal a cultivated thatch of hair and a gold icon with an inset diamond the size of a quail's egg.

"It depends," she said.

"On what?" said the Prince.

"Whether he's a *mensch* or a *schmuck*."

"You have beautiful cheekbones. I would very much like to get to know you better."

"Why? I'm a Jewish make-up girl. You're a newsreader with a title. If those magazines my mother is always reading are to be believed you own about a fifth of Russia, as well as stretches of the Ukraine, Siberia and the Crimea."

"You forget Georgia, Tadjikistan and a golf course in Scotland. I own the highest mountain in the Crimea. It was given to my grandmother as a birthday present. Would you care for it? You are pretty. You could have pretty things."

"Like a mountain? I suppose you'd marry me, *hein*? Would you like having a Jewish mother-in-law? With all the things you own, why do you want to be a newsreader?"

He grinned as he lit a Sobranje with his flip-top Fabergé. "Because I want to be loved, and I'd love you to love me."

She laughed. "I can't possibly love you!"

"Whyever not?"

"Because I would have to admire and respect you. You'd have to prove your physical and moral courage, you'd have to be kind to children and animals and the poor. Tell you what: if you donate ten million roubles to the Petrograd Free Hospital, I'll let you take me to dinner."

"You're the most expensive whore I've ever met! You fascinate me, Cinzia Davidovna."

His hand was in her hair again. She shook it free.

"Shall I tell you something even more fascinating? Isaac Judaiovich has just been scrying the future. He tells me I am to marry a prince. It could be you, Felix Dimitrovich Yussupov, but I wouldn't sleep with you unless you gave away all your property to the poor. We could live comfortably on your newsreader's salary. My mother would have to live with us, of course."

He stubbed out his cigarette, bored. "I suppose a quick fuck in the carriage park's out of the question then?"

She nodded.

He got up. "I'll see you again, Cinzia Davidovna. Cheerio, Asimov."

The newsreader strode off, jacket flouncing *en pelisse*.

"You should be mindful of him," said Isaac. "He's dangerous. Self-preservation should be your first law. Yussupoff is not above getting you jumped in a back alley and flown to some distant *dacha*."

"Then I'd have to hammer a tent-peg into his eye."

"You would too. You're quite a girl, Cinzia. You'd make a man very happy or very miserable. Nothing in between."

She raised her glass. "Here's to my prince. Just as long as it isn't Yussupov."

There was another flurry at the door. Middle-aged men marched in, handing coats to the ushers. At first sight, they did not belong in this gathering of glamorous and good-looking. Their boxy 1950s clothes suggested influence rather than fame. Cinzia recognised two television producers and a Member of the Duma. Among them was an unfamiliar face, a dignified, fastidious-looking type in an immaculate suit. He was obviously European, but the immense distance between his nose and top lip suggested something more exotic.

One of the producers spotted Isaac, waved, and ushered the strange-looking man towards their table.

Isaac stood and shook the producer's hand. "Bondarchuk! So you've come to Georgi's wake! Will you join us? May I introduce Cinzia Davidovna."

"Oh I know Cinzia. She's covers Georgi's vodka-blossoms," said Bondarchuk, taking her outstretched hand and kissing it. He was a little too old and formal to shake it. "Normally we have make-up girls, but Cinzia Davidovna is a make-up *artist*."

Bondarchuk pulled up a chair for his guest. "Permit me to introduce Sir Anthony Blunt. Personal assistant to the Dowager Duchess of York. He has come from London to help with the imperial wedding."

Sir Anthony nodded curtly. Because of her fluent English, Cinzia was assigned to work double shifts during the wedding story. She supposed she should be grateful.

Sir Anthony was about to sit down when he noticed one of the pictures. A framed 1920s Rodchenko poster, advertising baby pacifiers. THERE HAVE NEVER BEEN SUCH GOOD DUMMIES! SUCK 'EM 'TIL YOU'RE OLD! The Englishman took a closer look while Bondarchuk whistled up champagne.

Blunt moved further along the wall to some Lissitzky posters for Red Wedge beer, and more Rodchenkos, with the pithy slogans by Mayakovsky. The Happy Guys Club was decorated almost exclusively with the products of "Advertisement Constructors, Mayakovsky-Rodchenko".

When Sir Anthony was out of earshot, Bondarchuk leaned his head towards Isaac and the table. "Isaac Judaiovich, humour this fish. He's a courtier straight out of the *ancien regime*. I've baby-sat him all day and I'd pay two years' salary to see him guillotined."

Sir Anthony sat down next to her. She smiled at him. He ignored her and eyed the champagne disdainfully.

Bondarchuk continued talking to them, smiling and nodding at his guest, "This prick Blunt doesn't want any of the engagement and wedding to be on tele in the first place. He's worried that it interferes with the monarchical dignity of the occasion. It's okay Isaac, he doesn't speak a word of Russian. Dignity of the monarchy! Who's madder, Nicky or his sainted Edward VIII?"

Cinzia spoke to Sir Anthony in English, "you are interested in advertising, Sir Anthony?"

"No, I am interested in art. Rodchenko intrigues me. Idealistic and brutal at the same time. One cannot help but feel that his talents would have been better employed by a totalitarian regime."

From the corner of her eye she saw Bondarchuk nudging Isaac in the ribs.

"Do you not think, Sir Anthony, that some advertising aspires to art?"

"Much great art was produced to glorify a wealthy patron. Advertising is the same, but the patron is a corporation. Charles I favoured Van Dyck because he made him look like a king."

"So now," she said, rubbing the lip of her glass with her finger, carefully avoiding Sir Anthony's eye, "our Tsar wants tele to take up the brush of Van Dyck."

Isaac, she knew, spoke English. So, she assumed, did Bondarchuk. Both looked into the air, pursing lips, nodding as though she had said something wise.

Sir Anthony looked at her. "Your English is very good. Almost accentless. Are you British?"

"My mother is."

"The medium is neutral, whether paint or a cathode ray tube. What matters is the way in which the medium is employed. Van Dyck did not paint Charles stuffing his face with fowl, or scratching his fleas, or sitting on the commode. From what little I know, Russian television is solely interested in royalty on the commode."

"Bondarchuk, that's a great idea!" said Isaac. "I could interview people on the crapper...just a little cabalist humour."

Sir Anthony's disapproval was jarred by a feedback whine. "Weepy" Krasnevin, Director of Current Affairs Broadcasting, had picked up the microphone and was waiting for silence. Quiet came, but was instantly interrupted by a click and relief as someone else in Kuriakin's group didn't shoot his toes off.

"My friends," said Krasnevin, eyes dribbling crocodile tears, "this is a sad day for us all."

Except Prince Yussupov, she thought.

"Georgi Sanders is, one might say, a giant. He is the father of Russian current affairs broadcasting. His voice carried us through the dark days of the Great Patriotic War, the Alsace-Lorraine missile crisis, the assassination of Premier Smoktunovsky. You must all join me in wishing him the best for the future..."

Everyone clapped and cheered, banged fists on tables, stamped on the floor as Georgi bounded onto the low stage. Krasnevin, who had schemed for years to be rid of the newscaster, sobbed deeply and embraced the man he had just fired.

Cinzia saw the slightly smelly, bum-grasping salon snake she had sometimes thickly powdered, but recalled the suave, clear-sighted Sanders of wartime wireless and '50s television. The first Russian newsman to penetrate Capone's America. His sarcasm had been the single greatest factor in derailing the hysterical anti-Red pogroms of Ayn Rand. And he had tricked ITV into broadcasting footage taken amid the bloody shambles of the Duma's Indo-Chinese police action.

Georgi bowed to his audience, but did not smile.

Krasnevin took a carriage clock in the shape of Misha the Prime Time Bear from an impossibly beautiful girl and shoved it at Georgi. Between gales of tears, he garbled about "a small token of our affection".

Georgi's lip curled. He swayed as though on the deck of a Baltic steamer in a bracing wind. He took the mike.

"I asked for a Fabergé egg full of cocaine, but you got me a fucking clock."

"It's solid gold you ungrateful old bastard!" shouted Yussupoff.

Georgi bit into one of Misha's huge ears.

"So it is. Well, I'm touched. No, really I am."

There was an uncomfortable silence as Georgi carefully laid the Misha clock down on the floor, with more concern for his dignity than the clock's safety.

"Most careers end in tears and mine is one of them. I don't really want to go because I know retirement will bore me to suicide."

A huge monitor on a big wooden stand was wheeled towards the stage by minions.

"I hope you're looking forward to tele with *pedigree*. All the news the Tsar will own up to, read by pretty boys with lineages back to the Tartar bum chums of Peter the Great. As a farewell, I'd like to show you some film not broadcast on the orders of our magnificent emperor. A last taste of the sort of thing you won't be seeing on tele for a long time."

Everyone was listening now. Cinzia half-expected the Okhrana to burst in and arrest Georgi for sedition. Georgi signalled, and minions worked the machines.

"Can someone get the lights?"

The room went dark and chairs were turned towards the front, glasses were refilled, spectacles discreetly fished from inside pockets.

"Go on Illya," said someone, "a last time. Double or quits."

The screen came to light, first a fuzzy grey snowstorm, then bars.

There was a deafening discharge, screeches, a yelp of manly pain. Sir Anthony cringed as if he was the one the revolver had been shot at.

Brynner said, "get an ice-bucket, put the toe in it and take him to the hospital. The new Chinese surgeon might be able to sew it back on."

Onscreen: a pockmarked landscape with no vegetation. It looked like a far-Eastern desert, except the sky was completely black. Two figures bounced into view, encumbered by bulbous pressure suits.

"Bozhe moi!" said Bondarchuk.

Everyone knew what this was. In July 1969, the Imperial Space Program culminated with the lunar expedition. Count Rennenkampf and Count Ignatieff had died in the crash-landing of the *Star of Russia* and hailed as heroes of the motherland. But there were rumours that the landing had been successful and the cosmonauts perished later in some terrible manner that had been hushed up.

"*This is Baikonur, talk to us, excellencies,*" crackled the soundtrack.

- bleep -

Cinzia heard wild tales that the cosmonauts had been eaten by some fabulous monster out of the Strugatsky paperbacks her brother read.

"No hospital," said Kuriakin. "This I have to see."

"*Baikonur, this is Baikonur. Respectfully, talk to us, excellencies. Your wireless is not down.*"

She recognised Valentin Bondarenko, Russia's first-ever cosmonaut and Director of the Space Program.

The Counts bounded around the lunar desert, light as children's balloons.

"*This is Baikonur, excellencies. You are making us all look extremely foolish.*"

No reply.

Another voice: "*Velikovsky here. If you two titled pricks don't start acting like cosmonauts, I'll...*"

Finally, from one of the lunar explorers: "*You'll do what, Jew?*" *- bleep! -*

Immanuel Velikovsky was President of the Bureau of Space Exploration. He had single-handedly built it from government department to semi-public corporation. When the Duma wanted to cut its funding to spare taxpayers' purses in an election year, Velikovsky enlisted private money by creating corporations to exploit spinoffs from space research, from technology through to television rights. Not one of these companies was in profit. Shareholders tended to be Strugatsky fans, people who believed they might be fabulously rich in thirty years' time, and the Imperial family. The Tsar had gained enormous influence over the space program.

"*I'll see to it you are disgraced and sent to Siberia, your estates sequestered, your farms burned, your first-born slain...*"

One cosmonaut picked up a spade. The other picked up an Imperial flag that had been planted in grey lunar soil.

"*Stop this at once!*" *- bleep!*

"*You don't understand. You're a commoner, a Jew. Honour means nothing to you. In the capsule, Count Michael insulted my family. Honour must be satisfied.*"

They faced one another like medieval warriors about to do single combat.

"You're going to fight a duel? The first men on the moon spend ten minutes walking around, then kill one another! Has the journey driven you both mad!"

- bleep! -

The two faced off, neither moving.

"Couldn't you kill each other when you get back? I want to push back the frontiers of knowledge, to build a future in space, and you behave like Neanderthals. Bondarenko, get us a link to Tsarskoye Selo, *maybe* Batiushka *can talk sense to these fuckwits."*

- bleep! -

The one with the flagstaff had a longer reach. He lunged at the one with the spade, who parried the blow easily. Using weapons in the moon's atmosphere was like fighting underwater.

The Tsar, with his newly-acquired interest in outer space, insisted cosmonauts on prestige missions be aristocrats. Any glory they earned— even death—would reflect well on the monarchy, on the old, pre-democracy system.

The one with the spade landed a blow on the helmet of his opponent, to no effect. The latter dropped his flagstaff and tried to close with the spade-man.

They wrestled for brief seconds and pulled hoses from their bulky back-packs. They parted and struggled to re-connect the hoses, but neither could reach far enough behind his back. That they could help one another seemed not to occur to them. After half a minute, they came together again, and lay down, holding hands. Both bodies convulsed a little.

Velikovsky was emotional. *"Twelve billion roubles. Twelve billion roubles we've spent on this. The Duma will impale us when they see this! Imperial Majesty, I respectfully resign!"*

- Bleep! -

"Can someone get the lights?" said Georgi.

The lights came on again. Something over two hundred men and women sat or stood in stunned silence. Sir Anthony was blinking, bewildered. Asimov's face was in his hands. Harlan, glasses off, was goggling: if he was a spy, he had stumbled onto a genuine secret.

"The space program is on ice until air force officers with no breeding whatsoever can be trained," said Georgi, picking up his clock. "Illya, care for another round? I have a bauble I can wager. Chuck me that revolver, there's a good little game-show host."

"Now the De Havilland Comet of the King's Flight of the Royal Air Force touches down at Catherine the Great Airport, here in Petrograd on this glorious spring afternoon and as the great crowd assemble here to get their first glimpse of the Duke of Cornwall. Some people suggested that since the Duke is an officer in the Royal Navy he should have arrived by sea, but he didn't. And here is the aircraft now taxiing towards the apron. And there's the little man with the orange table-tennis bats signalling to the plane. Left a bit, right a bit, forwards a bit. I understand from Airport Director Gromyko that they bought him a brand new pair of orange table-tennis bats for the occasion. This must be a proud moment for him. He would normally spend his time making signals to tourists and businessmen, the occasional diplomat, no doubt, perhaps the odd ballet personality. This is surely the only time he has made signals to a plane carrying the future husband of a Princess of the Imperial family, and probably the next King of England. A very proud moment for him indeed."

Cinzia sat cross-legged on the sofa next to her mother watching television. They drank tea in the English style, with milk and the sugar stirred in. Cinzia was taking it easy. Today would probably be the last day off she would have for several weeks. Thanks to the Duke of Cornwall.

Her mother kept pushing her spectacles back onto the bridge of her nose, so she wouldn't miss a moment. She affected not to be impressed by the imperial carnival but was at heart an obsessive monarchist. Cinzia's late father joked that once she lost her religion, royalty was the only magic left to her.

"Now, as the aircraft's mighty engines die down, the steps are wheeled up to the door. And there are the men getting ready to roll out the red carpet, a detachment of the Preobrazhensky Guards, lining up on either side. Magnificent green uniforms, red facings. Boots as well. Bayonets glistening in the sun. For state occasions like this, each soldier has to polish his boots for a total of fifteen hours."

Mother was tense with excitement. It was unfair to sneer. She didn't have much pleasure in her life. She had met David Leonovich Bronstein while he was stationed in England during the War, and had come to Petrograd as a "cossack bride" in 1946. His health was affected by a wound sustained in Normandy, and he never progressed beyond junior civil servant. Being the son of a once-notorious seditionist circus clown had probably not helped him either.

Mother had to get by on a meagre pension and her job as an office-cleaner. Now Cinzia was earning, things were better, but Cinzia's brother was still a dependent. All lived in a three-room apartment in Gorokhovaya Street.

"*And now, the door on the aircraft opens, and...*"

The floor shook, noise erupted through the whole building, the shattering blare of an electric guitar. Cinzia put down her tea and leapt from the sofa.

She rushed straight into Vladimir's room. He sat on the edge of his bed, eyes closed in artistic ecstasy, hacking chords out of his guitar. She fell to her knees and furiously yanked the amplifier-plug from the socket.

"Hey!" he said.

"Mother is trying to watch tele," she said evenly. "Later she will walk three miles to work. She will not take the tram because she wants to save the fare. And all so she can keep you in cigarettes and clothes. I think a tiny consideration would be in order."

Vladimir shrugged. "What's she watching? The parasites flying in from London to gorge themselves on the sweat of the Russian people?"

"Why don't you save mixed metaphors for your songs, Vladi? You parrot them all from grandfather's old routines. If we're talking about parasites I suggest you take a good look in the mirror. You contribute nothing to the household budget. You don't even have the decency to go off and live in a commune."

Vladimir snorted. "*Girlchik*, you've bought the System in a big way. Times are changing. The people are waking: the 'Chine, corrupt politicians, subject races wanting freedom. There's a revolution coming, baby."

"Just postpone the revolution until Mother's had a couple of hours rest and cheap pleasure."

"Mother needs educating, *girlchik*. She's buying this whole ridiculous reactionary peepshow. She must know this is the last desperate play of a System with no future."

"Some other time, Vladi. Otherwise the Petrograd Military District gets an anonymous letter alleging that the medical certificate which rendered Vladimir Davidovich Bronstein unfit for military service is a forgery."

"I object to participating in the imperialist war in Indo-China on grounds of conscience."

"Conscience? Hah! Here's the deal, Vladi. First, you stop smoking *bhang* here. Secondly, you stop abusing your guitar when Mother is in the house. They can hear you from the Fontanka Canal. If you don't, someone tells the Army they ought to get you re-examined."

She hadn't seen Vladimir look so rattled since she first beat him at chess. For all that, he tucked the plectrum into the strings of his guitar and lay back on his bed. On the poster behind him, Ernesto "Che" Guevara—the pro-American guerilla killed fighting a Revolution in Angola—stared resolutely ahead into a bright new dawn of international socialism, managing perfectly well without Vladimir's help.

Cinzia returned to the living-room.

"As you know, protocol forbids senior members of the Imperial family from being present here to meet the Duke. The formal meeting will take place tomorrow. And as the Duke comes down the steps, two girls in traditional costume come to greet him with the traditional bread and salt."

"Look, there he is," said Mother, pointing to the tele. At the top of the steps to the aircraft, a young man of medium build stood wearing a dark blue overcoat belted with gold braid. His white-topped peaked cap didn't disguise ears that stuck out like the doors of a taxi-cab.

"Not exactly handsome."

"I suppose not," said Mother. "But he's brave. He flew helicopters in Indo-China. And he's clever as well. Until the war, he was studying to be an architect. He'll probably have to give up his studies to concentrate on duties of state."

Cinzia knew the feeling. She could have carried on at medical school, but after Father died, the scholarship wouldn't stretch far enough. She'd had to get a job.

"And coming to greet the Duke is Felix Dimitrovich Yussupov. Viewers will have noticed Prince Felix, the new newsreader on ITV, is dressed strangely, all in white. This is the uniform of a cricket-player. Prince Yussupov is a great lover of English culture. He in fact owns an estate in Scotlandshire. He told me this morning that he would wear the traditional cricketing costume to make the Duke feel at home. And there's the Duke now shaking his hand. And that's the Duke's uncle, the Earl of Balham, standing by them. He finds something immensely amusing. Perhaps Prince Yussupov has said something witty."

"That man," said Mother pointing to Prince Yussupov, "is a clown."

"I know, Mother."

"You've met him?"

"Yes."

She shook her head and smiled. "It's funny. I think of television as full of intelligent, witty, good-looking people. And my own little girl sees them every day. Will you meet the Duke and Grand Duchess Ekaterina?"

"Possibly. More likely, I'll be making up courtiers and military officers. Everyone else in the department will fight one another to do the high hats."

"*Now they're inspecting the Guard of Honour, and…Oh, the Earl of Balham is looking at their rifles, and looking under their caps, shouting at some of them, and the Duke is giving him a stern look. The Earl was a famous entertainer in his country before he married the Duke's Aunt Margaret.*"

"Isaac Asimov read my future for me last night. I'm going to marry a prince."

"Asimov read your future? In person? Gosh!"

"I have to go, Mother. I promised I'd do an extra shift at the Free Hospital."

She got up to get ready. Mother might struggle to support her deadbeat brother, but the Bronsteins didn't go without light and heat in winter, they had enough to eat and a colour tele. Many in Petrograd were worse off; sooner or later, they all ended up in the Free Hospital.

"*The piece of wood the Prince is holding is made of seasoned English willow, by the way. It's called a Marylebone Cricket Club.*"

The staff assembled in the canteen at Broadcasting House at eight a.m. for a final briefing with Sergo Paradjanov, Producer-in-Chief of the wedding coverage. Cinzia sat with the drivers, secretaries and electricians. ITV was assigning 130 personnel to the project and would broadcast an average three hours a day of coverage for the next month until the grand climax, the wedding itself.

Paradjanov, a bearded wrestler with green eye make-up and rouge-spotted cheeks, wore an eye-abusing orange-red Georgian robe. His huge lapels glinted, fragments of coloured glass and mirror woven into the fabric. He looked like Misha the Prime Time Bear ready for an evening in the nearest exquisite bar.

"Today," Paradjanov began, "three crews will go to the Winter Palace, which is opening for the Grand Imperial Ball this evening. This is where the Duke and the Grand Duchess supposedly meet for the first time. As you know, the pair have met on at least one previous occasion but the purpose of this event is to give the pond-scum a fairy tale. Every fool knows this is an old-fashioned dynastic marriage, but I want you to sell the fantasy. Eyes meet across the sumptuous room…They are introduced…They dance, they fall in love! Flop gauze over the lenses!

Smear petroleum jelly over everything! Fluttering silk scarves the length of a football pitch! My partners in dissolution, I want this to be the most romantic evening Russia has choked on since the Tsarevich Alexei Nicolaevich died on his wedding night at the Livadia Palace in 1925, spluttering blood among the vines and the heavy scent of summer flowers overlooking the sea.

"One more crew will cover the route from the Antchikov Palace to the Winter Palace. Another will be stationed at the Antchikov, where the British and Russian parties are preparing themselves for this evening.

"One last thing, rose-petals. It is my impression that after weeks of briefings, many of you sluggards *still* don't know who the Duke of Cornwall is. This is unacceptable. For the last time, he is a nephew of King Edward VIII. You may recall that Edward nearly lost his throne in 1936 because of his marriage to a White Yank divorcée. Remember the mini-series and Grand Duchess Anastasia's book? The upshot of that was that any children the couple had would not succeed to the throne. As it happens, they didn't have children. The King has a tiny penis, I'm told. Even monkey glands didn't help. Very romantic, *hein*? Succession therefore passes through the line of Edward's younger brother, the Duke of Pork. He died in 1952, though his wife, the Dowager Duchess of Pork, is still horribly alive and busily hating Princess Consort Wallis. Succession then passed to the daughters of the Duke of Earl. Elizabeth, Duchess of Edinburger, died in 1968, of that London fog respiratory disease. Her sister Margaret converted to Catholicism and married a lunatic, disqualifying herself. Elizabeth's oldest son Charles, until recently a naval officer nobody had heard of, has been created Duke of Cornwall, and is due to come into the crown on the death of King Edward VIII. *That*'s our Prince Charming. Got it? Now, let's get *royal* out there."

The footman held open gilt-encrusted doors, and Cinzia stepped through. Grand Duchess Ekaterina Nicolaievna was sprawled across an empress-sized bed, howling like a hyena with toothache. Her governess, Mrs. Orchard, had apparently been dismissed.

Cinzia put her make-up case on the floor and coughed politely.

The Tsar's eldest daughter looked up. "Who are you?"

"I'm from ITV. I've come to make up Your Imperial Highness for the ball. I can return later if you want."

The Grand Duchess sat and stared at her. No, *through* her. At nineteen, she looked younger. Still losing her puppy fat, she was becoming a beauty. Perfect skin, fall of dark hair, flashing green eyes. Cinzia's grandfather would cheerfully have bashed in her skull with a rifle-butt, and no wonder.

"I'm ill," said the Grand Duchess. "I'm delicate. I might die at any minute."

"I'm sorry to hear that. Shall I fetch a doctor?"

"Yes. Tell them to fetch Dr. Lysenko. Now."

Cinzia went back to the door and told the footman to summon Dr. Lysenko.

She returned. The Grand Duchess was pulling off her jeans and purple silk blouse. She fell into the bed and pulled covers over her head.

The kid was no more ill than Vladi. She was feeling the withdrawal symptoms of ten minutes' lack of attention. Cinzia almost felt sorry for the Duke of Cornwall.

A hand emerged from the covers and fumbled around the bedside table. Cinzia went over. Just out of the hand's reach was a box of Swiss truffles. According to the label, they had been flown in the previous day. She pushed the box towards the fingers, which took three chocolates and disappeared. Chewing motions shook the eiderdown.

No wonder the Grand Duchess was sick.

Cinzia settled in an armchair. The Antchikov Palace was turned upside down to accommodate the British and Russian royal parties, but the Grand Duchess had been allowed to keep her apartments.

The room, a mixture of bedroom and *boudoir*, was what every Russian teenager dreamed of. Between court paintings, the walls bore posters of cartoon characters and music stars, all centred on a framed poster of Nureyev as Agent 007 of SMERSH in *From America With Love*. In one corner was a huge stereo system with Quarrymen longplays scattered around it. In another, a vast dressing-table with a vaster triptych mirror. Huge windows, dotted over with see-through purple and turquoise plastic flower decals, added to the feeling of space. Beside the bed was the entrance to a wardrobe the size of the Bronstein apartment.

There was a commotion at the door. A group of people burst in. Some were obviously *pridvorny*, court people, dressed in the powdered wigs, tailcoats and knee-breeches of palace grooms. The leader was a small, chubby, elderly man in an old-fashioned pinstriped suit.

"What is the matter, Imperial Highness?" he said, bowing as he approached the bed, even though Ekaterina was hidden under the covers.

"Thank goodness you've come, Dr. Lysenko," said the Grand Duchess in a feeble voice. "I'm having another attack."

Half a dozen courtiers and servants stood around looking nervous, Dr. Lysenko and his assistant coaxed the Grand Duchess from under the covers and examined her at length, prodding, poking and asking her to cough. She showed no self-consciousness when the Doctor enquired about the condition of her bodily wastes.

"There's no doubt," said Dr. Lysenko, partly to the Grand Duchess, partly to his audience. "You suffer from chronic Smedley's Chorea."

Admittedly Cinzia hadn't finished medical school, but she'd never heard of Smedley's Chorea.

"There! You see? All of you! I'm going to die soon! I just hope I'll make it to the wedding. I'm sure the strain of that will finish me off. Like Great Uncle Alexei!"

"Your Imperial Highness, please don't say such terrible things," said Lysenko. "With enough rest and the right medication, there is no reason why you should not make a complete recovery in as little as three years."

"By which time, I will be expected to have given birth to three haemophilic sons and spent my summers being rained on in a nasty foreign country."

There was another commotion at the door. Everyone fell to their knees. Cinzia followed suit before she fully realised why.

The Tsar had entered the room, and was not pleased.

Her mother would never believe this.

"You! I thought I'd had you fired. Or shot!"

Lysenko bowed.

"I had him re-hired," said the Grand Duchess. "He's the only doctor who truly understands my condition."

Tsar Nicholas III was smaller in person than he seemed on television, but then everyone was. He was still impressive. The Russian Bear personified. Big, barrel-chested, strong. His full, rounded face was mostly covered by tightly-cropped beard. He wore a rough peasant smock, a thick leather belt and baggy trousers. His fondness for chopping wood and other "peasant" activities was well-known. It was also said he could bend a rouble coin in his teeth.

"Get out, Lysenko. And the rest of you."

Nobody needed prompting. Cinzia picked up her make-up case and made for the door with the others.

"Wait! You, girl! Who are you?"

He was talking to her. She turned and bowed. "I am from ITV. I have come to apply make-up to Her Imperial Highness."

"Then stay. You will start work in a moment."

The Tsar picked up the box of chocolates.

"You will need wallpaper and paste if *Katiusha* keeps filling herself with these pollutants."

He tossed the chocolates away.

"Hah," he said. "Wallpaper. Paste."

Evidently, his remark was an imperial joke. She tried a dutiful laugh, but it came out as a cough.

Nicholas walked over to the bed and hugged his daughter. The Grand Duchess sniffed, then started crying. "You don't care about me! Nobody cares about me!"

"We all care about you. Your mother and I love you very much. So do your sisters and brother. That's why we arranged this marvellous wedding for you. All over Russia, all over the world, millions and millions of girls will go to bed tonight dreaming that they could swap places with you. Isn't that true, make-up girl?"

"Absolutely sire," said Cinzia, nodding.

"Then let them swap!" sobbed the Grand Duchess. "I don't want to go through with this silly wedding."

The Tsar stood upright, stuck hands into his belt and spoke evenly. "Ekaterina, I grow tired of this nonsense. You always forget that you and I are not as ordinary people. We are endowed by the Almighty with power and wealth because we have duties and obligations ordinary people don't have."

"I'll abdicate. I'll go and be an ordinary person—just like her."

She pointed at Cinzia. Something inside boiled over. This spoiled brat was wasting her time, time she could be spending at home reading a book, listening to music, playing cards with Mother. Time she could be helping people who needed help at the Free Hospital.

"Your Imperial Highness wouldn't like it very much. If you want to swap places, let's do it. I live near a particularly smelly canal. I share three rooms with my mother and a bone-idle brother. Most months we have to get by on less than three hundred roubles. It's been a while since we had truffles flown in from Switzerland."

The Tsar fixed her with chilling blue eyes. For a few seconds, she was hypnotised, glimpsing an avenue of stakes, each with someone impaled on it. Had she gone too far?

The Tsar nodded, grunted agreement, almost smiled.

"Do you hear that, *Katiusha*. It is the voice of the great Russian people who love you. You must do your duty for this girl and for others like her. If you do not, I shall have to do mine, regardless."

Cinzia did not doubt he meant it. Tsar Peter had his own son tortured to death. And they called him Peter the Great.

Grand Duchess Ekaterina whimpered, "you don't love me."

"Yes I bloody well do! But I didn't father children to love them. I fathered them for the Russian Empire and the Romanov dynasty."

Cinzia believed this, too. Before Nicholas acceded to the throne, his childless marriage to Princess Flavia of Ruritania was dissolved. His subsequent marriage to Elisabeth-Mathilde Kshesinska was a model of heir-begetting fruitfulness, but Flavia kept apartments in Moscow, Petrograd and a dacha near the palace at Tsarskoye Selo. The Tsar still visited her almost daily.

"I don't want to leave Russia," Ekaterina sobbed. "The King of England is mad. Who's to say the Duke isn't the same? Look at his *ears*! And I don't want to be Queen of *England*. The peasants eat dogs there and they don't have colour tele."

There was a loud, firm knock at the door.

"Yes? What now?" shouted the Tsar.

In walked a hussar officer. Cinzia was used to thinking of cavalrymen driving tanks on the news reports from Indo-China, but this man looked as though he was on his way to Borodino. His jacket was red, covered in gold lace; over his shoulder was slung the hussar's pelisse, a short brown overcoat lined with black fur, also plastered with braid. His fur cap boasted a white cockade and a brass plate of the imperial two-headed eagle. Straps of white leather complicated his attire even further. From some of the straps dangled what appeared to be a flattish handbag, while others were attached to the scabbard of a sabre, which he held in his white-gloved right hand.

"Well?" snapped the Tsar.

The officer saluted, slammed boot-heels together and bowed. Cinzia was secretly relieved that all of his get-up survived the agitation.

"Apologies, sire," he said crisply, "I did not know His Imperial Highness was present. I have come to make my report to the Grand Duchess."

"Go on then." said the Tsar.

The officer turned to the Grand Duchess and saluted once more.

"Ensign Pavel Chekhov, First Troop, First Squadron of the Akhtirska hussar regiment respectfully wishes to inform her Imperial Highness Grand Duchess Ekaterina Nicolaievna that her personal escort awaits the pleasure of her orders."

"Ensign Chekhov," said the Grand Duchess. "You in command of my escort again? I thought you had applied for a transfer to the space program?"

"I did, Imperial Highness. It was recently decided all aristocrats were to be disqualified from becoming cosmonauts."

Cinzia remembered lunar duellists. *Krokodil*, the fortnightly satirical magazine, had carried a full report of Georgi Sanders' presentation. Count Ignatieff's younger brother thrashed Editor Solzhenitsyn through the streets of Moscow with the flat of a sabre until the self-proclaimed Funniest Man in Russia grabbed the staff of an imperial flag and defended himself. Now Solzhenitsyn was the Funniest Man Lying Low for a While in Sweden.

The Grand Duchess had evidently stopped feeling sorry for herself. She held a silk sheets in front of her face. The Tsar might assume this was to protect her modesty, or be smart enough to figure Ekaterina didn't want Chekhov to see her with red puffy eyes and mascara-stained cheeks. Cinzia recognised the symptoms: the Grand Duchess was smitten with her ensign in his tight pants. Maybe he looked less ridiculous on a horse.

"Thank you, Ensign," said the Tsar. "The Grand Duchess will come down when she is ready."

Chekhov saluted, spun round on one heel and marched out of the room. Through the door, she saw a pair of troopers bending down and cross-linking their hands to provide a seat for Chekhov. They carried him away. He'd probably had a regiment of servants smartening his uniform, shining leather, polishing brass and sewing on lace and he wasn't going to risk a speck of dirt spoiling things. The Grand Duchess sighed, let the sheet down and addressed Cinzia.

"Come on, soul of mother Russia, we'd better get started."

"Bronstein, I look like a *houri*," said Ekaterina, swivelling her head to one side and another, making eyes at the mirror.

"Under the lights you'll be radiant. You don't want to look like a ghost on tele."

The Grand Duchess now wore a pink satin ball-gown fit to grace the cover of a million women's magazines, even the snooty Viennese ones.

Cinzia tried to use little powder on that fine skin, and concentrated on eyes and lips. The Grand Duchess's hair hung loose over her shoulders, held by a small tiara set with rubies and diamonds. Without trying, she would outshine every other woman at the ball.

Maybe it was true. Maybe royals were more than human.

"I wish I could wear my hair Afrikan style," the Grand Duchess pouted. "It's too long. Perhaps I should cut it."

"You do and I'll assassinate you," said Cinzia.

They were surrounded by maids, dressers and flunkies, sewing, fussing and whispering. One or two gasped at her impertinence.

"I might as well be dead anyway," Ekaterina smiled. "I've decided I'm not going through with this marriage unless you are my personal make-up artist. I hope he likes it."

"If the Duke doesn't like you there's something wrong with him."

"The Duke...Oh. Yes. Him."

"Cinzia! Thank God I've found you," said Bondarchuk, out of breath. He bowed to the Grand Duchess. "Are you finished? We need you urgently in the Duke's suite. Half the British team are stranded at Croydon airport. An engine fell off their Bristol Brabazon. All the BBC make-up people are still there. I've got the rest of the girls working on his entourage, but I need you to do the Duke himself."

The Grand Duchess sniggered and waved her away. "I'll be fine now," she said.

Cinzia scooped her bits and pieces into the case.

It was wasted on her, really. Her mother should be here.

It took five minutes to negotiate their way across the palace, clambering over cables, lights and cameras, pushing through knots of soldiers and courtiers making last-minute adjustments to suits, dresses and uniforms.

And this was just an Imperial Ball. The wedding would be worse. It would bankrupt some of the Empire's most distinguished families. Duchesses could not wear the same dresses twice while there were cameras around.

In the Duke's quarters, things were even more chaotic. Luggage had gone missing, or had never come to Russia in the first place, and people rushed around trying to borrow jewellery, combs, razors, scissors, lipstick from the Russians.

Sir Anthony Blunt stood in the middle of this, looking miserable. The Duke of Edinburgh, the Duke's Father, who Paradjanov had identified as the widower of Elizabeth, Duchess of Edinburgh, was trying to get Sir Anthony to arrange a wild boar hunt.

Sir Anthony broke free and hurried Bondarchuk and Cinzia into a small side-room where the Duke of Cornwall stood in his shirtsleeves looking out of the window.

"Sir Anthony," said the Duke. "We must try and do a bit of sightseeing."

"Your Grace, this young lady speaks fluent English. She'll see to your make-up."

He turned to her, smiled and nodded. "Where do you want me, Miss?"

There was no dressing table. There was an armchair. It would have to do. She pointed to it. Bondarchuk made excuses and left.

The Duke sat down. She opened her case on the floor next to the chair, took out a large cotton sheet and spread it over the Duke, tucking it into the collar of his shirt.

She crouched in front of him and looked into his face. He was more of a challenge than the Grand Duchess. Though only in his mid-twenties, hardly older than her, Charles had lines. He'd been around. She was prepared to dismiss the talk of recklessly flying his helicopter into battle zones in Indo-China as propaganda, but something had added ten years to his face.

He was tense.

"You are nervous, sire?" she asked him.

A man cleared his throat behind her. "The correct form of address is 'your grace'." She had forgotten Sir Anthony was in the room.

The Duke shrugged and smiled apologetically.

"I rather suppose I am. It's not every day one meets one's future wife. With four hundred million people watching."

He spoke with a curious, clipped accent. Not at all like the affected "upper-class twit" English accent Mother used to entertain her with.

It was a question, she decided, of smoothing out some lines and emphasising a few others. Then she noticed the ears again.

She laughed. She couldn't help it.

The Duke smiled. "What's so funny?"

Her face was on fire. She hadn't blushed like this for years. Soon she'd be too old to. "It's nothing, your grace. Nothing at all."

"I hope you'll not think it remiss of me if I tell you that you have lovely eyes. Now go on, share the joke. I can take it."

She swallowed. "Making a professional appraisal of your grace's face, it occurs to me that your grace has rather prominent ears. I was wondering if sticky tape might be of use."

The Duke froze and gave her a murderous look. Blunt muttered words in English that she didn't recognise and stormed out.

"Blunt has gone out to find someone to have you shot. Now get on with it."

She set to work, wondering if she'd still have a job in the morning. Or a head.

Moments later, a voice behind her snapped, "ACH GD 22230333 Earl of Balham reporting for duty, *sah!*"

She turned. It was the man who had laughed at Yussupov at the airport. Now he stood wore an Asiatic turban, a blue jacket, a tutu and ankle-boots.

The Duke grinned at him. "You can't meet my bride-to-be dressed like that, Sellers,"

"Why on earth not, old fruity substance?" he said, in the upper-class twit accent her Mother imitated.

"You're not wearing your decorations. It states clearly on the invitation that medals and orders must be worn."

Both laughed. The Earl took a hip-flask from the breast pocket of his jacket and offered it to the Duke, who refused. He took a hefty guzzle himself and then noticed her.

"Well *hellaaao,*" he growled, crouching next to her and twiddling his moustache, "now you're a gorgeous bit of tottie, and no mistake. Are you coming to the *palais de danse,* my little Russian doll?"

She resumed work. "I am, but I shall be busy. I have to stay behind the scenes in case anyone's face falls off."

"I'd love my face to fall off for you, my little boiling samovar."

"You'd better get dressed for the ball. The British party has to leave for the Winter Palace inside the hour."

"But I'm going like this, *mein führer.* This is my formal evening dress. The turban's in honour of wartime service in Injah, RAF battledress because I was in the RAF."

"They let *you* fly an aeroplane?"

Oh dear, there she went again.

"Heavens no!" he said, switching accents. "Put me in ENSA, give 'em a song an' a dance, tell a few jokes, that was me. Every Night Something Awful. That's why I'm wearing the old tutu and boots don't you see, laddie."

Sir Anthony returned, pulling in Bondarchuk.

"I want her fired! At once. And I want all her family fired. Her insult to the Duke was unforgivable."

"Oh forget it, Tony!" said the Duke, waving him away.

The Earl of Balham went up to Blunt, puffing out his chest.

"You're talking about the woman I love, Tones. If you fire her, you'll have to fire me, too."

Blunt turned, threw his hands up in the air and walked off.

"I have deaded him, swine rotter that he is," shrilled Balham in a high squeak, "deaded him proper."

"Thank you, Earl," Cinzia said. "To return the favour, I'll remind you that you have less than half an hour to change into clothes more appropriate to the occasion. I've met his Imperial Highness the Tsar and my estimate of his character is that he could well lock you into a dungeon and throw away the dungeon if you do anything to spoil his little girl's big day."

"You are right, my Captain. I will go and do that thing. I will. I will. I will go and put on my brown paper suit and make a dress sword from Mum's old drawers."

The Duke laughed. Balham left.

Cinzia was losing count of mad royals. She wished she had Paradjanov's handbook of who was who.

More people appeared at the door. Cinzia looked up and was surprised to see the Grand Duchess standing there.

"Is everything to your satisfaction?" she asked the Duke in heavily accented English.

"Fine thanks," he nodded politely.

"Cinzia Davidovna has done an excellent job. Would you approve if she was personally responsible for your make up and mine until the wedding's over?"

"Fine with me," said the Duke, "as long as she brings her sticky tape".

Nobody had asked Cinzia if it was fine by her. It wasn't. Not without a big pay-rise anyway.

"Do you have any idea who that insane person in the ballet skirt was?"

The Duke had no explanation.

The vast rotors of the Sikorsky gunship cut up the air with a low roar, but the ride was smooth. Whether this was an inherent property of the aircraft or whether it was because the Duke of Cornwall was at the controls, Cinzia didn't know.

For all the noise, she heard Bondarchuk muttering into his wireless behind her. "You've got to just trust me on this. No close-ups of the happy couple when we come in to land."

At least one camera-crew would be waiting on the ground when the aircraft landed at the Imperial complex at Tsarskoye Selo.

Charles, Duke of Cornwall, and Grand Duchess Ekaterina Nicolaievna had carried on their televisioned engagement for three days. From the glittering Grand Ball at the Winter Palace through the couple's various subsequent public engagements, everything on-screen had been just fine. With three hours of live broadcast daily, ITV had captured immense ratings which still climbed. All Soyuz TV, the opposition, could offer was the remarkably unpopular comedy series *Mother Courage's Flying Circus* and repeats of *On the Trams*.

"Dear God! What I wouldn't give for a rifle right now!" said the Duke's father. She looked out of the gunport and saw, down on the ground 200 feet below, a herd of deer running, frightened by the helicopter's noise.

Edinburgh still sulked because he was not allowed to shoot anything.

The Duke of Cornwall was following the line of a stream, and banked the helicopter slightly to the left. Cinzia fell against the Grand Duchess sitting next to her.

"I've warned you how I get air-sick! Do you want me to spew all over you?"

Yes, why not? She could scrape Her Imperial Highness's dried-up vomit into cheap lockets and sell it at a huge profit to all the poor, deluded people who hung on her antics on tele every night.

She thought of her Mother, who had for the first time in her life taken a day off from her cleaning job: to watch the Imperial Ball on tele. When Cinzia got home that night, she'd had to stay up another two hours describing who she had met. She had told Mother about the Grand Duchess's tantrums, how the Duke had heartily disliked her crack about his ears, how she had seen with her own eyes how this was emphatically, definitely, utterly, absolutely not a love match. And still at the end of it all, Mother sighed about how wonderful it was to see "two young people falling in love." Mother had listened to her, enraptured that her little girl had touched this magic, but had not heard a word she was saying.

She had not realised how powerful television was. It encouraged people to believe what they wanted to. In the hands of a tyrant it could be a force for great evil. And the Tsar of all the Russias owned ITV.

There were fifteen of them in the gunship, on metal bucket seats covered with fraying canvas: the Duke, Edinburgh, Sir Anthony, the Earl of Balham, the Grand Duchess, and the ghastly old Grand Duchess Anastasia, who had appointed herself her great-niece's official chaperone. There were a couple of maids, a pilot, co-pilot and the ITV crew. Behind flew three other gunships, one carrying the Tsar his entourage, the others carrying security specialists from the Okhrana and medical teams. The Tsar's Sikorsky was armed, in case it became necessary to fire on a cheering crowd of his beloved subjects.

It was no longer a question of would something go wrong. Now it was a question of when. The atmosphere in their own gunship was sour, and getting worse with every hour. Everything came back to Ekaterina.

Though nobody watching proceedings on television would have noticed anything amiss, the Grand Duchess was fast becoming unmanageable. Like a lumbering goods-train on the Trans-Siberia, she threatened to leave the rails at the next bend.

When visiting a hospital, the Grand Duchess insisted the sick people be removed and replaced by actors in case she caught anything. They had met crowds on the streets of Petrograd and the Grand Duchess had had to take a bath immediately afterwards, though she had not come closer than ten feet to any of them. On the same occasion, the police failed to contain an anti-war demonstration and placards had been waved from the back of the crowd. The Grand Duchess insisted that the city's police commissioner be sacked. The couple attended a charity premiere screening of *The Tempest*, the new film by the British director Michael Powell, at the *Narodny Dom*. The Grand Duchess had to be carried out with a fit of the vapours before the opening credits. The director's trademark of arrows hitting a target had given her "a terrible premonition of assassination."

"She carries on like this and I'll be the one that does it," Bondarchuk muttered when she was being carried out of the cinema. Then he crossed himself, in case the Okhrana heard.

Today was the worst. They were supposed to go on a deer hunt on the imperial estates around Tsarskoye Selo. First the Grand Duchess insisted that the helicopter's olive green and brown camouflage colour scheme be replaced with shocking pink—"exactly the same colour as that," she said, pointing to one of the lipsticks in Cinzia's case. Grand Duchess Anastasia, who only ever wore pink, agreed this would be an appropriate way of making the nasty, brutal helicopter more feminine.

The Tsar shouted that idea down. Then the Grand Duchess pouted and said shooting deer was cruel. Great Aunt Anastasia agreed. So had Edinburgh, to everyone's surprise. He then suggested the helicopter be fitted with missile-pods to ensure a quick and painless death for the deer. At this point, the Balham collapsed in a fit of laughter, while the Tsar said it was impossible. The Grand Duchess flatly refused to go if any animals were going to be killed.

So they went for an afternoon spin instead. They had made an impromptu visit to a "typical" farmhouse and had an excellent discussion with a farmer about fertiliser. They had a picnic at which nobody said much to one another, and now they were going back again. The Grand Duchess was in a vile mood, which was why Bondarchuk was dissuading Paradjanov from taking close-ups.

The helicopter swooped down low over the town of Tsarskoye Selo. Beneath them was the railway station, and then the broad tree-lined boulevard with dozens of mansions to either side. This was where the aristocracy lived in the old days; it was where some of them still lived, though many of these elegant houses had long since been divided into apartments where the bourgeois of Petrograd commuted each evening to escape the noises and stinks of the city.

At the end of the boulevard, the gates to the Imperial Park. The eight hundred acres of Tsarskoye Selo proper—the "Tsar's Village"—had once been completely surrounded by iron railings, though these had been taken away to make munitions during the Great Patriotic War. Now, the boundaries were mainly wire and post, but still patrolled by cossacks and handpicked units of the Imperial Guard, with dogs, guns, wirelesses, even remote-control cameras.

"This is great," Bondarchuk said. "We can't get decent pictures just pointing a camera out of the window, but if you can get the ITV chopper to do this in a few minutes' time we can cut it into the evening prog with majestic music on top."

The Duke took the machine down lower over the Imperial Park. It was probably the first time he had seen the place. It was certainly the first time Cinzia had been here. She had seen photographs and paintings, but the Tsar—and his mother before him—had guarded its privacy fiercely.

The Park was designed to provide nothing but pleasant walks. Every inch was landscaped carefully with meticulously tended grass, or painstakingly trained woods. There were statues and monuments and flowerbeds and a huge artificial lake. The Sikorsky swooped over a *tyrannosaurus rex*.

As a boy, Nicholas had been fascinated by paleontology. Tsarina Tatiana commissioned life-sized dinosaurs from S. Eisenstein, the motion picture special effects genius behind the 1932 classic *Tsar Saur*. They were equipped with clockwork mechanisms that made them jerk to life.

The grounds were completely empty. It was as though they were for the pleasure of the Tsar alone. He might wander among his flowers and jurassic pets, undisturbed by the millions of his subjects still tied to the dirt or crowded into city slums.

The Duke banked slightly to avoid a small hill, on top of which was an exquisite red and gold Chinese pagoda. Then the palaces came into view. Cinzia gasped when she saw the Catherine Palace, an ornate blue and white confection with immensely tall windows. The simpler Alexander Palace, five hundred yards from it, was dowdy by comparison.

She was getting to know palaces. The Antchikov merely reminded her of an expensive hotel, while the Winter Palace was big and cold, but this was a place of real majesty. This was where the handsome prince carried his bride, or where a canny monarch kept his or her uppity nobles from getting up to any mischief by engaging them in ludicrous ceremonial. Inside would be long, polished halls, mirrors and mahogany, silk and velvet, marble and crystal and gold.

She was still staring out of the window when she realised the helicopter blades were slowing and that everyone around was unbuckling seatbelts.

"That's it for the day," Bondarchuk told his crew. "There's nothing else tonight. Everyone's got the evening off."

An arm snaked around her waist. The Earl of Balham.

"Come with me to the Casbah, Cindy."

"I'm going home for a shower and an early night."

"*Quel* shame, laddie. The Duke and I have decided to toddle into town for the evening. We were hoping you'd show us the real Petrograd. These court flunkeys and pomaded pillocks don't have a clue where to go for good time. Go on, say you'll do it. Pretty please? Not for my sake, but the Duke's."

She looked at the Duke. He was taking off the headset and engaged in technical discussion with the helicopter's regular pilot.

"Just a few drinks," she said. "And no funny business."

Balham chuckled and swore loyalty.

"Compliments of Nikita's," said the waiter, placing a champagne-bucket on the table.

"This is a bit of allright," said Balham around a *blini*. "Well done, Cind."

"Bottoms up," said Balham raising his champagne flute, "here's to our host."

They turned to the table where the proprietor sat with cronies. He raised his glass and beamed, a benevolent great uncle dispensing presents at Easter. Bringing the party here was divine inspiration. Old Kruschev, the most important gangster in Petrograd and a devoted monarchist, would see no harm came to his precious guests. It was lively and more-or-less respectable. Kruschev kept his less salubrious properties at arms' length.

"Chas, d'you recognise the fellows sitting on the table next to Niki's?"

"No," said the Duke to the Earl, "should we?"

Cinzia glanced. To one side was a tall, bespectacled man in early middle age with close-cropped, wiry hair. A little too careful with his appearance to be an intellectual.

"We were introduced to him at the reception for civil serviles the other morning," said Balham. "He had a meaningless job title, something with the Ministry of the Interior."

"Andropov. I remember. A senior civil servant hanging around in a shady night-club. Bit fishy, isn't it?"

"It's more than fishy, Moriarty," said Balham, slipping into a Georgi Sanders purr, "I had him down as one of the head mummers in the cloak-and-dagger brigade. Okhrana, and all that."

"*Sapristi!*" said the Duke, a word she'd never heard before.

"I'll tell you something else, old fruitgum," said the Earl. "If you turn around—nyet yet!—and steal a look in the next minute you'll notice Mr. Andropopoff popping off. The fellah sneaking with him happens to be Harold Philby, Russia correspondent of *The Times*."

"I wonder what they were plotting?" said the Duke.

"Overthrow of civilisation as we know it. What do you think, Cindy?"

"Probably nothing important. Russians love to plot for its own sake. It's why we always knock you out of the first round in the World Chess Championships."

"We always beat you at soccer, though," said the Duke. "It's the Accrington Stanley game tomorrow. Bobby Moore at centre-forward, Gordon Banks in goal. We can't lose."

A woman in her late twenties wobbled past them. She wore a Chinese *cheongsam* so tight she could barely walk properly. Her head was shaved and a dozen ping-pong balls were magically stuck to her scalp.

"Oh I say," said Balham.

She sat alone at a table close by and took a packet of Fribourg and Treyer cigarettes and a gold lighter from a tiny handbag. Cinzia decided she must be a whore. An experienced, expert, expensive one.

Balham had barely raised his hand when the head waiter appeared at his side.

"Would you be so kind as to convey my compliments to the lady with the lumps and ask if she would care to join us."

The waiter made the slightest gesture with his eye. The woman scooped belongings from the table and tottered over. The waiter held out the chair for her to sit down. Her jaw dropped when she realised who the Duke was.

"This is jolly, isn't it?" said Balham, "and what's your name, my dear?"

"Mariella Novotny," she said, recovering her composure. Her skin had a faint olive sheen. She might be a gypsy.

Cinzia looked at the Duke, expecting him to be discomforted by his uncle's philandering. He smiled faintly. He had seen all this before.

Balham busied himself with Mariella. Her English was basic, and he had no Russian. They communicated in broken French. Balham's accent was comically extreme, almost strangling the few words Mariella could recognise. He took her hand and ran his finger over it, pretending he could tell her fortune. Isaac would have been proud of him.

Scattered applause came as a men in evening dress filed onto a small raised platform and picked up instruments. The band launched into a silky-smooth, melodious Israel Baline tune, "Always". Piano, sax and clarinet took turns at the theme. It was seductive, tinged with longing or regret. Perfect music for falling in love, or getting drunk.

Some couples took the floor to dance. Balham and Mariella joined them.

She was alone with the Duke and didn't much like it. He was still frostily polite to her for the Grand Duchess's sake, but hadn't forgiven the remark about ears.

"How do you like Mother Russia?" she asked, trying to fill an embarrassing silence.

"Very interesting. Splendid architecture. Petrograd is a beautiful city."

She wanted to tell him of the city he wouldn't see, soulless acres of low-rise concrete apartments where the plumbing never worked, but thought better of it. Another long silence.

"Look," he said at last, "I wanted to..."

"Cinz-doll!" interrupted a whiny voice, "Is it copacetic if I make like a carpenter and join you?"

Allen Martinovich. The last person she wanted to see right now, but here he was. Drunk.

He sat down, uninvited, at the table and helped himself to one of Mariella's cigarettes. "Who's your *dybbuk* friend? He looks like that English idiot the Grand Duchess is going to marry. *Babychik*, I need a favour."

"Whatever it is, the answer is no, *nein, non*..."

"I gotta get a gig." She looked him in the face. As usual, his eyes skittered away from hers. He hid behind oversize eyeglasses. "I need to get on my horn again, Cinz. You could talk to someone at ITV. They've got house bands. They have to need a clarinet-player. Put in a word, please-please?"

"If I say yes, will you go away?"

"I'll make like a train and depart, I'll make like a family photo and fade, I'll make like a tree and..."

"Enough already."

"Do you know anyone who needs a musician?" he asked the Duke. "What's your angle, anyway?"

"He's the future King of England, Allen Martinovich. He doesn't need a clarinet player."

"Don't be silly, everybody needs a clarinet player."

Hands swallowed Allen's arms as the biggest men she had ever seen lifted him from the chair and carried him from the room.

"The proprietor sends humble apologies for the unpleasant imposition," said their waiter, signalling for a minion to bring a plate of *baklava* cakes and a jug of hot honey and rosewater sauce.

"Sorry about that," she said. The Duke refilled her flute.

"Skeleton from your cupboard?"

"I went with Allen for a long time. We were betrothed. He was going to be a famous musician. Like an idiot, I believed him. I supported him while he was waiting to be famous. He nearly made it, too. He had a band, Allen Konigsberg and the Bananas. They performed at the opening

255

of the Moscow Olympiad in '70. At the party afterwards, I caught him fooling around with a jail-bait Wallachian gymnast."

"Ouch."

"He sickens me. He ruined everything. He's the *dybbuk*."

The Duke grasped her hand across the table. "Everything will turn out fine, Cinzia," he said.

"It did," she giggled, half-hysterically. "He was pitifully infatuated with his bendy toy. He wrote a swing oratorio for her to perform to, *The Purple Rose of Cluj*. But she ran off with the novelist, Nabokov."

Her eyes stung. She drained her champagne flute at a gulp.

"What are we supposed to do with these?" said the Duke, indicating the *baklava*. He still held her hand. She poured the sauce over the cakes.

"You have to eat the cakes while the sauce is still hot."

"I wonder where our lovebirds have got to?"

"There are rooms upstairs. I wouldn't be surprised if Miss Bubblehead was an employee."

The Duke nodded. He ate a pair of *baklavas*. "These are very good."

"The country is wild for Turkish food. A new Turkish restaurant opens in Petrograd every week."

The Duke took his hand back and was oddly formal for a moment.

"I owe you an apology. Normally, I wouldn't bother. Being heir to the throne means never having to say you're sorry, but I want to say sorry to you. You didn't deserve my rudeness."

"What do you mean?"

"I got chilly when you said the thing about my ears. I don't give a damn about my appearance. If I was only Lieutenant Charles Windsor, we could laugh at my bloody ears all night long. But I have to protect the dignity of the future king. At times, I hate this job. Being a royal *is* a job, you know. Sometimes I think it's important. Sometimes I think it's ludicrous farce. I see you looking at me and the Tsar and my Father and Blunt and the Grand Duchess. You think we're idiots acting out some kind of comic opera."

"I never..."

"Don't interrupt, Cinzia Davidovna. Several times in the last few days, I'd gladly have resigned. But I would let too many people down."

"Your family? The Imperial family?"

"No. The blade wouldn't fall on their necks if I was to quit. I mean the lads."

"I'm sorry. I don't follow you."

"I served in the Navy. Eighteen months in Indo-China, flying Sea Kings off carriers, evacuating the wounded. For the first time in my life, something real. At Khe Sanh, I flew sixty-two missions in three days, didn't sleep at all. Brought in the bus three hundred yards short of the enemy's forward positions. Loaded with dying men, mutilated men, men maddened by combat, men who'd never walk or see again. I can't pretend I was happy because I absolutely wasn't, but I was more alive than I am now. Civvies can't understand. In Britain and here in Russia, people are sick of the War. We're pulling out as messily as possible. At the moment, Indo-China veterans, able-bodied and maimed alike, are merely despised, spat on by the longhairs. Soon, the men who served will be forgotten. That's my good reason for becoming King. I'll do all I can for the men; I won't have much political power, but I can get things done. The price I must pay for that is to appear regal, to be popular. Dress in silly suits and go through this happy-ever-after charade."

He shook his head, raised his hand. A fresh bottle of champagne appeared instantly. Both their flutes were filled. Even in the low light, she could tell he was blushing.

"I shouldn't really have said all that. We're not to show our feelings, don't you know?"

"Do you love the Grand Duchess?"

He shook his head slightly. "What's love got to do with it? Duty comes first. My opinion of Ekaterina is of no importance."

She was crying. And trying not to.

"There are worse prospects. I could be stuck with blue-blooded English neurotic with a fashionable eating disorder and a brain the size of a pea."

Through blurry eyes, she saw Sir Anthony Blunt striding towards them.

"Thank heavens we've found your grace. There's a flap on out there. Half Petrograd is looking for you. Where is the Earl?"

The Duke poured himself another fluteful of champagne.

"Balham's in an upstairs room, Blunt. He's having a shag, so knock before you go in, there's a good fellow."

"Your Imperial Highness will be presented to the British Prime Minister, Enoch Powell," said Tatischeff, the court's Chief of Protocol, a spry man in purple pantaloons and red tailcoat. He wore a transparent plastic rain hat over his powdered wig. "Then Foreign Minister Sir Alec Douglas-Home and Minister of the Interior, Jimmy Edwards. If Your

Imperial Highness might permit a humorous aside, Professor Edwards is known as 'Whacko', English onomatopoeia for the effect of one object hitting another. He sponsored a law for the birching of young criminals."

The Grand Duchess turned to Cinzia and snorted. "These English are perverts. What good is birching? If they want to instil discipline and respect in the peasants, they should *knout* them and have done with it."

It was early evening. The Grand Duchess was supposed to be getting ready for a state dinner at the Winter Palace which would be attended by British and Russian politicians.

"You will then be presented to our Russian government. Prime Minister Henryk Kissinger and his minsters. I am sure I need not remind your Imperial Highness of their names and titles."

"You do actually," said the Grand Duchess, from inside her vast wardrobe. "No, don't bother. They're all bloody crooks anyway. I'm surprised they've bothered to come up from Moscow. How can they tear themselves away from their money and mistresses?"

"And their tape-recorders," said Cinzia. The Grand Duchess laughed.

The imperial engagement was almost upstaged by daily corruption revelations. Two nights ago, Kremlin men were caught planting electronic listening devices in the Moscow HQ of the Social Democratic Party. The Mensheviks, faking outrage, were calling for an immediate election. Vladimir said the crisis aided the cause of the Tsar more than that of the Opposition. He was convinced *Batiushka* was responsible for leaking Moscow scandals to put all politicians out of public favour. Certainly, Prince Yussopoff was celebrated for his inside knowledge of Duma dirty-doings and ITV played up the break-in as a big story. Vladi claimed a military coup in the Tsar's name was being planned at the huge army camp at Krasnoe Selo. Cinzia told her brother to stop believing the conspiracy theories he read in Bolshevik underground comics, but wasn't too sure.

"Then you come to what is called His Majesty's Loyal Opposition," Tatischeff was saying. "The leader of the Labour Party is Dennis Potter, a capable man with bad skin. His deputy, called the Shadow Foreign Secretary, is Alan Bennett. He is a very pleasant gentleman whose conversation your Imperial Highness may well find charming, though I have been warned by a foreign ministry official to beware lest he try to tell lengthy anecdotes about his elderly female relatives."

"That will be quite enough," said the Grand Duchess emerging from the wardrobe. Cinzia guessed she had taken in none of the briefing. The man bowed, back creaking, and left.

"I don't have a thing to wear," said the Grand Duchess, leaping onto her bed. "The court dressmaker must provide a miracle."

The Grand Duchess had heard of Cinzia's adventures with her fiancé and the Earl of Balham, and was evidently amused. She wanted to know about Nikita's, and about the Earl absenting himself with a woman of easy repute. She thought the escapade hilarious. Cinzia did not talk about the Duke's confession that he hated his job.

"Put the tele on," said the Grand Duchess. "It's time for *The Rostovs*."

Cinzia got up and walked to the set at the end of the bed and switched it on. The Afrikan beat 1812 Overture was already playing over a series of postcard views of domes.

There was a tap at the door, and a small procession of women entered. A stout matron bearing a green silk dress. The Grand Duchess leapt off her bed and greeted the dress. She took it and held it against her body. She turned to a mirror.

"This is horrible. The colour makes me look as though I have an unpleasant disease!"

There was an embarrassed pause. Cinzia thought the dress beautiful. It had a simple, understated elegance. The colour perfectly matched the Grand Duchess's eyes.

"The decolletage is immense. Obviously, none of you have been to the Winter Palace in a low-cut gown. Ladies, they don't call it the Winter Fucking Palace because it's hot! If I wore this I'd get a chill and probably die! Then you'd feel pretty terrible. Remember the Egyptian Royals who had their servants buried with them. No, not you Cinzia; you'd have to stay alive to make me look nice in the sarcophagus...Out! All of you!"

The Grand Duchess steamed in exasperation as the panicked women scurried out. She flopped back down on her bed to watch *The Rostovs*. Cinzia sat next to her.

"That's it!" said the Grand Duchess suddenly. "The dress I want!"

Onscreen, Natasha burst into Prince Bolkonsky's office to abuse him for bankrupting her Uncle Vanya. She wore a loose cotton *djellaba*, printed with bright colour swirls.

The Grand Duchess pushed a buzzer at her bedside. Mrs. Orchard emerged through a hidden side-door.

She pointed to the screen. "I want that dress, Mrs. O. Get it for me. *Now.*"

The woman's eyes bulged. "That's *The Rostovs*, isn't it? It's broadcast live."

"So?"

"We can't get you the dress immediately. We'll have to wait an hour."

"We don't have time, Mrs. O. In an hour, I have to be at a banquet for the civilised world's most important criminals and perverts and I want to wear that dress. Get it for me!"

Mrs. Orchard, clearly regretting that she had not punished her charge more when she was little, left the room.

On tele, Talia Gurdin and Yul Brynner worked the sexual chemistry that made Natasha and Prince Bolkonsky a hit with the viewers. They circled each other, shouting and lashing out, occasionally making soothing noises and embracing.

"My marriage is going to be like that," said the Grand Duchess. "Only without the interesting bits."

The next scene was laid in a lavish drawing room where Pyotr Bezukhov (Romek Polanski), son of Prince Bolkonsky's best friend, told his great grandmother (Maria Ouspenskaya) how much he was in love with a gypsy singer, Yelena (Nana Mouskori). Pyotr burst into tears (he was a poet) and said his sacred duty was to follow the dictates of his heart, even if he died.

The Grand Duchess sighed "if only".

Back in the Prince's office, Natasha was still screaming. She paced towards the door. The zip at the back of her dress was undone. She wasn't wearing a brassiere.

The camera cut to the Prince, furiously justifying his decision to send his mad brother Nikki (Stefan Berkoff) to Siberia.

The camera cut back to a close-up of Gurdin, looking downwards, displaying unfeigned anger and anxiety. The camera pulled back: a man in a brown overalls held a towel in front of the actress's chest and midriff, while a woman in a white coat busied herself around her hips.

There was a brief snowstorm and the picture returned to Brynner, eyebrows an inch upwards from their usual position. He stuttered his lines.

Cinzia collapsed into fits of painful laughter. "It must be fun to be a Grand Duchess."

"No fun at all. It might be fun to be a Grand Duke, or a Tsarevich like my big brother. Men in the Imperial family are allowed to fall in love. They must marry out of duty, but can keep mistresses. It's different for women."

The Grand Duchess got off her bed. "I've been reading this book by an Australian commoner. *The Female Eunuch*."

Cinzia had heard of it.

There was a timid tap. Mrs. Orchard came in, triumphantly bearing Natasha Bolkonskaya's colouful *djellaba*.

"It was rushed over here in a police car."

"Bring it back tomorrow. Tonight I'm going to strike a blow for women."

The Grand Duchess disappeared into her wardrobe and emerged holding a scarlet trouser-suit.

"Time to put my face on, Cindy. As little makeup as possible. Enough to stop me looking like a corpse, but not so much that it seems I've tarted up just to please some man."

Another knock at the door.

"Enter," said the Grand Duchess.

An officer strode in, saluted. It took Cinzia a moment to recognise Chekhov without his hussar get-up. He was in the more usual dress uniform: green tunic, green trousers, peaked cap worn at an angle. He still had more than enough gold braid.

"Her Imperial Highness's escort awaits orders."

"Pavel Andreievich, I'm trying to decide what to wear. A ball gown or this suit. What do you think?"

Chekhov's eyes widened. He smiled like a kid awarded a pound of sweets and a day off school.

"You'd look smashing in a potato sack, Ek."

Smashing? *Ek?*

The Grand Duchess walked up to Chekhov, scarlet suit held to her body. "Make my decision for me, Ensign."

"We were provoked," said the President of the Dynamo Petrograd Claque, talking straight to the camera. In the background, ambulance-crews busied themselves with casualties. Police-car lights flashed. Officers shouted at one another, talked urgently into radios.

The Grand Duchess had dismissed Cinzia. Bondarchuk didn't need her for the evening, so she could get an early night.

After her weekly shower, she sat in her bathrobe, watching Yussopoff smirk through the main evening news. The lead story was that Leonid Brezhnev, the Social Democrat leader, was accused of taking a heavy percentage of the bribes paid to Menshevik local authorities for building contracts.

"We were absolutely provoked," said the President, who was being interviewed. "When their team won, the *Angliskis* sang anti-Russian songs.

We had to protect the honour of the Motherland. Any group of honest patriots would do what we did. Steamed in and give a well-deserved spanking. End of story."

The man had a scar running from below his ear to the side of his mouth. The friendly between Dynamo and Accrington Stanley had ended in a riot.

"I see you're carrying a sabre," said the interviewer. "Is that strictly necessary?"

"A lot of the Claque carry sabres. With this fashion for big baggy trousers it's easy to slip one inside 'em and get into the stadium. You've got to look after yourself. Football, right, well it's a game of two halves, isn't it? First, there's the bit where the players play the match. Then there's the fighting, where the fans prove loyalty to their team and protect its honour."

The telephone rang. The only people who ever called were her bosses, needing her in a crisis. It was Zhivago, Director of the Free Hospital.

"I know how busy you are at the moment, I wouldn't bother you if it wasn't an emergency."

On tele, the news showed the Dynamo Claque were armed with sabres, coshes, razors and, in a couple of cases, revolvers. The English fans were cheerful sporting spirits in scarves and bobble hats, carrying nothing more lethal than wooden rattles.

"I haven't seen this since the War. We've hundreds of *Angliskis* in here. I need every medic I can get."

The news cut to the Free Hospital. A middle-aged man with a toothbrush moustache sat upright in bed, heavily bandaged. He still wore an English flat cap.

"I never thought I'd see the day when footer fans would go at one another with blimmin' swords."

"You're one of the few English-speaking nurses we've got. Some of these men are bleeding to death. I need donors, too."

She hung up and turned to her brother. "Get your coat on, Vladi. You're going to be a blood donor."

"Will it hurt?" asked Vladimir.

"It'll hurt a lot more if you don't come," she said.

Her watch said ten to midnight but it felt later. She had administered countless injections and pills, put a few limbs in plaster and stitched a dozen wounds.

In a side office off the Casualty Ward, Cinzia gratefully accepted a mug of coffee. A nurse passed around a half-pint bottle of vodka. Everyone added a dash to their drink.

All sat on chairs or the floor. Some kicked off their shoes, lit cigarettes. Most of the patients were comfortable now; sent back to their cheap hotels or put to bed here.

"Where's that dishy brother of yours?" asked Lara, one of the younger nurses.

"I only brought him to drain his juice. He's still here?"

"He's been helping, lifting patients. It's wonderful to have a strong pair of arms around."

"You didn't let him near drugs?"

Vladimir wouldn't hang around the hospital without a good reason. Maybe he fancied Lara.

"Ladies!" said Colonel Yevgeny Ivanov, appearing at the door. "My butchers and I will take our leave in a moment."

With the Free Hospital overwhelmed with casualties, Ivanov—Chief of Medical Services, Petrograd Military District—had come from Krasnoe with two helicopters loaded with hundreds of units of conscripted blood and a team of army surgeons. The military sawbones were the sweepings of the medical schools, but they had experience cleaning and closing wounds in Indo-China.

The Colonel was handed a mug of coffee and the vodka. He poured himself a generous shot and raised the mug.

"I toast you, ladies. I would be a proud man indeed if any one of you served at one of my field-hospitals."

Vladimir appeared. Somewhere he had found a white coat and stethoscope. He saw the Colonel and made to leave again. A sheaf of papers fell from under his coat.

Ivanov put down his mug and bent to help Vladimir with the documents.

"I saw you work earlier. You are a medical orderly, yes?"

"I volunteered, just for tonight," said Vladimir, face reddening.

"It is gratifying to see a youth with a sense of social responsibility. This must be important paperwork for Dr. Zhivago?"

"Very urgent. If you will excuse me..."

"Before you go, what is your name?"

"Bronstein. Vladimir Davidovich Bronstein."

"I couldn't help but notice that you have there a batch of Exemption from Military Service Blanks. It's disgraceful but there is a black market in Exemption Certificates. Here in Russia, there are unpatriotic, antisocial elements who steal these papers from hospitals and sell them to cowards who would shirk their duty to their country. Shocking."

Vladimir sighed and shook his head unconvincingly.

"I expect you've done your military service Vladimir. Or are you still a student?"

"I'm sorry to say I was exempted, Colonel. Weak chest."

"Really? A strapping lad like you? I saw you helping this pretty nurse lift men off stretchers earlier on. I'd say the doctor who denied you the chance to perform your sacred duty to the Motherland was a quack. You're a born medical orderly. We need men like you in the 'Chine."

Vladimir looked pleading. She shrugged. He deserved what was coming to him. She hoped, for Mother's sake, he wouldn't be sent to the front line.

Ivanov punched Vladimir playfully in the stomach. "I'm going to help you, Vladimir Davidovich. You must have been devastated to miss the chance to serve your country. I see there's nothing wrong with you. I'm giving you a second opinion. A few months training will sort out your chest problems: assault courses, route marches, cross-country runs, small-arms training, lots of parade-ground drill. Make a man of you. Then we'll fly you first class to Indo-China. Sadly, as a medico you probably won't be assigned to an operational zone. If you would prefer a combat unit, I can arrange it."

"No, no," said Vladimir quickly. "I've always been interested in, um, bandaging people and such."

"Splendid. I'll have the papers sent. Don't worry, we'll have your address on file."

The Colonel retrieved his coffee, drained it in one go and marched out. He turned at the door. "I bid you ravishing ladies fond adieu. It is a privilege to work beside such dedicated professionals. Should any of you wish to volunteer for the Army Medical Service—pay's lousy, but company's great, you'll all find soldier husbands within the week—phone Krasnoe camp and ask for Colonel Yevgeny Ivanov."

He grasped Vladimir's head in both hands and kissed him on either cheek. then left.

"Bozhe moi!" said Vladimir.

The noise of rattling bottles came from the corridor. She looked out. Three men in suits carried crates of large brown bottles. A fourth, the

Earl of Balham, carried cartons of Strand cigarettes. The Duke of Cornwall was with him, too, hands clasped behind his back.

"Cinds!" said Balham. "Delightful to see you here! Small world, isn't it? Chas and I thought we should come over after the bunfest and bring home comforts to the troops."

Despite the hour, the lights in the ward were on. Most patients weren't yet asleep. They sat up in bed, playing cards or discussing the evening's adventures.

"Ho! Ho! Ho!" said Balham, striding into the ward. "Merry Christmas everybody!"

When they recognised their visitors, the men raised a cheer. The Earl and the Duke went up and down the ward handing out Strands and India Pale Ale. "Flown in from Blighty at enormous expense."

Both men stopped to chat with the patients as tops were cracked off the bottles on the edges of bedside tables. Cinzia noticed they were more interested in getting Balham's autograph on their plaster casts and cigarette packets than the Duke's. Cornwall gravitated towards the men who had fought in Indo-China and would chat quietly with each for a while.

Balham disappeared behind a screen and emerged completely naked. He waited a moment for everyone to notice him.

"I say, you fellows, can anyone tell me where I can find a decent tailor round here?"

The men laughed as Balham, still naked, climbed on top of a table and went into a long and utterly meaningless speech. As she realised Balham was pretending to be a politician, the Duke appeared at her side.

"You're a long way from the fairy tale tonight."

"I work here, as a volunteer. I didn't want to let my medical training go completely to waste."

"You prefer this to being a make-up girl?"

"The tele pays better than nursing, and we need every penny we can get. But this is more useful. And rewarding."

"Thank you for helping the lads," said the Duke, pointing to the men, now enjoying beer, tobacco and Balham's clowning.

She shrugged. "It was good of you to come and see them."

"I thought we'd never escape that bloody banquet and all those politicians."

She was home by 1:30. The telephone rang. She rushed to answer it before it woke Mother.

"Hello."

"Cinzia?"

"Yes."

"It's Charles here. Duke of Cornwall, that is."

"Hello."

"I just wanted to…thank you again. For all you did for the lads. Much appreciated."

"It was nothing."

"I'll say goodnight, then."

"Okay, goodnight."

A she set down the receiver, mother came into the living room.

"Who was that at this time of night?"

"Just the Duke of Cornwall. Goodnight Mum."

The elegant drawing room, furnished approximately in the rococo style, was knee-deep in cables and drowning in light. An elderly lady dressed in pink sat on a sofa, a massive pink handbag in her lap, smiling at technicians buzzing around her.

"Two minutes, everyone," said Paradjanov. "That's two minutes, Imperial Highness."

Day eight of the Royal and Imperial engagement, Sunday, was to be a strictly televised affair. All four crews had moved to yet another Imperial palace, the Gatchina, twenty miles south of Petrograd, for a three-hour special about both families.

Several members of the Duke's family who had not been here before had been flown in and would stay until the wedding took place. Cinzia had been presented to the Duke's grandmother, the Dowager Duchess of York, who seemed very charming but struck her as a formidable character. She'd also met Balham's wife, the Duke's aunt, whom she overheard some of the others in the British party refer to as "Lady Bluebottle" or even "Lady Gin-Bottle". King Edward and Princess Consort Wallis had not yet come. They would only arrive for the wedding itself. The Tsar, likewise, was considered above this kind of thing.

"Everyone clear the floor," said Paradjanov.

Prince Yussupov emerged, sporting a black kaftan with violent *eau-de-nil* splotches. He bowed to the pink lady and sat on the sofa next to her.

The Grand Duchess Anastasia Nicolaievna was the Tsar's aunt. Even if she had not been born into of the Imperial family, Anastasia would have been rich. For as long as anyone could remember, she had written romantic novels with historical settings. Cinzia had been briefly addicted when she was thirteen, but quickly tired of them. The amazingly-prolific Grand Duchess was still a regular fixture in the bestseller lists. Well into her seventies, she knew the royal families of Europe intimately (she was related to all of them). Since her stories were regularly televised, she was completely at home among TV people. Paradjanov, director of *Catherine, the Woman* and *Ivan, You're Not So Terrible*, was one of the few she trusted to do justice to her sumptuous tales of love among the aristocracy.

Cinzia and other crew members withdrew to the adjoining ballroom where British and Russian dignitaries were being dressed or made up. They took coffee and watched the monitors, awaiting their cues to go in and chat with the Prince and the Grand Duchess.

"It looks hot under those lights," said Cornwall. He was behind her, so close she could feel his breath on her neck.

"Whatever you do, try not to look uncomfortable. People notice."

He pulled back from her slightly, and smiled. "Do you think I should try and hold Kate's hand?"

"Kate? The Grand Duchess Ekaterina? I don't know. You could ask her."

"I don't know where she is. To be honest, I'm terrified she might slap me in the face for my forwardness if I try to take her hand on tele."

"She won't. The only person in the world she's afraid of is Grand Duchess Anastasia Romanova."

"She frightens the life out of me, too."

Yussupov was on fawning form, explaining to the camera that Anastasia was the last surviving daughter of Nicholas the Good, the Tsar who dedicated his life to the peaceful transformation of Russia from absolutism to democracy. The Grand Duchess replied in French, which she spoke fluently. She also spoke perfect English and German, but never spoke Russian. Vladi said she was "a reactionary old bat" who refused to speak the language of the ordinary people the Romanovs no longer ruled.

"My father was a generous man who worked tirelessly for the good of Russia," said Anastasia. "Some say he was far-sighted in conceding a Duma and a democratic constitution, but my view is that he was blackmailed into it by scoundrels and demagogues when we were weakened during the First Patriotic War. You look at politicians nowadays, all the corruption and spying on one another. They're a shabby lot. I know people say I'm old-fashioned, but I know with all my heart that the old

267

system was better. An autocratic Tsar takes no backhanders. He does not try to curry favour because there's an election around the corner. He does not get surprised in a hotel room with a can-can dancer."

"I say!" said Balham loudly. "What's the bally point in being Tsar then?"

Cinzia looked towards him. Lady Balham elegantly drew a cigarette-holder to her lips. Maybe smoke caused her eyelids to droop so much. Or perhaps it was contempt.

Behind Lady Balham stood her mother, Dowager Duchess of York. And she was looking straight at Cinzia with what seemed intense curiosity. Her head was inclined slightly: a result of some ailment of old age, or maybe force of habit. Tilting your head a little made for better photographs.

Cinzia looked away to see the Duke looking at her.

"What is it? Have I got a piece of cabbage stuck on my teeth?"

"There's nothing wrong with you at all," said the Duke, turning back to the monitor.

With the help of brief clips, Yussupov was ran through the recent history of the Romanov dynasty for the benefit of schoolchildren and foreign viewers: the funeral of Tsarevich Alexis in 1925; the constitutional change that allowed women to succeed to the throne; the marriage of Tatiana, Nicholas' second-eldest daughter, to Prince Louis of Bourbon-Parma; the cannonade announcing the birth of their only child Nicholas, the present Tsar.

There was nothing in the film about the marriage of Grand Duchess Olga, Nicholas' eldest daughter, to Crown Prince Carol of Rumania. Small wonder. Olga had not wanted to leave Russia. When she learned of her husband's womanising, she shot him and retired to a convent.

More film: the death of Prince Louis while attempting the world land speed record at Brooklands in 1931; the death of Tsar Nicholas in 1940; Tsarina Tatiana in nurse's uniform, Tatiana at the wheel of a truck taking food across the frozen Lake Ladoga, Tatiana standing on a tank near the front showing kneeling troops an icon, Tatiana lighting the great bonfire of captured German standards at the victory parade in 1945.

Mother would be watching this with tears in her eyes. The backdrop to the best years of her life was etched in the career of the indomitable empress. Even in old age the tall, willowy Tatiana, with her dark hair and grey eyes, had a cold, enchanting beauty. Born to command, she was the saviour of Petrograd, if not her country, in the Great Patriotic War. While politicians cowered in Moscow bunkers or fled beyond the Urals, a woman with less formal power than the Duma's Doorkeeper stayed through the German siege of Petrograd, vowing to die with the defenders. When Tatiana died in 1970, Cinzia's mother—an Englishwoman—had cried for two days.

Onscreen, Grand Duchess Anastasia reminisced about Tatiana's funeral. A million people had surrounded the Cathedral of Our Lady of Kazan. Cinzia was there, with Mother, surprised to see so many young people with long hair among middle-aged and elderly war veterans. One hair-head held up a sign saying GOD BLESS EMPRESS TATIANA, HEROINE OF A RIGHTEOUS WAR. The point about the current unrighteous one was lost on nobody.

"I'm on in forty minutes," said the Duke. "Could you touch me up?"

She led him to a corner of the vast ballroom that was curtained-off like a hospital bed. It was a makeshift dressing room. She sat him in front of the mirror and tucked a sheet into his collar.

"You're tense," she said. "Still nervous about holding your fiancée's hand on tele?"

The Duke's hand slipped out from under the sheet and patted her on the hip. It was not unprecedented: Georgi Sanders, among others, often took the opportunity of having her bend over him to paint his face to snatch a feel of her bottom. The Duke's touch was more tentative, affectionate rather than lecherous. His hand stayed on her hip. No, she admitted, his touch was shading into lechery.

"Was there something, your highness?" she said, tapping his hand. He took it back as if scalded.

"Charles," he said.

"Charles."

He looked oddly sheepish, like a little boy caught out. On impulse, she kissed his forehead. Looking at his face in the mirror, he was bright red under his powder. His hand emerged again and took hers, gently. His throat worked, as if he were swallowing: his adam's apple was as prominent as his ears.

The curtain twitched aside and a man popped his head in, breaking the moment.

Charles went redder and started sweating. He looked guiltier than Kissinger.

"I'm frightfully sorry," said the person from Porlock. "I was looking for someone. George Smiley. Security wallah. Have you seen him?"

They both shrugged. The intruder showed no sign of departing.

She remembered the man. He had been at Nikita's: Balham had recognised him as Philby, a senior English journalist. He was a very well-connected newspaperman if he could breeze unsupervised about the Gatchina.

"You're British, aren't you?" Charles said. Philby nodded. "Good. You'd be obliged to obey an order from your future king."

"Certainly, highness."

"Well, push off then, there's a loyal subject, would you."

Philby looked at them both. She had an impression of canny intellect. "I'd be delighted, highness."

Philby withdrew and Charles got out of the chair, the sheet falling from his collar. She had to look up to him. The red had faded from his face. He still held her hand.

"Cinzia…"

Oh hell, she thought, letting him kiss her.

The polite, formal, etiquette school kiss escalated gently. He didn't taste more royal than other men, though his tongue was sweeter than the Allen's nicotine-permeated one.

She closed her eyes and felt his pull. He held her hands in the small of her back, pinning her to him. Medals pressed against her blouse.

Somewhere, "Always" was playing.

A tiny soothsayer of panic sparked in her mind. Whatever Isaac might prophesy, make-up girls did not win Princes. At least, not for long.

She broke the kiss and pulled back, letting go his hands.

"Cinzia…"

"No," she said, kindly. "I don't want to hear it. I think you're better than that. And I am too."

She couldn't read his face. Royalty were trained to obscure their feelings. But she had *felt*: appreciated the tentative, trembling touch. She knew enough simple leches to recognise deeper feeling.

This was not fair. This was impossible.

Damn it, she kissed him. He was surprised, but responded. She knew she would stop kissing him soon. When she wanted to.

There was a warning commotion outside the curtained area. She stood away from Charles. The Grand Duchess had arrived.

"You're on," she told him. He sighed and adjusted his uniform.

"You could tell they were in love," Mother told her. She had faithfully watched Yussopoff's interview with Anastasia and the Royal

Couple. "It may have been a political thing at first, but it's a matter of the heart now. I know you're still a cynic, dear, but he was just *glowing*. And she's so *lovely*."

The Grand Duchess Ekaterina had been attended by her hussar, Chekhov. He was the only subject in all the Russias who would think of calling her "Ek".

Cinzia could have told Mother more about Charles's glow, but hadn't sorted it out in her mind yet. She knew from the sick feeling in her stomach that she was stuck; it hadn't been this bad since the first week with Allen. She also knew from alarms ringing in her brain that she'd never been involved with a man who could get her into more trouble. Including Allen.

If this came out and it were down to Anastasia, Cinzia would be lucky to get off with an *oubliette*. For ruining the fairy tale, she would most likely be beheaded with a scimitar.

"They held hands but never looked each other in the eye," Mother said, meaning Charles and Ekaterina. "That means something."

She should resign from ITV, work full-time as a nurse, marry a doctor, bear a half-dozen sons for Russia, get out before it got worse.

"He's changed, the Duke of Cornwall," Mother said. "He looked so gawky when he first came to Russia, so ill-at-ease. Now, he's become handsome. That's love for you."

Cinzia wanted to strangle her mother with her Imperial Wedding Souvenir towel.

She had recognised the voice on the telephone, speaking English with a comical Russian accent, as one of Balham's characters. With conspiratorial glee, he told her to be on the steps of Our Lady of Kazan the next morning at nine, wearing an orchid in her hair. She did not bother with the flower, but had turned up at the cathedral.

Hordes of the devout swarmed around. On the steps was a permanent vigil of Russian mothers who'd lost boys in Indo-China. They handed out snowdrops for peace. Cinzia took one and fiddled with it, waiting. A longhair strummed a balalaika, wailing a song about the War, "Sonia, Don't Take Your Love to Kiev". He wore fingerless gloves and had a transparent scraggle of beard like Che Guevara's.

Vladimir had cleared out of the flat, taking his guitar and records. He would lie low or flee to Finland until Ivanov forgot about rescinding his certificate of exemption. Or the war ended.

A pilgrim tottered towards her, weighed down by a bearskin coat and a huge fur hat. Despite the false moustaches, she recognised Charles.

He kissed her before she could giggle too much.

After a while, she pushed him away to look at his disguise. She professionally adjusted his sticky moustache.

"I hope you used the proper gum or your upper lip will be skinned."

"One had help."

"Let me guess, the Earl…"

"…never travels without his old stage make-up kit."

"Charles," she said, seriously.

"No. Today one is just Old Karol, Humble Sight-Seer. And you are my Tour Guide."

She looked around. There were two obvious Okhrana men huddled by a chestnut stove, eyes on the peace protesters.

"Do you know the penalty for two-timing a daughter of the Tsar?" she asked.

"Castration, one believes. And forfeiture of estates and titles."

"You can laugh. The blood of Catherine the Great flows in that little twit's veins. Our heads could be book-ends."

A mounted guardsman trotted by, plumes bobbing. Longhaired kids chanted at the toy soldier. "*Nothing could be finer than to be in Indo-China killing chi-i-ildren…*"

Charles was surprised.

"That's not fair," he said. "Our lads are brave souls."

"And that guardsman's for show, not for the 'Chine."

"They don't know what they're saying."

The guardsman was gone, but the kids still jeered, sloganising while the balalaika man strummed. They sang "*Nothing could be nicer than to massacre a ricer…*"

Captain Lucan, an English aristocrat, was standing trial at the Old Bailey, having ordered the slaughter of an Indo-Chinese village. Around the ITV news room, Cinzia heard stories of worse atrocities committed by Russians.

Charles was reddening, not with embarrassment. She had to intervene before he laid into the kids.

"Remember your disguise, Old Karol," she said, holding his shoulder, nuzzling his false moustache.

"I'm sorry, Cinzia. But they don't know what it's like."

She slipped an arm around his waist and steered him away from the Cathedral.

"Kings in disguise always hear things they don't want to," she said. "That's the whole point of the exercise."

His arm was light on her shoulder.

"Not this time."

"So this is where you live. It's very..."

"Small?"

Mother was still at work. She had brought the Duke of Cornwall back to the apartment.

Charles stood in their front room, uneasy in a domicile with fewer than a hundred rooms.

"Cosy," he said, at last, deciding.

She laughed.

"Well, all right, small."

"Dingy, too. Cold in winter, hot in summer. Cramped. Hard to fit three difficult people into."

"Which is your room?"

"Usually, I sleep on the couch. But with Vladi underground, I can stretch out on his floor-cushions. It won't last."

They had spent the day walking around Petrograd, pretending to be ordinary. Well, Charles pretended. Cinzia was the genuine article, though she didn't feel ordinary just now. Not every girl walks out with the future husband of a daughter of the Tsar.

In Alix's, her favourite cheap restaurant ("You can get your kixes at Alix's"), a waiter thought he recognised Charles. She said "Karol made a record once, but it didn't sell." Charles flashed the peace sign and solemnly said "man" like a longhair. She laughed for minutes.

Without meaning to, she opened Vladi's door. A herbal scent still clung to everything inside. Charles lead her into the room.

"Who's that?" he indicated Che. "A relative?"

"You don't get out at all, do you?"

He looked sad and silly in his absurd moustache. She sat down cross-legged on the crimson and yellow cushions. Awkwardly, Charles folded his legs and joined her.

Most of the books on the shelves were by French or American communists. French reds had more style, Cinzia understood, which was why kids followed Chairman Godard's Paris line rather than the stolid grimness of First Secretary Goldwater's USSA.

They were holding hands.

How does one set about seducing Royalty? She had imagined from Anastasia's novels that it would be easier. The room should be a lot bigger, more luxuriously appointed, and have a four-poster bed in it. She should be in a ball-gown with three yards of silver train.

Charles was in his embarrassed phase again. Like Balham, he was only confident when pretending to be someone else: Old Karol, or the fairy tale prince engaged to Ekaterina. As himself, he was terminally uncertain.

She wondered if Vladi had left any *bhang* behind.

His eyes were fixed on her chest. A lot of men were like that. But this was just a way of not meeting her eyes.

She tilted his chin upwards and looked at him. He was not that much older than her. She peeled his moustache off in one easy pull and stuck it to her own upper lip, twitching it in an exaggerated manner. She looked like The Little Anarchist, the character her grandfather played in his silent films.

"Kiss me and tell me if it tickles."

Emerging from the lobby of the apartment house as evening fell and lamps flickered unreliably, Cinzia was sure every passerby and loiterer was watching them.

For her, this was a first. Having made love with a Prince, an interesting enough addition to her repertoire of experience, she was certain the whole world knew about it. It was ridiculous to assume that a big furry hat and a fake 'tache could enable Charles to avoid his Okhrana shepherds and whichever agencies, foreign and domestic, who might take an interest in his affairs. In his affair, in this case.

She kissed Charles goodbye as he slipped back for his evening's televised fireworks display. He walked off jauntily, like any other man who has spent an afternoon with his girlfriend.

She looked up and down the street. The man with a dog might have been stirred by Charles's appearance and be following him in the pretence of exercising the animal. And the big German car prowling towards the canal seemed slower than it should be.

Charles turned and blew her a kiss. He looked about twelve. His ears kept his oversize hat from falling over his whole head.

She told herself not to be paranoid. Not everybody was a spy.

Charles hurried off, whistling.

A man in an expensive coat, who had stood shadowed in a doorway opposite, stepped forward and clicked a camera, startling her. She realised she was wearing Charles's false moustache.

She recognised the attache from the Happy Guys Club. Not everyone might be a spy, but Isaac had told her that Harlan was. The American smiled with genuine friendliness and took a picture of Charles turning the corner.

Cinzia looked to the sky, a grey wedge above the black building-tops. Now, she was of interest to Great Powers.

She worried about what Mother would think.

In the upstairs bar of the Happy Guys Club, Isaac Asimov and Georgi Sanders played *faro*. A half-empty litre of vodka sat between them.

Cinzia was unsurprised to see Allen's Wallachian moppet, still not old enough for liquor, at the bar. She'd dumped her novelist for *Rostovs* star Romek Polanski, who was cajoling her into sampling an ice cream topped with three inches of assorted fruit.

"Weren't you going to shoot yourself?" she asked Georgi.

He didn't look up from his cards.

"Thought I'd wait, my dear," he purred. "This damn Imperial Wedding is getting all the air-time. My suicide would be relegated to a humorous item before the weather forecast. I await a slow news season."

"Isaac, things are complicated," she explained. "Can we talk?"

"Of course, child."

"Don't mind me," said Sanders. "I have no one to tell your secrets."

She sat down and poured herself a shot of Stoli. She took it in a swallow. Hot tears pricked her eyes as her throat burned.

"That's supposed to clear the head," Isaac said.

She took another.

"And that's supposed to fog it up again," said Sanders.

She looked around. Polanski cuddled up to the gymnast, who shrank away, playing with a cherry plucked from her sundae.

"Cinzia," Isaac said. "I scry something is the matter?"

She laughed. "What are you, a fortune teller?"

She was leaking hot tears, but not crying.

"You said I'd marry a Prince, Isaac Judaiovich. You were nearly right. I seem to have slept with one."

"Not Yussopoff!"

She felt sick. "No. It's not *that* bad. It's Charles, the Duke of Cornwall. The fiancé of Grand Duchess Ekaterina."

"Big Ears," said Sanders, still pondering his hand.

"They aren't that big," she snapped. "It's the way he wears his hair. He can look quite nice with some work."

"Cinzia Davidovna, you're in love!"

"No. Yes. Maybe. I don't know. You're supposed to see all, you old fraud."

"There are mysteries impenetrable even to my powers."

"Stow it, Isaac. I need help, not mumbo-jumbo. I'm being followed. Your friend the American cultural attaché, Harlan. And someone I'm sure is Okhrana."

Isaac was still shocked. Obviously, he had not foreseen this.

"They can make me disappear, can't they?"

"They made me disappear," Sanders said.

"I don't see it's any of their business, whoever they might be," Isaac said.

"But with the wedding..."

"That's it. Harming you would raise questions. Your little affair would come out. That would spoil the story. Nobody wants that. Not the Tsar, not the Brits, not ITV..."

"Soyuz TV would broadcast your confession," Sanders said. "They've offered me an aristocratic game show, *What's My Lineage?* You could go public, piddle on the parade. Scupper Yussopoff's ratings."

"I don't want trouble. I don't want to spoil the wedding."

"Is that why you're sleeping with the groom?"

"Have slept."

"There's a difference?"

"This thing with the Duke," Isaac said. "It was a one-time occurrence?"

"So far."

"I thought better of you."

"So did I."

"You haven't slept with either of us," Sanders grumbled. "And it's not as if you haven't had the opportunity."

She looked at the pair of them and was tempted to laugh. The gymnast slapped Polanski, who burst into tears as he did every week on *The Rostovs*.

"Are you going to see him again?" Isaac asked

"I have to. I'm doing make-up for the wedding."

"Not like that."

"I don't know."

"Look into your heart and scry the truth, Cinzia."

"Don't be silly, Isaac."

"It's so beautiful, loves," sobbed Paradjanov as he fluttered a length of see-through orange silk over the camera, one eye on the couple on horseback, the other on the monitor. "So poetic."

Cinzia wanted to be sick. At the moment, as fine rain fell on the lawns of Tsarskoye Selo, only Paradjanov, who had earlier told *the Tsar* to stand aside to aid the composition of one of his long shots, saw the beauty.

Charles and Ekaterina were returning from a ride through the grounds, unchaperoned though Ensign Chekhov and a detachment of guards dogged their tracks, hanging back a hundred yards or so. Chekhov looked as if he would like to use his sword on someone. Security men in slick raincoats flitted through the woods like foxes, looking for snipers in the trees.

Cinzia stood under the pagoda-like marquee with a crowd of Royals and hangers-on. The Earl of Balham was subdued in the presence of his wife. The Tsar, who must be wondering whether to have Paradjanov shot or appoint him First Minister, discussed diplodocus knees with Sir Anthony Blunt. Anastasia and the Duchess of York sighed in tandem, cooing over the couple.

Ekaterina was uncomfortable on her horse and kept shifting on her ladies' saddle, held in place mainly by the weight of her dress. Charles, raised as a rider, slouched like a cossack and looked miserable. Cinzia hoped he was miserable thinking about her.

She had not slept much last night. Her head throbbed from Sanders' vodka. Vladi's cushions were faintly scented with the Duke's hair oil.

"*Perfecto,*" sighed Paradjanov. A rainbow shone through drizzle, settling a multicoloured glow around the mounted couple. "Mr. Duke, lean across and kiss the Grand Duchess. Your public demands it."

The couple were startled by the demand. Cinzia thought her heart would stop as Charles bent in the saddle, bringing his lips to Ekaterina's cheek. Spooked, the Grand Duchess's horse jittered away a few yards. Ekaterina lurched badly and slipped to one side, clutching reins.

Paradjanov was pleased with the moment.

"That mount they've dug up for Chas," Balham mused. "He's not a gelding, is he?"

"I don't think so. Why?"

"It might be better if he were, Mags. Look."

Balham pointed to the monitor. Paradjanov's camera zoomed steadily in on the couple. Cinzia saw what the Earl meant. Charles's horse, obviously a stallion, was obviously aroused by Ekaterina's mare.

"The symbolism, the earthy beauties..."

Cinzia thought ITV brass might not share Paradjanov's enthusiasm for equine erections.

Charles's horse reared, waving its hoofs at the flanks of the Grand Duchess's mount. What seemed like a foot of throbbing horse penis bobbed in front of a hundred million tele viewers worldwide.

Balham was laughing. He turned to his wife.

"Reminds me of our wedding snaps. Remember the one with the custard and the handcuffs."

The Tsar's impassive, bearded face flickered with rigidly suppressed humour. He issued an order and Chekhov dashed into the field to rescue the Grand Duchess.

"Can't have dear old Ek coming between true lovers," Balham said, winking at Cinzia. "It'd spoil everything."

Now, Cinzia *was* going to be sick. Charles must have told the Earl.

Chekhov gallantly scooped the Grand Duchess from her saddle and, staggering under the weight of the girl's dress, got her out of the way. Charles dismounted gracefully, showing off the curve of his rear in riding trousers, and let his horse off the rein.

The Royal horses nuzzled and manoeuvred into position. The stallion pressed the mare down, and his pole-like organ slipped neatly in.

Cinzia had to sit down. She was not sure if the pain in her stomach and heart came from trying not to laugh or trying not to cry.

"Stop filming, you Georgian exquisite!" the Tsar roared at Paradjanov. "There must be dignity in all things."

"No dignity in that," Balham said, smiling at the noisily copulating animals. "And no shame either."

Ensign Chekhov put the Grand Duchess down on the lawn and began to fan her with his hat. She had fainted.

Cinzia had to escape.

"Where are you off to, Cinds," Balham shouted as she ran for the gate house.

"Cinzia...Cindy..."

She looked up, and he was there, as cute in his riding outfit as an auricular freak could be.

She was sitting against a stegosaurus leg, racked with fear. She was afraid of going on and afraid of going back.

He took her hands and hauled her upright.

"Cinzia."

He kissed her, expertly now. There was no false moustache between them.

"This is dangerous, Charles."

She pulled him behind the model dinosaur, checking that no one could see them, and responded to his kiss. It was not wise, but it was impossible to resist.

"They'll notice you've gone. Search parties will be sent out. Worse, Sergo will happen along with his orange silk and live outside broadcast camera. You'll be seen betraying the Tsar's daughter in millions of homes."

"I don't care."

He pressed her against the stegosaurus. She was reminded of his horse.

"Of course you *care*, Charles. You told me how much you care."

He hesitated and gulped.

"I love you, Cinzia Davidovna."

It was like a rabbit punch.

"And I love you, Charles Edinburgovich," she wanted to say back, wondering instantly if it were true. She kept it to herself.

She wanted this, but she knew better. She struggled, pushing his chest, fending him off.

"It's just because I'm the first real woman you've met, Charles. You've been spoiled by princesses. I'm not a saint, believe me."

"That's not true. I was in the Navy. When my mother was expected to inherit the throne. I've met real women."

"Girl in every port?"

"Every *British* port."

He kissed her again, his hands in her hair, his right leg pressed between hers. She felt the knobbled iron dinosaur hide against her back and did not care.

His mouth was on her throat, in her hair, tasting her, smelling her. She looked, cross-eyed, up at the canopy of branches. Perched in an old oak was a statue pterodactyl, with glass eyes like those of the Grand Duchess Anastasia.

These woods were the heart of Europe, stretching trackless across the continent. They might be alone with the extinct animals. Safe from all harm.

Her hands were under his riding jacket, loosening it from his shoulders. The buttons of her blouse were undone.

He might be a huntsman, and she a hermit's daughter. Away from the world and uncaring.

His warm mouth was on her skin above her heart.

She thought of Marie Antoinette, pretending to be a shepherdess. Of the young Nicholas walking in his Jurassic playground. Of Anastasia, lying about the past to keep people from asking about the future.

With great difficulty, fighting herself as much as him, she broke the embrace, and fastened herself up.

"I won't be a Royal mistress, Charles. better than that."

"I don't want a mistress. I want a wife."

"You'll have one soon."

He shook his head. "Marry me, Cinzia."

"You can't ask that. You're not free."

"I'll be a king. I can do what I want."

She was crying now.

"No you *can't*. No king is more powerful than the Tsar, and he had to marry whom he must."

"Then I won't be king."

She shook her head and mopped her eyes with her hankie. The world was spinning.

"*Cave canem*, Chas," shouted Balham. Cinzia realised Charles must have left the Earl as a look-out. "Tsar Nick's in a bate, and you'll be missed."

Balham loped out of the wood, a camera slung around his neck, light-meter at his hip.

"Say cheese," he smiled, snapping off a shot. "Magic memories, children."

Now, Cinzia was afraid again.

Charles stood away from her and walked towards the Earl, shoulders slumped, back bent. She knew he felt as good as she did.

And she felt horrible.

Even Balham was serious for a moment. She wondered what *his* Royal Marriage was really like.

"You stay here for a bit, love," the Earl said. "We'll see you at the picnic later."

Cinzia nodded and watched Balham and Charles walk away, through the trees towards the palace.

The ITV crew were billeted in the gatehouse, which was itself the size of several of the smaller palaces she had seen recently. Cinzia had been given what must have been a maid's room. High up in the roof somewhere, it had a gable window the size of an icon. The child-sized bed was piled thick with eiderdowns and pillows. Lying on it, looking up at the ceiling, Cinzia felt she was sinking. The pillows would close over her, and she would be forgotten.

During the picnic—a thousand guests gussied up for the tele and endless toasts to the happy couple—she had resisted the temptation to get drunk again, and concentrated on doing her job. She went into remote control to work on Charles and Ekaterina, resisting the temptation to write "SHAM" in lipstick letters on their foreheads. Charles made one attempt to talk to her but she silenced him with a look. The Grand Duchess wanted to chat about something trivial, but Cinzia could not concentrate on it.

Now, she wanted to sleep.

It had not been this bad before, even when she found out about Allen and the gymnast. Nothing had ever been this bad for anyone ever.

At the very edge of the picnic, staying away from the lights and the cameras, she had noticed a veiled lady, very chic, very mysterious. It was Princess Flavia, Nicholas's one-time wife and long-time mistress. She stayed away from the Tsar, who was surrounded by his children, and drifted like a ghost.

Cinzia could imagine.

Also, she was getting good at spotting the spies. Besides the men in raincoats, she knew which waiters, guests, tele crew were secret agents. It was impossible, however, to tell for whom they were spying. It might be, from what she understood of the trade of deception, that they themselves were not fully aware of who their masters were.

A tinkle resounded. There was a stand-up telephone on the night-table. This could not be good news.

She picked up and heard his voice.

"I wish I were with you, darling. In bed."

She knew what he meant. Yesterday had been the first good sex for her in nearly a year. She could do with some more.

"I wish I were your sanitary towel."

"*What?*" she exclaimed. "That's *ridiculous!* You wish you were my *what?* I hope this line isn't being tapped, Mr. Windsor."

"Cinzia .."

"Good night and God bless."

She hung up and took the phone off the hook. Thinking about it, she put the receiver back and waited. It did not tinkle again.

She waited…

She was woken up by a knock at the door. She had fallen asleep in her clothes and not dreamed.

She could reach and open the door without getting out of bed. She huddled back against pillows as her visitor entered.

It was not who she had expected.

Sir Anthony Blunt looked down on her as if she were a forged painting. Or, worse, a real one by someone of whose work he disapproved.

"Miss Bronstein, I'll come to the point…"

"You do that," she said, prepared to be outraged.

Blunt took a manila envelope out of his jacket. It was bulked out fatly.

"One million roubles. You can count it if you like."

She felt expensive and yet cheap.

"Who do you represent?"

"Interests, Miss Bronstein. We have a great deal tied up in the Imperial Wedding, and we are not going to lose it through your wayward *amours.*"

He dropped the envelope on the bed. It bounced.

"It's yours if you leave the country, and don't come back for six months. At least."

She touched the envelope as if it were a big squashed slug.

"There are other ways of dealing with you."

There was a chill in the room. She looked closely at the long face and cold eyes and was frightened. All courts had people like this: hatchet men.

"Think of it as a patriotic duty. Your influence is making the Duke of Cornwall unhappy with things that must be."

She shoved the envelope away, angrier now than she was scared.

"You've a low opinion of me, Sir Anthony."

He stepped into the room, bumping his head on the low lintel. He seemed a giant, bowed under the ceiling. His big hands reached out, long fingers closing around his money.

"You won't be missed. In a month, he won't remember your face. No one will."

"I'd advise you to be careful with your words, Anth," said a male voice, in English. Someone else stood in the door. "You never know if a room is bugged these days. Especially in the Russias."

The newcomer was Harold Philby, looking cheerfully unkempt as if he had been at the picnic all night. He had turned up before, like Blunt. They seemed to know each other. Sir Anthony froze with detestation as Philby slipped into the room.

They were all seriously cramped now.

"Hello, Miss," Philby said, kindly. "You shouldn't mind what grumpy old Anth says. He's all wind. Wouldn't hurt a fly. *Couldn't*, in fact. Not when some of us know his home truths."

Blunt might have been swallowing hemlock *frappé*.

"Don't he look British?" Philby said, nodding at Sir Anthony. He sat on the corner of the bed and patted her knee with an avuncular, conspiratorial look. "With his title and all, and so close to the dear old Royal Family. So valued, so trusted."

Blunt hissed like an angry cobra.

"He's not so trustworthy, though. Used to be a spy for the Americans. Caught Communism at Cambridge, read his Marx and Debs between sodomy and champagne. Ferreted out secrets and posted them off to Uncle Al Capone. During the War, he was careless and got found out. Wasn't sent down because strings were pulled on his behalf. Besides the jolly Yankee Red Americans were Allies back then. Shoulder to shoulder against the beastly Nazis and all."

"This is all very educational," Blunt said. "But..."

"How'd it be, I wonder, if I were to write it up in the *Times*. The Duchess of York's closest adviser in the pay of the Americans since the 1930s. Somebody's nice comfortable life would go down the drain. You'd make lots of close friends in prison, though."

Blunt glared fire.

"No, not a very happy thought is it, Anth. Now, beetle off back to the Duchess and the Tsar and tell them this young woman has no intention of disrupting anything."

Blunt got up and barged out, rigid with rage. Philby shrugged and smiled as the door slammed.

"Why are you doing this?" Cinzia asked.

"Think of me as a Fairy Godmother," Philby said. "No, that has *associations*. A good Samaritan, then. Fear not, all will be for the best in the best of all possible worlds. Voltaire, you know."

"*Candide*. And it's meant ironically."

"Good girl. Better than Charlie deserves."

She thought he might try to kiss her but he didn't. Philby patted her knee again, got up, and slipped out of the door.

Now she was just confused.

"The Metropolitan is waiting in the chapel," the Tsar bellowed at the closed door of Grand Duchess Ekaterina's suite. "Paradjanov says he will lose the light through the stained glass windows. *Katiusha*, you must come down."

Cinzia, summoned by imperial messenger, joined the queue in the corridor. The Tsar was at its head, like a desperate man waiting for his turn in the lavatory. Behind him, in full fancy dress, was Ensign Chekhov.

Paradjanov was at a window, sternly looking at the sun, mentally forbidding it to rise further. Today, the director wore a medieval padded hunting jacket studded with tiny crystal balls, and tight-like leggings cross-gartered, with scarlet rope sandals and an embroidered codpiece.

"You, *girl*," said the Tsar, pointing at her...

...this was it, an imperial decree of banishment or death. Perhaps with torture.

"...you are the only one she will see."

Thank the Saints, it was only Ekaterina being unreasonable. She was still not found out.

"Your friend is here, *Katiusha*," said the Tsar, signalling furiously that Cinzia should approach.

The would-be autocrat of all the Russias was sweating heavily and seemed to have lost bulk. If he could not rule one daughter, his chances of ruling most of two continents were looking weaker.

There was a whining mumble from behind the door.

"We could charge when she opens up, imperial highness," said Chekhov, thinking like a cavalry officer. "Strike fast and establish a beachhead."

"We are trying to coax this minx to a church service, you idiot. Not mounting an offensive patrol on the Mekong Delta."

Chekhov was put in his place.

The door opened a crack and Cinzia slipped in. Ekaterina, in a short nightie with Misha the Bear on it, slammed and locked the door behind them. Her rooms were dark and she had obviously been crying.

The Grand Duchess hugged her and sobbed into her shoulder.

"There, there…um, Ekaterina."

"Call me Ek."

"There, there, Ek."

That set her sobbing again.

"*He* calls me Ek."

Kindly, she sat her down and began wiping her face with a tissue.

There was a serious conflict of interests here, but first she must calm this poor girl. Maybe the Grand Duchess would be less likely to ask for her head later.

"This is the worst thing that has ever happened to anyone, Cinzia. I shall have to enter a convent."

"Come on, Ek."

"No, I have been true to my heart and betrayed my country. I'm torn in two."

"There's a lot of that about."

"I can't understand it. Andropov must have known, but he had Pavel Andreievich transferred from the space program."

Cinzia's head hurt.

"Andropov? Of the Okhrana?"

Ekaterina nodded miserably.

"What's he to do with Ensign Chekhov?"

"Yuri Andropov is in charge of all personnel attached to the Royal household for the period of the Imperial Engagement. It's some silly security measure. When I first felt, ah, *stirrings*, I tried to have Pavel Andreievich sent away. I *tried*, Cinzia. I tried to do my duty."

The kopeck was beginning to drop.

"You and Pavel, you are…"

"We are lovers, Cinzia. I could not help myself. And neither could he."

Cinzia could have been listening to herself.

"I'm so *miserable*. I don't want to be a Grand Duchess and end up a pink elephant like Great Auntie Anastasia. I want to go to Star City and watch Pavel Andreievich take off in his rocketship for the final frontier. I want to go to the moon with him. I want to make love in zero gravity."

Cinzia could imagine the possibilities.

"But I have to marry this cold fish from England and live in a freezing palace in Scotland. What is to be done?"

Cinzia had often heard of people wringing their hands, but had never actually seen anybody do it. Ekaterina buried her face in slightly chubby fingers and keened like a gutted seal. It was not pretty.

Suddenly calm, Cinzia got up and unlocked the door. The Tsar's face hung outside, a mask of wretchedness. Cinzia detected a goaty smugness in Chekhov. The Grand Duchess and the cosmonaut would make an interesting couple, zero gee or not.

"Imperial Highness," Cinzia said, "there's a problem with the wedding."

At the end of the corridor, standing beside Paradjanov, was the veiled lady, Princess Flavia. Cinzia wondered if this woman would end up ruling the country.

"I think you'd better come in and listen to your daughter."

In the corridor, everyone listened. Ekaterina's tiny voice was indistinct, but the Tsar's bellow would have been clear through ten inches of lead shielding.

"What do you mean, you love someone else? Who is this foul adder of a betrayer?"

Chekhov was pale with fear.

Cinzia was quite enjoying this. It made a change for other people to have a miserable, complicated love life.

Paradjanov had given up on the chapel and summoned a crew to snatch shots of expectant courtiers. He was especially keen on images of Flavia drifting mysteriously like a ghost past huge paintings.

To complete the cast, the crowd was swelled by Grand Duchess Anastasia and the Dowager Duchess of York, Sir Anthony Blunt (who looked at Cinzia with loathing), the Earl of Balham and Lady Balham, Harold Philby and Yuri Andropov (spies!), some British dignitaries gone astray from the chapel, a couple of Okhrana footmen, and, at last, Charles.

"A *cosmonaut*!" yelled the Tsar.

Chekhov fell to his knees and began praying.

Charles looked at Cinzia, and she shrugged. It was possible the Imperial Engagement would fall apart without *her* taking the blame. She felt sorry for Chekhov.

"I hear an unmanned probe is leaving for Jupiter next month," Balham said to the Ensign. "Maybe you should volunteer to be on it."

There was a quiet moment.

The door opened and Tsar Nicholas issued orders. "Everybody, in here. And somebody bring me a revolver."

The Tsar looked around at the faces. Paradjanov's cameraman had hefted his instrument on his shoulder. Andropov ordered him to turn it off and, at a nod from the director, the functionary fiddled with some switches and pointed the lens askance at the room. The little red light was still on, suggesting that for an ITV man a director outranked the Okhrana.

"I want you all to bear witness to the shame of my wretch of a daughter," thundered Nicholas. "Tell them, *Katiusha*."

"I can't go through with the marriage," Ekaterina said, directing herself to Charles. "I'm in love. With someone else."

The Grand Duchess looked at Chekhov.

"With him, in fact. Pavel Andreievich Chekhov."

Anastasia fainted dead away in the arms of Sir Anthony Blunt. The Duchess of York looked intensely jealous.

"Oh dear," said the English Shadow Foreign Secretary.

Nicholas waved his revolver for emphasis. Chekhov flinched as the barrel pointed in his direction.

"Bad show, what?" Charles said. "Fearful disappointment. One will try and get over it."

He was trying not to laugh, the rat.

Balham snapped a photograph.

"One for the album there, Chas. I call it Disappointed Bridegroom."

Cinzia tried to suppress hysterical giggles and hoped the Tsar didn't notice.

With quiet determination that made her seem a little like Tsarina Tatiana, Ekaterina said, "I am prepared to give up my title to marry the man I love."

She held out her hand and took Chekhov by the glove, pulling him to her. Balham took a photograph. Paradjanov, weeping openly, nudged the cameraman to frame the shot perfectly.

Ekaterina stood up, regal in her nightie, beautiful through teary smudges, and kissed Ensign Chekhov. Anastasia, revived, fainted again.

Extraordinarily, Philby stepped in front of Paradjanov's camera and began talking in Russian.

"For those of you joining us late and expecting to see Prince Yussopoff hosting the Metropolitan's Engagement Mass from Tsarskoye Selo, we have a change of program. In a dramatic reversal, it has been announced that questions are being asked about the impending wedding of Charles, Duke of Cornwall, and the Grand Duchess Ekaterina…"

Cinzia realised this was going out live. She had never been on television before. She suppressed an urge to wave to Mother. She would have stayed home to watch the mass and must now be as stunned as Anastasia.

The Tsar pointed his revolver at Philby's head—did he even know who the Englishman was?—but Flavia laid a hand on his arm and made him drop his aim.

"I, too, have an announcement," Charles said, in English. Philby translated for the viewers.

Paradjanov waved at a minion—*Andropov!*—to open the curtains. Glorious light flooded the room as Charles tugged Cinzia to him.

"Since my engagement to the Grand Duchess is at an end, I wish to ask Cinzia Davidovna Bronstein to be my bride."

There was cheering. Out of camera range, Flavia gave the Tsar a squeeze.

"Cinzia, will you marry one?"

The camera swerved her way.

"Marry one what?"

"Um, Duke of Cornwall."

"No," she said.

Mouths fell open. Paradjanov was chewing his hat.

"I'll marry Charles Windsor," she said. "The man, not the title."

In the Happy Guys Club, Charles was recognised but not given special treatment. After all, the waiters and cigarette girls all wanted to work in tele and he could do a lot less for them than the producers and directors who swanned through.

For the first time, the big television set in the upstairs room was tuned not to ITV but to Soyuz. Since Georgi Sanders and Isaac Asimov began to broadcast opposite ITV's *Nine O'Clock News* with an irreverent current affairs program called *Not a Pack of Lies*, ITV's ratings monolith had been dented. With the departure of Talia Gurdin and the defection of Yul Brynner to the movies, *The Rostovs* was pulling in fewer viewers than Soyuz' rival "realistic" beet opera, *The Lower Depths*.

Cinzia sat with Charles and Balham, watching Sanders interview Harold Philby. The Englishman explained that he had been obliged to take advantage of the situation at Tsarskoye Selo and provide a commentary on the extraordinary events that had been broadcast.

"I still don't understand what that man was up to," Cinzia said. "He seemed in with Andropov."

"I've been giving it a bit of an old think with the mighty brain-box, Cind. Putting it all together, I think I've come up with the real story."

"Everybody likes a love story, Georgi," said Philby. "I'm just a softie."

"Chas, your starter for ten," Balham began. "Who is Andropov working for? The Tsar or the politicians?"

"Pass," said Charles.

"My theory is that our Gospodin Andropov is in fact Comrade Andropov. Working for the Americans. He's a communist."

"What?" said Cinzia, "the head of the Okhrana a communist?"

"Why not? The British secret service is riddled with reds. Last year, it came out that Sir Alexander Waverly, head of MI6, was a commie. Philby used to work for Waverly."

On tele, Isaac admitted that Philby's future was shrouded in mystery. "Like my past," the Englishman commented.

"I'll bet he's a commie too. Anyway, assume Philby is a red. Doesn't it strike you queer that he and Andropov are hob-nobbing with one another?"

"What about Blunt?" Cinzia asked. "Philby told me he was the communist."

"Tones got caught. Dead embarrassing. And, unlike Philby, he's got lots to lose. If he's found dabbling in political intrigue again, he'll spend the rest of his life in the Scrubs. Blunt enjoys the life he has too much. If he had to live under communism there'd be no more champagne and fine art for him. Just Bourbon and Norman Rockwell prints. He's no more a commie now than I am. He's just the loyal servant and tool of the Dowager Duchess of York, God bless her and all who sail in her. Dear old mum-in-law."

"So they are reds," said Charles, "What were they up to?"

"Trying to put the kibosh on your nuptials, dear boy. All the time you and Ek were on tele, you were doing a propaganda job for Royals everywhere. Meanwhile, Tsar Nick was drip-dripping all this dirt on the politicians. Why do you think he owns a television station and twelve newspapers? He was, and perhaps still is, preparing a *coup d'etat*. Everyone knows that. The big wedding, with its orgy of pomp and grandeur, was to be the first step in the restoration of an absolute monarchy."

It was news to Cinzia.

"Nick was going to seize power, like Tsars of old. His nice, clean, new government could rule by decree. He'd get out of Indo-China at once, which would make him hugely popular. He'd also send every corrupt politician and bureaucrat to Siberia and crack down on any discontent. Russia would effectively become a dictatorship. It'd be unpleasant but, for the next few years at least, very efficient. Nick is not an idiot. He'd be a very effective ruler. The gnomes in Debs D.C. would far prefer it if their rival superpower was run by incompetent crooks."

"And they achieve this by stopping my marriage to the Grand Duchess?"

"Not completely, but it goes a long way towards it. Now the wedding is off, the masses realise you and Ek were never in love. They see what a sham the whole thing was. People who were loyal monarchists realise they've been sold a lie by the Tsar's own tele station. They won't like that. They'll start looking to the politicians for their salvation again. Stupid bastards."

"But this is ridiculous. The plot didn't stop the wedding. Charles and Ekaterina stopped it. They realised they didn't love one another and it would have been hypocritical and damaging to go through with it."

"Pish and fiddlesticks, Cinds. Most royal weddings are between people who don't love one another. Am I right, Chas, or am I right?"

"Most," Charles admitted.

"Remember, Blunt tried to keep you out of the picture. Philby's job was to mark him and jolly you two together. At the same time, Andropov saw to it that the handsome young hussar officer Ek had a crush on was returned to Petrograd to be right at her side just as she was about to marry someone else. They didn't stoop to assassination to stop the wedding, just provided the happy couple with happier alternatives. My guess is that the plotters concentrated on Pavel the Patsy and you were just an unexpected opportunity they took advantage of."

Charles raised his champagne flute and toasted "God bless the USSA."

She looked around, wondering if anyone heard. Harlan, the American attaché, was distracted from chatting up an Olympic skater and grinned at them.

"I feel like a puppet in a show," she said, almost annoyed.

"I've felt like that for most of my life," said Charles. "But not now."

"Won't Ekaterina's marriage to the handsome ensign prove just as popular with the masses? When they polled people on tele, everyone wanted to see her happy."

Balham smiled slyly. "But, Cinzia, you must have seen how tiny Chekhov looks on tele, surrounded by all the scrambled egg."

Shiploads of Imperial Engagement souvenirs had been recalled and reissued with Chekhov's face stuck over Charles's. The ensign would transfer back to the space program after the wedding and had requested a moon mission.

"And have you noticed how Ek cosies up to that young Austrian they brought in as a bodyguard?"

"*Leutnant* Schwarzenegger?"

"The very same. If I were that Asimov chappie, I'd foresee storm clouds over that marriage."

"Isaac has been right about some things," she said.

Charles held her hand. They would return to Britain for a decent period and then have a quiet wedding in Westminster Abbey, which Cinzia understood was quite small. She had to convert to the Church of England, which would probably set Grandfather a-spin in his grave.

Mother would be moving back with them, and Vladi—who wanted Brynner to play him in the Paradjanov miniseries Anastasia was writing about *l'affaire Cinzia*—said he would consider moving to Britain if the obligation to perform National Service were waived.

Another bottle arrived, complements of Harlan. Cinzia doubted Charles had ever bought champagne in his life.

"Oh good," said Balham to the pretty waitress. "Can we have the fish eggs with that, there's an antelope. And don't tell me fish eggs are off, love."

Harlan grinned. In the dark corner with the Ice Queen and the attaché.

"Cheers, you scheming commie bastards," Balham toasted.

"So who won?" she asked.

"We did," said Charles.

They toasted each other and drank. The Earl washed down a lump of caviar with champagne.

"Cindy," he gulped, "has the future King of England taught you the English National Anthem?"

"I already know it, my Mother taught me. She's English, remember. *God save our gracious King, long live our noble...*"

"No, not that one," interrupted Balham, cackling. "The real one."

Charles and the Earl looked at each other, wickedness sparking in their eyes, and began to shrill at the tops of their voices, startling everyone in the room.

"*Ying tong ying tong ying tong ying tong ying tong iddle-eye-po...*"

Eventually, she joined in.

ON THE ROAD

1998

Oak Park, Illinois

"Remember alternative comedy? Boffo in Europe in the early-to-mid-'80s?"

Lowe nodded, cornered by Hunt Thompson. He had actually been at the Windmill Theatre the night Mary Millington shot Rik Mayall in the throat, the fabled Gig That Stopped the Laughter.

"The Okhrana were behind the scenes," continued Thompson. "The fiendish Russkies figured it'd be cool to have obnoxious types get up and be unbelievably rude about your system of government. The idea was that the comics were so personally horrible your docile population would equate them with their message and react against anyone who dared complain about anything. So they came up with psychiatric profiles of the sort of person who'd piss off the most people. You know, clever college-boys without girlfriends."

Chugging Vimto, he did his best to look attentive while Thompson declaimed. This was his marquee and the party-thrower was in a fever of expansive, post-Communist reminiscence. The condition was widespread and, Lowe feared, incurable.

"The intelligence boys recruited misfits, trained them in irritating vocal mannerisms, designed off-putting stage outfits. Even their haircuts were calculated to offend. The spooks paid *mucho dinero* to get the movement off the ground, then let the gullible stand-ups do the rest."

Lowe had heard the rumour before. He didn't really credit it. For a while, with that explosion of irreverence, it had seemed things in stifling

293

grey Britain were genuinely about to get out of hand. And a good job too. The Dangerous Brothers called Bill Grundy a pillock on live television, a defining moment. But the next year, Tarby and Brucie were back on the Home Service and the shiny-suited, arrogant iconoclasts were out of work or dead. Now, the survivors were doing advertisements for banks.

"Kinda clever, we thought," drawled Thompson. "You know, prove to the world how tolerant the democracies were. For a while it was my job to go around rounding up illegal tapes of Alexei Sayle and Ben Elton."

Sayle would have been an especial problem in the USSA. The showpiece of his act was a combined impersonation of George "Mr. Woo" Formby and President Al "Scarface" Capone. At the height of his career, the self-styled "fat bastard" was probably a sincerer Marxist than anyone in the American government.

"I was seconded to the Ministry of the Interior," continued Thompson. "We didn't understand alternative comedy at all. We even thought for a while that it might be the precursor of some sort of socialist youth movement in Europe. That's why we were so keen to stop it coming into America. Last thing we wanted was for American kids to catch socialism."

Lowe laughed dutifully.

Nine years ago, when Lowe first met him, Hunt Thompson was a minor official. Lowe had been in Chicago to interview Charles H. Holley, one of the troubadours of the New Deal, for *The Sun*. The CP lived on for a few years after Vonnegut was swept to power, and Thompson was the singer's Party minder.

Then, America was different. Full of hope, bursting with strange energy, letting out the stench of two generations of corrupt dictatorship. Now? Disillusioned, wary, uncontrolled. Fragmenting into half a dozen near civil wars and squabbling states, petty crime and medium-sized rackets on every street. And overrun, poor bastards, by European God-botherers and double glazing salesmen like Sir Robert Maxwell.

Lowe wanted to ask Thompson if he'd heard from Holley.

"The bad days are behind us now. My people and I have very high hopes of your Sir Robert and this tour. This is a big country, Mr. Lowe, a very big country, with big opportunities."

That much was true, as long as you understood the way the system worked. Where most European hucksters failed was in simply not understanding that nothing would happen if you didn't pay off the right people, from the local mobsters all the way down to the janitors.

Thompson, the prissy little official of nine years ago had reinvented himself as a capitalist. He had obviously blagged his old Party connections into new business connections and made a fair old wedge in something or other, buying himself a big house on the proceeds. He probably sold army surplus to the secessionists and militias springing up all over the country.

Thompson was organising the Yank end of Sir Bob's "Freedom and Enterprise Roadshow", a circus that would spend eight weeks travelling from Chicago to Los Angeles, bringing Americans the gospels of capitalism and Christianity—and selling them all sorts of rubbish along the way.

Christ! Two months of dealing with idiots like Thompson, all the while hacking out adulatory nonsense about Sir Bob for the *Mirror*.

"What have you been doing with yourself since we last met?"

"I left the *Sun* a few months after I got home" shrugged Lowe. "The new owner wanted to take it "down market". Bathing beauties and bingo. There was talk of going tabloid. I moved into the wireless for a while, but came back here three years ago, as North America correspondent for the *Daily Mirror*."

"Yes sir, it must be satisfying being a newspaperman. Travel, meeting people, being at the centre of world events…"

Lowe's glass was empty. He needed to get away.

"Fact is I had to take the *Mirror* job. All an old Fleet Street hand could get at the age of 51. Auntie BeeBee fired me."

Hunt's jaw dropped a little.

"Live on *The World at One*, I referred to the Home Secretary, the Right Honourable Francis Urquhart MP, as 'a murdering cunt'. So you see, communism or capitalism, it's all the same. Always a struggle to get the truth out."

He walked off to the bar, leaving Thompson wide-eyed.

The bar served only British soft drinks. Lowe took a Vimto refill from a young man with a yard-wide smile and a celluloid bow tie. The barman —HI PARDNER! MY NAME IS TOM on his lapel badge—insisted on demonstrating his juggling, decanting the drink from a bottle in mid-air, snatching the full glass from free-fall to hand it over.

Lowe quite liked Vimto, but couldn't quite understand how an unexceptional fruit-flavoured cordial had come to symbolise, for New Americans, the best in democratic style and youthful chic.

The Freedom and Enterprise Roadshow was kicking off right here, right now in a marquee in Hunt's spacious garden. Along with the various British stars and "businessmen" of the roadshow, *Le Tout* Chicago was here. Hard-faced, crop-haired men in dark suits moved like sharks through the crowds, accompanied by big minders in expensive British-made shell suits with gun-bulges under their armpits. The womenfolk were all under 30, with long legs, short dresses, big hair and too much panstick.

"Lowe!" boomed His Master's Voice.

Sir Robert Maxwell barrelled towards Lowe, displacing the air like a whale shifting water, planet-shaped body exerting a repellent force like gravity in reverse. The proprietor of the *Daily Mirror* was a moving mountain in a purple tux, half a dozen chins pinning his dickie bow to his sternum, fists swinging like hams. Rivulets of pungent sweat flowed from his coal-black hairline down through the deep folds in his face.

"I've decided you're opening bat."

Part of the Roadshow's remit was to introduce Americans to the joys of cricket. Maxwell was captain of the team, and a firm of sports equipment manufacturers had donated a vanload of gear, mostly seconds.

"Me?" said Lowe. "I'm hopeless. They made us play cricket at school. I don't think I scored more than three runs in all that time. And dropped every catch I ever got near."

"Well, practice, you pillock! And make sure you give the team a decent write-up in the next few days."

When Maxwell, whose real name was something Czech and unpronounceable, took over the Mirror he had promised he would not interfere in the running of the paper.

Maxwell sighted Mr. Gekko, a hungry-looking American entrepreneur, and bore down on him like a sweaty avalanche in evening dress. Lowe, as always, was relieved by the passing of his boss.

Someone asked HI PARDNER! MY NAME IS TOM for a glass of Tizer. The newcomer was British, with a firm, clear voice that radiated friendliness and decency. It could only be a vicar, Lowe bet himself, and turned to look.

He won. He caught the eye of a thin man in his late 30s. He had an unlikely mop of unruly hair and a dog collar.

"Hello," said the vicar. "What do you think of it so far?"

"Rubbish," said Lowe. "And you?"

"Needs must when the Devil drives." He held out his hand. "John Beverley, roving Anglican evangelist, at your service."

Lowe saw something in the Reverend's eye, at odds with his mild manner and clerical suit. A tic, maybe, but also a tick-tick-tick. The vicar would bear watching.

"I'm Lowe of the *Mirror*."

A vast shadow fell over them: Sir Robert returning like a happy dirigible, arm heavy on the shoulders of Mr. Gekko, breathing business opportunities into the American's face, insisting he meet the minions.

Lowe decided to venture forth and mingle.

Part of the Roadshow was sponsored by Strand cigarettes. Lowe helped himself to a handful from a tray carried by a girl dressed as a can-can dancer. Her pretty face was a frozen mask of utter misery, but her legs, in fishnet stockings, were worth a second glance. He was distracted from the legs by a tall, elegant blonde in a pink twin-set. She was nodding intently, the losing half of a one-sided conversation. She was tapping her cheek with her two middle fingers, the universal secret sign of boredom distress, requesting rescue from anyone who picked up the signal.

The blonde's borer was Blair, a young-looking man with fifty-two teeth. The Cheshire piranha was coiner of the slogan "New Britain, New Hope" and currently working triple-time to get attention for the Roadshow. He paused in mid-tirade to draw breath, and his victim cut him off, making a "there's someone I really must say hello to" gesture. She advanced towards Lowe, arms outstretched, pink lips puckered for a double-cheek air kiss.

As the woman got close Lowe realised who she was. Lady Penelope Creighton-Ward. A minor Royal, great-grandchild of Queen Victoria by one of the youngest of her immense brood. He remembered hearing something about how she'd been hammered by death duties and didn't qualify for the civil list. She was persona non grata with the *pridvorny* of King Andrew's court because of some sordid row with Queen Sarah.

"Thank God you're here, darling," Lady Penelope breathed at him. "Do you have a gun? Or a spear? That ghastly man needs murdering. Wipe the *risus sardonicus* off his fizzog. Give me one of those dreadful fag things, smile like we're old friends, and snag me a drink will you, lovie."

Lowe noticed the deft way Lady Penelope managed to hug and kiss him without any physical contact. She smelled of something expensive.

He lit up two cigarettes and gave her one, which she jammed into a pink holder that she sucked languidly. Then he fetched her a Vimto.

Lady Penelope was well into her forties, but looked a sight better than her pictures. Her skirt seemed to restrict her movements, forcing her to bob in tiny steps as if she were on wires. A wide-brimmed pink hat, with a functionless veil, perched on her stiff blonde hair. Her eyes were huge and fascinating, her mouth generous and red; these features seemed almost too big for her small, smooth face.

"What do you think of it so far?" he asked.

"If, as I suspect from your seedy manner and general grubbiness, you're a journo, I want it understood anything I say to you between now and the day I die is strictly off the record."

Lowe grinned. "Done."

Lady Penelope took a deep breath, and let it out in a torrent of smoke and tiny words.

"This is no kind of work for a lady, the Yank criminals are unspeakably vulgar, and that Maxwell creature gives me the screaming willies. And Mr. Blair is a complete phoney. D'you know my principal function right here, right now? What it is I'm supposed to be here for?"

"To add aristocratic glamour to the Freedom and Enterprise Roadshow, what the Americans call 'a touch of class'?"

"Balls. At this particular do, I'm to allow my posterior to be manhandled by American oafs. It's astonishing how much loudmouthed criminals want to grope the bum of a minor, financially-strapped British royal. If things carry on like this, I shall set up a stall and charge a million dollars a time. Would you like to be my barker? It's a very presentable bum, I'm told. Who are you, by the way."

"I'm Lowe."

"Of course you are, darling."

"It's my name too."

Having run out of patter, Lady Penelope blew a smoke ring and looked through her veil at a tall man in dark glasses who stood alone at the far end of the bar.

"There's a bit of rough, and no mistake," she said.

The man was in late middle age, but obviously kept in shape. Like all of the British government cloak-and-dagger brigade at public functions, he had a cheap camera dangling like a charm bracelet, to give the effect he was a tourist, a visitor, a member of the family.

"I know him," Lowe said. "He used to be famous."

"Bloody dangerous is what he is," said Lady Penelope. "Some of my silly girlfriends dream of a night of brutal intimacy with someone like that. Personally I'd rather sleep on top of a live volcano."

"Brown," Lowe said, pulling up the name from memory, "William Brown. Just William, they called him. Used to be with one of those tearaway outfits in Indo. A necklace of small human ears sort of fellow. Then a couple of dozen other brushfire wars. The whisper is that he's the one who topped Gerry Adams. Wonder what he's up to here?"

"Keeping tabs on Fatty Maxwell. Or perhaps something more sinister?"

Lady Penelope seemed excited by the idea.

Lowe let his thoughts run on. "Half a dozen secessionist movements or state governments in this country would pay handsomely for a consultant like Just William. Maybe he's checking out freelance opportunities."

Lady Penelope turned back to him. "Oh well, killers on top of criminals. Hardly unexpected, what? Now then, Mr. Oh So Lowe, as a newspaperman you ought to be able to tell me what a girl has to do to get a drink in this wretched place."

"Sorry. I've been asking exactly the same question."

Lady Penelope lifted her veil and looked at the barman with big eyes. "Oh pardner," she sang.

"Yes, ma'am," said HI PARDNER! MY NAME'S TOM.

"If you were to procure me an alcoholic beverage, I'd sleep with you."

"I'm sorry, ma'am, but I've taken a vow of celibacy. I'm of the Futurian faith."

Lady Penelope's mouth sagged open, leaking smoke.

"Futurian faith?"

"You should have heard of it," HI PARDNER! explained, juggling three empty glasses. "The Church of Futurity was founded by an Englishman, Arthur Clarke. I'll give you a card that's good for a free personality test at our down-town temple."

"No thank you, darling. I already have a personality."

"Alcohol craving and sexual incontinence are unknown among true Futurians, ma'am."

"You poor dear. Let me give you a card that's good for French at any brothel in Mayfair."

HI PARDNER! dropped a glass, and looked none too pleased. Lady Penelope linked arms with Lowe and dragged him towards the exit.

"I've got the car out the back," she said. "It has a wet bar."

They weaved between the orbits of Sir Robert and Hunt Thompson, and escaped from the crowded marquee.

In the grounds of Thompson's mansion, a stage was erected by an ornamental lake. A band were tuning up as Lady Penelope led Lowe to the backstage area car-park. The best of Britpop was due on soon, filling his gut with dread. Her Ladyship posed as if for a rotogravure photograph by a pink Rolls Royce, as curvy and elegant as a swan, as potentially powerful as a panther. He thought he was in love.

"Fab," he said, struck dumb.

"Would you like to drive her?"

"Is the bear a Catholic?"

"Can you assure me you don't have a drink problem?"

"I've driven from London to Edinburgh and back again in a single day on a bottle and a half of Scotch without any accidents. Well, nothing fatal."

"Then you get the job as chauffeur," she smiled graciously, tossing him the keys. He held the rear door open for her to get inside.

As she settled into her seat, he took the wheel. He breathed in the aroma of leather and walnut. A fresh cut rose was propped in a test-tube-shaped dashboard vase.

"Your orders are to take us away from this dry hell to somewhere we can get a drink."

Lowe started the engine as Sir Cliff took the stage. Partly because the Roller was a beautiful piece of work, and partly to avoid listening to much more of "Living Doll", he opened her right up. The clock said 60 as they swept past the Group 4 rentacops on the main gate, but the Rolls Royce seemed to glide out onto the road.

Having joined Lady Penelope on the spacious backseat and sampled some of the Scotch from the discreet bar, Lowe found himself humming a tune under his breath between liquoury kisses. It was most inappropriate: here he was, about to make love with Royalty in an upholstered dream machine, and he couldn't get Sir Cliff's "Living Doll" out of his mind.

She still wore her pearls. He rolled them between his teeth, recognising from the smoothness that they were real. She held his head to her body, tickling behind his ears, encouraging him to tongue wet patterns on her gloriously unmarked skin. She was soft yet supple, as if her muscles were factory-fresh and had not yet been used. Maybe it was Royal blood.

He licked a tracing of moisture down between her breasts, past her neat navel, to her perfect triangle of pubic hair. It was twenty hours since his last shave: he gently sandpapered Lady Penelope's inner thighs with his chin.

"Go low, Lowe, oh go," she cooed.

Crying, talking, sleeping, walking, he thought, tongue active.

Her thighs pressed tight on his cheeks. He gripped the taut velvet of her sides, feeling her ripple.

...best to please her...just 'cause she's a...

"Oh, Lowe, well done," she said.

St Louis, Mo.

Perched on the edge of the motor hotel bed in his Y-Fronts, Lowe hit the "Finish Edit" key on his portable Amstrad WP. Sir Bob insisted every detail of the Freedom and Enterprise Roadshow be a showcase for "the best of everything British". The Amstrad was marvellous if you liked gadgets and certainly British-designed and owned, though manufactured in Mexican sweatshops. Lowe preferred his old Imperial travelling typewriter: it was lighter, cheaper to replace when (not if, in America) it got stolen, and you didn't need to find a telly with compatible sockets to plug it in to.

The Dis-United Ex-Socialist States of America is in trouble. Since he was shot two years ago, President John Ross Ewing has not been a healthy man. Like one of those red gerontocrats from the late '70s and early '80s, Ewing clings to power because the people who work for him have too much to lose. If you talk to senior government figures or the eager young reformers who form the backbone of the administration, you have to think of the Raft of the Medusa. Starving, thirsty, maddened people clinging to one another atop waterlogged pieces of wood lashed together in a desperate hurry. If anyone falls off, they won't just drown quietly, they'll be torn to pieces by sharks. The predators who want to gorge on the carcass of a ruined country range from old CP hacks reinvented as democrats (Newton Gingrich, Hal Phillip Walker) to new millionaires with shady reputations (Ivan Boesky, Milo Minderbinder).

Policy is made up on the hoof in an attempt to cope with major insurrectionist or secessionist movements in California and Texas (which would have gone by now were Ewing not himself Texan). Washington State wants to federate with Canada, Alaska wants to re-join wealthy Russia, Florida is trying to become part of the "Caribbean Rim" economy. In places like Montana and Wyoming, ex-Communists, fundamentalist Christians, Mormons and other lunatic backwoodsmen form communities —protected by armed militias—which recognise no government at all. Those plains Indians (or "First Americans" as they call themselves) who survived collectivisation, purge and genocide in the '30s demand the return of their lands. The former slave states have effectively introduced apartheid, which they call "separate development" or "democratic segregation". Swedish Lutheran missionaries who started out encouraging negroes to use the law to challenge the system have ended up supplying them with weapons.

For all practical purposes, the Confederation of Independent North American States (CINAS), as we're trying to remember to call it, exists as a geographical expression only. It would take Garibaldi, Bismarck, Joan of Arc and Garth to re-unite this country.

One of the things you notice very quickly is how patriotic Yanks are. In Britain, especially since Indo-China, patriotism is rather quaint, the preserve of *Daily Torygraph* readers in the golf club bar. In America, it has all the power of religion. Yanks of every age and class see their country falling to pieces in a wave of crime, swamped by capitalist hucksters like Robert Maxwell, their young people corrupted by trashy telly, by porn masquerading as sexual freedom, by European and Russian evangelists, by tawdry consumerism. They compare this with the days when people respected the police, when there was free schooling, medical care, libraries, and very little crime. Most Americans forget the disappearances (which, after all, happened to other people), the shortages of food and consumer goods. Then they feel a profound, visceral anger that their country has turned from global superpower to banana republic in under five years.

It's not that there are no contenders for the title of Saviour of America. There are too many, all soldiers. In messes up and down the land junior and middle ranking officers drink to the day when General Colin Powell leads them to power to form a government of national salvation. Powell seems to be humane, he is certainly immensely able (he defeated the Panama uprising a few years ago with almost no bloodshed) and is popular with all ranks. There's only one problem. He's a negro. 98% of the population could beg him to become President tomorrow, but racialists and fascists would take pot-shots until they eventually got him. The thing is, Powell might still do it anyway. He is only the sanest and best-known of a pack of Caesars-in-waiting. Of the others, several should have been cashiered for insubordination before now for making political speeches. The most dangerous is undoubtedly the deranged, incontinent old General "Buck" Turgidson who famously claimed he could restore the country to red glory by using the nuclear arsenal on secessionist states. But one would do well to keep an eye on a whole string of Generals and Colonels: Ross Perot, Oliver North, Nicholas Fury, Dale Dye, William Calley, James M. Scott.

God help America!

Not very funny, perhaps, but horribly truthful. He should go through it and put in more jokes. Or even some.

Penny leaned over his shoulder, pushed a cigarette into his mouth and lit it with her Fabergé.

"What are you writing?" she asked.

"The truth," he said.

"For Fatty Maxwell? Poor baby, you're ill, let me get you a drinkie."

"No, not for Bob."

She bounded off the bed, naked, and fetched a bottle of Scotch from her overnight bag. She poured a generous slug into the motor hotel tooth-mug, drank half in one go, and handed the rest to him.

"So, man of mystery," she smiled. "Special report for MI5, perhaps?"

He smiled, "Look…"

"Don't worry," she said, jumping back onto the bed. "Your secret's safe with me." She nibbled his ear-lobe and whispered, "…Joanna."

He tried to turn around. She darted away and held up a grottily-produced magazine, open to a column headlined by a picture of a chain-smoking slut with a typewriter.

"How did you know?" he asked.

"Didn't. Educated guess. When you socialise for a living, you learn to read people. I saw you as someone who could only function as an employee of Repellent Robbie through the strategic use of conscience-appeasing treachery. Besides, I'm a huge fan of Joanna Houseman's 'Letter from America'. I noticed at once that you talk like she writes."

For three years, Lowe had been contributing "Letter from America" to *Lilliput*, the gadfly magazine owned by Viv Stanshall, co-edited by Michael Foot and John Lennon. America was a haven for every sort of

British weirdo, fraudster and crook; there was a ready market back home for humorously cynical tales of their activities. Naturally, Sir Robert's travelling freak-show was next up for the satirical chop.

"You should do this full-time," said Penelope, pointing to his latest column. "This is what people need to know."

Lowe shook his head and smiled. She shot him a don't-patronise-me-you-bastard look. He raised his hands in surrender.

"*Lilliput* don't pay, Penny. Unless you count the odd parcel of Marmite, HP Sauce and Branston Pickle that John sends me. It's all they can afford. The money is spent defending libel cases. That civil servant Hislop nearly bankrupted John and Michael for calling him a 'smug baldie get'. It may be what folk need to know, but it's not what most of them want. The great unwashed want the *Daily Mirror* and its crime and celeb tittle-tattle."

"You swine," Penny said, mock-swatting him with the magazine. "All this time you've had Marmite and refused to share!"

The door barged open. Maxwell exploded in, sporting a shiny plastic bowler hat and an immense Union Jack waistcoat.

"Come on, Ladyship," he roared. "Time to meet and greet the good people of Saint Lewis. You, too, Lowe. I want you to write about how Sir Cliff is taking the country by...Fucking hell!"

Most women would have grabbed for the bedclothes to cover themselves or snapped something about the basic courtesies of knocking. Penny stood up stark naked and faced the tycoon, one hand on her hip, the other fanning her breasts with *Lilliput*.

Maxwell stared, not at Penny's body but at the magazine he had made his life's work to sue out of existence. It was always running stories about his bullying, monstrous bombast and financial irregularities. Lowe ought to know: he was the main source funnelling the stories.

Maxwell detested *Lilliput* mostly because it spared no effort to make him look ridiculous. Lennon and Foot were counting on "Joanna Houseman" to feed them tit-bits about Sir Bob's adventures in America. If Maxwell found out Lowe was Joanna, it wouldn't just mean the end of his career, but of his functioning testicles. He tried to cover the trail with a female pseudonym and regular hints in the column that "Joanna"'s business in the States was organising cultural and educational exchange visits.

"If I find any of my employees reading that toilet paper," Maxwell growled, eyebrows converging like angry earwigs, "they are fired. Brutally."

He tore the magazine out of Penny's grasp and ripped it in half, like a circus strong-man destroying a telephone book.

"Now put some clothes on and bloody well get to work. Mill and swill, you two."

Joplin, Mo.

The Roadshow had set up at the Missouri State Southern College. The place had once trained engineers, chemists and farm managers but was now trying to get by teaching accounting, marketing and business management. About one window in ten was broken, the chill kept out with cardboard and sticky-tape.

There was a huge brass mural of Debs, Capone and Goldwater shoulder-to-shoulder at the barricades. An embarrassed lecturer in Creative Advertising had explained to Lowe that it would be torn down as soon as the college had funds for the demolition. In the meantime, it was feebly plastered over with posters hawking free enterprise.

The crowd was huge. Much bigger than in Oak Park or St Louis, sprawled across the college grounds, most of it in front of the scaffolding stage hung with a huge banner reading "VIMTO—THE TASTE OF FREEDOM". Beneath it, Sir Cliff and his band belted out "Summer Holiday". Someone had decided to change the words to "summer vacation" so as not to confuse the Americans. It didn't sound right at all.

Officially, the population of Joplin ran to something between forty and fifty thousand. About half had turned out to see the show, not to mention several thousand more in from the sticks.

Lowe had started mingling with the crowd at the beginning of the show, as Sir Robert delivered a matey lecture about the wonders of capitalism. He'd arrived in Britain as a penniless refugee during the War, he claimed, and pulled himself up by his bootstraps. Lowe's story idea for the day, relayed from the boss's desk, was to describe how the people of Joplin, Missouri were inspired to go out and start their own businesses by Captain Bob's inspirational speech.

The only quote he had in his notebook was "what does that fat old asshole know? Probably got rich by stealing it."

Oh well, he'd just make it up as usual...*This is just what we need to turn this town round. I'm gwine go out there starting tomorrow morning first thing an' set up a shoe-shine stall. Yeah, Captain Bob, he's dang right—I'll start me a protection racket.*

Few had turned out just to see Sir Robert or Sir Cliff; few had even heard of them. They were here because it was something to do, a day out. Joplin was that kind of place; once upon a time, its air and rivers had been polluted by the by-products of heavy industry: zinc and lead, machine tools and chemicals, aircraft parts and slaughterhouses. Now, exposed to the chill winds of the global economy, most of the old factories had closed down or put their workers on part-time shifts. Driving through the rusted, mostly-abandoned industrial estate in a pink Roller was an entirely apt introduction to the place. Along the highway from the factories to the town were dotted dusty white concrete oblongs, apartment buildings built block-on-block on the Lego principle.

This was USSA *Profonde*, the sort of place no-one had much heard of, even in America, a place that communist politicians hadn't cared about as long as production targets were met. Now nobody cared at all, apart from the people living here, lured to the Freedom and Enterprise Roadshow by the promise of a free show, not to mention free bottles of Vimto and packs of Strands.

The audience applauded politely. Sir Cliff thankyoued and asked Joplin if it was feeling good. A few people mumbled a mild "yurp". When asked a second time, the response wasn't any louder, so the Peter Pan of Britpop turned to the band and waved them into "Jolly Jolly Sixpence".

Lowe started towards the VIP enclosure in the backstage area.

"He's got jolly jolly what?" someone asked.

Lowe turned. Two white men stood, hands in pockets, one short and fat, one tall and thin. They wore black suits, white shirts, black ties, black trilby hats and sunglasses, and expressions of amused contempt.

"Sixpence," Lowe said to them. He reached into his pocket and fished out the 1946 tanner he always had on him. It wasn't legal tender anymore, but it was as old as he was. He carried it for luck, and for tossing when a difficult decision had to be made.

"About a dime, huh?" said the taller man, inspecting the coin in Lowe's outstretched hand. "Shoot, we don't even have that much."

Lowe introduced himself. The two men were Jake Papageorge and Elwood Delaney, musicians who specialised in what had once been condemned in the USSA as "degenerate negro music".

"Excuse the funeral outfits," Elwood explained. "Stage gear, and the only clothes we've got left anyway."

They'd been touring the country, hadn't made any money, the rest of the band had left, their van was kaput and they'd just lost everything else in a poker game trying to raise the price of escape from Joplin.

"Still, like the fat guy said, mustn't grumble."

Elwood managed a fair Maxwell impersonation. Lowe gave them five dollars and continued on his way. At the VIP enclosure he discovered the Access All Areas laminate clipped to his lapel was gone.

"Can't let you through without accreditation," said the jobsworth at the gate.

The mysterious William Brown appeared out of nowhere and just touched the guard on the shoulder. Lowe was admitted, no further questions, have a nice day. He said "thanks" to Brown, who gave the faintest nod and was gone again.

So Brown was in charge of security, was he? Was there a story there?

The marquee was quiet. There might be a huge crowd outside, but Joplin was notably thin on VIPs, or at any rate the kind of VIPs Maxwell would want to cosy up to. There were a few civic types, a chief of police and a couple of businessmen, but most of the people here were with the Roadshow.

Bottles of Vimto and Corona were laid out on a table. Lowe uncapped a Vimto as Blair sidled up. The glow of his smile preceded him, as if his teeth were luminous.

"Sir Cliff is a marvel, isn't he?" the PR man said.

"Certainly is."

From the corner of his eye, Lowe noticed Elwood and Jake assaulting the buffet. Jake had Lowe's laminate clipped to his hat. Elwood piled up chicken legs, vol-au-vents and sausage rolls into a heap on a cardboard plate, while Jake tried to conceal an entire Black Forest Gateau in his mouth, easing its passage with swigs of Vimto.

"It's a privilege to be able to bring such British energy to this tired country, don't you think?"

The miracle was that Blair talked like that off the record.

Jake and Elwood sauntered nearby. Now, they were weighed down with guitars, a saxophone and an electric keyboard.

"You can sense the people waking up," Blair said, eyes shining.

"When I wake up, I'm usually angry."

Jake passed directly behind Blair. The PR supremo shrieked, surprising Lowe no end. How the hell had Jake goosed him with his hands full of musical instruments? Elwood touched the lip-piece of the sax to his hat-brim and smiled. Lowe had to admire them.

The Reverend Beverley appeared, accompanied by an attractive, demure woman in a floral print dress.

"Lady Penelope! Mr. Lowe! Mr. Blair!" he beamed. "Meet my wife, Nancy."

Nancy's handshake was a wet fish. She looked at the ground, and Lowe looked at her forehead.

"Nancy is American," said the vicar. "We met in New York. At the Chelsea Hotel. I suppose you could say it was then that my love-affair with America began."

On stage, the final bars of "Congratulations" thumped flat. Applause was faint to non-existent. Sir Cliff thanked Joplin for their warm welcome.

"I think that's my cue," said the Reverend. He licked his hand and tried to slick back his hair. "Time to go out there and get Evangelical!"

If Cliff hadn't actually died on stage, then he certainly hadn't done too well. Now the mild-mannered cleric was going to go out there and give them a Thought for the Day. ("You know, I often feel that the Love of God is a lot like a Brussels sprout.")

Lowe's heart sank. He could take a certain pleasure in the humiliation of a pop singer he'd never particularly enjoyed, but it seemed a shame such a manifestly decent, modest sort as John Beverley should follow him to the lions of incomprehension and boredom.

Beverley and his wife made for the stage entrance.

"Have you seen him in action yet?" asked Penny.

"No. I don't know if I can bear to."

"I rather think you should see this," she said. "It's quite a spectacle."

He shrugged and followed her from the tent to the ramp at the side of the stage, past members of Sir Cliff's band wondering what had happened to various instruments.

The Reverend took a radio-microphone and strode out to the front of the stage. He assumed a sort of strutting swagger, almost like a drunken man. Lowe wondered if he'd given himself an electric shock.

"Good evening Joplin," he yelled, triggering a feedback whine from the big speakers. The crowd cringed, but paid attention. The electricity was coming out of him.

"I want to talk about *Salvation*, about the Love of *God*. About how even in your *darkest* hours, when things look like they can't get any *worse*, the *Lord* is always there for *you*, for *me*, for *everyone*..."

His limp Home-counties accent was gone, lost in the force of his voice.

Lowe looked around, at the smugly-smiling Penny. Sir Cliff was struck open-mouthed, either in envy or sudden enthusiasm. Blair was rapt, a worshipper at the temple of British Energy.

Beverley gripped the mike as if choking the serpent of Eden.

"I know you got *trouble*, Joplin," he said, almost sneering, "I know you're all *hurt*. You've got fuck-all *jobs*, or jobs that pay *jack-shit*, or your marriage is a hideous *trap*, or maybe the *Anti-Christ* is stalking your kids…Am I *right*?"

"*Amen!*" yelled a lone voice, not from the audience, but from the other side of the stage. Little Nancy had turned into a wide-eyed acolyte.

"*Am I right*? C'mon Joplin, lemme hear you say *Amen!*"

Joplin said Amen.

"Say it *louder*, Joplin," he shouted. "*Shame the Anti-Christ!*"

Joplin said Amen a lot more as the Rev. Bev. stomped across the stage, thrashing his arms, enunciating every conceivable milestone in the vale of tears, promising the Almighty was there for them, all of them.

Lowe had seen Baptist preachers in Virginia and South Carolina, but never a performance as frenzied as this, and never from a white man. If Beverley had been working in Britain, the Anglican establishment would have kicked him out for excessive fervour, but here in America he'd found his true voice and calling. Lowe had never heard an Anglican swear in a pulpit, but it went over big.

After ten minutes of frenzied ranting, Beverley's voice fell to a croak.

"Brothers and sisters, beloved people of Joplin, I shall call upon the *Holy Spirit* to descend upon this town and fill it with the *light* and *strength* of the *Almighty!*"

Beverley looked down, mumbling. Words poured through the speakers.

"*And now…the end is near…*"

It took a moment for it to become clear that the Reverend was singing, quietly first, almost to himself, but growing louder. Lowe vaguely recognised the words of some old song Ken Dodd used to sing.

"I did it…*God's Way!*" yelled Beverley

He went stiff as if impaled by a spear from above, every muscle stretched tight. Sweat shone on his twisted, ecstatic face. Lowe was still concerned for his health, but Penny's amused calm suggested this was all part of the usual show.

Beverley collapsed onstage, tearing at his clothes with his free hand, jamming the mike to his mouth.

"I feel *His* presence," he shouted. "*He* is come among us! *He* is come to give this town *His* blessing!"

Then he stopped making sense altogether, mumbling loudly in Double-Dutch.

"I believe it's called glossolalia," said Penny. "Speaking in tongues."

"This sort of thing never happened at St Botolph's when I was a kid," he said.

"You think he's remarkable, you should see the crowd."

"Are they liking it?"

"A lot of them are, yes. The Rev. has a dozen helpers at the front of the stage to sign up new believers. Then he'll send an organiser to live here for a year or two to get a church started."

Beverley twisted, shouting what sounded like Babylonian obscenities at the crowds. There were indeed minions with forms mingling with the thunderstruck Joplinites.

Penny let him kiss her cheek. Already, everyone from Blair to the roustabouts knew they were an item.

The Reverend Beverly came offstage, half-crawling, half-carried. He seemed to have sweated a stone off his scarecrow frame, and his suit was shredded. His wife scurried along next to him, dabbing at several cuts on his face with a hankie. He wiped froth (puke?) off his chin with a tattered sleeve.

The crowd were howling amen and hallelujah like a hurricane.

"You know, my dear," Beverley said to Nancy, "I do believe that went off rather well."

His wife agreed with him.

"I need a drink," Lowe said to Penny.

Joplin was still rejoicing.

"Darling," she said, "I fear we've reached the bottom of the barrel, and it's time to give it a good old scrape."

"Meaning?"

"Meaning a crate of something I've saved for desperate times. Come on. It's in the car."

From the tour vehicle park, they saw the crowds start to drift home, though a few thousand remained by the front of the stage, signing up for the Reverend Beverley's crusade to bring God to America.

Penny tossed him the keys of the Roller.

"In the boot," she said. "Sorry, what do they call it here? Trunk. Like an elephant."

Lowe remembered he needed to get into the boot on business of his own. He opened it up and took a *Concise Oxford English Dictionary* from his holdall. Then he saw the box of bottles.

"Those are the fellows," Penny said. "Fetch us one, would you?"

He took out a bottle. Its label was Russian.

He joined Penny on the back seat and screwed the cap off the bottle. Its contents smelled vile. He could read the Cyrillic label, but not translate it.

"*Chernobyl*? What's that mean, then?"

"Wormwood."

"What? The Star of the Apocalypse?"

"An educated man, eh? What this particular Wormwood means is that we haven't got any proper booze left, so we've got to drink Russian *absinthe*. I bought it in Canada, from a naval officer. Probably a spy, actually."

She took the bottle from him and downed a hefty swig. Her big eyes started watering.

"Any old port in a storm," he said.

"It's interesting," she admitted. "No glowing insects yet."

He took the bottle and had an experimental sip. *Absinthe* didn't just get you drunk, it made you hallucinate. It didn't taste that rough, so he took a hefty gulp, warming his throat and tummy.

He passed the bottle back to Penny and started to work with his notebook and dictionary, first drafting his message and then finding the page number, column number and paragraph number that each word appeared in.

"A secret message?" she asked. She lit up a Strand and screwed it into her holder.

"Tomorrow, I'll telegraph this to a friend in London. I need some detective-work done."

"Why not use the telephone like everyone else?"

"The deeper you get into America, the more useless the phone service becomes. Even if I manage to put a call through to London, there's no guarantee we'll be able to hear one another. Also, I've a strong inkling calls made by anyone on the Freedom and Enterprise Roadshow are listened to with great interest by the gnomes in Cheltenham."

"GCHQ? That's illegal, isn't it?"

"Never stopped 'em before. It's the beauty of an unwritten constitution. What our beloved Prime Minister Alan Clark likes to call 'the most mature democracy in the world' when he's being patronising to foreigners is actually a cloak for a bunch of self-serving, casually corrupt crooks who don't give a monkeys about anyone except themselves."

"Poor baby," she said. "Can I have the soap-box when you've finished?"

There was a bitter aftertaste in his mouth.

"You're a bloody aristocrat. What would you know?"

He hadn't meant that. His tongue was possessed. It slithered in his mouth like an open razor.

She shrugged and looked out of the window.

"In my blue-blooded parasitical way, I may not know much. But I'm pretty certain that those two in the black hats are driving off with all the cricket gear."

A four-ton Scammel—loaded with pads, bats, balls and stumps—pulled out of the car park. While Elwood wrestled with the immense steering-wheel, Jake leaned out of the window on the passenger side of the cab, smoking a Strand.

"Who are those fellows?" Penny asked.

"They said they were musicians."

Oklahoma City

"D'you think they'll do Watney's Red Barrel?" he asked as he unscrewed the Spirit of Ecstasy ornament from the bonnet and pocketed it.

"I'll settle for a gin and tonic," said Penny, putting on her sunglasses. "Anything but *absinthe*."

He took the windscreen-wipers off, too, dropped them on the driver's seat and locked the car. Anything that could be removed from a car in the new America could be stolen. The streetwise motorist always took precautions.

They had fled the inanities of the Roadshow, currently setting up shop in the big park in the middle of town. Lowe had chauffeured Penny off in search of a half-decent bar in a part of town where a pink Rolls Royce wouldn't be vandalised or stolen. Limey Louie's Authentic British Pub looked like a prospect both fascinating and appalling. They hadn't been able to resist pulling in for a look.

Aside from the spittoons, the pub looked authentic enough: sawdust on the floor, those mahogany-topped wrought-iron tables, a bar with ceramic pump-handles. The walls were hung with pictures of the Royal Family. Queen Sarah looked quite slimline in her wedding snaps. There was even the rare shot of King Andrew and his last-but-one Royal Mistress, Patsy Stone.

"Good arfternoon folks, wot'll you have to drink, then?" said the man behind the bar. He wore a butcher's apron and a pork pie hat. Limey Louie himself, presumably.

"A gin and tonic for the lady, and I'll have a pint of bitter," said Lowe.

"Sorry mite, but we're aht've gin at the moment, an' I don't keep bitter."

Lowe had heard such an accent before. Three decades ago, he had tried and failed to get off with a girl studying fine art at the Slade and she'd dragged him to several dreary American socialist realism films at the Everyman. He had endured the "genius" David O. Selznick's ham-fisted stabs at *Hard Times*, *The Ragged-Trousered Philanthropist* and *A Child of the Jago*. Back then, the commies liked to think London a mid-Victorian hellhole of gruesome industrial accidents, filthy rookeries and bloated, whiskered capitalists. The cockney proletarians of those films all spoke like Limey Louie, in an adenoidal whine somewhere between Brummie and Australian.

"Okay," said Penny, "do you have any Scotch?"

"Sorry," said Limey Louie. "That's way too expensive. All I 'ave in that line is Bourbon."

Penny shrugged.

"What beers do you do?" Lowe asked.

"Bud. Might 'ave some malt liquor out the back, mind."

"Enough," said Penny. "I'll have a triple Bourbon on the rocks and he'll have a jug of Budweiser."

"Sorry, can't do jugs Ma'am. This is an authentic British pub. We only serves beer in pints and half-pints."

"Whatever. Just get us some drinks."

Limey Louie looked at his pocket watch. "Sorry, I can't serve you alcohol now."

"In the name of God, why?" said Penny through clenched teeth, delicate little hands balling into fists.

"It's quarter to three. I called time ten minutes ago."

"So you're closed for the afternoon? Why didn't you tell us when we came in?"

"I'm not closing," he said indignantly. "That'd be terrible for business. This is supposed to be an authentic British pub, so I keep to British pub hours. They call them licensing hours in Britain, you know. They shut the pubs at half past two so's the workers will go back to the factories. I can sell you soft drinks and mineral water."

"Let me get this right," said Lowe. "There's no local law against you selling alcohol in the afternoon." Louie smiled and nodded. "But you won't because it'd spoil the gimmick of this place." Another nod and smile. "Well, how about you break your rule just this once? There's no-one else here to see you do it, and I promise we won't tell."

Limey Louie looked pained. "I'm sorry, sir, truly I am, but this is my vision. I've been to night classes to learn how to run my own business, and Mr. Leeson from the London School of Business Excellence said that to make it work you've got to have a vision, and stick with it. I've never been to Great Britain myself, but I'm a great admirer of everything British, and my vision was to make my pub as bloomin' authentic as possible."

"So how's business?" said Lowe.

"Not so good, but it'll come right any day now, I just know it…Listen, sorry to disappoint you over the drinks. Tell you what I'll do. I'll give you both a nice glass of Vimto. On the house."

Lowe glanced at Penny, assuming she'd be all for going somewhere else or back to the *Chernobyl* in the boot. Instead she shook her head resignedly. They both felt sorry for Limey Louie, who had doubtless sunk his life savings into this idiotic business after listening to bullshit from some wanker who probably wasn't good enough to lecture in Britain.

"I can tell from your accents," said Limey Louie as he poured the drinks, "that you're not from round these 'ere parts. Where you from, then? Canada?"

"Something like that," said Lowe. If they admitted they were British, they might never escape.

They took their Vimto and sat at a table by the window. Lowe reached into one of the inside pockets of his jacket, pulled out his hip-flask and unscrewed the top. Without bothering to hide the fact, he poured a hefty tot into Penny's glass and something likewise into his own.

"Cheers," she said as they clinked glasses.

The Vimto masked the hideous, bitter taste of the *Chernobyl* rather well.

"I think you've stumbled on a drink that could be the sensation of the Home Counties Set next season," said Penny, licking her lips. "My one social indulgence is a marquee for a few friends at the Henley Regatta, and next year I shall serve *absinthe* and Vimto."

"Isn't it illegal in Britain?"

"Who cares? So is *bhang*, but everyone smokes it these days. *Absinthe* on the other hand is truly decadent. *Absinthe* and Vimto. A new cocktail. I name it...Meltdown."

They downed their drinks in one.

Lowe felt as if a sledge-hammer had been taken to his forehead.

"Mr. Louie!" Penny shouted, "my companion and I will have another two glasses of your vintage Vimto, please."

"Okay, Ma'am," said Louie, opening two bottles, "just as long as you understand that I can't bring it over to you. You or the gentleman have to come to the bar to fetch it because..."

"...this is an authentic British pub."

At that moment, the window shattered, spilling away from its frame as though the glass had turned to water. Penny raised her hands to brush away the fragments. Lowe thought for a moment that he had been hit, but it was just another *absinthe* kick.

Louie was beside them in an instant, holding a sawn-off shotgun. Having checked that they weren't hurt, he flew out of the front door. Lowe looked out. A pick-up truck was pulling away. Red stars were painted on its sides. Three men stood in the back, jeering and waving fists.

"Are you all right," he asked Penny.

"Yes," she said. "Fine thanks."

The shotgun boomed outside. Limey Louie swore extensively, in his original Okie accent.

Penny stood up and walked over to the bar, glass splinters tinkling as they fell off her skirt. "What was all that about, then?" she asked, letting herself in behind the counter and helping herself to a triple Bourbon.

"Old-style commies, I suppose," he said, joining her and looking for a beer glass. "Lots of people are nostalgic for the good old days, when there was law and order and prohibition and the USSA was a superpower. You wouldn't expect them to be mad keen on a place like this."

He found a glass and pulled a pint of frothy, yellow beer.

Louie came back in and began to inspect the damage.

"Louie," said Lowe, putting a five-dollar note down on the counter, 'for goodness' sake have a drink. Break your rule just once. You need it."

"Sure," said Louie, sweeping pieces of glass across the floor with his shoe. "That's the third time this has happened this year. Militia bastards."

The door opened. Louie trained his gun on two men, one tall and thin, the other short and fat. They wore white pads on their legs and arms, and carried cricket bats and stumps.

"Thought we'd find you here," said Elwood. "We saw your Ladyness's pink car outside. We need to talk about something. Can you buy us a drink, Mr. Lowe?"

"Piss off."

"No harm in asking."

"Is that your Rolls Royce out there?" Limey Louie asked Penny. "Say, are you British? You must be an aristocrat? In my pub, what an honour!"

"Louie," said Lowe, "I'd like you to meet Jake Papageorge and Elwood Delaney. They're not British, but they can probably sell you a few cricketing mementoes. I'm afraid we have to go."

"Mr. Lowe!" pleaded Jake. "We've got a truckload of useless sporting goods."

"Leastways, we think they're sporting goods," said Elwood. "Could be some kind of martial arts implements. Or marital aids for real tight-ass Brits."

"We can't fence them or sell them to anyone," said Jake.

"We can't even live in the truck because it's full of bats and sticks and these white things with straps on," said Elwood

"We were wondering," said Jake, "if your Sir Bob would want to buy them back?"

Amarillo, Tex.

"This just bloody isn't good enough, Lowe," said Maxwell. "How much do I pay you?"

Not enough.

"Twenty-one thousand a year."

"Plus a generous expense account, I expect. Champers all the way, and strawberries out your schnozzle. Bleeding journos. You're worse than gannets."

Maxwell's face contorted. The flesh pouches around his nose and under his chins blew up and went scarlet like haemorrhoids. Malteser-sized droplets of sweat grew on his forehead. Peristaltic movement started in his flabby neck and worked its way down through the rings of fat upon fat that clung to his torso and belly, forcing what must be a large bolus of faecal matter into his lower bowel.

Lowe imagined the shit concentrating into a bullet-shaped turd for expulsion.

Sir Robert's doughy arse-cheeks overflowed the wooden seat and hung like mottled saddlebags. Veins in his face pulsed like mating earthworms, as if he were defecating a large cactus. He roared relief, and there was a splash in the pan.

Then the process started again.

Getting a dressing-down was one thing. Getting it in the bathroom of Maxwell's hotel suite was altogether another. Sir Robert loved to rant at his minions while stark naked on the bog, moving his considerable bowels.

One of the vans on the Roadshow hauled a load of soft, European toilet paper purely for use on His Master's Arse. Sir Robert insisted there be an armed guard on it at all times. Penny also had a stash of pink Andrex, which she was unwilling to share even with an intimate friend. Everyone else was learning about the joys of scratchy cardboard Yank loo-paper. You had to pay twenty cents a sheet to gouging attendants in any public place.

Lowe said nothing, and tried not to breathe.

The bathroom was brown, with earth-coloured tiles and a Western longhorn motif on all the fittings. It was larger than the room Lowe was sharing with Penny. The shower stall was larger than the single he would have been allocated if he hadn't shacked up with the nobility.

Another epochal clenching of intestine began deep inside Maxwell, as he squeezed a turd the size of the *Titanic* through his bowels. Sail On, Great Sir Robert, the Shit That Will Never Go Down...

Maxwell held a week-old copy of the *Mirror* flown in from London. It was the Saturday edition, with a special 16-page colour pull-out featuring all the wonderful things Sir Bob was doing for the benighted peoples of America.

"I grant you you've scrawled a puff piece about Sir Cliff, and tried not to be too sarky about Beverley's sermon. But there's something missing, isn't there?"

"Is there, Sir Robert?"

Another minute in this room and he'd throw up. In Sir Robert's armpits, clusters of pink, worm-like extrusions writhed in with his iron-grey underarm hair.

Lowe was sure the worms were alive, looking at him.

"There's next to nothing about me, you cringing toad! Apart from the pathetic intro. Where's the piece I told you to write about *Mirror* Group's big deal to buy newsprint from that plant in Joplin?"

Sir Robert could read about that in Joanna Houseman's next "Letter From America". She was focusing on the two hundred workers back in Dundee who would be put on the dole because, even after shipping costs, American paper was only half the price of British.

We're going to get you, Lowe, whispered the armpit worms. *We know all about Joanna.*

It was infernally hot in the hotel bathroom. Green squiggles gnawed the edges of his vision.

You're just the *absinthe* talking, he told the worms.

No, said a new voice, *I'm the fucking* absinthe *talking!*

It was a deep voice, like a brutal Arthur Mullard, and echoed in the saxophone-shaped porcelain bowl beneath Maxwell's oversize buttocks.

Yes, me, growled the *absinthe*. *I'm talking to you out of Sir Robert's arsehole. Do you have a problem with that.*

"Fuck, yes."

"What's that?" snapped Maxwell, momentarily interrupting his harangue. "And where's the piece about the enormous influence I have with top Yank businessmen and politicians? Didn't I tell you to write a big caption for that picture of me with Gordon Gekko and Bob Roberts?"

"In my judgement…"

You're fucking fucked, fuckface, said Sir Robert's arsehole.

"I do not pay you good money to exercise judgement," said Maxwell coldly. "I pay you to do as you're bloody told."

"All I was going to say, Sir Robert," said Lowe, trying to ignore the continual burble-farting of the talking arsehole, "was that I thought the best way to impress the readers with what we're doing here is to find the gossip behind the headlines. Most *Mirror* readers aren't interested in American businessmen unless they affect their lives."

"Enough! The readers are interested in everything I do. I am a man of power, wealth and influence and I am prepared to make great sacrifices to help the people of America. The *Mirror's* readers want to know about that. They will be interested. From now on, you'll do exactly as I tell you! If you don't we'll drop you and your P45 off in the desert somewhere. Now get out."

Lowe actually said "thank you". It was involuntary. Like you'd thank the torturer who stopped stretching you on the rack to go off for a tea-break. Now, he wanted to take another gulp of *absinthe* and go deeper into *Chernobyl* country, beyond the talking arseholes, into new territory.

Good-bye, Joanna, rumbled the arse-hole. *Kissy-kissy.*

Gallup, N.M.

BILL APPARENT FREELANCE. RUMOUR: WORK VERYX2
HUSHX2. NOT MILITARY OR SECURITY. RUMOUR TOP CITY
& HOUSE INVOLVE, INCLUDE ERR CART. ASSUME NOTHING.
BUT MIGHTX2 BE PLOT VERSUS MAC SWELL. LOVE,
WHACKER.

Lowe looked at his watch. He'd been parked at the side of the highway
for fifteen minutes, translating the message from John Lennon that had
been waiting for him in an airmail envelope at the Gallup main post
office.

He'd told Penny he was borrowing the car to go and look for
newspapers and booze, but not to worry if he was away a while. He was
going to stooge around and get himself one of his periodic fixes on the
real America. Maybe something to fill Joanna's column.

He took the letter and the page of his notepad he'd used to translate
its sequence of page, column and paragraph numbers in the 1987 edition
of the Shorter *OED*. He got out of the car, touched his lighter to both
and dropped them to the ground.

In the semi-desert light, he couldn't see the flame. The flimsy blue
paper and the lined white paper turned brown then black, and
disintegrated to little fragments of ash. There were still green squiggles
at the edges, but he was used to them now. They didn't stop him thinking.

Second only to a matter of "national security", this was about as heavy
as it got. William Brown, who in his time had almost certainly been an
assassin, was working for influential politicos and businessmen. If Sir
Francis Urquhart was one of those politicos, anyone who crossed him
was in very deep trouble indeed.

And you called him a cunt, said the disembodied arsehole.

Shaking a little, he got back into the car and sat in the driver's seat.
He considered getting out his hip-flask for a tot of *Chernobyl*, but decided
against it.

He needed to think.

The *Mirror* was the only big-selling daily to support the Opposition.
Sir Robert would have loved to be a top Tory, would have given anything
to be accepted by the British establishment, but they regarded him as an
outsider, a foreigner and a buffoon. Buying up aristos like Lady Penelope

and telling *Mirror* readers to vote Lib-Lab was his revenge on his tormentors, who only despised him all the more for it.

Some folk would love to get their hands on the hugely-profitable *Mirror*, others would be happy to see its politics slant rightwards. Maxwell wasn't invulnerable. At least half the stories *Lilliput* printed about his financial irregularities were true. The *Mirror* was profitable, but most other businesses the bungling, arrogant tycoon touched—and there were a lot of them—turned to manure on the double. There was even a story going round that Maxwell had come personally on this jaunt to escape problems back home. One little flick of William Brown's finger in precisely the right place, and an empire might go pear-shaped.

"How do we feel about this?" he said out loud.

Good question, replied the arsehole. *On the one hand, you'd like to see Maxwell get fucked up me with a chainsaw. On the other hand, you'd not like to be out of a job. You like your job, don't you? Yes. And for all that the place is falling to bits, you love America and the American people, don't you? Yes. And you have no reason to go back home to Blighty, do you? No. All you have there is an embittered slapper of an ex-wife and a surly lout of a teenaged son who for some reason hates your drunken guts. Furthermore, M'Lud, I'd submit that much as you'd love to see Sir Bob roast in hell for all eternity, you're not in the business of doing Sir Francis Urquhart any favours. He is, as I believe you rather famously said on the steam radio, a cunt. Maxwell is just an arsehole. I can vouch for that. Or possibly a prick. Certainly worse than a tit, but not a cunt.*

That settles that then.

He heard a distant roar, heavy metal thunder, and glanced into the rear-view mirror. Sunlight glared off something metallic, and clouds of dust rose.

Lowe knew it was Brown, coming for him. The Thought Copper knew what was in his mind, and would clean it out for him with a couple of bullets.

It was two motorcycles, with three riders.

Out here, the roads were ill-maintained, nothing like the motorways Enoch Powell had run up and down and around and across everything green in the UK. There were pot-holes and years-old roadkill skeletons. Flattened old cartridge cases were as common as fag-butts, drifting to the verges or pressed into the soft asphalt.

The bikes were big Detroit machines, like the ones the police outriders used to escort top Party Suits on special occasions, with horn-shaped handlebars and more chrome than an espresso machine in an Old Compton Street cafe. One rider had a Stetson hat and an Old west moustache a size and a half too big for his face; the other wore a crash helmet painted with the Stars and Stripes and Hammer and Scythe; behind him was an unshaven man in an American football helmet.

Lowe didn't relax. There were a lot of these cycle tramps on the People's Roads, now. Ex-USS army types, mostly, living off the land, keeping ahead of the authorities, pitching into local disputes.

Some were scavengers.

The cycles slowed as they neared. Lowe's mouth went dry. The cycles stopped just in front of him. Riders dismounted.

"Howdy," said the cowboy, wandering over to his open window. "I'm Billy, and this is Comrade America."

The other biker touched his helmet.

Comrade America was a comic book character from World War II.

"And this is Hanson. He's a lawyer."

The unshaven man grinned. His eyeballs were flying.

"I'm Lowe," he said.

Billy grinned. "We're lower."

There was no threat in the smile. Lowe relaxed. There might be a Joanna Houseman in these bums. He got out of the car.

They reminded him of the pair Charlie Holley had told him about, the outlaws of the 50s, Howie Hughes and Jack Kerouac.

"I'm a British journalist."

"You want to buy any weed?"

"Weed?"

"What you call *bhang*. Maryjane."

He didn't use the stuff, but Penny might like some.

"How much?"

"What you got? Burberry?"

"I wish."

All Americans dreamed of owning a Burberry overcoat.

"That's a cream machine," Comrade America commented, looking over Penny's Rolls.

"Wish it were mine," Lowe said.

"You got a lot of wishin' in you," Hanson drawled, eyebrows flexing like pianists' fingers.

"I could cut you a deal," Billy, the businessman, continued.

In the end, Lowe swapped a battered Penguin paperback of Colin

Wilson's *The Outsider* for a small brown paper bag of loosely-rolled leaf that looked like green tobacco but smelled sweeter.

He learned a little about the cycle bums. They'd picked up Hanson in a county lock-up a few states back, and he'd left his dying town to come along on their quest.

"We're looking for America," the Comrade said.

"If I see it, I'll tell it you're coming."

"You do that."

Billy had been in the army, but the Comrade—who claimed to have no real name, but allowed that he'd answer to Wyatt—turned out to be a second generation "invisible", one of those who fall through the gaps inefficiency creates in the system. His Daddy before him had been a vagrant.

"Maybe you've heard of him. Tom Joad?"

Lowe thought Tom Joad was a legend, like Robin Hood or John Henry.

"Nope, he was real. Didn't do all they said he did, but he did some of it."

Lowe assumed this was just talking. Like Tommy Atkins or Jimmie Higgins, Tom Joad was a name used when someone small did something big. If Joe Shmoe saved a kid from drowning and hit the road, why then he must have been Tom Joad.

"Have you heard of Howie Hughes? Or a Canadian named Kerouac?"

They hadn't. But they knew Elwood and Jake.

"Bastards still owe us for a couple of keys."

Lowe didn't think Billy meant the kind you need for doors.

Lowe offered them warm Vimto and shots of *absinthe*. They made a fire and sat around it, watching the rainbow squiggles in the flames.

The sun set. Briefly, before full night, the desert was red and alive and beautiful.

"This used to be a hell of a country," Hanson said. "Whatever happened to it?"

The Roadshow had set up shop in the grounds of the home of Jonas Cord, a local big-shot. Another former Party boss who'd taken to capitalism enthusiastically, Cord now ran most of the local oil and gasoline businesses. One of his big indulgences was grass. He'd spent a fortune bringing in turf from somewhere and employed a small army of gardeners watering, rolling and tending it. It was the nearest thing to a proper cricket pitch in the whole state.

Lowe parked the car in the VIP enclosure, his clothes still stinking of last night's campfire.

Jake and Elwood came out to greet him, pads and gloves over their black suits. They carried bats under their arms like violin cases.

He'd persuaded the Blues Brothers—the name of their band—to return the truckload of gear in return for no money at all by simply explaining that the Roadshow's head of security was a professional killer. Jake and Elwood thought about this for a few days before showing up one night to say they'd found the van abandoned on the road, and wanted to return it to its rightful owner. Maxwell said the pair of them were splendid examples of all the finest aspirations of the American people. He rewarded them with jobs in the tour's road crew and had his photograph taken hugging them like a proud father. Lowe hoped the *Mirror*'s picture editor knew enough to crop Jake and Elwood's hands out of frame when the shot was printed, but few people in England understood the meaning of that extended middle-finger gesture.

"We're having our first ever cricket-ball game this afternoon," said Elwood. "Mr. Maxwell says we're to tell you that you're playing as well."

"Leave it out," groaned Lowe. All he wanted was a shower and a shave.

"Can't be worse than baseball," said Elwood, slashing dangerously at the air with his bat.

"Bloody can, you know," said Lowe.

"All out for *thirty-seven*," growled Maxwell. Practically incandescent with fury, he was beginning to sound alarmingly like his arsehole.

"I thought it all went rather well, actually," said Blair breezily, polishing a ball against his whites. "We get up a game against a scratch team of our American cousins and they win. Ought to make them more enthusiastic. More new. More energetic."

"We're not supposed to lose," said Maxwell. He had graced the game by deciding to captain the British team and had been bowled out for a duck. "It makes us look stupid. It makes *me* look stupid."

There was a summerhouse hidden in the grounds of Cord's mansion, which they used as a changing-room.

"No use crying over spilt milk," said the Rev. Bev, filling an embarrassed silence. "I'm looking forward to tucking into the cucumber sandwiches."

"You'll do nothing of the sort," fumed Maxwell, face almost purple. If he wasn't careful, thought Lowe, he'd have a coronary. It was just a question of whether his arsehole could hold out longer than his heart. "The game didn't last long. There's still plenty of time left. I'm going to demand a re-match."

"But..." said at least three people.

"I won't have arguments. I'm demanding a re-match," said Maxwell, picking up a bat and pointing it at Blair. "And I want to know how you propose to win this time?"

"I suppose we could start by putting them in to bat first," said Blair. "We'll have to give them everything we've got, get some good fast bowlers, throw a few googlies."

It was just possible that one or two of the locals might have played cricket before, but what had done for them was the homecoming queen, who'd been grenade-throwing champion of the women's branch of the New Mexico Military Reserve. Then, for all his hatred of baseball, Elwood turned out to be a demon batsman, notching up a whole over's worth of sixes against Penny's underarm bowling.

"Sir Robert," said Beverley, "I do think perhaps we should be a bit more sporting about this. Whether they beat us fairly or not, our hosts will think us terribly childish."

Maxwell threw his bat in impotent rage. It crashed through a window.

"I own the biggest-selling newspaper in Britain. I have a business empire with interests stretching around the globe. During the War, I killed Germans with my bare hands. A lot of them. But I can't organise a cricket team to beat a bunch of thick provincial Yanks. It makes me angry, and when I'm angry I'm very dangerous."

Someone somewhere out of Maxwell's view sniggered.

"Who was that?!" he roared.

Penny burst through the door. "Sir Robert," she said, "the local big-shots are just dying to meet you. I told them about your wartime exploits. They want to hear more about your adventures."

Maxwell harrumphed, brightened a little.

"Lowe," he said as he left. "You're still on sufferance. Don't think I'm going to forget those two easy catches you dropped. Now I want you to write a report on this game, and I want the result to be the correct one. Understand."

Flagstaff, Ariz.

Letter from America, by Joanna Houseman

A very strange place, is Flagstaff. Under the old regime, it was a resort; bigwigs from Arizona and even Texas owned ranches here, while the Party maintained a couple of hostels where quota-busting farm or factory workers would be rewarded with family holidays. Now, Flagstaff is a bizarre melting-pot for the desperate. Accommodation is cheap, if not actually free; ranches and resort cabins have been taken over by squatters. The owners are too far away and with too many worries of their own to go to the trouble of evicting them. Many squatters are stalled migrants, people on their way to California who ran out of gas (petrol), or suffered breakdowns (mechanical or otherwise), or just didn't feel like carrying on.

Most bizarre of all, Flagstaff has become a spiritual capital—the Glastonbury, if you will, of North America. Under the New Deal, First Americans started holding an annual "Pow-Wow" here in July. I don't know if the region is especially sacred to the Indians, but naturally the gatherings included medicine-men and shamans. These attracted the white kids and spiritual seekers. The streets are thick with American beetniki (known as "hippies") panhandling for "spare change" or handing out leaflets. They claim the Great Spirit or a spaceship or plain old Jesus Christ, is going to descend on Arizona any time now and take them all to a better place.

In the wake of the hippies came other zealots and charlatans. British and German Buddhists vie with Russian Hindus for pitches on street corners. The clean-cut, sinisterly wholesome Bavarian Catholic missionaries are the biggest act in town because they have the most money. About 2,000 people attend their midday prayer services for the free bread and soup afterwards. Danish Lutherans at least made themselves useful with a free clinic and contraceptive advice, but their HQ was fire-bombed last month. No one knows who did it, but everyone has a conspiracy theory.

The ones everyone keeps a wary eye on are the repellent Russian doomsday cultists, the *Khlysty* and the *Skoptzy*, who preach that the day of judgement is at hand. They occupy two ranches on the edge of town where they are rumoured to have regular orgies. To become a full initiate of either sect, however, the males have to castrate themselves. Sheriff

Robertson would dearly like to run the *Khlysty* and the *Skoptzy* out of town, but he has two deputies, four rifles, three pistols and not much ammunition. The bitter irony of this is that there used to be a huge military arsenal in Flagstaff until one night guards who hadn't been paid for two years were persuaded to look the other way. By the following morning, the arsenal had been emptied. By coincidence or not, the Russian cultists are extremely well-armed.

Both factions have American leaders: the *Khlysty* are represented by a fire-eyed prophet named Charles Manson, the *Skoptzy* by a guitar-playing egomaniac named David Koresh. Interestingly, both of these men were failed musicians before they discovered their religious calling. Neither man, by the way, is castrated; as leaders of the sects they have already "transcended" the temptations of the flesh.

"Yeah, sure," as Sheriff Robertson would say.

The Sheriff asked the Federal Government to send in help nine months ago, but the government has more pressing problems to see to. In the meantime, Manson and Koresh skirmish with each other, and the town trembles. Everyone in America talks about Apocalypse like the British talk about the weather. The sky is filled with signs and portents. Rumours of war fly thick. Dark strangers stalk the roads. Flagstaff is on People's Road 66, the mostly derelict interstate constructed under Capone for cross-country military traffic. All the signs have an extra "6" spray-painted in red. This is now PR 666.

Kingman, Ariz

The only car ahead was the antenna-festooned Bentley from which Maxwell controlled his empire. Further past, maybe a mile on, was what appeared to be a roadblock.

A motorcycle tore past them. William Brown wore dark glasses and black leather but no helmet. Slung across his back was a gun.

"SIG 540 machine-pistol," commented Lowe. "Swiss. Very expensive, very efficient. A cold little cutie from the cantons. Not quite state-of-the-art, though. An '80s thing. Brown's obviously a connoisseur."

In the back of the Roller, Penny stirred from reading a three-month old issue of The Lady. "I didn't have you marked down as a gun nut."

"I'm not. It's a legacy of one of several failed novels. I read up on guns when I was trying to write a best-seller a few years ago, about an attempt to assassinate the French President-Chairman Jean-Luc Godard. Wasn't such a bad stab, too. Got up to page 70 before binning it."

Brown stopped up ahead in the middle of the road, signalled to Maxwell's driver to slow right down, then rode back past the convoy like a hired gun marshalling a wagon-train.

"Are we in trouble?" said Penny.

"Hard to say. Someone up at the front wants us to stop. Maybe the local boss wants us to pay the toll."

"There's a gun hidden under the glove-compartment," she said.

"I know."

He'd accidentally found the Czech vz61 Skorpion gaffer-taped under the walnut dashboard when rooting around on the floor for a dropped cigarette. Just ten inches long, it was a little war all by itself. "If we need it, we're probably already dead. Better trust in God almighty and William Brown."

There was a clicking noise from the back seat. He glanced in the mirror in time to see her push the chrome-plated and pearl-handled Tokarev automatic back into her handbag.

"This, my dear, is why I'm an aristocrat and you're not. We're always ready to fight. It's how my ancestors seized your ancestors' land, livestock, women and dignity."

Maxwell's car slowed to 20mph. Brown's bike rumbled past them once more and on towards the roadblock.

A distant throbbing noise rapidly grew louder. In a few moments, two matt black helicopters hovered overhead, no more than 30 feet from the ground. The car shuddered in the rotor down-draught. Dust swirled all around.

Both the huge black insects carried missile-pods, and had sinister arrangements of gun-barrels beneath their noses. Chain-guns. The helicopters hovered over the road just in front of the roadblock. Tumbleweed twisted in with the sand-storm. Brown rode his bike into the dust.

The helicopters landed, side-on, to either side of the road.

Maxwell's car pulled to a halt. Lowe stopped the Roller, pulled the handbrake and shut off the engine. His hip-flask was on the passenger-seat. He reached for it, unscrewed the top and offered it to Penny.

"No thanks," she said.

The *absinthe* burned his throat. He thought of taking a second slug, then thought again. The dust in front of the choppers was thinning.

Brown had parked his bike in front of them and was walking back towards Maxwell's car accompanied by a tall, muscular blonde man in an olive green uniform

He'd never seen the infamous black helicopters before, but knew them now.

"Put the safety-catch back on, Penny. We're in friendly hands."

"I never took it off. Who are they?"

"The United Nations."

As if on cue, the man in green pulled a sky blue beret from the pocket of his immaculately-ironed trousers and put it on.

Two years ago, during a Russian general election campaign, Menshevik incumbent Mikhail Gorbachev—his administration undermined by allegations of corruption, mismanagement and incompetence—had tried to wrest back the moral high ground by getting together with the British Prime Minister, the EU and the United Nations to declare a "New World Order". The world's leaders committed themselves to a visionary plan to eradicate world poverty and hunger and protect human rights.

It was 99% electioneering bluster, of course (and for Gorbachev, it worked), but probably achieved some good in a few places. The EU and Russia put a few million quid into development projects and a lot of earnest, serious young university graduates signed up for Voluntary Service Overseas. Hospitals, dairies, water purification plants, fish canneries and concrete factories got built in various parts of Africa and Asia. Gorbachev twisted Ewing's arm to let UN human rights monitors into certain American states.

And here they were.

"Time to be a reporter," said Lowe, getting out of the car.

The UN presence had probably prevented several massacres and minor local wars, but most Yanks regarded it as an ultimate humiliation. At first, the UN sent unarmed civilians in Land Rovers: some witnessed things they didn't live long enough to report. Then, Ewing was pressured into allowing the UN to deploy heavily-armed soldiers in distinctively unmarked black helicopters.

More or less everyone believed the story that the statue of Abe in Washington's Lincoln Memorial cried tears of blood on the day the first UN troops arrived. Lots of Americans—some of them otherwise intelligent individuals—believed the story that Gorbachev's New World Order was in fact a Jewish conspiracy to enslave or wipe out honest

Americans. The black choppers were paving the way, reconnoitring the best places to land the invasion army and set up the extermination camps.

"This is Colonel van Damme, of the Belgian army. He commands a mixed Belgian and Irish unit operating in this area." Brown introduced the big man to Maxwell. The Colonel saluted and said something in French. Maxwell embraced the startled officer, and one of the staff photographers emerged from Maxwell's car to take pictures of the historic event. Van Damme writhed in the tycoon's bear-hug and presented a cheeky grin to the camera, turning to show off his profile and jaunty cap.

Another man walked up. A slightly chubby youngster with thick black hair and eyebrows. He wore a slightly outlandish sky-blue uniform.

Lowe introduced himself to the younger man.

"Scott Tracy," said the man in an American accent. "International Rescue."

They watched Colonel Van Damme dazzle the photographers, while Maxwell tried to get into the pictures. The Colonel hopped up on the roadblock and did the splits between two trestles, grinning like Sabu in *The Thief of Bagdad*.

"You're an American?" Lowe said to Tracy.

"We Tracys prefer to think of ourselves as citizens of the world," he said, letting the accent slip towards something more British-sounding.

"International Rescue?"

"Specialists in the prevention or relief of accidents and disasters."

He couldn't decide if young Tracy was an arrogant little prick or just a bit on the serious side.

"What are you doing with the UN?"

"Helping whatever way we can. We have some special equipment. Excavation and lifting gear. We're only semi-officially here, but the Colonel seems to find us useful."

"What's your business around here?"

Tracy pointed towards the gentle slope away from the road. In the yellowish-grass, something shiny caught the light, an affair of spokes and chrome tubes. There were UN men poking around.

Lowe and Tracy strolled.

Lowe's stomach flipped as he realised what he was looking at. In the grass were the tangled relics of a pair of motorcycles. The petrol tanks had exploded, and there was a brown burned patch.

"Been here for a while," Tracy said. "Days."

Green blankets had been thrown over two man-shaped patches.

A Belgian brought something to show Tracy. It was a crash helmet painted with the Stars and Stripes and the Hammer and Scythe. There was a ragged hole in it.

"Good marksmanship," Tracy commented. "Especially with a moving target. And probably fired from a vehicle too. You all right?"

Lowe's stomach was upside-down, and bars of bright black and orange ran across his vision. He held his knees and willed himself not to be sick.

"I knew them. No. I met them. Once. There were three. Billy, Wyatt and…some other name."

"Only two here. The other one'll show up somewhere. We see this all the time. Crime of opportunity. Hippies on bikes come into view, there's a shotgun under the dashboard, nobody cares about road flotsam, so why not score a couple of kills? Bam bam bam. Yank bastards."

Evidently, young Tracy was not an American after all.

Two men lifted one of the bike skeletons up. There was a bullet-hole in the gas tank.

"Maybe it's this stretch of road?" Tracy said.

"What do you mean?" Lowe asked.

He gently escorted Lowe past the motorcycles. They went down an incline and up a slope, then crested what seemed at first like an archaeological dig. A crater of bare earth was being picked over by men with cloth masks and rubber gloves.

"We'd never have found it if it weren't for the easy riders."

Lowe saw the bones. They were recent enough not to come easily away from the bodies. The UN and International Rescue were sorting it all out. Skulls were arranged neatly in groups of ten. There was a central collection point for spectacles, wallets, intact clothing, shoes, papers. Anything that might be of use in identification.

There was a dry, nasty smell. Dust was blowing from the crater, across the road.

"What happened?" Lowe asked, the journo's most feeble question.

"Seems that two years ago a few hundred Oklahomans settled themselves in a valley just inside Californ-i-ay, raised a few crops, minded their own business. Someone rounded the Okies up, took 'em over the border and killed the lot of 'em. Some of them were shot, some were beaten or stabbed. I guess whoever did it didn't want to waste too many bullets. Hence, this mass grave here."

"Any idea who did it?"

Tracy shook his head. "Not yet. But Colonel van Damme will find out. Might be one of the So-Cal militias, might be a landowner tried to drive them out."

Most of the skulls were crushed. Lowe tried to envision it, but couldn't. Some damper in his imagination cut in. He could conceive of the bikers being shot dead, one then another. It was horror, but he could see it. Two shots, an explosion, corpses by the road, waiting to be found. He could conceive of ten, a dozen, twenty, more, dying in a battle, a brisk firefight and casualties all over the ground. He had seen traffic pile-ups on these People's Roads, attended executions, watched a couple of shoot-outs, witnessed murders. But this was outside the scope of his understanding.

Two hundred people.

How long did it take? Were the murderers efficient and dispassionate, or hysterical and sadistic? Did someone think it out and give orders— that touch about not wasting bullets suggested calculation—or did the killers just keep on killing until the job was done? Was it a job, or a crusade, or a spasm of hate, or a natural phenomenon like sunspots?

Two hundred people.

Lowe took out a pack of Strands and offered them. Tracy looked faintly disdainful as he refused. He still couldn't figure this guy out; serious, cool professional, or fucking boy-scout? Then he notices that Tracy's hands were shaking, just like his own. That was sort of comforting.

"Do the perpetrators get punished?" asked Lowe.

"The ringleaders are supposed to be handed over to the Federal Government for trial. But first you have to catch them. Even then, Federal Prosecutors are often reluctant to bring suit. They're all related to each other."

"People who commit crimes like this get off scot-free?"

"Not always," said Tracy. "The way I hear it, the Irish-Belgian UN battalion takes a very pro-active approach to its own self-defence. I'd say that Colonel van Damme would regard whoever did this as a threat to his unit's safety. Action will probably be taken to eliminate that threat."

"What about the due process of law? A fair trial and all that?"

Tracy shrugged. "As one of the Irish officers said to me, 'there's no justice, there's just us'."

The wind whistled, blowing the corpse dust back at the Roadshow. The convoy of lorries, buses, low-loaders and cars stretched out about a quarter of mile behind them. Tracy asked what was going on, and Lowe told him in neutral tones about Captain Bob's travelling circus.

The young man whistled. "That's insane."

Lowe looked at the neat piles of dented skulls. Their eyesockets looked at him. Turquoise glowworms writhed in the shadow-circles.

In a few more minutes, these bones would walk around.

Lowe didn't want to be here for that.

He didn't want hallucinations, but he didn't want this reality either. He didn't want more *absinthe*, but he knew he needed it.

The worst of it was the short bones, the skulls no bigger than apples. Men, women, kids.

Maxwell stood nearby, still talking to, no, talking at, Colonel van Damme. He had the upper hand, because he controlled the photographer. Van Damme's grin was like ice about to crack.

"You're a reporter, right?," said Tracy. "Report this. Tell the folks back home what a grand job the UN are doing. The poor soldiers never get any thanks for anything. Tell the tax-payers something else, too. They're not vigilantes or hired killers, but sometimes they do unpleasant things to stop matters getting worse. Tell your readers this poor damn country is being crucified by ignorance, greed and hate. Tell them not to let the politicians pull the troops out. We're the only hope people like these ragged bones used to be have got."

Lowe nodded. He'd heard the Danish Lutherans say the same back in Flagstaff. He heard Maxwell say something similar every day. America was dying from the attention of too many doctors, each with a different cure.

Up ahead, the rotors on the helicopters started up. The Land Rovers blocking the road were backed away. Van Damme saluted Maxwell and Brown and strode off.

"So long, then," nodded Tracy.

The kid was probably right, but Maxwell wasn't about to let Lowe write anything on mass-graves. Being rocketed by Sir Bob for depressing *Mirror* readers would be bad enough, but what he wouldn't be able to take would be dealing with Blair's hurt and disappointed tones for "negative reporting".

But he had next week's *Lilliput* column, no problem. He doubted if he could think of many Okie massacre jokes, but the humour seemed to be leeching out of Joanna Houseman as she travelled further along PR 666.

Maxwell seemed unaware of the burying ground a few yards away from his convoy. He'd had his photo taken with some heroes, and that's what the *Mirror* readers were interested in. Lowe remembered Billy's grin and Hanson's—that was the name—rolling eyes. And he imagined the others, the two hundred individuals shovelled under out here in the nowhere.

Lowe got back into the Roller and started the engine. Penny sat in the back, and picked up her magazine again.

Maxwell's car moved forward. Lowe put the Roller into gear and drove.

"What in heaven's name are we doing here?"

"Earning a living the only way we can," said Penny, without looking up from her magazine.

Barstow, Calif

The nearer you got to the Pacific, the more the edge of America frayed. Before they crossed into California, William Brown told everyone to travel in groups of at least four. Barstow, though, he said was okay. A sheriff had brought law and order to the town. Lowe didn't like to think what the rest of the state was like.

It was early evening, and they were heading for the Roadshow to do their bit.

"Not as shabby as some of the places we've been through lately," he admitted.

"It's feudal," said Penny, looking across the road at a busy-sounding saloon. A sign at the entrance said (in English and Spanish) that all weapons were to be left with the gun-check girl at the door.

"How so?" said Lowe.

The saloon looked tempting, but kind of rough.

"All the townsfolk have been telling us Barstow has law and order. This, as I understand it, is thanks to the activities of the town sheriff, a mysterious stranger who came in, shot some local trouble-makers and is now hailed as a wise and just ruler."

"I didn't think that there was anything wise and just about the feudal system."

Two of the townsfolk, elderly gentlemen in Stetson hats sitting on the porch of the dry goods store, wished them a good evening.

"There isn't and that's not what I meant," said Penny. "People are moving into Barstow from outlying areas because the Man with No Name will protect them. They accord him respect, give him so much of their money or produce, and he protects them. The feudal system was exactly the same."

"You make it all sound so simple."

"It is," she said, as they turned a corner. "There's nothing more simple" —she pointed—"than that."

In the middle of the street, the corpse of a man dangled from a gibbet. Around his neck hung a sign, "SHEEP-RUSTLER AND THEEF". His boots had been stolen, and fungussy dead toes poked through holes in his socks.

A lorry swerved past them and pulled up. In the back were stacked the biggest amplifiers Lowe had ever seen. Elwood leaned out of the cab, ignoring the grotesque display further on.

"Evening, pilgrims!" he called. "Coming to the show this evening? I'll see to it you get VIP seats."

Jake leaned across his brother's lap. "He ain't talking about the Maxwell show. Bob fired us for rustling his lobsters." Jake maraca-rattled a pair of claws. "We're putting on a show of our own. Got the old band together."

"Be just like old times," grinned Elwood.

"Be a damn sight better than listening to that hundred-year-old crooner Cliffy or the mad preacher or Maxwell telling us we should start our own businesses."

"Even more fun than cricket," said Elwood.

"Are you sure it's wise to annoy Sir Robert like this?" said Lowe. "I expect he's bought the sheriff of this town. And the sheriff, from what I can see, is very keen on law and order."

He pointed to the corpse, swaying gently in the breeze.

"We'll be fine," laughed Elwood. "It was the sheriff loaned us these babies. There's an old military depot in town. Them's Marine battlefield amplifiers. Supposed to be for broadcasting propaganda and inviting the enemy to surrender. You can hear 'em 30 miles away. Don't be late now, y'hear. We're on a mission from God."

In the marquee at the back of the stage, what passed for local society was tucking into sausage rolls and Penny was trying, and failing, to start a conversation with the Sheriff. He stood still as a rock, polite, not bored, just not very talkative. He looked like a hobo, in his tattered cowboy hat and a filthy poncho. Sir Cliff was onstage. Back here, behind the PA, a distorted, bass-heavy "Bachelor Boy" rumbled, but not so loud that you couldn't hold a conversation.

Lowe held a half-hearted chat about politics with Mr. Blair. The PR man was thinking of standing as a Lib-Lab candidate in the council elections when he got home, but wondered if he wasn't too young for the burden of office. Blair never said anything without qualifying it, as if all his remarks were going to be quoted back at him at the tribunal. Lowe wanted to ask him what his position was on mass murder. "On the one hand, it's very bad. But on the other..."

Everyone was saying Alan Clark's government was so unpopular that the next general election would see John Noakes in Number 10; but the Tories had been in power since World War Two. It had been predicted that they would lose each and every general election that came along, until a last-minute landslide kept the Opposition in opposition and the Conservatives in power.

Lowe realised he was experiencing slight pangs of jealousy about Penny and the Man with No Name. Sure, they'd told one another this affair was expedient. She'd told him she had no strings attached, but...

He kept trying to edge closer to Penny, Blair occasionally taking a step to keep up with him. Blair reckoned Noakes was PM material, but had doubts about the Lib sidekick, David Icke, who had taken to wearing white robes at the hustings and sometimes claimed to be God.

"Bachelor Boy" finished. Cliff thanked the audience, which ran to several thousand people sitting out here on the edge of the desert. He began "My Old Man's a Dustman", but another, louder noise started up. High-ish chords on an electric guitar tore the night air, backed by a fast tom-tom beat. Cliff was entirely drowned.

"Good EEEE-vening, Barstow!"

The voice didn't sound like Jake or Elwood.

The Sheriff's immobile, granite face momentarily cracked upwards. "He's here," Lowe heard him say, as much to himself as to Penny. "Excuse me, Ma'am. I've gotta go."

Jake and Elwood had set up their rival attraction about half a mile away, but their battlefield amplification easily squelched Sir Cliff. On stage, the eternal cheeky lad looked as if he would cry.

"Bloody shame," Lowe smiled, going over to Penny.

"You're just jealous. You thought I was trying to seduce the Sheriff." She was watching the Sheriff's slim shanks scissor as he strode away.

"I didn't mean that."

"I don't see what's so funny," said Blair. "After all the trouble Sir Cliff's been to to bring some British pep to this dried-up desert."

"*If you knew...*" sang the voice half a mile away.

"Good grief!" blurted Lowe. "I know who that is!"

"*...Peggy Sue...*"

Penny arched her eyebrow.

"That's Charles Hardin Holley. Penny, Mr. Blair, talk about pep! That man is a legend. The Blues Brothers have brought Charlie Holley to town. You have got to see this!"

Sir Cliff and his band descended from the stage, shrugging. They made for the food and drink. Maxwell waddled in at speed. "Just what the hell do you think you're doing, Bachelor Boy? You're not finished yet. Get back out there and play. Turn everything up."

"It's up as far as it can go," said Sir Cliff politely. "We can't compete with that rig."

"Get on stage at once!" Maxwell yelled. Cliff shrugged and led the band back towards the stage. "Brown, I want you to put a stop to that other racket."

Brown appeared out of shadows and shook his head. Maxwell looked as though his brain was about to burst.

"The Sheriff approves," said Brown quietly.

Maxwell roared.

Outside, the crowd drifted toward the Blues Brothers show in a single, quiet and compact mass. Lowe dragged Penny along. For all his protest, Blair came with them.

The Blues Brothers' stage was a huge scaffold in the middle of the desert, sited at the bottom of a gentle slope. Behind it, at least half a dozen generators fed power to the enormous amps and to a few lights. Up ahead, as Holley played through his best-known song—the first to get banned by the Communist Party back in the 1950s—people had already reached the front of the stage and were dancing.

"I think this is far enough," said Lowe. "We get too near, we'll be deafened."

He took off his jacket and spread it on the ground. Penny sat on it. He sat next to her. He took out his hip-flask, she produced a bottle of Vimto and some plastic cups. Lowe turned to Blair to ask him if he wanted a drink, but he stood there, smile fixed across his face like a cut throat, lost in the music, nodding his head back and forth like he was praying at the Wailing Wall.

"Beats 'Bachelor Boy', doesn't it?" he yelled, but Blair couldn't hear him.

The crowd applauded wildly as Holley wrapped the song up. The tiny figures of Jake and Elwood appeared quite distinct in mid-stage and bowed. Other musicians appeared. A brass section. Then a pianist.

At a signal from Elwood, two trumpets, bass, drums and piano burst into a tune every American over the age of ten knew better than the national anthem.

"My socialist heart," sang Elwood, *"will play its socialist part..."*

The song was a huge hit for Sinatra back in the early '50s. The party suits were worried about it when it first came out, because they weren't sure it was altogether respectful.

"Wanna be a good loyal communist, increase the quota of lips I've kissed..."

In Chairman Capone's eyes, Sinatra could do no wrong. He was an Italian from Hoboken and an official Friend of the Friends. Even without talent, he'd have been the USSA's most popular singer. Nobody knew whether Sinatra was being ironic or not.

"Wanna look into your reflective eyes," Holley took up the verse, *"let's you and me collectivise."*

Irony became fashionable in Capone's America. Once Chairman Al died and the threat of late night visits from the FBI and the rumours of dissenters being tortured to death in deep underground cells started to recede, it became the national religion. That was what made the song so popular.

"Whenever you are standing near," sang Holley, *"I wanna be a good little pioneer."*

Holley passed it to the horns, who blew a break fit to blast you into the middle of next week. At the end of it, the audience clapped, cheered and held up lit matches.

"Remember folks," announced Holley over a drum and bass holding pattern, "it ain't over 'til the fat guy sings!"

Jake came forward. *"Come on baby, be a smartie...Let's you and me form a vanguard party...Come on baby, what do you say...Let's tell this whole big beautiful USSA!"*

The band wrapped it up, the military amps fell silent for a moment. The roar of the crowd reminded Lowe of the time he'd watched Accrington Stanley take the F.A. Cup at Wembley. Even poor Mr. Blair was jumping up and down, clapping, saying, "Oh really good show! Quite splendid!"

"Whoo! Thank you, thank you," said Jake, waddling around the stage, jerking arms and legs this way and that. He might have been possessed by one of Beverley's angels. "Did you hear that, you jerk, Bobby Fatwell?"

"Yeah!" said Elwood. "Any day of the week, my socialist heart can whup your capitalist ass!"

The crowd agreed. "Oh dear!" said Blair quietly. Penny clapped enthusiastically. It took Lowe a moment to realise he was clapping, too.

"Strap yourselves in folks," said Elwood. "We're going to party— *awwwll niiiight llooong!!*"

San Bernardino, Calif.

He was out ahead again, on his own. That made it worse. He'd have liked to ask Penny if she was seeing what he thought he was seeing. The driving was slow, because of the objects strewn across a lot of the roads.

Some of the offices and shops were boarded up, as though by people who were planning to come back. A lot of the houses back in the suburbs had just been left. Curtains flapped out of broken windows. Screen-doors slammed back and forth. There were abandoned cars. Faded smiles, pock-marked with rips, beamed from out-of-date advertisements.

Lowe drove in slow motion. Dust blew across the windscreen, and he had to use the automatic wipers. The few feeble squirts of water turned the dust to grit. The wipers scraped.

He was seriously spooked.

It wasn't as though the place had been left to rot. To rot, you needed moisture, and that was the one thing there didn't seem to be any supply of.

Lowe was thirsty.

It was only when he parked the car outside the boarded-up main post office that Lowe was certain this really was a ghost-town. His copy of the *Rough Guide to America*, admittedly five years old, put the population of San Bernardino at 165,000. Driving in, he hadn't seen a soul. However, he couldn't shake the feeling that he was being watched.

The eyes in posters moved as he passed.

In a place like this, you could be jumped by bandits and left lying in the middle of the street. It would have been best just to drive away, back to the safety in numbers of the Roadshow, the sheltering arm of William Brown and his matt black Swiss machine-gun.

Curiosity got the better of him. He wrenched the Skorpion from under the dashboard, peeled off the tape and got out of the car. He pretended to himself that he was Agent 007 of SMERSH, coolly proficient with deadly weapons.

There weren't even any dogs or cats. Maybe there weren't even any rats. Nothing to eat.

He walked up to the door of the post office and peered through a crack in the boarding. Inside, it looked neat and orderly enough. Next to the door was a peeling sign giving the times of collections and deliveries of mail. But he didn't think there'd be a coded message from John Lennon waiting for him here.

Further along the sidewalk was a large bar. MURPHY'S SHEBEEN, said the sign, which had shamrocks to either side of it. Evidently an Irish-style bar that had sprung up during the New Deal with no more success than Limey Louie's. This, too, had been boarded up. Peering through a crack, he saw the place was neat and tidy. Tables and chairs had been stacked against one wall. The bar was empty, no broken glass anywhere, no signs of looting. Whoever had left Murphy's had not left in a desperate hurry. The abandonment of San Berdoo had been orderly and deliberate. Which probably ruled out radioactive or chemical contamination.

He looked around for mutant gila monsters. There were none. The only truly monstrous thing to hand was a life-sized plastic cut-out of a happy family with very white teeth. It was advertising Freedom, a British company which ostensibly sold toiletries and household cleaning materials, but which was in reality a pyramid-selling scheme which relied on members recruiting new "representatives" all the time. Thousands of Americans had put everything they had into the scheme and its "business excellence" and "customer service" courses only to lose it all when the scheme went belly-up.

No sign of life anywhere. He peered through the doors of the bar again.

"I'm afraid you're going to have to search a little further afield if you want a drink."

The man was between him and the sun. A black shadowshape. He tried to cock the machine-gun and instead got the muzzle tangled in his shirt cuff.

"You're obviously lacking in skill-at-arms, old fellow."

The accent, amazingly, was English. Upper class.

The stranger was elderly and dapper, hankie folded in his pocket, wearing a panama hat. He looked just like Alec Guinness in the film of Graham Greene's *Our Man in Marseilles*.

"I'm sorry," said Lowe, still trying to untangle the gun from his clothes. "You startled me."

"Are you British?"

Lowe got a good look at the old gent.

"Good grief, I know who you are."

The man smiled.

"Really? I should think I'd been forgotten a while ago. I am pleased, though. They remember Guy Fawkes, so they should remember me. Gunpowder, treason and plot and all that."

It was Harold "Kim" Philby. The diplomat, then journalist, but always the spy. The traitor.

"So you know who I am. That means you're a diplomat, a journalist, or that you've come to kill me. Are you here to settle accounts?" Philby asked.

"No, of course not. I need to air-mail something to England."

Joanna Houseman's latest column.

The man was amused.

"You won't be able to do it here."

It hit Lowe that William Brown might indeed have come all this way to tidy up a loose end like Philby. Philby had done a bunk in 1977, leaving chaos and scandal in his wake. It was suggested that, through Philby and others, Britain's post-war intelligence service had almost entirely been run from Debs, D.C. Yet another occasion on which the government had almost been brought down.

"I seem to have backed the wrong side," Philby said, smiling almost regretfully. "The Yanks have kept me in what they think of as the lap of luxury out here in the land of the orange. But now I must be something of an embarrassment. Well, no, to tell the truth, I've been forgotten."

"Did they all leave town to get away from you?"

Philby laughed.

"Oh, no. Nice thought. The British turncoat oversleeps one day, and wakes up to find everyone has sneaked out at night. Not like that at all, I'm afraid. I'm not the only relic here, by the way. There are a few other retired gentlemen pottering around empty haciendas, missing their houseboys and their gin fizzes."

"What happened?"

Philby shrugged. "You know what the most valuable commodity is in California?"

"Guns? Oil? Gold bullion? Teenage girls?"

"Water. Just old-fashioned H_2O. Some months ago, someone came from out of town with some hired guns, bought the mayor and cut off the city's water supply. She says the water is hers."

"And that someone is…?"

"You are a hack, aren't you?"

It was Lowe's turn to shrug.

There was a faint rumbling sound. They both looked. Something further up the street was raising the dust. Vehicles. A lot of them, coming through quickly.

"I'd lose that thing if I were you, old boy," said Philby, glancing towards the Skorpion. Lowe laid the gun down on the sidewalk, behind the happy Freedom family.

The roar of the vehicles grew nearer.

"It's a very long, dull story," said Philby, "but I've had little to do in my retirement but study the queerer eddies of American history. The water-snatcher is a perfectly sweet, but curiously twisted, old dear named Katherine Mulwray. Her grandfather—or father as some say—was Noah Cross, whom you might remember as the most reptilian of the pre-Revolutionary robber barons. Old Noah—apt name, all considered—fled the country in '18, leaving behind a huge amount of property. Little Katie hobbled back to America during the New Deal to buy herself a private army of Nicaraguans and ex-Marines and reclaim what she called "her rightful inheritance". Which means stealing back the things the reds stole from Noah that he stole from some cowboys who stole it from the Spanish who stole from the Indians, who robbed the Heavens to found this golden land. Noah allegedly bought San Berdoo's water in 1912."

Lowe's thirst was growing. He could taste the powdery dust in his throat. Philby stood in the open sun, almost transparent, like a ghost.

"But why cut off the supply? If it was money she was after, why didn't she just raise the price?"

"She doesn't want money."

"Eh?"

"She wants the future, Mr. Lowe. The future." Philby shouted over the noise of two dozen powerful engines.

They were Russian-built Moskvich pick-up trucks, big wide-bottomed low-slung things that held a low profile and couldn't be knocked over easily. Each one mounted either a heavy machine-gun or an anti-tank rocket launcher. They were camouflage-painted in a garish mixture of yellows, browns, oranges and pinks. The men driving them or sitting in the back of them were casual, but alert-looking, all wearing the same khaki fatigues and slouch hats. They were not the usual crowd of redneck cut-throats, all piss and wind. This lot would have had Rommel's *Afrika Korps* for breakfast.

And they were stopping.

"I think we're about to be graced with a visit from Miss Mulwray," said Philby.

Half the convoy pulled up further along the street. A green Land Rover stopped opposite them. A sprightly old lady in paisley headscarf, green wellies and Barbour jacket jumped out. Without the immense mirrorshades, she would have looked like the wife of a gentleman-farmer off to the County Stores for the week's groceries.

She smiled at Philby, but with her eyes hidden behind the glasses there was no telling what the smile meant.

There was a commotion in the back of the Land Rover. Two, maybe three dogs started barking.

"Oh do shut up, you lot," she shouted back over her shoulder. Her accent was even more plummy-Brit than Philby's.

The Land Rover's little tailgate burst open, the canvas flapped and a man rolled out and fell to the road. His wrists and ankles were bound with what appeared to be razor wire. Two immense Alsatian dogs jumped out after him and growled at him. He was covered in dried blood and bruises.

Miss Mulwray sighed in exasperation. Two of her soldiers ran up, kicked the man several times and bundled him back into the truck.

"Caught him trying to steal water up in the hills," she said. Her tone was sorry-for-the-inconvenience apologetic. "Well anyway, good morning, Mr. Philby."

"And a very good morning to you, Miss Mulwray. I must say you're looking very well today."

"Stuff and nonsense, man," she said. "This old biddy's not long for this world. Who's your friend?"

"This is Mr. Lowe. He arrived here hoping to find somewhere to post a letter but found it was early closing day. He and I have been passing the time of day. He's British, you know."

"Are you really?" she said, advancing towards him, mouth cracked into a fixed half-smile. "And this must be your car?" she pointed to the Roller parked further back.

"Alas no, ma'am." he said, breaking unconsciously into the sort of tones he'd use with royalty. "I am merely a chauffeur. The car belongs to someone else."

"The only person I know who drives a pink Rolls-Royce is Penny Ward," she said. "She's not here by any chance is she?"

The old dear was mad. She had emptied a town out and had her own private army. Lowe knew that for her every question would have a right and a wrong answer. If, by any chance, Miss Mulwray didn't like Penny she could have Captain's Bob's entire roadshow slaughtered. It reminded him of the night he was stopped by a gang of lads on the streets of Glasgow and asked if he was Catholic or Protestant, Rangers or Celtic. Arsenal Atheist wouldn't have done.

"She is," he said. "I'm her driver."

Protestant. Rangers.

"Are you *really*," she brayed in a completely authentic county set voice. It figured. Miss Mulwray would have spent most, if not all, of her life as an exile in England and old Noah Cross would have taken plenty of his White Yank gold with him when he'd fled.

"Tell her we simply must meet up while she's over here," said Miss Mulwray. "She and I weren't exactly part of the same set, but I always remember her as one of the nice aristos. Never looked down her nose at me like some of 'em. Now here's my card. Tell her to call me soon."

Lowe took the card. It had her name in copperplate and a mobile phone number.

"Now Harold," she turned to Philby, "are you alright for water?"

"Yes thanks," said Philby brightly. "Your man with his tanker comes by my little cottage three times a week."

"Good." she said. "I like to see the tenants looked after."

The dogs jumped out of the Land Rover once more. She bent down and fussed over them, then briskly commanded them to get into the vehicle's cab with her.

Miss Mulwray and her convoy left as suddenly as they had appeared.

Lowe sighed. "Mr. Philby, what the hell is she about?

Philby smiled and shrugged. "Look around. What do you see? An immense piece of property with vacant possession. At the moment, California is falling to pieces along with the rest of the country. But there's an independence movement. If California becomes independent, kills enough of its trouble-makers and resists becoming Northern Mexico, it has the potential to be a very wealthy place. Wouldn't you like to own a whole city in a prosperous state the size of Great Britain? Every last house, shop, office, factory and patch of land here can be bought for a fraction of the price people would have sold out for even a year ago. And Miss Mulwray is sitting on it all, like a mother dinosaur waiting for her eggs to hatch. Who could have foreseen that the extinct species would return? I myself am looking forward to a brief spell as a tiny, hopping mammal in some Jurassic park. When I get noticed, I'll get eaten by the big robber reptiles. You can understand why I thought you were to be my executioner."

"But…But she's an old lady. Has she any children to leave it all to?"

"Not that I know of."

"But that's the most insane thing I've heard all…Well, all day."

"On the surface, you'd think that she wants to own all this land. In truth, she's not all that bothered about owning it. What she wants, what she really wants, is not to have the land belong to her, she wants to belong to the land. She's an elderly White Yank come back from a lifetime's exile in a place where she was made to feel she didn't belong. Now she's back, now she's going to found a great city, and nothing can take that future away from her. Trust me, Mr. Lowe, I'm an exile myself. I understand. She knows I do—that's why she lets me live here. That and the fact that I proved such an embarrassment to the English establishment that cut her dead for all those years."

Cliff Richard was a velvet-collared choir-boy. His backing band were Philby's velociraptors, reptilian things with long tails, scaly skin and row upon row of sharp teeth. Lowe wondered if he should be frightened, but instead he found it funny.

"Do share the joke," said Penny in slow-motion.

Sir Cliff sang with surprising gusto and professionalism, given that he didn't have an audience.

"Sorry," said Lowe. "I've started seeing things."

"Not really surprising," said Penny. "Another Meltdown?"

"Don't mind if I do. After all, we may not be the young ones very long."

He held out his glass. Penny filled it with bottled Vimto from her cool-box and added half a gill of *Chernobyl*.

They sat on the baked mud about 150 yards from the stage, picnicked out on a tartan rug. They had a clear view, sharing the area with maybe twenty locals—crawled out like Philby from under their rocks—and around a hundred other members of the Roadshow. All the others were busy manning their stalls. Blair trying to sell cricketing gear, two dozen others selling or promoting the best of British culture and commerce to a non-existent population. The fastest seller, unsurprisingly was bottled Malvern water, actually brackish New Mexico tap-water refilling empty bottles.

Nobody had even bothered objecting when Maxwell insisted that, population or no population, the show should go on. Lowe had cornered William Brown to tell him about Katherine Mulwray and her private army. Brown had shrugged. "She won't be interested in this. And she won't tolerate any other bandits in the area. We're safe." It was the most that Lowe had ever heard him say.

The stage began to rot. Like a time-lapse film of a wilting flower, it started to go yellow, then brown and crinkly at the edges.

"How can that happen?" Lowe asked aloud. "I mean, it's night. The edges of the stage are dark. I wouldn't be able to tell what colour they are."

Pieces of the stage floated gently to the ground. The big Vimto banner at the top shrivelled. But no matter how much fell off, the structure seemed to remain fully intact.

Sir Cliff and the band played "Congratulations". Lowe didn't know what a congratulation looked like, but there appeared to be one of them flying from the stage towards him. Just as the congratulation was about to hit him in the face, just as he shielded his eyes with his arm, it burst on his nose like a soap-bubble.

Uh-oh! Here came more congratulations! These wouldn't be nice bubble ones like the first. These would be the evil congratulations. They were going to hurt him. They swarmed like locusts and came for him.

"Stop whimpering," said Penny. "It's time we got you to bed."

He shook his head. The congratulations had gone.

"You're right," he said. "I've much too had."

But then if you were in an area with no water and you were bored, what else was there to do but drink Vimto and *absinthe* all day?

The hotel had been deserted. The Roadshow had simply taken the place over like an invading army. Brown explained that toilets could be flushed with sand.

Penny helped him through the door of his room. There was a large envelope on the floor just inside the door.

The envelope snarled at him, became an angry Rottweiler. Its back was a satanic black colour, its belly the colour of shit, it smelled like a dying man with halitosis and its huge yellow and brown-stained teeth glistened. Saliva dripped from its jaws.

"Don't touch it," he said to Penny.

"Nonsense, it's just an envelope," she said, swiping it up off the floor. "You're just hallucinating."

He shook his head. "I'm not sure I am."

Los Angeles, Cal.

"So when do we get to Los Angeles?" Penny asked.

"We've been there for three hours."

She looked out at the bungalows lining the boulevards.

"It looks like Surbiton with palm trees."

"And guns."

The Roadshow had picked up motorcycle escorts from the LAPD, who wore reflective silvered sunglasses and enough black leather to induce instant orgasm in an SS officer. Each officer was adorned with an amazing variety of chrome-shiny weaponry.

"If I'd brought along my *I Spy Book of Firearms*, I could tick off the lot." Penny laughed.

Lowe was worried. The LA cops were made of liquid metal and black leather, and kept changing shape with oily, serpentine sneakiness. If they took off their glasses, they'd have sewn-shut eyes.

Los Angeles was like the Balkans in 1912, a collection of mutually hostile fiefdoms packed with trigger-happy trouble-makers out to set off the big one.

Just before the New Deal, the Junior Communist League schismed into two feuding "vanguards", the Hammers and the Scythes. Barely half a decade later, the original vanguardists were mostly dead of violence, but their younger brothers and sisters (or children) had taken their place and, augmenting their pocket money with protection rackets and drug deals, had stocked up on military hardware.

Without the cop escort, the Roadshow would have been raided by one or other of the big vanguards, and left to be picked clean by any of the dozens of other, smaller factions that operated on a block-level.

This was Scythe territory.

Knots of kids in Grim Reaper robes hung out on street corners, the famous "Boyz in the hood". Sickle-shapes were spray-painted everywhere.

"At least, the weather's lovely," said Penny.

Having played the Hollywood Bowl, the Roadshow's last gig was on the Santa Monica Pier. Everyone was checked into a sea-front resort complex. From their balcony, Lowe and Penny watched the sun go down on the Pacific, sipping at their Meltdowns. The sea rippled and reflected like dragon scales, red and gold and green and turquoise.

"It's beautiful," she said, holding his arm, laying her head on his shoulder.

"It's pollution."

The refineries up the coast had been pouring filth into the sea for the better part of a century. Now they stood idle, while international environmental inspectors tried to impose emission standards on factories that had only ever heard of output quotas and which had a very big pond outside for throwing garbage into.

"Every summer, it catches fire. Sometimes, the fire spreads across the beaches. There used to be a Party Boss colony up near Malibu, but it was burned out in '92. Los Angeles has earthquakes too."

"Why does everyone in America want to come here?"

"It's the end of the dream. Since Chris Columbus's day, people have been coming west across this continent running away from nightmares or chasing after the American dream. This is where the trail stops."

They finished their Meltdowns and went inside.

The envelope lay on the table. Lowe had looked over everything in San Berdoo, Penny had only just finished reading the documents.

"What about all this?" she asked. "Is it genuine?"

"What do you think?"

There were photocopies and carbons and flimsies. Enough evidence to put Sir Robert Maxwell in jail for a thousand years, if they still sent rich people to jail. Of course, if this was all kosher, Sir Bob wasn't even rich.

Spent it all, didn't I? growled the arse-hole.

"It's the pension fund that's the worst," said Penny. "People who've worked for the newspaper all their lives, long before Maxwell bought it, have paid into the fund. And there's nothing there. They'll be on the scrap-heap, without a bean."

"You sound like a socialist."

"He's supposed to be one."

All for one, and that one is me.

There was more than just the pension fund scam. There was solid evidence here of a vast spectrum of illegal business practice, from insider-trading to colossal tax fraud. It was no wonder that Maxwell wanted to be in America if all this was about to come out back home. He might well want to get to California because there was no way of extraditing him.

There was a Bonfire Night rattle outside. Someone firing a machine-gun, probably into the air. Then a rumble of explosion. The first time, Lowe and Penny had been certain it was an earthquake. It was just the usual LA firefight, Officer Fuhrman—of the security squad—explained, "spics and the spooks offing each other, saving the community the trouble."

"I suppose Joanna will publish this," Penny ventured.

Lowe felt queasy.

"Of course, that's what should happen. John and Michael will be delighted. *Lilliput* can bring the bastard down. And there's no question but that he deserves it. But I can't help feeling like a puppet."

"I know what you mean."

Penny waved her arms up and down, as if on wires like Muffin the Mule.

"Someone carefully assembled this, and gave it to me. I can't help but feel that some sinister, smirking, snakelike superman is snickering."

"This land is blighted by Satan," said Beverley. "This is where I shall found my ministry."

Nancy's eyes glowed.

Lowe wasn't surprised.

At the Hollywood Bowl, Beverley's speaking in tongues had provoked a minor riot. Worshippers had rushed the stage and, in a mad rapture of devotion, nearly killed the vicar.

His dark suit had been shredded, and was now held together only by safety-pins. His face was scabbed and scarred. He had lost weight as he gained intensity. His hands were wrung out and red with stigmata.

"*Fucking gobshite bollocks cunt!*" Beverly yelled.

Nobody thought the language unusual. Lowe realised how close glossolalia was to Tourette's.

"Amen," said Nancy.

And the word was fucking gobshite.

Lowe saw the divine green spark flickering in Beverley's eyes. But he had been seeing Blair as a red-eyed demon with horns and fangs. And Sir Cliff was ageing rapidly, like Dracula exposed to sunlight.

He was used to the Meltdown visions.

"I shall make this truly the City of the Angels," declared the Rev. Bev.

"Alleilua," breathed Nancy.

Officer Fuhrman provided an armed escort so Penny and Lowe could go shopping on Rodeo Drive. The most luxurious Party Stores in the USSA had been here, and they were still open for business, with murderous-looking, olive-uniformed killer guards at every door. It was said in America that you could buy anything on Rodeo Drive. There were certainly fourteen-year-old boys and girls in abundance, some in the obvious gear of whores the world over, others crisply-dressed and clean-cut. There were even a few still in perfect Junior Pioneer uniforms, with red caps and socialist merit badges. Some wealthy remnants of former regimes wanted to stay with their old pleasures. Everyone in sight was armed, but then again so was Lady Penelope.

She was disappointed. The clothes were out of date by London and Vienna standards, and not especially well made. Californians believed in pastel and dayglo, sequins and rhinestones.

In the most exclusive vest shop on the Drive, Lowe searched in vain for a present to send his son. He had said he would try to find a picture vest with a typically American image—President Ewing, an old-time cowboy or Al Capone with a cigar. Instead, there were only left-over Russian or British icons—Ken Dodd, Rudolf Nureyev, King Andrew and Queen Sarah, Doctor Who. In Los Angeles, everyone wanted to be foreign.

He wasn't too concerned with shopping. He was still struggling with the Maxwell problem.

He had written up a blazing Joanna Houseman exposé, packing in as much of the dirt as could be contained in a single article. It was devastating, his best piece of writing in ten years, and if published would utterly destroy a loathsome personage. The scoop of a lifetime, the stuff that every news hack dreamed of.

But...

After me, the deluge, said the arsehole. *A deluge of shit.*

"Look," said Penny, jogging him out of his thoughts. "It's those fellows in the hats."

It was Jake and Elwood, weaving around the rows of garments like shoppers in Tesco's, piling their arms with purchases.

"I didn't think of you as pastel types," Lowe said.

Jake and Elwood caught themselves up short, looked at each other, and at the draping of mildly-coloured clothes they had no intention of paying for, and threw them up in the air.

An armed guard shot at them.

"They have the death penalty for littering in California," Lowe said.

Jake and Elwood adjusted their sunglasses and ran out of the back door. Two guards jogged after them, and piled into an alley-full of ash-cans.

"It's never going to work, is it?" Penny said. "America?"

The door of their room was unlocked. Not forced and broken, but unlocked.

Lowe felt the handle warming in his grip.

The eyehole blinked at him.

Take the money, open the box, said the arse-hole.

He signalled to Penny, clattering up after him with her bags of purchases, to be quiet.

He turned the handle and stepped in.

William Brown was sitting at the desk, reading the Joanna article. His machine-pistol rested on top of the Maxwell documents, like a paperweight.

"You shouldn't leave sensitive material like this out in the open," Brown said. "There are spies everywhere."

Lowe relaxed, realising Brown wasn't about to kill him. People who were killed by Just William didn't see him first. But anger boiled up.

"Come to check up, have you?"

"You puzzle me, Mr. Lowe. Or should I say Miss Houseman?"

"Why?"

Penny leaned on the door and lit up a fag. If the worst came to the worst, she had a gun. She might even surprise the trained killer.

"Because you haven't delivered this excellent article to your friends at *Lilliput*."

"I'm saving up for the postage."

Brown put the article down.

"It's Urquhart, isn't it?" Lowe said. "He's pulled Alan Clark out of the fire three times already. If Maxwell goes down, that's the only pro-Lab-Lib paper out of the race. Then maybe the government can survive the next election."

"What about all the poor *Mirror* pensioners?"

Lowe wished he had the gun now.

"Don't tell me you care about them!"

"Funnily enough, I do. My entire career has been based on an overdeveloped sense of what is right and what is wrong."

For a moment, Brown reminded Lowe of Philby.

"If I don't do it," Lowe said. "Someone else will."

"And you won't have to be involved," said Brown. "You can sit on the sidelines again, Mr. Lowe. Taking notes, kidding yourself you're a neutral observer. Deliberately dropping catches to get the match over with. Pouring poison into your stomach."

"He's right," said Penny.

"I know he's right. That's why I hate him."

The final show was a let-down.

The Rev. Bev. was off the bill, hospitalised with heat prostration. It was the two knights, Sir Cliff and Sir Bob. At the end of the pier, like a Punch and Judy show.

If it weren't for a hefty kickback, the pier wouldn't have passed the safety inspections. It creaked and cracked under the weight of the invited, VIP-only audience.

Lowe thought the enormously obese Maxwell, whose weight could be gauged in large fractions of a ton, might plunge through the weakened floor into the sea. Best thing for him.

Before Maxwell began his speech, a ripple went through the audience and a lot of uniformed folks—militia leaders, top cops, vanguard generals —scrambled out of their canvas chairs and headed for their bulletproof cars and, in a couple of cases, armoured personnel carriers. Even Miss Mulwray had shown up; she had picked thirty of her best-looking Nicaraguans and former Green Berets to form her bodyguard, then dressed them in Ruritanian uniforms, all scrambled egg and lanyards and lace. Their guns were real enough, though.

The sounds of gunfire drifted from the shore. Serious shooting. Helicopters buzzed low over the pier and swooped across the city.

"At last," said someone nearby.

"What's happening?" Lowe asked.

"The crack-down. Restoration of the rule of law."

A column of fire rose from somewhere in Santa Monica.

"By dawn, it'll be finished."

Sir Robert droned on.

Brown had taken the Joanna exposé and arranged for its priority delivery—in a diplomatic pouch?—to *Lilliput*. It was out of Lowe's hands.

Maxwell talked about new business opportunities.

Helicopters dropped fire on people.

Maxwell was talking through his arsehole.

Almost all of the Americans were gone. They had grabbed their guns and got into the action. Only Miss Mulwray and her Praetorian Guard remained. The old girl was deep in conversation with Penny, catching up on a couple of years' worth of gossip about the various "sets" of people they knew back home.

Before the show, Lowe had run into a BBC-TV crew scrabbling for some shots of the stars. Maxwell posed with Lowe and Penny, smiling like a happy ogre showing off his children. He was delighted that someone was finally paying attention. But the cameraman kept letting his equipment sag on his shoulder, and the interviewer seemed to be a twelve-year-old American girl. Now, even this pair had rushed back to the city, to get their chance with a big story.

They would be delighted.

The girl had explained that the BBC's A-list California crew were in Arizona, covering the big UN action there. It seemed that Van Damme had found evidence linking a vigilante militia with the Okie massacre, and there was a shooting war. There was a lot of controversy about the UN's right to take direct action, but Lowe remembered the field of bones.

Now, the action was in LA.

Sections of the city were burning.

Another wave of helicopters came in off the sea.

Sir Cliff tried to compete with the war. He called up a couple of remaining dignitaries from the audience, and tried to get them to sing along. Lowe noticed that the performer didn't cringe when bombs went off, and wondered if he might not be deaf.

Now was the time to get clean.

He made his way backstage, picking carefully through the tangle of overturned chairs. He had been drinking Meltdowns, but wasn't drunk.

He knew what was real.

Penny followed him. She helped him stand up straight when he tripped.

A chunk of the pier broke away, girders snapping. A stray mortar shot had landed.

"Did I do that?" he asked.

"No, dear."

"That's all right then."

Sir Cliff kept on singing. Staff with fire extinguishers sprayed a corner of the stage.

In the backstage area, Sir Robert Maxwell squatted on a tiny stool, looking like an over-the-hill sumo wrestler. After his speech, and the mass walk-out, he was drained. His face had collapsed, like an empty scrotum.

He looked at Lowe and Penny.

"They left," he said. "Yankee bastards walked out."

There was an enormous explosion on shore. Maxwell's face was briefly red-lit.

"It wasn't you, sir," Lowe said. "It was the fighting. Los Angeles has gone up like a firework."

"Ungrateful bastards."

Maxwell stood up, swelling like a sail.

"All I wanted to do was bring this godforsaken country the benefit of my expertise, to help them get back on their bloody feet again. And they walked out!"

This was not a good time for confession.

But it had to be made. First confession, then absolution. Then redemption.

Lowe had his eye on redemption.

But Penny had a gun just in case.

"Sir Robert, I cannot tell a lie..."

Penny laughed.

"...for I am the viper in your tit. I am Joanna Houseman."

Maxwell's eyes shrunk to points of suspicion.

"What?"

His hands opened and closed like an angry gorilla's.

"I've been writing the articles in *Lilliput*. The ones about you."

Maxwell took in a deep breath. He inhaled the fire and hate of Los Angeles. His dinner jacket split down the back. Horny spines projected.

"You're going to die, fuckface!"

It was the arsehole voice, amplified to a typhoon roar.

The huge hands closed on Lowe's throat. The enormous, pitted face loomed close. Burning shit was breathed into Lowe's eyes.

He felt his body going limp.

Strangely, the explosions and Cliff's cheer-up wailing faded. He heard only the gentle pounding of the waves. And a distant echo of Charlie Holley...

Every day, it's a-getting closer

This might not be a bad way to end.

Lowe was on the floor, and the enormous weight of Sir Robert was on top of him. This man, who had killed Germans with his bare hands, was squeezing the life out of him.

A silver tube pressed against Maxwell's temple.

"Let him go," said Penny.

The hands relaxed.

It didn't matter. Sir Bob's weight was enough to force every ounce of air from Lowe's lungs.

"Get off him, Fatty."

Maxwell rolled over, sobbing.

Lowe sat up. Penny was elegantly posed, her gun as perfect an accessory as her Fabergé lighter.

The press baron lay in a writhing heap.

Another face appeared in the gloom.

"When you reach the edge of the world, where do you go?" Brown asked.

Lowe looked down at Maxwell.

"Home," he said.

"What if you have no home?"

"Everyone has a home," said another voice. Miss Mulwray. "Sometimes they don't know where it is, or perhaps they can't go there, but there is always home, always a place that owns you."

"So what on earth am I doing here?" said Lowe, still sprawling on the ground. The question seemed more important than the pain in his windpipe or any possible broken ribs.

"I haven't a bloody clue, young man," said Miss Mulwray.

Brown helped him to his feet, then walked away. Penny took out a handkerchief and dabbed at what he realised was a cut on his forehead.

Miss Mulwray sat on the floor, cradling Maxwell's head in her lap. "They never gave you a chance, did they?" she was saying, as much to herself as to him. "Happy to take your money or accept your hospitality for the weekend, but most of 'em looked down their noses at you behind your back. Made snide remarks about how you weren't really 'one of us' while they were guzzling your champagne. I know, I know, there there..."

The pier was burning, and the remaining Roadshow personnel were escorted back to the shore. It took four men to help Maxwell, who was an untenanted hulk.

Lowe felt free.

But the city was burning.

This was the end of People's Road 666.

Dawn found them on the beach. The sun came up in time to cast some light on the pier as it finally collapsed. Then a cloud of thick, choking smoke blotted out the sky. Helicopters buzzed through the cloud, whipping the smoke to tatters.

Lowe and Penny huddled together, coughing.

"Look," said Penny, pointing.

The heap that was Sir Robert Maxwell gathered itself together. He ripped the last of his tuxedo from his back, and tore off the rest of his clothes.

Few people took notice. A few hours ago, someone had raked the beach with gunfire. There had been casualties. Everyone was keeping their head down. Sir Cliff and his band had dug fox-holes, which filled up with sea-water.

Maxwell stood, naked, and walked to the water's edge.

"He's going for a paddle," Penny said.

"No," Lowe replied, breaking away from her and standing up.

Maxwell walked into the water. It rose around him, lapping at his equator-like stomach.

Lowe staggered to the shore.

A rocket-like flare streaked overhead, fired from somewhere up in the city. It landed a hundred yards or so out to sea, in the middle of a blackish slick.

Fire blossomed.

Maxwell's head bobbed.

Lowe was knee-deep himself.

Fire spread in a circle. The sea was burning.

Maxwell's head went under.

Something vast and reptilian stirred in the depths of the Pacific, warmed by the burning film overhead. Lowe felt the tidal assault of displaced water. Limbs and tail were in motion. Snake eyes opened and looked up at the flame on the water. Lowe knew it would come, summoned by Maxwell's final breath bubbles, and would swarm out, striding across the city. Where its feet fell, thousands would die.

Lowe stood and looked out at the Pacific.

And cried like a baby.